Reading the Signs

Also by Keira Andrews

Contemporary

Honeymoon for One
Beyond the Sea
Ends of the Earth
Arctic Fire
The Chimera Affair

Holiday
Only One Bed
Merry Cherry Christmas
The Christmas Deal
Santa Daddy
In Case of Emergency
Eight Nights in December
If Only in My Dreams
Where the Lovelight Gleams
Gay Romance Holiday Collection

Sports
Kiss and Cry
Reading the Signs
Cold War
The Next Competitor
Love Match
Synchronicity (free read!)

Gay Amish Romance Series
A Forbidden Rumspringa
A Clean Break
A Way Home
A Very English Christmas

Valor Duology
Valor on the Move
Test of Valor
Complete Valor Duology

READING THE SIGNS

BY KEIRA ANDREWS

Reading the Signs
Written and published by Keira Andrews
Cover by Dar Albert

Copyright © 2016 by Keira Andrews

ISBN: 978-1-988260-07-5

This is a work of fiction. Names, characters, businesses, places, events and incidents are either the products of the author's imagination or used in a fictitious manner. No persons, living or dead, were harmed by the writing of this book. Any resemblance to any actual persons, living or dead, or actual events is purely coincidental.

Acknowledgements

Thank you to my wonderful friends and beta readers Anne-Marie, Becky, Dee, and Rachel. I really couldn't do it without your unflagging support and encouragement. Rachel, I know how much you *love* baseball and sportsing in general, so an extra thank you for soldiering through so gamely. <3

Special thanks to Mary for her vital assistance and generously sharing her family's experiences as Italians in Niagara Falls in the 1950s and '60s.

Author's Note

I've loved baseball since the Jays won the pennant in '85, and I tried my very best to realistically portray life in the clubhouse and on the field. That said, this is fiction, so certain liberties may have been taken, and any similarities to real life players or teams is entirely coincidental.

CHAPTER ONE

J AKE FITZGERALD WASN'T even in the room when his carefully contained life was smashed right out of the park.

It rocketed over the field, his pulse zooming as he followed his manager down the stairs from the dugout in the top of the ninth. Their footsteps echoed dully in the dank tunnel leading to the visitors' clubhouse in Boston, cleats scratching on concrete. Ted wouldn't look at him. Gruff and unsmiling was Ted's usual MO, but a different tension hunched his shoulders.

Jake had just been scratched from the lineup near the end of the game even though he wasn't injured. Sure, his left knee ached with every step, but that was nothing new, and he sure as hell hadn't complained about it. No, something was up, and as he followed Ted into the visiting manager's office and closed the door, nausea churned his gut.

They stood there on the faded carpet by the desk, a small fridge humming with a slight rattle beside a brown couch and fluorescent lights harsh overhead. Black and white prints of baseball greats watched from behind glass frames on the beige walls.

Ted took a deep breath and blew it out, his gaze still on the floor. When he raised his head, his eyes glistened, and an electric jolt of terror seized Jake.

"What is it? My mom?" Jake's voice came out hoarse. The

office smelled faintly of lemony disinfectant, and he thought of the hospital where his father had died. *Oh Jesus.*

"No, no. Nothing like that." Ted shook his head and took off his cap, scrubbing a hand over his buzzed black hair, his wrinkled face even more creased. "Hell, Fitz. You're traded. I can't believe it's going down like this, but here we are."

A bark of laughter scraped Jake's dry throat as the relief that his mom was okay butted up against incredulity. "But Norwalk said he'd give me a heads up if there were talks with other teams. We had an agreement." Verbal, but still. "He knew I wanted to finish out my career here. He promised if anything changed, he'd warn me. We shook on it."

Ted grimaced and looked like he wanted to spit. "I'm sorry, Fitz. I guess business is business and money is money, and a man's word don't mean shit anymore."

Traded. The word raked through Jake's mind, all sharp edges. He managed to get out, "Where?"

Trying to smile, Ted said, "Well, do you have your passport?"

An iron band constricted Jake's lungs. "Toronto?"

The memory of an easy smile and twinkling eyes burst into his mind. *Brandon.* Lost to Jake years ago. Only stony silence and avoidance existed between them now—if they had to play together again it would be a disaster. Jake had ruined everything, and Brandon would never forgive him. *Should* never forgive him.

"Ottawa."

Blinking, Jake's mind spun as he tried to remember everything he knew about the new Ottawa team, which wasn't a heck of a lot. The Capitals had been renamed and built from the ashes of a failed Florida franchise and were in their second year.

They'd visited San Fran the previous year, and Jake's team had gone up to Ottawa for two games, but hadn't met yet for interdivision play this season. The Ottawa crowds had been enthusiastic, and the Caps' new dome was state of the art.

"Ottawa," Jake repeated. He took off his cap, staring at the gray and green. He'd have new colors now. New uniform, new home, new life.

He didn't want any of it.

"They're not doing bad," Ted said. "Could actually nab the wild card this year or even the division title. You've got a better chance of making the playoffs with them."

Jake bit back the urge to scoff. That was a pipe dream for a team in only its second season. And God, he hated to even think it, but he didn't care about making the playoffs. He'd established a comfortable routine in San Fran over the last eight years. He had everything under control. Just the way he liked it. Now that control had been ripped away.

It was like a ball to the throat behind the plate, bouncing up and hammering the one spot his pads didn't quite cover. Unable to breathe, feeling like he might actually die right there.

Inevitably, the panic receded, and he would shakily gasp for air, waiting for the next pitch.

Jake inhaled now, rolling his knotted shoulders. "I only have two years left on my contract. I'll be thirty-six then, and I'm going to retire. Be lucky if my knees last that long. Why would they want me?"

Ted frowned. "They want you because you're a hell of a ball player. One of the best damn catchers I've ever coached. When you came to us I thought, 'Fuck me sideways, what am I going to do with a giant behind the plate?' You're not done yet. So don't give me that shit." His eyes blazed, gruff voice filling the room as he got fired up. "You know why they want you? Because they need a leader to set the tone. A vet with a cool head to inspire that new team. And damn it, you'll do it. I know you're blindsided right now, but this is gonna be a great change. Even if we'll miss the hell out of you. Got it?"

Jake nodded, his throat tight and eyes burning.

Ted slapped Jake's arm. "Okay then. Norwalk's waiting on the phone."

His throat closed up for a different reason. Nails digging into his palm, he snarled, "I don't have anything to say. Not anything he wants to hear, at least."

"I know, but you've got to talk to him anyway, so let's get it done." Ted turned to the phone on the desk and jabbed a few buttons. The speaker crackled to life, and he said, "I've got Fitz here with me. I've informed him of the trade."

Henry Norwalk's oily voice slithered from the speaker. "Hi, Fitz. We've got heavy hearts here in the office, but tough choices had to be made."

Rolling his eyes, Jake only said, "Uh-huh."

"I hope you know how much you've meant to this ball club and—"

"Not enough for you to be honest with me," he bit out. "You gave me your word that you'd warn me of trade negotiations."

Voices filled the hallway, a rumble of footsteps going by as the team headed to the clubhouse. Boston had been up by three runs, and Jake's team had apparently failed to tie it in the top of the ninth. He heard Sanchez's distinctive peal of laughter and someone's reply, probably Owen or Manheim.

Jake realized with a pang that they weren't his teammates anymore. This was how it went in baseball—players were traded around the league fairly regularly, part of a team one week and then facing them in different colors the next. His teammates were already in his rearview mirror, and he wasn't even behind the wheel.

Norwalk droned on, but Jake could only focus on the sick, clammy powerlessness of knowing he'd taken his last at-bat with his team. That he'd caught his last pitch with them and hadn't known it. He hadn't even been able to mark the moment. After eight long years with the same team it was over, and there was absolutely nothing he could do about it.

"—paying you the rest of your contract and you get that million-dollar trade bonus," Norwalk continued. "It's an excellent deal for you, Fitz."

Jake managed to speak evenly. "It's not about money. It's about my life."

Ted kept quiet in the corner while Norwalk said, "Well, I know it's a tough part of baseball. But at least you don't have a family to uproot. Heck, maybe you'll find Miss Right up there." He laughed awkwardly.

Jake had zero desire to find Mr. Right, let alone *Miss*. He'd already found the man he wanted to spend his life with, and it would never happen. Even if Brandon was gay or bi, which he wasn't, Jake had destroyed their friendship. He'd let himself fall in love, and he would never, ever make that mistake again.

A memory of the hospital surfaced, squeaky shoes on linoleum in the hush of night, disinfectant and death in the air. Jake's parents had been visiting him in San Francisco when his father had collapsed. They'd find out later the cancer was already in his bones.

Brandon had sat shoulder to shoulder with Jake in the hall outside his father's room all night, even though the first pitch was at 12:07 the next day. Murmuring the stupidest jokes he could think of...

"Hey, J—why'd the girl smear peanut butter all over the road? To go with the traffic jam."

Jake had to smile, a little piece of his heart lightening amid the sorrow.

"Why do bananas have to put on sunscreen before they go to the beach? Because they might peel."

In the silence, Norwalk added, "You're Canadian—this'll be a homecoming for you. The fans will be thrilled."

Jake shrugged even though Norwalk couldn't see him. Sure,

but he'd prefer to keep his life exactly the way it was.

Ted cleared his throat. "Okay, Henry. Can you patch us through to Ottawa now?"

"Will do. Fitz, I hope you understand. Tough business decisions have to be made sometimes. None of us enjoy it. But I have to do what's right for the team."

"Then don't shake my hand and make promises you won't keep." Jake slumped on the couch, stretching out his long legs. Reddish dirt marred the green of his jersey where he'd slid into second in the fourth inning on a blooper from Moreno. He rubbed at it uselessly.

It was true trades were part of the game, and it was up to team owners to wheel and deal, no matter what the players wanted. It still sucked. He wondered what Norwalk had gotten in return from Ottawa. Probably pitching prospects, but it didn't really matter. Either way, Jake was traded.

Traded.

He tuned out until another voice came down the line, this one belonging to Martin Tyson, Ottawa's general manager and leader in the front office. From what Jake vaguely recalled, Tyson had been GM in San Diego before making the move north.

"Hey there, Jake. You're probably a bit thrown right now, but I want you to know how thrilled we are to have you on the team."

Ted watched silently, leaning on a corner of the desk as Jake cleared his throat and sat up straighter on the couch. "Thank you. I didn't see this coming, but…yeah. Um, thank you."

"We need leadership, and I know you're the perfect man to provide it. Your pitch-framing skills and command behind the plate are among the best in the majors. We've got a few young pitchers who need a firm hand and a more experienced catcher guiding them. Especially Agresta. He could be a Cy Young one day, but he needs discipline."

"Agresta? Marco's little brother?" Jake remembered an intense stare, a pimply face, untamed dark curls, and shy silence.

The season had started six weeks ago—how had Jake not even heard that little Nico was in the majors? Deep down, he knew the answer. He did his job, but his heart wasn't in it. If he was honest, he knew when the leak started, like air escaping a tire so slowly you don't notice at first. Since Brandon, baseball hadn't been the same. Life hadn't.

Tyson laughed. "The kid's twenty-two. His rookie season."

"Wow. And you're having problems with him? I haven't seen him in years, but I can't imagine him being a prima donna."

"Nah. He's a little cocky at times, but he stays to himself in the clubhouse; keeps his head down. It's his temper and impatience. First sign of trouble, he unravels. His command of the ball is outstanding, but he needs to control his emotions."

"Okay, good to know." It'd be interesting to see what kind of man Marco's brother had become.

"Can't wait to see you up here tomorrow, Fitz. Can I call you that?"

He blinked. No one had ever actually asked. "Of course. Everyone does."

"Terrific. I know the team's going to be just as excited as we are in the office. We'll email you the flight info, okay?"

It wasn't as if he had a choice, but Tyson seemed to be waiting for an answer. Jake said, "Yes. Thank you."

"I know this is a big shakeup, but you'll love it here. I'll make sure of it personally. Have a good night and see you soon."

Jake said his goodbyes, and Ted hung up the phone.

Tomorrow.

He wouldn't even have a chance to go home from Boston first. The next time he saw the stadium in San Francisco, it would be from the visitors' dugout. His chest ached as grief spasmed through him. He'd expected his retirement game to be there. He'd wanted to go out on his terms, and now his life was going to change completely, whether he liked it or not.

The truth was, he'd been considering walking on the rest of his contract. He didn't need the money—had more millions than he'd ever know what to do with. If he'd gone to management, they'd probably have been delighted to save the cash and cut him loose early, get some young prospects to build the team. But that wouldn't happen in Ottawa. They had their fill of rookies and wanted experience.

"Well, you know I hate to see you go," Ted said. "But you're going to do a bang-up job up there."

Jake sat there on the couch in his dirty uniform—a uniform he'd never wear again. "This doesn't feel real."

"I hear you." He opened the fridge and tossed Jake a can of beer before taking one for himself and flopping down beside him with a low groan. "Jesus, my sciatica. Take my advice—don't ever get old."

The cold can was already wet with condensation in his hand, and Jake popped the top and guzzled. "I'll drink to that."

After a few sips and moments of silence, Ted said quietly, "Sometimes change is just what the doctor ordered, even if we can't see it at first."

Jake took another gulp. The ball was long gone over the wall, and he had to circle the bases or get left behind in the dust.

"*OTTAWA? ISN'T IT* too cold for baseball up there?" On the tablet screen, Ron's green eyes twinkled.

Despite himself, Jake huffed out a laugh. "You realize it's almost June and we do have summer in Canada. But there's a dome just in case."

"That's cool. Brand-new stadium to play in." Ron sat back in his desk chair with a sigh. Books lined the shelves behind him.

"But damn, I'll miss you. Who's going to tie me up and spank me now?"

A voice off-camera piped up, "Don't look at me, honey." Steve, Ron's husband, appeared behind Ron's chair. He leaned over and waved to the camera, light reflecting off his graying hair. "Hey, Fitz. Sorry to eavesdrop, but this one turns the volume up to eleven. How are you doing? Must be a real shock."

"Yeah. I guess I'm processing." In his boxers, Jake leaned back against the pillows on the king bed in his navy and cream hotel room, his tablet propped against the ice packs on his knees.

Beside him, his phone buzzed again, probably another teammate asking if he was okay. News of the trade wouldn't go out until the morning, and Jake just didn't have it in him to tell them right now.

"Well, Ron and his ass will really miss you," Steve said with a wink. "He's going to be a bear until he finds someone else to give him what he needs." His smile faded. "But really, I hope you're okay."

"Thanks. I'll survive. There are worse things in life, right?"

"I'm sure there are." Steve gave Ron's shoulders a squeeze. "Dinner's ready in ten, but don't rush. I'll keep it warm." To the camera, he added, "Take care of yourself in the great white north, and don't be a stranger."

"Will do."

When Steve was gone, Ron sighed again, his dark, bushy eyebrows drawing together. "I really will miss you. Who am I going to watch *Survivor* with now? Steve would rather eat glass."

Jake chuckled. It was his and Ron's standard weekly routine when he was at home—fuck for an hour or so, then catch up on the latest episode on the DVR with beer and pizza. Ron was in his late forties now, Steve a decade older, and their open marriage worked better than most relationships Jake had ever seen.

"We'll have to Skype it. And I'll be back in the Bay Area once in a while. I'll miss hanging with you too."

"You bet you will. You'll have to find a new friend in Ottawa."

Jake groaned, rubbing a hand over his head. In the small window in the corner of the screen, he saw that his sandy brown hair stuck up on end and his eyes already had dark circles beneath them. Surely they'd been there before, but he hadn't noticed. "I'm too old to find someone else."

Ron put on a faux sad face. "I know, it's so hard being a thirty-year-old baseball star with millions of dollars, a square jaw, blue eyes, and an outrageously hot body. Oh, and you're six-five. However will you find someone else to fuck?"

"I'm thirty-four," Jake grumbled. "And you know it's not… It's hard, okay? I can't trust just anyone. If I hook up with some random guy, next thing I know he's tweeting about it."

Ron sobered. "I know, man. I'm sorry."

It had taken several interviews with Ron, who worked at a local newspaper, for Jake to trust him enough to go for friendly drinks off the record. Their mutual love for trashy reality shows had led to viewing nights at Jake's house, and after too many drinks once they'd eventually discovered a mutual affinity for light BDSM.

It was the perfect arrangement—Jake took care of himself on the road and scratched his itch to get sweaty and dominant a few times during home stands.

"I'll just stick to jerking off. I'm pretty good at it."

"That you are. Although I still say coming out would go just fine."

Jake's neck tensed, and he rolled it back and forth. "It would be such a *thing.*" The idea of the headlines and questions and worry about how his teammates and fans would respond sent needles of sticky apprehension down his spine. "Most of the guys in the clubhouse wouldn't mind, but some would. There's still a conservative streak in baseball; a religious one. Although the league brass are making a real effort on inclusion, I'll give them that. They've made it clear gay players will be supported. I just…" He sighed.

"It's still tough. I hear you."

"Growing up, homophobic comments flew around the locker room. Guys ribbing each other. Even if they don't mean it, you still hear that shit. Not much now in the majors, but once in a while. I just want to do my job."

Ron grimaced. "God, high school. The hateful things other kids said, and I never spoke up because I was terrified they'd know. They'd see right through me and turn on me instead of the nerdy kids who couldn't throw a football or dunk a basketball the way I could. I was such a coward."

Jake shifted uncomfortably, a hot flush spreading on his skin. "I know I'm being a coward now. There's no excuse for it."

"No, no. Coming out is personal for everyone. Who you tell and when you tell them should be your choice. I'm sorry. We live in a different world now, but despite everything that's changed, there's still a lot of hatred out there. Jesus, look at the anti-LGBT laws some states are trying to pass. It's scary."

"It is. Two steps forward, three back." He scrubbed a hand over his head. "I just want to be judged for what I do on the field. What does it matter anyway? I'd still be the same player whether the world knows who I fuck or not."

"There's the rub, isn't it? If you came out, it would show people that a gay man can play ball and be damn good at it. That sexuality doesn't matter and we're all equal. But coming out puts the spotlight on your sexuality and personal life. We all know there are gay and bi players in the majors, but none of you want to be the poster boy. And I don't blame you."

Jake exhaled slowly. "Thanks. I'm almost done. Two more seasons after this one. Then I can just fade away and have a normal life."

"You could actually try dating."

Scoffing, Jake rolled his eyes. "Yes, Mother."

Dating wasn't for him. *Love* wasn't either. Love had cost him his best friend, and he was never going down that road again. He'd find another fuck buddy or two wherever he ended up after retirement, and that would be that. No muss, no fuss.

Ron asked, "Speaking of which, have you told your mom yet? She's going to be over the moon."

"It's too late here now; she's in bed by nine-thirty. I'll call her in the morning." He smiled. This was at least the one good thing about the trade—his mom would indeed be thrilled to have him closer to home, even if Ottawa was still at least a five-hour drive from Midland.

"Is Ottawa nice? I've never been."

Jake pondered it as he shifted the ice packs slightly to get another angle on his knees. "Yeah, it's nice. Pretty small and clean. I visited as a kid, and we were up there once last season, but I didn't really pay attention. There are parliament buildings and stuff by the new stadium. I'm sure it'll be fine. Whatever, I won't be there too long."

"I sure hope you're going to fake some enthusiasm when you meet the press up there. Or—and this is a crazy idea, I know— you might actually look at the bright side for once and feel some. Get out of your rut. The Caps have had a good start, haven't they? Who knows, you might make the postseason."

"You sound like Ted giving me a pep talk. There's no way it'll happen. It doesn't matter anyway. I don't need the playoffs. Everything was good in San Francisco."

"No, everything was comfortable. There's a difference."

Jake pressed his lips into a thin line.

"Okay, that's enough tough love for now. I'd better go eat, and you'd better get some sleep. But just think about this: When you were a little kid playing baseball instead of hockey up on the northern tundra—"

"Ontario is not tundra."

Ron continued as if Jake hadn't spoken. "Did you dream of a ho-hum career playing for a middling team? Cashing in your huge paycheck and not really giving a shit? Or did you dream about the big time? About winning it all? Did you eat and sleep baseball and *love* it?"

Memories flashed through Jake's mind: *In the backyard playing catch with Dad even after the frost came. Mom baking hundreds of butter tarts for the community fundraiser to buy him a ball machine, the house smelling like sweetness for days. Making the provincial team, so proud of the trillium flower on his jersey and his name sewn on the back in real lettering, not just an iron-on stencil.*

Scholarship to college in Florida, the humidity unbearable but a funny, cool, sexy roommate in Brandon Kennedy. Drafted by Chicago, quick path to the majors as a catcher. Traded to Philly after a year, rooming with Brandon again while they played minor league ball— cheap beer and pretzels and late nights. Called back up to the Show, teammates again until Jake was traded. Brandon's gleaming smile when he landed in San Fran a couple years later too.

Jake cleared his throat, looking away from the screen at the faint pattern of squares on the cream duvet. "That was a long time ago."

"You're not so old as you think you are. Just remember that. Talk soon, okay?"

"Yeah. Thanks, Ron. Enjoy dinner." He put the tablet aside and flopped back on the pillows. His phone buzzed again, and he switched it off completely, rolling over to snap off the light. His ice packs slipped onto the duvet, and he kicked them onto the floor with dull thuds.

In the darkness behind the blackout curtains, Jake closed his eyes and tried not to think about how his life was changing. He tried very hard not to think about anything at all.

CHAPTER TWO

"**B**ABY?"

Nico gritted his teeth as Julie—no, Jenny's—voice echoed from the other side of the bathroom door. They'd known each other all of two hours, and he sure as hell wasn't her *baby*, or sweetie or darling or boo. He choked down his dickish reply and cleared his throat. "Think the shrimp was off."

"Oh, you poor thing! I'll call down for some ginger ale and crackers."

"Thanks."

Rubbing his face, he leaned against the door, the fluffy hotel bathrobe soft at his back. The sex had been short and pretty terrible, so he wasn't sure why Jenny would even want to stick around. When he'd spotted her in the hotel restaurant, her red hair gleaming and magnificent tits showcased by her clingy dress, he'd thought, *Maybe…*

Snorting, he caught his reflection in the mirror, a mess of curls on his head, his brown eyes bleary. He muttered under his breath, "You thought she'd have a magic pussy that would turn your faggot ass straight?"

A dull headache throbbed. He'd had way too many shots. Now he wanted to chug some water, pop a few Advil, and forget the world. He and the team had a short flight back to Ottawa from Toronto in the morning, and he was already dreading the day of training.

Should have stopped at five drinks. Never should have even started. Never should have done a lot of things.

He could imagine the messages waiting on his phone from his father. A string of texts sent during the game, and then a voicemail outlining everything the team had done wrong, just in case the texts weren't clear enough. Even though his father had been an outfielder, he was an expert in all things baseball.

Especially pitching. Especially *Nico's* pitching. Especially everything fucking wrong with it. Even the days when he pitched well or was only sitting in the dugout supporting his team, he avoided his father's messages for as long as possible.

Jenny's tinkling voice came through the door. "Feeling any better, baby? Can I help?"

You can go away, please, please, please. He kept his tone soft. "Just need a minute. Sorry."

"Don't be sorry!" Her Canadian accent lilted, making it sound like *sore-y*. "It's not your fault."

Nico turned away from the mirror and took a piss, staring at a framed black and white photo of a tree-lined street in Paris or some place with cobblestones. What was that saying about the definition of insanity? Doing the same thing over and over and expecting a different result.

There had been dozens of Jennys, starting when he was drafted to the minors in Arizona at eighteen. In high school, he'd had a steady girlfriend who wanted to wait for marriage, which had been hella convenient in hindsight.

In Phoenix, he'd started this ritual of Jennys and booze and, more often than not, pretending to be sick. When he garnered their sympathy, they were less likely to complain about the crappy sex.

After the first few drinks came the optimism stage. With a buzz on and a beautiful girl smiling and pressing close, he'd think,

Maybe. Maybe I'll like it this time. Maybe it'll be enough. But the orgasms hollowed him out, the images in his mind of rough stubble and broad muscles, and fantasies of hard cock in his mouth and ass giving way to the reality of sweet perfume and soft curves.

So he'd escape to the bathroom and pretend to be sick, knowing the Jennys deserved a hell of a lot better than him. He splashed his face with water now and avoided the mirror, opening the door with a deep breath. Wearing one of his T-shirts, which draped her petite body to mid-thigh, Jenny closed the front door and brought a tray with ginger ale and saltines over to the bed.

"Here, try nibbling on these."

Nico sat on the side of the messy bed and did as he was told. The crackers tasted like cardboard. "Thanks. I know this sucks."

"Don't be silly. You can't help it. Did you get it out? Always feels better after."

He tried to smile. "Yeah." He sipped the ginger ale, the nausea nothing to do with seafood. There was a soft tapping, and he glanced over sharply. "No pictures!"

Jenny jerked, eyes wide, still holding her phone. She said tentatively, "I wasn't going to. Just texting my mom to say I won't be home until morning. See?" She held up the screen. "I swear."

"Sorry. Management gives us shit if we end up on Instagram doing anything that's not clean and wholesome."

"Oh, I bet." She winked. "Don't worry, it'll be our little secret."

His stomach churned. "Maybe you should go home. Don't want your mom to worry."

Her smile fell. "Oh. Okay."

"I had an awesome time, but I feel like shit. I'll pay for your cab."

"Right. Sure, I understand." She put on a smile and, in awkward silence, slipped back into her dress and strappy sandals. She tapped her phone. "I ordered an Uber, so don't worry about it. I don't live far."

"Are you sure?" Ugh, this was the worst stage. He didn't want to be an asshole, but he always, always was.

"When are you back in town? Maybe we can hang out again. Or I could take the train up to Ottawa. It's not that far. I kind of like the train. It's relaxing, you know?" She stopped talking and fidgeted with the hem of her dress.

"Yeah, maybe. That would be cool."

"Let me get your number." She tapped her phone again, then paused. "Oh, my friend Lorraine—from downstairs, with blond hair? Anyway, she says you're getting a new catcher? Are you excited? She says he's really good." Jenny laughed and rolled her eyes. "And hot."

"New catcher?" Nico asked dumbly.

She squinted at the screen. "Jake Fitzgerald? Apparently was just traded from San Francisco. Do you know him?"

In a mighty whoosh, all the oxygen was sucked from the room. Jake. Fitzgerald. *Jake Fitzgerald.* JAKE FITZGERALD.

"Are you okay?"

Heart hammering as if he was on the mound with a million people watching, Nico tried to catch a breath.

Jenny's brows drew together, and she reached out. "Sweetie, you look like you're going to puke again."

He nodded and stumbled into the bathroom, locking the door behind him. He really did taste bile in his throat, and he ran the taps, leaning heavily on the sink.

"Are you sure you're okay?" Jenny asked through the door. "Maybe you shouldn't be alone."

He practically growled, "Just go!"

There was no reply, but soon he heard the faint thud of the front door closing over the rushing water and thumping of his heart. Lips parted, he gulped for air.

Jake Fitzgerald.

Suddenly Nico was thirteen again in Chicago, gangly and covered in zits, his hair in his eyes and headphones almost permanently shoved in his ears. Dad so proud of Marco making the big leagues, Marco and his teammate Jake coming over all the time for Nonna's ziti.

Jake playing catch with Nico by the pool for hours, insisting he didn't mind, paying attention to him while Marco and Dad went over game tapes. Towering over him, a forceful high-five with a huge hand and a strong arm around Nico's shoulders after a good session, smelling like musky sweat and grass.

The little divot scar on Jake's temple, his blue eyes so fucking *pretty*. His big body somehow folding down into a perfect catcher's crouch, all coiled power and easy smiles, thick thighs that could crack walnuts. Taking the sting out of Nico's dad's criticisms, offering up a compliment for every complaint, earning an extra helping of cannoli from Nonna.

That summer, Nico had let himself wallow in Jake Fitzgerald, jerking off multiple times a day to thoughts of Jake's big hands on him when he should have been thinking about tits and pussy.

Then that day in the living room watching the big-screen TV: a marriage equality rally on the news, Nonna clucking her tongue in disapproval and making the sign of the cross, Valentina glued to her laptop chat window, and Dad gulping beer and sneering at the screen.

"This country's going down the shitter. Queers wanting to get married—next thing we know, they'll want to play baseball too!" He laughed and flipped the channel, and it was already forgotten as he watched a golfer miss a putt. "Ah, come on! I could have made that with one hand tied behind my back!"

Nine years later, sweat still broke out on Nico's brow, his hands clutching the bathroom counter, knees shaking as he fought the wave of nausea. He'd sat on the couch, his throat dry, knowing without a doubt that he was this laughable thing, this *queer* who wanted to play baseball. Knowing that he was *wrong*.

So he'd tried to stop fantasizing about Jake Fitzgerald, or any other guys. He'd tried over and over to find the right girl. The girl who could fix him. The Jenny who could be so perfect he'd only want to fuck her. So he could be the way he was supposed to.

Splashing his face again, Nico turned away, avoiding the mirror. The hotel room was blissfully empty, and he shook out a few Advil into his palm and washed them down with ginger ale.

There was a note in gracefully scripted writing on the desk with Jenny's number and an "xo" and "feel better." The words on the starkly white hotel notepad stared up at him accusingly, and he tore the note into thin shreds.

Jake Fitzgerald. He was going to have to play with Jake Fitzgerald. See him every day. Practice with him.

Nico wasn't the way he was supposed to be, no matter how hard he tried. No matter how diligently he worked to ignore his hot teammates in the locker room, keeping his head down and mind somewhere else while they laughed and joked.

Because at the thought of Jake Fitzgerald, all the sticky, desperate lust came roaring back. So did the fantasies Nico had tried to bury over the years.

Worshiping a dick, swallowing it so deep he choked. Sucking heavy balls and licking ass. On his hands and knees, spreading himself open for a thick cock, rammed by it so hard he'd feel it for days. Smothered by a heavy, hairy, sweaty body with muscles. Consumed.

In the past few years, he'd only allowed these faceless fantasies in moments of weakness. Now Nico fought not to imagine himself at Jake's feet, or in Jake's bed. It'd been a struggle to get it up for Jenny earlier, but now he was rock hard without even touching himself.

Fuck. He had to get in control.

"There are no queers in baseball," he muttered hoarsely.

It obviously wasn't true—a minor leaguer had come out the year before, and Billy Bean and Glenn Burke had publicly revealed their sexuality after retiring. Statistically, with hundreds of players in the league, some of them had to be gay.

It can't just be me.

But it sure as shit felt like it. It didn't matter that gay marriage was legal now, and that things were changing. Because nothing had changed for Nico's father, and even though the pope had kind of said LGBT people were maybe okay, Nonna still crossed herself if the subject ever came up.

His aunts and uncles and cousins probably hated queers too, and Nico tried not to think about what his mother would have thought. His hazy memories of her were so few he didn't want to risk tainting them.

Flowery perfume that couldn't cover the stench of sickness, a silver cross nestled against her throat, reading him Curious George *in bed, her skin tissue paper thin and arms practically bones around him...*

Guilt swirled, familiar and grasping. If he hadn't been born, she wouldn't have gotten sick. Would still be alive and beautiful like she was in the old pictures without him. Dad would smile the way he did in those pictures, before Nico destroyed everything.

The pictures still hung on the walls of their big house in Chicago, but Nico hadn't heard Dad speak her name since the funeral. Nonna never talked about her daughter, and Nico's brother and sister had only mentioned Mom in fleeting whispers.

Even as a kid, Nico had known why. He'd kept his head down and played quietly, never breathing a word. He'd wanted to beg for forgiveness, but silence was easier, and then the years passed, and there didn't seem to be any point. His father tolerated him, but Nico knew he was never as good as Val or Marco. And how could he be? Not only had he killed their mother, he was secretly queer.

Nico had never had the guts to tell his brother and sister. He didn't think he could stand to see the disdain—or worse, disgust—on their faces.

Or Jake's.

God, how horrified he'd be if he knew the dirty things Nico had imagined. Nico picked up the tray off the bed and hurled it across the room, crackers flying and the glass of ginger ale shattering against the wall, his chest heaving and cock stubbornly rigid.

Jake fisting his hand in Nico's curls, fucking his mouth. Coming all over his face. Bending Nico over a table and holding him down, not letting him move an inch as he pounded his ass, filling him with cum until it dripped out, until he was covered in it like a slut, still begging for more.

Gritting his teeth, Nico gave in with a groan, dropping on his back on the mattress. Tearing open the robe, he spread his bent legs and jerked himself dry and rough. He squirmed his left hand under his body and jammed a finger into his hole, welcoming the burning pain. His dick leaked, curving to the right in his palm, the cut head glistening.

He knew he should think of anyone else, but Nico could only close his eyes and imagined Jake on top of him, so heavy and big, his body hair scratching, stubble scraping as he dominated Nico's mouth and filled his ass, ramming with long strokes, pushing his knees up to his shoulders, bending him in half, the headboard thumping, heavy balls slapping against Nico's skin—

Gasping, Nico spurted over his chest, his ass gripping his finger as he shuddered and wrung himself out. His legs flopped down, but he kept his finger in his hole, giving himself another minute to imagine it was Jake.

Another minute to imagine Jake was kissing him now, whispering words of praise, holding him close, warm and safe. It would never happen, but Nico closed his eyes and dreamed.

When the minute was up, he stumbled to the shower and

turned it on as hot as he could stand, scrubbing his skin raw. That had to be the last time he let himself think of Jake Fitzgerald like that. He'd always known he'd never be able to act on his desires, but with Jake about to be around all the time, even fantasizing was reckless. If Nico let something slip… He shuddered.

But it would be okay. He'd gotten it out of his system now, and he could focus on the game—on being perfect. Then nothing else would matter.

CHAPTER THREE

THE PHONE WOULD not stop ringing.

Jake's cell was surely blowing up with messages too, but he'd muted it hours ago. He stupidly hadn't thought to have his room calls held, and when the third one came, he jerked out from under his pillows and grabbed for the phone on the nightstand, barking, "What?"

"Well, isn't that a fine way to greet your mother?" His mother Helen's English accent had faded over her thirty years in Canada, but now it sharpened in annoyance.

Groaning, Jake rubbed his face in the dark room, the hard plastic of the phone cradled between his ear and shoulder. "Sorry. Hi, Mom. What's up? Everything okay?" He stretched, wincing. The bruises and weariness always caught up with him in mornings, the rush of game-time adrenaline gone.

"What's up? What's up is Janice called me at six o'clock this morning to say how exciting it is that you've been traded to Ottawa."

Oh, right. That had actually happened. It wasn't a dream. "I was going to call you as soon as I got up. I didn't want to wake you last night."

"It's after nine, Jake. I showed admirable restraint in waiting three hours to track you down at your hotel."

"True, but you know I don't usually get up until ten-thirty

after a night game." Flopped on his back, the covers tangled around his legs, Jake stared at the dark ceiling, a crack of sunlight coming through the curtains. "But I really am sorry you didn't hear it from me. So, yeah. I got traded to Ottawa. Surprise!"

"It is a surprise. What happened?"

With a sigh, he gave her the rundown on his conversations with Ted and Norwalk. "So there's nothing I can do about it. I'll finish out my contract in Ottawa."

"You know it's not a prison sentence."

"I know. But I have everything the way I like it in San Fran. My house, my friends, the team."

"No boyfriend, though."

"*Mom.*"

"What? I'm just pointing it out. In all these years, I don't understand why a wonderful man like you hasn't found anyone yet. It's not like San Francisco is lacking in options. Did you ever go down to that Castro place? I saw a program on TV about—"

"Stop."

"Okay, okay. Maybe you'll have more luck in Ottawa. It's small, but they must have a gay bar. And I'm sure people use those apps. I downloaded one on my iPad to see what it was all about. Some handsome men on there!"

Sweet Jesus. "I'm not going to a bar or putting my face on an app. I can just see the headlines now."

She sighed. "I don't think people will care. It's 2016. You know Phyllis in my ladies' golf league? She lives in Penetang? Her daughter's a lesbian and no one minds at all."

"Good for her. She's not playing professional baseball. Can we not do this right now?"

"Sorry, sorry. You're right. It's up to you, and I shouldn't nag. I only want what's best for you. Now I know you're not happy, but…" He could imagine a smile lighting up her face, the wrinkles around her eyes getting deeper, her gray-blond hair waving around her chin. "Oh, Jake, I'm so happy you're coming home! The Capitals are a good young team! Doing better than those bums in Toronto so far this season. When's your first game? Tomorrow? Janice is going to organize a bus trip next month for the seniors' center, but obviously I'm driving up to see you!"

Affection for her warmed Jake inside out, and he smiled in the darkness. "I'm assuming it'll be tomorrow, but maybe tonight. It's not a long flight from Boston. I'll find out for you. So how are you? Did you play yesterday? How was your putting?"

She tsked. "I'm sure it would have been terrible, but we were rained out. Went to Hustle and Muscle at the center instead. Did I tell you Betty had a fall the other night? Poor thing twisted her knee, so I made her a lasagna and a tuna casserole."

While his mother filled him in on the latest seniors' news from their small town, Jake made listening noises at the right times, in no rush at all to get out of bed and face the day.

"Patty sent me a picture of the new baby. Cute little girl. Strange name—Sailor. But it's not so bad as some you hear these days. Honestly, *Boomer*? That's a name for a golden retriever, not a child. I think all that chlorine has affected Michael Phelps's brain, I'm just saying."

He chuckled, squirming a bit at the mention of his cousin. His family was quite small, and he certainly had affection for Patty, who'd been the closest thing he had to a sibling growing up. But any mention of her would lead to—

"That's her third child now, can you believe it? Time flies. Tom and Louise are so thrilled to have another grandchild."

Here we go. "Yes, I'm sure they are."

"Oh, and the neighbors across the street, you know, the Duponts? Their daughter-in-law is expecting. I'm going to help with the shower."

Guilt and irritation fought for dominance, irritation winning. "Great. Look, you know why I don't have kids, so do we have to have this conversation *again?*"

She huffed. "No, I don't know why you don't have kids. Gay people can have children, Jake. There's adoption, or a surrogate, or plenty of ways. Of course you need a husband first."

"I'm not interested! It's my life, Mother."

After a few moments of silence, she sighed. "You're right. I'm sorry." Her voice was soft now and so terribly sad.

And there was the guilt. "I'm sorry I snapped at you. It's just…I don't know if I can be the son you want me to be."

"Oh, Jake. Don't ever think that. You know I love you exactly the way you are. I just worry about you. Worry that you're not happy. I'm sorry, I know I'm an old nag."

"Of course you're not. Look, let's just deal with the trade before any other life changes."

"All right. Love you, my boy, and see you soon. This is exciting!"

He smiled fondly. "Love you too."

After they hung up, Jake stared at the ceiling for another minute, the crack of sunlight in his peripheral vision. With a sigh, he heaved himself off the bed, threw back the curtains, and opened his suitcase. He was off to join the Caps whether he liked it or not.

"Welcome to Ottawa!"

Jake dutifully smiled at Ryan, the front office staffer who'd been sent to pick him up at the airport. The clean-cut young man—a kid, really—insisted on taking Jake's suitcase, and they walked through the small terminal chatting about weather and the flight. Jake's sneakers squeaked on the floor, and he kept his hands in his jeans pockets.

"It's good to be home, eh?" Ryan asked.

Home. Aside from the quick series against the Caps last season,

Jake hadn't been to Ottawa since a school trip to see the parliament buildings and the civilization museum across the river in Hull. Was Canada even home anymore?

He'd grown up in Midland, but hadn't lived there since he was eighteen. He realized with disbelief that he'd almost spent as long living in the States as he had in Canada.

"It is," he answered, since he couldn't exactly say no. "A little surreal."

Yesterday, he'd woken up, worked out with the team, and prepared like he had a thousand times, getting ready to call the game with his starting pitcher. It had been just another Tuesday. Now everything had changed—his team, his home, his life. He had to make all new routines.

Shoving his hands in his pockets, he fought the urge to rip his suitcase away from Ryan and race back to the gate for the first flight to anywhere. Hell, he'd rent a car and drive. Anything to get back behind the wheel of his damn life.

At six-five, Jake was used to people looking twice at him, but as they made their way through the terminal, he could feel stares and hear the murmurs of whispers. He hadn't even looked to see how the trade had been reported in the Ottawa media, but apparently the news had traveled quickly. Good thing he'd worn a plain gray hoodie and not one of his San Francisco ones. Pics of him in his old team's apparel would probably launch some Twitter rants.

As they passed the airport convenience store, he asked, "Hey, mind if I grab a Crispy Crunch? It's been a while."

Of course Ryan didn't mind, and when Jake tried to pay with American cash—which the cashier would have happily accepted—Ryan insisted on paying, handing a silver and gold two-dollar coin to the cashier.

"You'll have to get used to using loonies and toonies again!" Ryan laughed.

Jake laughed along, wishing he was in California, heading back to his nice, familiar house in Marin, where he had all his stuff and his nice, orderly life.

His cheeks went hot as he thought about the ridiculous salary he received to play baseball—a game he'd loved once upon a time. *It's not like you're hauling rocks in Siberia. Jesus, you make millions; more than most people ever see in their lives. Stop being an entitled douche already. Enjoy the little things.*

"Everything okay?" Ryan asked.

"Absolutely." Jake unwrapped the chocolate bar and took a bite, moaning appreciatively at the chocolate-covered, flaky peanut layers.

A small voice asked, "Mr. Fitzgerald?"

Jake turned to find two kids around eight or nine staring up at him. The girl's black hair was tucked up beneath a red and white Capitals hat, the red maple leaf embossed with threads of silver. The wide-eyed boy, presumably her brother, had his mouth open.

"Hey, guys. How are you doing?"

Still staring up, the girl hissed, "I told you it was him!"

"Guilty as charged." Jake smiled. "I haven't worn the uniform yet, but do you want me to sign your cap?"

She nodded vigorously. "Thank you."

Her brother's lips trembled. "Mine's at home."

A woman Jake assumed was their mother stepped forward and squeezed his shoulders. "It's okay, Sunil. You can share Rina's hat."

Rina whirled to her mother. "What? But this is *my* hat! It's not fair!"

Jake glanced around the store, spotting a display of Capitals merch in the corner. "No worries. I'll buy you a new one, okay, buddy?" He asked the cashier, "Do you sell Sharpies?"

The mother said, "Oh no, I can't let you do that!"

Jake smiled. "I insist. It's my pleasure."

Once Sunil had picked a new hat, Jake insisted on T-shirts for both kids and signed them on the counter, giving the cashier his credit card before Ryan could argue. A small crowd had gathered, and Jake was aware of cell phones photographing and probably recording him. Smiling, he posed for pictures with the kids, and then selfies with a host of other travelers as well.

"Sorry, folks, Jake's got to get to the ballpark," Ryan said loudly, guiding him past the magazine stands at the entrance. "Time to get him in a Caps' uniform, what do you say?"

Now everyone applauded, and Jake waved and smiled, and okay, that felt pretty damn good. He didn't stop smiling as they reached the parking lot. Ryan enthused about the encounter, tapping his phone. "I got some awesome shots of you and the kids. PR's gonna love this."

"Great." Jake pulled the rest of the chocolate bar from his pocket and savored the sweet peanut-chocolate flavors.

"The guys are psyched to meet you. Everyone's really excited to have you on the team."

"Thanks. It's…yeah, it's great."

Don't be an entitled douche. Find the silver lining.

But as they drove downtown, Jake felt a growing sensation of dread. After eight seasons on the same team, he was going to be the new guy again. He was going to have to get used to a new way of doing things; a new stadium and clubhouse and trainers and managers and teammates. A few of the guys were acquaintances, and he'd known Marco's little brother a little bit, but that had been a million years ago.

"How do you like the new dome?" Ryan asked, immediately answering his own question with a chipper, "Pretty great, eh?"

The Capital Dome was open in the distance as they approached, and from what Jake recalled, it was a nice ballpark with good facilities. "Yeah. Surprised they found room for it downtown."

"Had to partner with U of O to get the space, but the city brokered the deal. The owners really wanted the park here in the city and not out in Kanata."

"How's attendance?"

"Fantastic. Seats just over thirty-five thousand, and we've been near capacity since the first game. Ottawa's super loyal to its teams, and a lot of people come over from Quebec too. Montreal really wanted a team back, but it's only two hours away. There are a bunch of bus trips that come for every game."

"Cool." It was definitely overdue for Canada to have another ball club.

Ryan drove into the dome's underground parking, and Jake took a deep breath, readying himself for a hundred handshakes. He could do this. It was his job, and he'd do it damn well.

His smile stayed in place as he encountered more people from the front office and met Martin Tyson in person. Tyson shepherded him through the bowels of the stadium. He was about forty, tall and African American, his suit and tie immaculate on his muscled frame, cuff links gleaming at his wrists. His legs were almost as long as Jake's, and they strode quickly through the tunnels.

"Everything is state of the art. Conditioning and physio are vital, and we'll take care of all your needs. But if there's something we've overlooked, speak up. I want you to feel at home here." Tyson gave Jake's shoulder a light slap. "You and Garcia are exactly the shot in the arm we need. Everyone says a club takes years to win, but I'm not a patient man." He grinned.

"Garcia?" Jake's heart thumped a little faster. *Which Garcia?* "You made another trade?"

"Sorry, thought you would have heard. It came together quickly, just like it did with you. We acquired Diego Garcia from Houston for Johnson and two pitching prospects. We need your leadership behind the plate, and Garcia in the infield. He's struggled at bat, but I know he can turn it around, and his defense is some of the best in the game. You two played together in Philly, right?"

A murky soup of apprehension and regret simmered in Jake's gut. "Briefly, yeah. Great guy. Great second baseman too. Which you're well aware of, obviously."

Tyson laughed, a low rumble. "Still good to hear that you concur."

He did—Garcia was indeed a great second baseman and person, but Jake had largely avoided him for years. Now that was clearly at an end, and it was one more element he couldn't control. His skin prickled, armpits growing damp.

As they neared the clubhouse, he spotted the team's manager in the hallway under the bright fluorescent lights, pacing back and forth with his hands in the back pockets of his uniform pants. Skip Jankowski's jaw worked his trademark bubblegum like one of the stitching machines at the luggage factory Jake's dad had toiled in.

Skip's hair was mostly gray under his Capitals hat, and he was a compact man, built like a barrel now as he aged. He'd been one of the best shortstops in his day, wiry and tough. He spotted Jake and Tyson approaching and strode over, his hand extended.

"Good to have you on board, Fitz." He pumped Jake's hand as vigorously as he chewed his gum. "Call me Skip."

Jake wasn't actually sure what the man's given name was; he'd been known as "Skip" or "Skipper" since his player days for the way he could fire a ball while in motion, his feet barely touching the ground like a stone on the surface of a pond. The name had transitioned perfectly into his leadership role. "Great to be here, Skip."

"The guys are doing BP, so come see your new home in the meantime."

Home. There was that word again. Jake pasted on a smile,

hoping the team was in no rush to wrap up batting practice. He was used to meeting new people but wished there was some way to avoid the endless handshakes, at least for the day.

He followed Skip and Tyson through double frosted-glass doors into the multiroom clubhouse. They walked down a hallway through to the locker room, an open rectangle of a space, carpeted in navy with the Caps name and maple leaf logo emblazoned in red across the open part of the floor.

The players' wide, open-design lockers lined three walls, names and numbers on a plaque above each. High cubbies held bats and equipment, while cleats were below. Spare shirts and pants hung on a rod, and a spotless uniform and hat for that night's game were displayed on a hanger.

In front of each locker sat a padded, black leather office chair on wheels with the logo stitched on the backrest in red and white. The middle of the room contained a ping-pong table and leather couches, with several flat-screen TVs high up on the walls.

There wasn't a speck of the green that dominated San Francisco's clubhouse, and when Skip stopped in front of a locker, Jake read his own name and number from the plaque. He smiled weakly. "That was fast."

Skip clapped his shoulder. "Wanted to make you feel right at home. I know it can be a punch in the nuts getting traded. I've been there."

It took a second for Jake to realize his number, 19, was the same as it had been in San Francisco. His smile broadened. "Thanks for the number."

"Our pleasure," Tyson said. "Like Skip mentioned, we want you to feel comfortable. In the clubhouse and on the field."

"Speaking of which, we'll play you as DH tomorrow and behind the plate Friday," Skip said. "Carter's a knuckleballer, and he and Baldoni have a good thing going, so we're keeping Baldoni as his primary."

"Absolutely." It wasn't uncommon to pair certain pitchers with catchers they connected with, even if the catcher wasn't the usual starter. "I'm excited to get out there in a Caps uniform." His gut tightened at the thought, but he grinned through it. As designated hitter, the pressure was on to have a good night at the plate.

It was a long season, but he'd been having a decent year so far—.273 batting average with seventeen RBIs and a handful of homers. Definitely wanted to get his RBI number up—batting in runs was vital. His on-base percentage was strong, well up over three hundred since he had the patience to draw his fair share of walks. As much as he hadn't wanted to play for Ottawa, he wanted to do a good job.

Skip continued. "So that'll give you and the starter time to drill and coordinate signs for Friday and get your ducks in a row with the relievers too. We've got scouting reports on Baltimore's hitters for you to call the game. I trust your judgment on which pitches should be thrown. I know we're in good hands with you taking the lead on the field."

The confidence sent a warm flush through Jake. He'd clashed in Philly with a manager who liked to micromanage, wanting Jake to look to him for signs before every pitch like it was college ball. But most major league managers trusted their catcher to call the game, and he was relieved Skip was one of them.

Jake asked, "Who's starting Friday?" They'd have two days to get familiar with each other, and he'd have to spend time with the other pitchers too.

"Agresta." Skip's lips quirked into a smile, and he blew a forceful bubble with his gum. "The kid's got a hell of an arm, but you'll have your hands full keeping him in check. He's got a temper, and when he gets rattled it can go to shit in a soup can real quick. He needs discipline. Patience. Needs to calm the hell down when he gets behind in the count. Obviously you'll talk with our pitching coach, Loyola. He's got lots of thoughts on the matter. He'll brief you on the rest of the starters and bullpen too."

"Sounds good." Jake had gotten to know the pitchers in San Fran well over the years, their quirks and habits and the best way to keep them focused and effective. It was daunting to start from scratch again, but that's why they were paying him millions. In the past, he'd loved to take on a new challenge. When had that fire died out?

When you fucked up the best friendship you ever had.

Jesus, it had been five years. How had he let himself get so complacent? So *bored?* He'd always liked control, but he'd cut out spontaneity and risk on the field—and in the bedroom. The arrangement with Ron had been safe and uncomplicated. Playing for a team that didn't contend year after year had been safe too.

Pushing away thoughts of Brandon's easy smile, Jake cleared his throat. "Thanks for your faith in me. I'm really excited to join the team and see what we can do together."

Tyson grinned. "We're going to make this a winning ball club, Fitz."

"Damn straight," Skip agreed.

There were voices outside, and the clubhouse door opened. Diego Garcia walked in with a few front office staffers, his handsome face breaking into a grin and his arms going wide. "Together again, Fitz!"

The guilt flared, prickly and sharp, as Jake met Diego in a back-slapping hug. Diego was just over six foot, his white smile straight and almost blinding, stubble on his tan skin, his thick hair neatly coiffed, swooping back gracefully from his forehead.

He smelled like pine with a hint of citrus. Jake was struck by the memory of sitting together in a bar on the road in Minneapolis or maybe Detroit, their shoulders brushing in the booth by the pool table, heads together and voices low as Jake had confessed his secrets, too much tequila loosening his tongue.

"It's good to see you, brother," Diego said as he stepped back with another slap, his smile warm.

"You too." By all rights, Diego should have cooled considerably to him after the way Jake had distanced himself over the years and blown off Diego's attempts to keep in touch. The last time San Fran had played in Houston, Diego had once again invited Jake over for dinner with his family, but Jake had canceled with a lame excuse. "How are Liz and the kids?"

"Good." Diego shot a glance at Tyson and Skip. "Obviously a bit upset at the moment, but we'll figure it all out. School year's just ending, but they're going to camp, so they're staying in Texas for the time being."

"Like I said, we'll do everything we can to help the transition," Tyson said. "Diego, here's your locker just over here. The equipment manager's going to talk bats and gloves and everything with you both."

A rectangular screen on a thick post in the middle of the room displayed that night's starting lineup, scrolling through different information, including weather and the start times of the anthems and first pitch. Diego's name was on the lineup, and he tried on his cap, wearing it as the tour continued into the players' lounge through another set of doors.

The carpeted lounge was like a small cafeteria, dotted with tables for four, salt and pepper shakers on top of each. A huge glass-fronted fridge with soda, water, sports drinks, juice, and several varieties of milk stood against the wall by the door next to shelves of nuts, candy, a vast array of gum, and sunflower seeds of every variety imaginable—including barbecue, bacon ranch, and dill pickle.

Tyson motioned to the industrial kitchen area beyond a wide pass-through, where several people chopped vegetables. "As you'd expect, there's a big spread here after every game, and you'll eat before the game after BP as well. If you have requests, just let us know."

Diego eyed the arcade-style video games against the walls, which also featured two TVs and framed pictures of Capitals players in action. Since the team was only in its second year, the same people cropped up in most of them. Diego said, "Jake, we definitely have to take the Golden Tee machine for a whirl. I bet I can beat you by three strokes."

Jake answered the way he was supposed to, with a grin. "You're on."

The double doors opened, the team streaming through, fresh from batting practice. Turning on his smile and being his best self, Jake shook hands and slapped backs, the room filling with chatter as he and Diego did the rounds.

Jake's cheeks ached from smiling, and a headache throbbed behind his left eye and vibrated through the little scar on his temple from a nasty foul ball in the minors that had jammed the corner of his catcher's mask into his face and gouged out a chunk of flesh.

He was just about to excuse himself when Skip caught his arm. "Fitz, come meet Agresta."

Ah right, Marco Agresta's gangly little brother. But when Jake turned, the man he saw frozen by the lounge doorway was most definitely not the kid he remembered. The mop of curls had been tamed, kept short on the back and sides, with a few locks tumbling over his forehead.

Nico had grown like a weed and had to be six-one or two now. Long and lean like many pitchers, he filled out the red and white uniform with sculpted muscles and narrow hips. He opened and closed his mouth, then licked his thick, red lips. A small cleft accentuated his strong jaw, and the white of the caps uniform set off his clear, golden skin perfectly, dark hair dusting his arms.

No, aside from the familiar intensity of his dark stare, Nico was not the child Jake remembered.

So he turned out hot. It's irrelevant. You have a job to do.

Jake realized he was staring, and jumped into action with another smile. "Hey, Nico. It's been a few years. You're all grown up now, huh?"

Nico swallowed hard. "Um...yeah." He extended his hand.

Chuckling awkwardly, Jake shook it and pulled him into a half hug and requisite back slap, inhaling the musky smell of cowhide, dirt, and sweat. "Good to see you."

Nico stepped back, breaking contact. "You too." Jittery, he wriggled his fingers and dropped his gaze.

Skip laughed. "You're not facing a firing squad, kid! Don't worry, Fitz'll take real good care of you."

Jake laughed on cue, wondering at the turmoil in Nico's dark eyes. Nico was a man now, but a surge of protectiveness had Jake reaching for his shoulder to give it a squeeze. "I'll go easy on you, I promise. How about we practice early? We'll work out our signs."

"Great." For a fleeting moment, a smile dimpled Nico's cheeks. He glanced at Skip and waved his hand. "I should...you know." With that, he bolted for the drink fridge.

Skip leaned in and murmured, "He's a weird kid. Doesn't say a whole hell of a lot until he gets mad, and then you can't shut him up. You'll get a handle on him. We're counting on you, Fitz."

"Absolutely."

"All right, make yourself at home. We'll talk more later." Skip headed to the kitchen, calling out something about a peanut butter sandwich.

Tyson and Diego were in conversation across the lounge, and Jake's gaze zeroed in on Nico Agresta sitting by himself at a table in the corner, peeling the label off a blue Gatorade, his broad shoulders hunched.

Nico was having an outstanding rookie season by the sound of it. He should have been on top of the world. Maybe he was partying too much. Jake had seen it before—guys getting swept up in the excitement of the big league, spending too much time at the bars with girls, too many late nights.

The headache was now accompanied by an uncomfortable flush over Jake's body, and he escaped into the hall to pop a couple aspirin, leaving his new teammates behind.

CHAPTER FOUR

"**I**'M THRILLED TO be back home in Canada. It really is a dream come true."

From the entrance to the shower area off the locker room, Nico listened to Jake's session with the media, a shoulder against the tiled wall. He could imagine the smile on Jake's face, the way his blue eyes lit up. Nico had put on his workout clothes—a red Caps tee and his usual white uniform pants with his red socks pulled up to his knees.

That's the way his father had worn his uniform, that's the way Marco wore his, and Nico wasn't about to mess with success. Besides, he liked the throwback look of socks over his pants, the tradition of it. Maybe he'd heard too many rants from his father about how the guys today were going to trip over their baggy pants. They had shorts to wear for practice once summer hit, but late spring had been surprisingly cool.

"Hey, Ag." Third baseman Aaron Crowe nodded as he came out of the bathroom area, running a hand through his reddish hair and over his bushy, hipster beard. He paused, his brows drawn together. "You okay, man?"

Nico straightened up off the wall. "Yeah. Just waiting." *And lurking like a creeper.* He followed Crowe out into the locker room, glancing at Jake, who wore his new Caps workout clothes. He didn't have his socks tugged up, but his uniform pants hugged his muscular legs above his catcher's pads. He caught Nico's eye with a nod.

"I've got to start earning my keep. Talk to you guys later." Jake grabbed his hat, glove, and catcher's mask and hustled to catch up with Nico, briefly laying a big hand on his shoulder.

Nico's stomach flip-flopped like he was thirteen again, and he shoved his own cap on his head, trying to think of something to say as he led the way up and out to the bullpen across the field, the artificial turf springy beneath their cleats.

The stadium was empty that morning but for cleaners sweeping up endless peanut shells in the rows and rows of stands. The rectangular bullpen for pitchers waited beyond the right field fence, and a shiver of anticipation tripped down Nico's spine.

Every time he went to the mound, whether it was in the pen or on the field, excitement bubbled in him. He could already feel the cowhide and seams, and he thumped his right hand into the thick baseball glove he wore on his left. The leather was worn and soft against his fingers, and he flexed them eagerly.

That Jake was walking beside him made the butterflies flap harder than ever. Nico wanted to impress him, show him how much he'd improved. No, he didn't just *want* to—he had to.

"How's Marco?" Jake asked. "Haven't played him this season yet. What's our schedule? Are we going to Chicago soon?"

Dread slithered through Nico, his excitement withering. "Next month before the all-star break. Four-game series."

"Cool, you'll get to see your family. Is your Nonna still making that amazing cannoli?"

He smiled softly, imagining the chocolate chips melting on his tongue. "Yeah."

Jake seemed to be waiting for him to say something else, and smiled after a few awkward beats. "Well, great. What about Valentina? Still breaking hearts?"

"Getting married, actually. She's good."

"Cool. Are they all going to come to a game while we're in Chicago?"

The fist of dread tightened in Nico's gut. "My dad will be at all of them."

At the bullpen door, Jake smiled. "He must be so proud of you."

Nico shrugged. "He has season tickets. Marco's still playing there."

"Well, I bet he's still proud. Your mom would be too."

If I hadn't killed her. He tried to smile.

Frowning, Jake blocked the door. "Sorry. I guess I like to think my dad can still see me. Even if it's a fairy tale, it's nice."

"No, it's okay. I get it." Nico wanted to think his mother was watching. Wanted to think she'd forgiven him. But thinking of her at all was like having his insides scooped out with a rusty spoon.

"That'll be weird, pitching to your brother. Media'll make a big deal about that."

"Yeah." Nico brushed by him, rolling out the tension in his neck.

In the corner of the bullpen where pitchers practiced during the day and relievers warmed up during games, Mike Andropoulos, the bullpen catcher, sat on a bench scuffing a box of new balls, a tub of Lena Blackburne's Baseball Rubbing Mud by his feet. In his forties with his dark hair graying at his temples, Mike glanced up.

"Hey, guys. You're out early." With a dab of mud on his fingers, Mike spit on them and rubbed the ball all over with sharp, rhythmic movements, the white glow dimming and becoming easier to grip.

Jake went over and extended his hand, clasping Mike's dirty one firmly as they made their introductions. "Good to meet you. Scuffing up those shiny new pearls for us?"

Mike grinned. "You know what they say about pearls and swine."

There were boxes of new balls—the slick "pearls"—stacked next to Mike, hard ball bags on his other side filled with the scuffed balls ready to be pitched. Mike also caught for the pitchers and threw during batting practice. He had been a minor leaguer who never made the Show, and Nico was pretty sure Mike worked harder, day in and day out, and for way less money than the guys on the team.

Mike tossed over a dirty ball, and Nico gripped the cowhide, tracing the red-stitched seams with his thumb. Mike carried on with his scuffing, engrossed in his work as Nico stood on the rectangular pitcher's rubber at one end of the pen and Jake went partway to the plate, holding up his glove for the ball. Still standing, he tossed it back to Nico as they warmed up.

"How's your splitter these days?"

Nico blinked. "You remember?" He'd been obsessed with mastering it the summer Jake had been around in Chicago, even though his hands were a little too small back then and he should have focused on his curveball.

"Sure. Does Loyola let you throw it at all?"

"Nope." Ed Loyola, the grizzled pitching coach, was stubbornly against it. "They think it strains the elbow too much, having the fingers so wide apart."

"Yeah, in San Francisco, none of the guys are doing it. Management thinks the risk is too high."

"Obviously I don't want to fuck up my arm, but when a splitter hits the mark…"

Jake grinned. "Nothing like seeing that ball rocket in as a strike and drop at the last second as they swing at thin air."

"Exactly." It really was the greatest feeling in the world when the batter swung and missed, especially to strike out.

As he and Jake talked pitches, they tossed the ball back and forth easily. If Nico squinted, they could be back in the huge yard at his dad's house in Chicago up in Highland Park on the North Shore. But nope, Nico was a major leaguer now too, and he was actually going to get the chance to pitch to Jake for real. If he'd told his scrawny, zit-faced self back then he'd ever see this day, he probably would have come in his pants before passing out.

"Do you have any preference on signs?" Jake asked. "Skip gave me the team's bible to get me up to speed. Looks standard for the most part—one finger for fastball, two for breaker, three for slider, four and wiggle for changeup?"

"Yeah. What would you do for a splitter if I ever get to throw it?"

"Hmm. How about thumb and first finger wide apart?" Jake made the shape of an upside-down gun, cocking his wrist and holding his first finger out, his thumb down. "Good?" At Nico's nod, he added, "Okay. Prefer pumps or outs?"

When a runner was on second and could see the signs, catchers would try to confuse them by making the pattern of signs more complex. Some used the number of outs in the inning as part of the code, others the number of times they initially flashed their fingers. "Doesn't matter to me."

"Let's do pumps then. We'll run through a few now."

"Cool."

After walking to the plate at the end of the bullpen, Jake squatted and pulled on his protective mask, thickly padded with a metal cage over his face. Nico had always been amazed by how Jake could fold his tall body so compactly. Most catchers were on the shorter side, but Jake somehow made it work. His bulk protected the plate, and it would be hard to get wild pitches past him.

In his crouch, Jake's fingers flew between his long legs, and Nico called out the pitches, trying not to focus on the fact that he was staring at Jake's crotch. There was nothing sexual about it, and never had been with other catchers he'd worked with. Yet with Jake, Nico was captivated by every movement of his long fingers.

"Nico?"

Blinking, he jerked his gaze up to Jake's. "Uh-huh?"

"Lost you there for a second. What was the last sign?"

"Sorry, can you do it again?" He concentrated as Jake flashed his fingers. "Breaking ball to the inside."

"Yep." A grin broke out over Jake's face, his blue eyes crinkling. "Just thinking about how your grandmother thought the catchers were playing with themselves when she first started watching baseball."

In the corner, Mike burst out laughing. "What did you say?"

Jake pulled his mask onto the top of his head and stood from his crouch, absently rubbing his left knee. "Seriously. It's the best story." He looked at Nico expectantly.

"Right." Jake and Mike were waiting, and Nico cleared his throat. "Well, she hadn't been in America long. Moved from Italy and didn't speak English hardly at all. Her daughter—my mom—was dating my dad, and Nonna thought she should see what he did for a living. She told Mom she was glad he was catching balls in the field and wasn't one of those dirty boys playing with themselves in front of all those people."

"I think she still side-eyes catchers," Jake said. "Doesn't quite believe we're not doing something nasty."

His hand moving in a blur over a ball, Mike called, "Can't really blame her, can we?"

Laughing, Jake called back, "Takes one to know one."

Nico laughed too, and it was still hard to believe he was in the bullpen with Jake. In the nine years since that summer in Chicago, he'd tried not to go looking for photos and clips of Jake, but he'd stumble across them every so often. It'd been so long since he'd seen him in the flesh that Jake had started to feel like a movie star

Nico had crushed on, distant and unattainable.

Not that he's attainable now.

As Jake took a break to chug some water, Nico stretched. From the corner of his eye, he watched Jake's throat work, gazing at the long line of his neck. Did he have a girlfriend in San Francisco? He'd never been married, that much Nico knew. Never seemed to really date either, or at least not that the media noticed. Nico had wondered sometimes, and thought, *Maybe...*

Wishful fucking thinking. Even if by some miracle Jake's queer, he'd never actually want *me.*

By the plate, Jake called, "What?"

Nico realized he'd laughed out loud at his own thoughts. "Nothing. Want to work sinkers?" It was his second-favorite pitch after the splitter.

Jake got back into his crouch and Nico took a deep breath. This was solid ground. This, he could do. He usually threw two-seam fastball sinkers to the inside of the plate and regular four-seam fastballs out. It was like muscle memory his coach in the minors had taught him—that when he gripped his fingers along the seams in his glove before the windup, he knew subconsciously that he was going to the inside. The fewer things he had to actively think about on the mound, the better.

But in the bullpen with birds chirping distantly, the sun-warm breeze on the back of his neck and Jake catching, he hardly had to think about anything at all. He lifted his knee to his chest and let the ball rip, going for placement and not putting his full force behind it yet.

In the pen, there was no hulking umpire keeping count behind the plate, no batter walking to first, no crowd muttering in disappointment, all eyes on him, cameras zooming as he tried to keep his expression blank.

There was only him and Jake and Mike off in the corner, the scuffing noise soothing as Mike worked through the bags of pearls.

Here, Nico could breathe.

Then he missed, pitching into the dirt.

He missed again, high this time.

"You're overcompensating," Jake called.

He was, but pitch after pitch, his rhythm faltered. He tried a few curveballs, but it was no good. Swearing under his breath, he clenched his jaw. "If there were hitters here they would have scored at least three times by now. Probably homered."

Jake jogged over. "It's okay. Take a deep breath and focus. Trust the process. Every pitch is a new opportunity." He headed back to his spot.

Closing his eyes, Nico did as he was told. He wound up and ripped a sinker across the plate.

"There you go!" Jake called.

But as he continued, the missed pitches looped through his mind like a Vine on Twitter. He wanted to impress Jake, but who'd be wowed with that kind of loss of control? If it had been a game, Skip would have yanked Nico for sure. He'd been feeling so good, but it'd fallen apart with just a couple pitches.

What if it happens tomorrow? My ERA will go up and I'll get pulled from the game, and I'll have to wait five more days to get another chance. And then what if I screw up that game too? Dad'll rip me a new one. Every pitch counts. Every pitch has to be—

"Nico."

Blinking, he realized Jake was standing in front of him again, mask up on his head. "Huh?" Nico asked.

Jake held up his hand to block the angle of the sun. "Where'd you go?"

Nico actually glanced around as if he'd find himself somewhere other than standing on the rubber in the pen. He shrugged and reached for the ball, but Jake held onto it. Their fingers met, skin flushed and warm. Nico whipped his hand back.

"You totally checked out. Lights were on, but no one was

home."

"Sorry." He took off his hat and lifted his arm to rub his sleeve against his damp temple.

"What were you thinking about?" When Nico shrugged again, Jake raised his eyebrows, dipping his chin. "Use your words. I know you've got them piled up in there."

He huffed out a breath. "I don't know. Was thinking about that run of bullshit pitches."

"Why?"

"Why do you think?" He tugged his hat back on. "Because if that was a game I'd be toast. I was way outside the zone, and the ones that were in didn't sink for shit."

"Okay, but it wasn't a game," Jake said calmly. "And you were getting your form back."

"Yeah, but—" He sputtered, trying to think of how to explain it.

"You can't let go of what happened before." Jake smiled ruefully. "Trust me, I get it. But the past is the past. It's done. We can't change it, no matter how damn much we wish we could. And this wasn't a game. Don't psych yourself out over what-ifs. Okay?" At Nico's nod, Jake gave his arm a pat, his fingers brushing against Nico's skin beneath his short sleeve.

Jake jogged back to the plate, the heat of his touch lingering. All Nico could do was think of the what-ifs, and they had nothing to do with baseball.

LEANING BACK IN his black leather chair in front of his locker in the corner, Nico answered the FaceTime call and smiled at his sister. "Hey, Val. What's up?"

Valentina tucked a dark curl behind her ear with a smile. "What, I can't call my baby brother for no reason?"

"You can, but you don't." To be fair, he didn't generally call her out of the blue either.

She grinned. "Touché. Is this a bad time? Looks like you're in the locker room."

"It's fine." He glanced around. The TVs played sports news and a few guys milled around. Game time was in three and a half hours, so most players were grabbing a bite to eat in the lounge before BP.

"Sorry, I just need to bug you about your plus-one. The wedding planner is ordering engraved bombonieres. Our names and the guest's name will be on the bottom with the wedding date."

"Engraved what?"

She rolled her green eyes. "Nic, you've been to enough Italian weddings to know what a bomboniere is."

"The stupid keepsakes that clutter up people's shelves until they get over the guilt and throw them out?"

"Hey! That's not necessarily true. And mine will be awesome. Crystal candle holders that you wouldn't even know came from a wedding unless you picked it up and read the inscription. I want it to be personalized for everyone."

"For five hundred people?"

"Yep. So I need to know who you're bringing."

"How am I supposed to know? It's in *November.*"

"Don't remind me. Because heaven forbid I get married during baseball season. Dad would be streaming games on his iPad during the ceremony." Her cheeks puffed out. "God, I hope it's a nice day. What if it's gray and rainy? What if it snows?"

Elbows on his knees, Nico leaned over his phone. He tried to look reassuring. "It won't. Don't worry." He wasn't sure what the stats were on sunny Chicago days in November vs. shitty ones, but had a feeling the odds were so-so at best.

"Ugh, I should have eloped. Nonna and the rest of the family would have murdered me, of course. Anyway, I know you're busy, but can you please lock down a date?"

"I'll try."

"You know what that little green muppet says about no try and only do."

Behind Nico, a voice said, "Did you seriously just call Yoda a muppet? He was a Jedi master, Val."

Heart thumping, Nico looked over his shoulder to find Jake standing there. Jake raised his hands. "Sorry to interrupt, but I had to defend Yoda's honor."

"Is that Jake Fitzgerald?" Valentina laughed. "Let me see that handsome mug."

Nico held up the phone while Jake leaned on the back of the chair, his face just above Nico's shoulder. Jake said, "Long time no see. I hear congratulations are in order."

Val beamed, her button nose scrunching as she lifted her hand to the camera, showing up a huge heart-shaped diamond. "Thank you! Had to kiss my fair share of frogs, but I finally found my prince. I never imagined my dream man would be a forensic accountant, but Ian's the best. Smart and handsome, he'll watch *The Bachelor* with me, and he brings Nonna flowers every time he sees her."

Jake laughed. "Is he Italian?"

"His parents are Irish. But he's Catholic, so Nonna will take it since she was despairing of me ever getting married now that I'm—gasp!—over thirty."

"My mom and your grandmother could probably talk for hours on the subject," Jake said.

"How's she doing?" Val asked. "Oh, she must be so excited to have you back in Canada, huh? Or should I say '*eh*'?"

Jake replied, "No, you shouldn't, especially since Americans never say it right. But yes, she's thrilled. She's coming to the game tonight."

"That's awesome, and congrats on the trade! Although I guess it probably threw you for a loop. I can't imagine having to pack up and move overnight with no say in the matter. I mean, you can cry into your millions, but still."

Jake said, "Yeah, it… Well, it was a surprise. But here I am, so I have to make the best of it." His smile was strained.

"You know, Dad thinks the Caps could get to the playoffs, and he's got a good nose for it." Valentina grinned. "And I was watching the baseball roundtable on ESPN last night—because of course I'm marrying a baseball fan and will never escape it—and they were throwing names around for Rookie of the Year. Guess whose name got mentioned?"

Nico's heart shot up to his throat. "Me?"

She laughed. "No, Dylan Price. Well, he was mentioned too, but yes, you. The experts agreed that you're in the running. What do you think, Fitz?"

"I think he's got a great shot."

"Gotta hold up that family tradition, Nic. Dad and Marco, and now you. I'm so proud of how well you're doing!"

Nico managed to smile, but the excitement and pleasure quickly hardened into another knot of pressure lodged in his chest. He'd been well aware of his father and brother's myriad accomplishments—all-stars, MVPs, proud owners of champion-ship rings—and now his heart beat in time with the same refrain.

Must win. Must win. Must win.

If he won, he could prove he was just as good as them. Could prove queers belonged on the diamond too. Maybe he wouldn't have to hide who he was anymore. Excitement, fear, and a sweet, secret beam of hope reverberated through him.

Valentina was still talking to Jake, and Nico refocused as she said, "And I'm so glad you'll be there with Nic. I can't believe my baby brother's playing in the big leagues. It seems like just yesterday he was trailing after you like a puppy."

Nico knew he was blushing, and he bit back a retort as Val

went on.

"Fitz, you'll take care of him, right? Keep him in line."

"Hello! I'm sitting right here." Nico glared at his sister.

Jake's breath gusted across Nico's cheek as he laughed. "I think he's doing just fine."

She winked. "Nic, you know I'm just teasing. Don't sulk."

I'm not! He pressed his lips together, barely resisting saying it out loud. Val *was* only teasing the way she had a million times, but this time it was in front of Jake. The red tide was rising, and Nico had to breathe deeply to keep a grip on his temper.

"You know I just worry about you up there in the wilds of Canada," she added.

Managing a smile, Nico rolled his eyes. "I haven't lived in Chicago for, like, four years."

"I know, I know. Can't I worry about you? Don't answer that. Anyway, it's so good to see you, Fitz." Her face lit up. "Hey, are you busy the weekend of November ninth? Want to come to my wedding with Nico? Otherwise he'll take forever to find a date and probably wind up coming alone. We'd love to have you, and you'd be doing me a huge favor. I'm super stressed, and I want to get everything locked down."

"Oh." Jake smiled, but Nico wasn't sure his heart was in it. "Well, sure. I'd love to."

"Awesome! Thank you so much. There, Nic—problem solved. You're welcome!" She glanced at her watch and looked back at the camera. "Gotta run. Kisses!" She kissed her palm and blew before the call disconnected.

What the fuck just happened?

Nico tucked his phone away and stood, nervous energy ricocheting through him as he rearranged his uniforms, looking anywhere but at Jake. "Um, sorry about that. You don't have to come. Val's being a bridezilla or whatever."

"No, it's cool. I said yes, so. It's not a problem."

Nico dared a glance at Jake, who smiled blandly. "Okay. Um, thanks. She would have been on my case for months."

"That's family, right? Mine's pretty small, but my mom picks up the slack with her nagging." He nodded to someone across the room and called, "Be right there!" before grabbing his mask. "Later. Good session today. It's going to be a great game tomorrow."

Nico nodded and watched Jake walk across the locker room, shaking hands with a few guys who were coming in. Nico's brain tried to catch up.

Seriously, what the fuck just happened?

With a sick twist of dismay and excitement, he realized Jake was his date to Valentina's wedding. Not that it was an *actual* date, but now he'd see Jake at least once after the season ended.

As Nico headed to the lounge, Lopez fell in beside him with a playful poke to his ribs. "What're you so happy about, Agresta? Shit, I didn't know you had that many teeth."

Nico realized he was grinning like an idiot. But quickly enough his smile vanished in the lounge as he pulled out his phone and googled his name and "Rookie of the Year." A page of hits came up, and he read the articles and blogs one by one, the command pulsing in him like a distant drum.

Must win.

CHAPTER FIVE

"S o?"

Holding his menu, Jake glanced at his mother across the linen-covered table. "Have you decided already?" If he knew Helen Fitzgerald, she'd looked up the menu online and picked all her dishes hours ago.

She laughed out a huff. "I don't care about what I'm going to eat. What was it like out there? And don't give me the canned responses you feed the press after every game. It's like cliché Mad Libs." She dropped her voice to a gruff growl. "'It's a marathon, not a sprint. Maybe we played a little too hard today. It is what it is. We gave a hundred and ten percent out there.'" Dropping the put-on voice, she added, "That's mathematically impossible. I'm just saying."

Jake had to laugh. "Look, if you had to answer the same questions from multiple people after every game, you'd start spouting that crap too."

"Maybe." She glanced at her menu, twisting a lock of her blondish bobbed hair around her finger. "I'm not sure what to order. I was planning on the scallop pasta with figs and goat cheese, but it might be too heavy. I never eat this late. It's after eleven!"

"Eat whatever you want, Mom. I'm getting the steak."

"Well, you're a growing boy."

They laughed and eventually placed their orders. Once a bottle of Cabernet Sauvignon had been delivered, they sipped from their glasses and Jake buttered a thick piece of bread.

His mother cleared her throat. "Back to my earlier question. How do you feel after your first game as a Capital?"

"It was fine. You were there, you saw. We won. It felt good to homer, and I'll take the two walks. Not a bad night."

"I also saw the fans give you a standing ovation for your first at-bat. And the home run."

"The fans are great. Absolutely. I really appreciate the warm welcome. I do."

"You should, young man. And you're catching tomorrow? For Marco Agresta's brother? What's he like?"

Intriguing. Jake blinked at the thought. "Uh, he's good. Has a great arm, and his control is quite impressive for a rookie. There's obviously room for improvement, but his potential is enormous. He's…" Jake swirled the wine in his glass. "I get the feeling there's an awful lot going on inside his head. Puts a ton of pressure on himself, probably wanting to live up to his father's and brother's legacies. I don't know. He doesn't say a lot. They tell me he's got a temper."

"I'm sure you can teach him a thing or twelve. He's lucky they brought you on board."

Jake waved off the praise, but had to admit, "I think I might enjoy teaching him. I knew him when he was a kid, that first year when I was in Chicago. Talked to his sister today for the first time in years. They were really good to me when I didn't know anyone. It feels kind of full circle, catching for Nico now in the majors when I used to do it in his backyard. It's nice, I guess."

Helen laughed. "Oh, sweetheart. You don't have to sound so surprised. I think it's wonderful that you can take him under your wing."

"Well, the pitching coaches will be doing the brunt of the

work."

"Don't underestimate yourself. You'll be on the field with him. They won't. The catcher's the most important player on the team, which of course is why my brilliant son is a catcher. They said you were too tall, but I knew you'd prove them wrong."

Jake smiled. "Thanks, Mom." Under the table, he straightened out his left leg and his aching knee, his lower back voicing its displeasure as well.

He'd popped his usual anti-inflammatories after the game, but should have taken longer to ice and go through his daily physio routine. But Mom had been waiting, and he didn't want to keep her up too late. "You've put in decades of strong work as president and CEO of my fan club."

"You bet I have." She winked.

They talked about a bit of everything as they ate, and soon it was time to order dessert.

Helen told the waiter, "I'll have to try the crème brûlée. And a decaf cappuccino, please."

Jake closed the menu. "Just an espresso for me."

Helen sighed loudly. "Surely you're not going to let your mother eat dessert alone. You know, the calories don't count if someone you love is eating them too."

Jake had to laugh. "All right, all right." Opening the dessert menu, he scanned the selection. "I'll have the berry pavlova." When the waiter had slipped away, Jake asked, "Did that argument work on Dad?"

"Every time. Now that I usually eat dessert alone, my girlish figure's taken a hit. Well, I suppose getting old might have something to do with it too."

"You're as beautiful as ever. Don't be ridiculous." He frowned and swirled the last of his wine in his glass. "And you're not *alone*. I mean, you're busier than most non-retired people. I don't know where you find time for all your activities."

"It's not that hard. Most people who say they don't have time for things watch hours and hours of TV a day. And I'm alone, but not lonely. There's a difference." She smoothed her palm over the white linen tablecloth. "That's why I'm such a nag."

"You're not," he replied automatically.

Eyes crinkling with laughter, Helen shook her head. "The best part is that you can say it with a straight face."

"What? You're not a nag. Usually. Most of the time."

"Only once in a blue moon, right?"

Chuckling, Jake thanked the waiter as he dropped off their drinks. The white foam on top of his mom's cappuccino was shaped into a flower, and she smiled down at it, clearly tickled.

"Looks too pretty to drink," she said. "Just like the Easter bunnies you were afraid to eat. 'But Mommy, I don't want to make them go deaf!' You were always the sweetest child."

"Yeah, for five minutes until I remembered how good choco- late tastes. Then it was bye-bye rabbit ears." He plopped a cube of sugar into his cup with tiny silver tongs.

"But really, I'm sorry for nagging."

"It's fine. But like you said, you're alone and you're not lonely. Neither am I."

"If you say so."

He smothered the spark of irritation. "Mom, I'm not lonely."

"Aren't you?"

"No. I'm not." *Liar*, a little voice hissed. "Some people aren't cut out for relationships, and they're happier alone."

"Yes, that's very true." She opened her mouth to say more, but then smiled at the waiter as their desserts arrived, tucking a lock of hair behind her ear. When they were alone again, she cracked the top of her crème brûlée, the spoon making a satisfying *thwack* on the top layer of caramelized sugar. "As I was saying, it is true that some people are perfectly happy alone. Happier, as a matter of fact. Aunt Carolyn, for example."

"And you, after Dad. You never even tried dating, did you?" He toyed with his pavlova, pushing his spoon through the whipped cream on top of the flaky meringue.

"Nope. Your father and I had a darn good life together, but there's something to be said for being able to turn the light on in the bedroom as late or early as I want. If I don't want to cook, I don't. And I don't have anyone making sarcastic comments from the sidelines if I want to watch a silly show about wedding makeovers. I'd give it up in a heartbeat to have your father back, but since that'll never happen, I'm enjoying the freedom of living on my own."

"Exactly. I like living on my own too. I'm much happier this way."

"Mmm." She swallowed a spoonful of thick cream.

The tables were well spaced for privacy, but Jake still glanced around to make sure they couldn't be overheard. "I'm not cut out to live with someone. Sleeping together every single night, sharing the bathroom. Sharing *everything*. It's a pain. You said it yourself."

"I also said I'd do it all again in a heartbeat with your father. When it's the right person, it's different. At least it was for me." Scooping her spoon into the white ramekin, she sighed. "I just wish you really were happy. About anything."

"I'm happy." Jake had a mouthful of pavlova, the chewy meringue and cream almost too sweet but for the raspberries on top. "Of course I'm happy."

She reached out and squeezed his wrist briefly. "You shouldn't lie to your mother, you know. It's bad karma. But I'll let you off the hook. For now. Once you—" She peered across the restaurant beyond Jake. "Oh, it's a couple of your teammates! Banner and Lopez. Those must be their wives or girlfriends. We should say hello."

Unable to choke down his groan, Jake resolutely didn't turn around. Maybe the guys wouldn't notice them. "It's late. I really need to get to bed soon. Let's just finish dinner."

Helen tried to laugh it off, but didn't quite succeed. "You don't want to introduce your friends to your mother?"

"It's not that. It's… They're not my friends. We just met."

"Yes, but you won't get to know them if you don't make an effort."

"I'll get to know them enough during the rest of the season. As long as we gel on the field, that's what matters."

Still holding her spoon, Helen blinked at him. "Why wouldn't you *want* more friends?"

"I have plenty," he lied. He could admit that he used to have far more. He ate another spoonful of pavlova, the meringue getting stuck in one of his molars. "I'm only here until my contract runs out. I don't need to make a bunch of new friends."

"But don't you play better as a team when you care about each other? When you want to succeed together?"

"New York does just fine without braiding each other's hair in the clubhouse. We're pros. Obviously I'll get to know my teammates, but we don't all need to be pals."

His mother watched him, her face drawn in unmistakable sadness. "Don't you *want* to win?"

"Of course." He shrugged. "It's my job."

"It used to be more than that. It used to be your dream, sweetheart. Don't you remember? All those years you spent with a glove on your hand and grass stains on your pants, throwing that ball with your father. And when you actually made it to the big leagues, you and Brandon—"

"Mom, I grew up." He dropped his spoon on his plate with a clatter and pushed it away, inhaling deeply, trying to banish the memories of Brandon—his high-fives and the stupid jokes he'd loved to lean in and tell while they sat shoulder to shoulder on the bench in the dugout.

"Hey, J, what do you call cheese that's not yours? Nacho cheese!"

"Growing up is all well and good. But since when does it mean you have to stop loving? Stop dreaming?" She motioned beyond him. "Stop making friends?"

"I did that in little league and high school and college and the minors. And in Chicago and then Philly for a season and then San Fran." He rubbed his face. "I'm tired. I didn't want to start over again. I can do my job without being everyone's buddy. There's no way the Caps will make the playoffs until they have a few more years together at least. They're dreaming if they think otherwise. And that's fine. I've made my peace with not getting a championship ring. I've had a good career. I'll play the best I can as I finish out my contract. It's a job, and it doesn't have to be more than that."

Helen stirred her cappuccino, the flower swirling out of existence. "No, it doesn't *have* to be. You're right. But it could be. You can still dream, sweetheart."

"You're as bad as Ron," he muttered, only realizing with a sinking sensation what he'd said once the words were beyond his grasp. "Anyway, I appreciate what you're saying, and—"

"Who's Ron?" She watched him like a hawk, even though she was clearly trying to act casual as she sipped from her cup.

"Just a friend." It was the truth, at least.

"A friend," she repeated. "Well, that's nice. Have long have you known this Ron? Does he live in San Francisco?"

Groaning internally, Jake answered, "A few years, and yes."

"Hmm. And he's a…special friend?"

As much as he loved his mother, he wasn't going to discuss his sex life with her. "He's married. Very happily."

Her eyes widened, and she leaned in, hissing, "Married? Jake, I expect better from you. That's just not right."

"He and his husband have an open relationship. So Ron and I have a…special friendship, and it's nothing more than that."

"So it's just sex."

"Oh God, what did I do to deserve this?" He rubbed his eyes. "Can we not?"

"You don't want anything more than—than *booty calls?*"

He had to laugh. "First off, please don't ever use that phrase again, and second, no. I don't. We had a good routine set up. It worked for me, okay? Now can we stop talking about this for the rest of my life? I'm begging."

"You're in luck. We can talk to one of your new friends instead." She beamed and waved at someone behind him. "Hello there!"

Pasting on a smile, Jake turned to greet Banner or Lopez, his pulse spiking as he saw Nico Agresta instead with a leggy blond on his arm, being led to a nearby table.

Nico looked incredibly fuckable in black slacks that hugged his slim hips and strong thighs, and a royal blue button-up shirt that made his tawny skin look even richer. His lashes were so long around his rich brown eyes that Jake wondered if he used mascara.

Nico stopped short. "Oh. Hey."

"Hey." Jake nodded and smiled at Nico's date.

Helen held out her hand and said, "I don't know if you remember, but I met you once when Jake played in Chicago that year. Your father invited me over for dinner, and I've never had gnocchi like your grandmother's before or since. Oh, and I'm Helen Fitzgerald. Like I said, it's been years. Look at you, all grown up!"

Smiling politely, Nico shook her hand. His shirt had three buttons undone at the throat, and Jake watched his Adam's apple bob. "Nice to see you again, Mrs. Fitzgerald."

"And who's this?" Helen reached toward the young woman.

From the momentary widening of Nico's eyes, Jake wasn't convinced he knew her name. Fortunately, she answered, "Amber Paige. So lovely to meet you, Mrs. Fitzgerald. And you, Jake. I'm a huge fan."

Jake half stood and shook her hand. "Thank you so much, Amber. Have a great meal. The food's delicious."

Amber smiled widely. "I'm so glad to hear it! Everyone's raving about this new chef, and I talked Nico into trying dessert before they close."

"The crème brûlée was exquisite," Helen said.

"We won't hold you up," Jake added.

With more nods and smiles, the torture was over, and Jake motioned to the waiter for the bill. He gulped down a mouthful of lukewarm coffee once the check was paid. "Ready?"

Helen nodded. "Thank you for dinner, hon. It was wonderful. And I have to apologize for nagging. Again."

His smile was genuine this time. "No you don't. It's your job." Once they got up, he leaned down and kissed her cheek. "Are you sure you don't want to stay another day?"

"No, I'm hosting Dorothy's birthday lunch on Saturday, and I need to drive home tomorrow and bake the cake. Don't worry, darling. Your mother will be visiting plenty of times this season."

They decided to detour to the bathrooms on their way out, and Jake unzipped at the urinal under low pot lights, faint music playing overhead that might have been sitar or perhaps a pan flute. The door opened, a wave of murmured noise coming from the restaurant before fading away.

"Oh."

Jake glanced over his shoulder to find Nico by the sinks. "Hey."

"I thought you left."

"Just on our way out."

Nico still stood there staring, and Jake had the strangest urge to ask him where he was headed next. *Why should I care? He probably can't wait to go home and fuck Amber.* Jake smiled to fill the awkward pause and turned back to the urinal to pull out his dick.

Nico took his place with one urinal between them, and they pissed in silence but for the sitar pan flute medley tinkling in the air. Despite himself, Jake watched Nico from the corner of his eye. *Gaze* UP, *for fuck's sake. He's your teammate. And a kid.*

Of course Nico Agresta wasn't a kid at all anymore, and he'd grown into a hell of a pitcher. Jake realized with a little jolt that he was actually excited to catch for Nico tomorrow. There was so much raw talent there, and there was something about him. He remembered how Nico used to grin back in the day when he nailed a pitch, two dimples creasing his cheeks deeply. Jake wondered if he could get him to smile like that again.

In the low lights, he could make out the strands of dark chest hair poking out at Nico's throat from the open collar of his blue shirt. He imagined what it would be like to tease his fingers through it...

Then Nico looked at him, their eyes locking, electricity flashing right to Jake's dick in his hand. His sore knees wavered, and he tore his gaze away.

Stuffing his tingling cock back in his slacks, Jake zipped up and slammed down the handle to flush. He washed his hands at the sink and called, "See ya," not waiting for a response.

On the walk back to the hotel, he asked his mom about the new charity project her seniors' group was spearheading to provide breakfast at school for kids. Obviously he donated a hefty amount to all her causes, but she insisted that local fund-raising was vital for a sense of community pride, and was surely right.

The late spring air was cool but fragrant, fresh and clean with the scent of budding flowers. As they strolled along the quiet sidewalks, not too many people out on a weeknight, Jake's mind drifted back to Nico and his throat, his warm skin with hints of rich gold, the hair on his chest...

Sighing inwardly, Jake admitted it. Fine, he was hot for Nico Agresta. And that was perfectly okay—Nico had grown into a hell of an attractive man. Jake was used to being around a lot of sexy guys, and as long as he kept it out of the clubhouse and off the field, the odd lustful thought or appreciation of a fine ass wasn't a problem.

And if there was something about the fixated way Nico looked at him through those thick lashes, that was fine too. Nico had always been an intense kid, and he probably looked at everyone like that.

Now that Jake had acknowledged his attraction, he could put it behind him and concentrate on his job.

"Do you think that sounds like a good plan?" Helen asked as they passed Parliament Hill.

Snapping his focus back, he nodded. "Sounds perfect."

WHEN JAKE ANSWERED the room phone Friday morning, he assumed it was his mother before remembering she'd gotten up early to make the drive back to Midland in time for her Zumba class that afternoon. But he couldn't hang up now. "Hello?"

"Fitz? It's Diego."

"Hey, man. What's up?"

"I sent you a couple texts, but not sure if I still have the right number? I know it's early, but I figured you'd be as wired as me."

"Sorry. Haven't turned my phone on yet today. Guess I'm in avoidance mode."

Diego chuckled. "I hear that. I was just wondering if you want to come down the hall to my suite for breakfast, but probably not."

Shame prickled the back of Jake's neck. Diego had made such an effort over the years, and the least he could do was have breakfast with the guy. "Sure, that would be great."

"Yeah? Cool. I'm in 1504. I'll order two lumberjack breakfasts? Get our strength up."

"Sounds good." After hanging up, he sighed and hustled into the shower. It wasn't that he didn't like Diego—he really did. But when Diego was around, memories of that night years ago inevitably surfaced.

Memories of the night Jake's best friend Brandon met Denise, an actress from a BET sitcom who was in town filming a movie. Denise, who would come in and out of Brandon's life until she was the sun he orbited, until Jake's jealousy boiled over and he destroyed the relationship that had meant the very most to him.

Standing under a powerful jet of hot water, Jake closed his eyes and was there again in a ragged heartbeat. He could hear the *thumpa-thumpa* of relentless dance music, the rippling buzz of shouted conversations throughout the bar.

Could feel the heft of another pint of beer in his hand, condensation on his palm, chasing the salt and lemon of too many tequila shots. His jeans tight and the sleeves on his button-up rolled to his elbows in the humidity that came from too many drunk people in close proximity.

The sticky table on the horseshoe-shaped back booth was too low for his long legs, his knees bumping against it as he watched Brandon elbow his way onto the crowded dance floor and make a beeline for the tall African-American woman with legs for days and a thousand-watt smile…

The colored lights circling over Brandon's dark skin, his own smile a flash of white, his eyes crinkling, head thrown back in the laughter that came so easily to him. The hopeless, helpless yearning burning through Jake, a low, ever-present pilot light catching fire when he let down his guard, when he allowed himself the luxury of really looking.

"Does he know?"

Blinking, Jake tore his gaze from Brandon to find Diego sitting beside him, a fresh pint in his hand and black shirt unbuttoned to his sternum. "Huh?"

One eyebrow raised, Diego looked pointedly at Brandon grinding up on the actress. *"I'll probably get punched for this, and maybe I'm completely out to lunch, but sometimes the way you look at him makes me think..."*

Jake's mouth went dry, bile rising in his throat. He gripped his pint glass. *"That's not... What? He's my best friend. I'm not—Why? No. You think we're..."* A panicked hamster spun on its wheel, Jake's heart in his throat. He jerked his head left and right, but they were surrounded by walls in the back corner, the closest booths empty in favor of the dance floor or patio out front.

"When you don't think anyone's watching, or you're too drunk to notice, you get this look around him."

A pathetic attempt at a laugh limped out. *"So, you think I'm what? In love with him?"*

"Is that so crazy?" Diego asked kindly.

He sputtered, *"Of course it is!"* and gulped the rest of his beer, still clutching the glass when it was empty, staring at the remaining foam residue.

"Hey, I'm sorry. I was clearly out of line." Diego laughed. *"My new brother-in-law's gay, so apparently I think I'm an expert now or some shit. Forget I said anything."*

Of course Jake couldn't forget a damn thing. Did other people suspect? Could they tell? If they could, how long until Brandon figured it out? The waitress came and said something with a cheery smile, and Jake nodded, relinquishing his glass and hoping she was bringing another.

His left leg was jammed against a bolt under the table, digging into his kneecap, and he focused on the discomfort, trying to get a handle on himself before he said—

"He doesn't know."

Jake wasn't positive he'd actually uttered the words aloud, but in his peripheral vision, Diego's head turned, and he leaned in, smelling of pine and maybe lemons.

"Hey man, it's okay. Shit, Fitz, breathe!"

His lungs couldn't expand, a tunnel of black closing in on his field of vision. Diego shook his shoulder, and Jake managed to suck in enough air for the blackness to recede. The hamster was still on its wheel, spinning frantically, each step more useless than the last. "Can everyone tell?"

"No, no. Not at all. I swear."

Then there was a glass of water in his hand and Diego was saying something else to the waitress, and it was probably for the best Jake hadn't been granted another beer. He guzzled the cool water, ice cubes clinking against his teeth. "I'm fucked, D."

"It's okay. Just breathe. And drink more water."

"He's my best friend. I tried not to feel this, but...fuck. Most of the time it's fine. I can ignore it."

"Yeah, but you can only ignore something like this so long. Maybe you should talk to him."

Jake whirled in the booth, a burst of pain from his jammed knee and blood rushing in his ears over the DJ's bass. "No fucking way. Never. It'll ruin everything. Look, you can't say a word. No one can know, least of all him. Jesus, if anyone finds out—"

Diego raised his hands. "I won't say a word. And—shit, here he comes."

Yes, there was Brandon strutting toward the table with the actress on his arm and two other women behind him. "Here we are, ladies, we found the party."

Jake was frozen, watching them slide into the booth, and the horror must have been stark on his face because Brandon's smooth smile faltered, his brows drawing together as he leaned over the table and whispered, "You good?"

The thought of playing nice with the girls and pretending his heart wasn't beating outside his body for everyone to see, his pathetic feelings splashed all over the sticky table, was torture, but Jake nodded. Thank God Diego was tugging his arm from the other side of the booth.

"We hate to be buzzkills, but I have to call my wife, and Fitz

promised to run some extra drills with me in the morning. I need to work on my throw to home plate."

"What? Come on," Brandon wheedled. "You're really going to leave me alone here? Defenseless?"

The women laughed, and Jake waved, following Diego through the crush of bodies, profoundly grateful for the fresh night air when they escaped the bar. Sweat slicked his skin, his collar damp, pulse thready. He put one foot in front of the other until he and Diego were turning the corner, the thump of the bar fading into the drone of traffic.

"Hotel's just another block," Diego assured him.

Jake's head spun, stomach revolting against all the tequila. "Thank you. I…"

"Anytime. And don't worry. Your secret's safe with me."

And it had been, almost seven years later. They hadn't played together much longer in Philly, and as Jake toweled dry and dressed in jeans and a tee, he realized he didn't even know how many kids Diego had now, only that he had at least two.

But Diego welcomed him with nothing but warmth, ushering him to the small table in the suite's living area. "You're just in time. Our lumberjack specials await. Apparently lumberjacks eat three kinds of breakfast meat and a ton of eggs, FYI."

"Good to know." Jake took a sip of orange juice. "How are you holding up?"

Diego's cheeks puffed out as he exhaled noisily. "Okay, I guess. It's good to talk to someone in the same boat."

"What did Liz say?"

He smirked. "Let's just say it was nothing I'd repeat in polite company. So I can tell you that the term cum-guzzling thunder-cunts was bandied about."

Jake laughed. "Remind me never to get on Liz's bad side."

"No worries. You being up here with me is a huge plus. She figures if I hang with you, I won't be out at the bar with groupies hitting on me."

Jake's smile became strained. "So she knows?" It wasn't like it was a *complete* secret. Jake's family in the UK and some of his mother's close friends knew. Ron and his husband. Diego, and apparently his wife.

"Yes." Diego grimaced. "I'm sorry. It was years ago. You were supposed to come for dinner, and she wanted to set you up with one of her girlfriends. She wouldn't let it go, and I figured it was better to tell her than subject you to a surprise blind date with a woman. Liz has never told a soul, I swear."

"It's okay." He exhaled. It really was. "I don't want my personal life to be public knowledge, but friends knowing is fine. I realize people must wonder. Thirty-four, unmarried, doesn't party at the bars, never seen with a girlfriend."

"Yeah. I think we've all had teammates that we wonder about. Does anyone ever ask?"

"Sometimes, in roundabout ways. Never directly. I just say I'm enjoying being single. It's the truth. Or at least *a* truth."

"That makes sense." Diego buttered a piece of toast. "So did you see your trade coming?"

"Nope. The owner and GM promised they'd keep me in the loop. Not so much, it turns out. I know it's business, but after so many years, I guess I thought a handshake meant something. It just would have been nice to get a little notice."

"Yeah, I was blindsided too. Liz and I are both from Fort Worth, so our families are freaking. I had one trade provision on my contract, so this was it. I'm going to be up here for six years. Now Liz and I have to decide if we move her and the kids up too. They'd have to change schools, and we'd stay year round. I've heard Ottawa winters are a little tougher than the ones in Texas."

Jake held his fingers up an inch apart. "Just a tiny bit."

Diego pushed around his scrambled eggs. "I really don't know what to do. If Liz and the kids stay in Houston, they'll be a lot closer to our folks. Liz's mom moved down there last year and got a condo nearby. She helps out so much, and we've got a good system going. If we move up here, we don't know anyone. No family. I know we'll make friends, but it's not the same. How's it been for you living in the States all these years?"

"It's been good. I still talk to my mom a lot, but my dad didn't have any family, and hers is in England. Obviously she's thrilled I'll be so much closer now."

"I bet. Silver lining, huh?"

"Yeah. She drove up yesterday. It was great to see her." Familiar guilt simmered in his gut. It *was* a silver lining that he'd be able to see much more of her, and he had to remember to be grateful for it. "I'd fly her down sometimes, but she's got so much going on. Runs a volunteer charity, and plays golf, and does a million things with her lady friends. I hope I've got half her energy at that age." He straightened out his left leg, giving his IT band on the side of his thigh a rub.

"I hear that. How are your knees holding up?"

"Hanging in there. Getting creaky."

Diego rolled his shoulders. "Yup. My rotator cuff will be demolished by the time I retire. But it's worth it." He cut into a thick sausage. "I just wish it wasn't so tough on my family. I mean, we've got money—I'm not complaining about that. But if Liz and the kids stay in Texas, I won't see them half the year. More than. Couple months in Florida for spring training, then six months up here. We can Skype, and they can visit, and we'll be in Texas to play once in a while. It's still not the same. Being with them for all our home stands in Houston made a big difference. The kids are growing up so fast."

"How old are they?"

"You know I'm going to bore you with pictures now, right?" He pulled out his phone and scrolled through pictures of his three kids—two girls of eight and six and a boy of three.

"They're adorable. Really."

Diego looked at the last pic, smiling goofily. "They really are, aren't they? You ever think about having any?"

"Did my mother tell you to ask that?" Jake glanced around with pretend suspicion. "She's hiding in the bathroom, isn't she? Come out, Mom! I'm onto you!"

Laughing, Diego said, "Sorry, sorry. My bad. I was just curious. I don't even know if you have a boyfriend."

Jake shifted in his seat and shoveled a forkful of eggs into his mouth.

"And I'm being nosy again." He ate a piece of bacon and washed it down with coffee. "I just... I hope you know I'm cool with it."

"I know. I appreciate it. It's not you—I don't like talking about that stuff with anyone. When you debrief my mom in the bathroom later, she'll tell you."

With a chuckle, Diego said, "She'll be extremely disappointed I couldn't get you to spill."

"Honestly, there's nothing to tell. There was a guy in San Francisco, just a weekly hookup when I was in town. We're friends. It's a good arrangement. I'm not interested in more."

"Fair enough."

They ate in silence for a minute, Jake squirting ketchup onto his eggs in a red blob. Why would he want more than sex? Why would he ever want to put himself through that torture again? He'd been powerless, his guts hanging out to get bruised and torn. He'd never intended to fall for his best friend, but it had spun out of control, an avalanche careening down a hill while he stumbled behind it, slipping and sliding, grasping for a handhold.

No. He'd never put himself through that again. Would never fall for *anyone.*

Diego scratched the back of his neck. "I have to admit I wondered what went down with you and Brandon before he got traded. I heard he punched you, and I just can't imagine it."

That certainly put an end to Jake's appetite. Eyes on his plate, he shrugged. "I was a prick. About Denise, when they got engaged." He cringed thinking about the awful shit he'd spewed. The explosion of pain in his cheek as Brandon's fist had connected had been nothing compared to the gaping hole Brandon's sudden and staggering absence had left behind.

"Ah."

"Got wasted and said some shitty stuff that wasn't true. Stuff I didn't mean. About how she was a gold digger and he was only thinking with his dick."

Diego whistled softly. "Ouch."

"Yeah. Asked the team to trade me, and they traded him instead. He's the one who threw the punch, so he paid the price. I would have punched me too."

"You guys have played each other since, right?"

Jake grimaced. "Yep. Awkward as hell, as you can imagine."

"You ever think about explaining it to him?"

His throat going dry at the thought, stomach swooping, Jake shook his head. "No way." The idea of Brandon knowing that Jake had loved him felt absolutely impossible.

"I'm sorry it went down like that." Diego smiled. "And I'm sorry you got hit with a surprise trade, but it's nice to have a familiar face up here. I think we could do some great things with this team. Agresta's got a hell of an arm. What's your take on him?"

A flash of Nico's intense stare filled Jake's mind, and he gulped down the rest of his juice, pulp sticking to his tongue. "Like you said, a hell of an arm. Speaking of which, I should get going. I've got a meeting with the pitching coaches to get up to speed."

"Cool. See you this afternoon. It's weird, isn't it? A few days ago we played for different teams thousands of miles away. But the routines are always pretty much the same. Just the colors change. I guess that's baseball, right? Hey, what are you going to do with your house in San Fran?"

"I…have no idea." He liked his house, a high-ceiled Craftsman with huge windows and lots of wood, but did it make sense to keep it now? Maybe for the off-season. Fuck, so much to think about, and he didn't want to deal with any of it. "I'll have to get my housekeeper to pack up some stuff and ship it up here. Shit. I'm going to be out of underwear really soon."

Diego laughed. "I guess that's baseball."

CHAPTER SIX

"NO, SERIOUSLY. THIS idea's going to make a million." Banner cleared his throat dramatically, sitting forward on the couch. "Did you ever wish you could get the latest scores and stats on your favorite team or player in an instant?"

Nico watched as the new second baseman, Diego Garcia, replied, "I'm pretty sure we can already do that. It's called Google."

"No, no, this is different!"

Pacing by his locker, acid churning his stomach, Nico tuned out the details of Banner's newest app idea. Garcia had apparently heard enough too, since he walked over to the other side of the room, where Jake was finishing a protein bar. Garcia leaned in and said something, and Jake laughed, a low rumble that went straight to Nico's dick as if it had ears.

Jake and Garcia seemed to know each other, and a quick search had turned up that they played together for most of a season in Philly years ago. Garcia's Wikipedia page also said he was married with kids, so Nico tried not to glare as the guy clapped Jake's shoulder.

Fingers twitching, Nico glanced at the huge clock above a TV on a pillar in the middle of the room.

The clock was apparently broken, because no time had passed, and it had to have been at least ten minutes. But the clock stubbornly read 6:10. Game time was 7:05. In one corner, guys sat around a table playing cards. Others leaned back in their leather chairs by their lockers, playing video games or whatever on their phones or tablets.

Baldoni, the backup catcher, strummed a guitar, playing an old Eagles song. Some of the guys were in the video room reviewing their swings from the previous game or scoping out the opposing pitcher.

But Nico could only pace, a few feet one way, and then the other.

At the locker beside him, Crowe said, "Shit, son. You know that carpet's still pretty new."

"Huh?"

Stroking his bushy red beard, Crowe laughed. "I was implying that you're going to wear a hole in it."

"Oh. Right." Nico stood still, tapping his thighs with his fingers.

Crowe leaned over and gave Nico's hip a good-natured slap. "Kid, do whatever you need to do. I'm not trying to bust your balls. But maybe you shouldn't get here so early. Makes for a long-ass day. As long as you're here for whatever you want to do in the bullpen before team stretch, you're good."

Nico's father had drilled into him to always be at the stadium by one p.m. for a night game. And Nico was well aware of the unwritten rules of the clubhouse—rookies show up early, and if they want to use the training room, they'd better get their asses in there before the veterans arrive.

Crowe had been playing in the majors seven years, so it was easy for him to say. Nico simply nodded. Some of the vets were early birds too—it just depended on the player.

Every club had its own variations on the schedule, but when the Caps were at home, team stretch was around four o'clock, followed by some catch and then batting practice at quarter to five. During batting practice, Nico and the other pitchers joined the outfielders shagging fly balls. Some of the pitchers did more chatting than anything else, but Nico enjoyed running down flies to get out some nervous energy, especially on a start day.

He waited five minutes, staring at the clock until it was time, then headed to the bathroom. Glancing around, he slipped into the very last stall. With the seat lifted, he bent at the waist, hands braced on his knees.

Over the years, he'd become an expert at puking without making much of a sound at all. He inhaled hard through his nose, staring at the white porcelain and clenching his gut muscles in just the right way.

When he was in high school, he'd vomited all over the mound during the most horrific, humiliating game of his life, and the terror of doing it again had his stomach roiling predictably now.

The remains of breakfast and lunch emptied into the toilet with a little splash, and he coughed once, getting out a little more before wiping his mouth with a wad of toilet paper. Standing straight, he flushed and leaned back against the stall door.

The relief was immediate, and now he could relax a fraction knowing he wouldn't toss his cookies in front of thousands of people and on national TV to boot. He'd sip Gatorade during the game to keep his electrolytes up, then wolf down dinner after. Well, if he got the win or at least pitched well. If not, he usually went right to bed.

By the sinks, he splashed his face with cold water and toweled off, avoiding looking in the mirror. Then it was back to the locker room and eight—he checked the clock—no, seven minutes to wait.

On cue around 6:30, the music, games, and chatter dropped off and a focused quiet descended, guys going into their pregame routines and rituals. Nico watched Crowe tie the laces on his left cleat before the right as always, and when he stood and circled his right ankle, frowning because the laces were probably too tight, he sat back down and took both cleats off, starting over again.

"Hey." Jake tapped Nico on the shoulder with his glove. "Ready to head out?"

Nodding, he put on his own glove and straightened his cap, tugging twice on the brim the way he always did before a start. He followed Jake into the tunnel, through the dugout, and across the field to the bullpen. The crowd was filing in, a low buzz in the stadium, the sun dipping beyond the open dome.

"What's your process?" Jake asked. "I'm going to guess you don't have a lot to say before a start."

Nico laughed softly, a tiny bit of tension loosening. "Not so much. I just… You know. Throw some pitches to warm up. Take the mound. Try to win."

Must win. Must win.

"Sounds like a plan." Jake glanced around. "Looks like it'll be a good crowd." As they neared the right field wall, some fans in the cheap seats shouted out a greeting and support. Jake gave them a little wave, but Nico kept his gaze on the bullpen.

Once inside, Nico took his spot by the rubber and Jake got into his crouch by the plate. They warmed up until the anthems, then made their way back onto the field. The crowd was really buzzing now with Friday night energy and twelve-dollar beers. Even though Nico had never worked a nine to five job, he noticed a definite difference, people in the stands eager to let go of the week's stress.

When he took the mound, he wished his stress wasn't just beginning.

Jake got a ball from the ump and jogged over. "Ready?" At Nico's nod, Jake deposited the ball in his hand, their fingertips brushing. "You got this. Take it pitch by pitch."

As he watched Jake return to his position, Nico concentrated on the feel of cowhide in his hand, running his fingers over the red stitches. Baldoni and other catchers Nico had worked with were great, but there was something about having Jake behind the plate that gave Nico the freedom to breathe a little easier. Jake was so confident, and Nico knew he was in good hands in a way he hadn't experienced before.

The ump pointed at him. "Play!"

CRACK!

Nico's heart sunk as the Baltimore DH hit the ball, and he spun to watch its trajectory over the field. *Please, please, please. Drop in. Don't go over.* It seemed to soar forever, center fielder Lopez back at the warning track with his glove up, and *yes*, it was dropping. Thank G—

The crowd groaned as Lopez somehow bobbled the catch and the ball skimmed past the edge of his glove to hit the ground. Nico swore, tension seizing him, the red tide roaring through him, rushing in his ears.

Fucking goddamn it!

The batter Nico had walked earlier was now at third, the DH at second. Two men in scoring position when the inning should have been over. Nico breathed hard, muttering to himself and watching Lopez, who stood there like nothing had happened, chomping on his gum. Nico turned to find Jake approaching.

Holding up his glove so no one could read his lips, Jake calmly said, "Stop glaring. You know everyone can see you, right?"

Nico lifted his glove too. "How the fuck did he drop that?"

"We all make mistakes."

"But he doesn't even care!" Nico hissed.

"Just because he's not stomping his foot and pouting doesn't mean he doesn't care. Cut the shit. We're all on the same team here. Lopez didn't shoot you stink eye when you walked Dibble.

Calm. Down."

He knew Jake was right, but tension ricocheted through him like he was a pinball machine. "I'm trying," he mumbled.

The hard lines of Jake's expression softened a few degrees. "I know. Think about the next pitch." He glanced behind him to where the ump was making a move toward the mound to break up the timeout. Jake gave Nico a pat with his glove and hurried back.

Inhaling forcefully, Nico caught the ball Jake threw him. The next pitch was a borderline changeup that Jake framed perfectly for a strike, closing his glove around it toward the plate. Then a ball almost in the dirt, and then another so high Jake had to stick his arm straight up to catch it, the crowd shifting restlessly.

The Caps had scored in the second, but it was only a run. Knowing the tying run was on third and the go-ahead on second sent a tremor through Nico. He couldn't screw this up.

Breathing hard again, he focused on reading the signs, Jake's fingers flying between his legs. Nico nodded and threw the curveball. The batter got a piece of it, grounding it toward the left field gap, where Crowe caught it and stepped on the bag at third base, taking out the DH running from second. The inning was over.

The Caps trotted back to the dugout, and Nico took his seat on the bench, zipping on his jacket to keep his arm warm. It was the bottom of the fourth, and aside from the last inning, so far, so good. He surreptitiously rapped his knuckles on the bench. No one sat right beside him or talked to him, which wasn't unusual. Most pitchers didn't like to be distracted during a game, and Nico was no different.

But he glanced at Lopez guzzling Gatorade at the other end of the dugout and squirmed with embarrassment. He hadn't even realized he'd been glaring and wearing his emotions on his sleeve. He needed to work on his poker face. And Jake was right, they all made mistakes. Nico damn well knew that, but in the moment it was hard to remember.

He'd made the mistake of checking the league stats that morning and saw that he was one win away from leading the division. Those were the kind of numbers that nailed down Rookie of the Year, and he just needed to rack up the wins.

Easy.

As the Caps went up to bat, Nico sipped a cup of Gatorade, tapping his foot. He hated this part, when he had no control at all over the game's outcome. He watched Crowe in the batter's box, wriggling his bat over his shoulder as he waited for the pitch, which—

The gasp was like a seismic wave, rippling over the stadium as the ball rocketed smack into Crowe's ribs even as he tried to spin away.

Alvarez shouted, "Son of a fucking bitch!" and the Caps dugout was on its feet, jaws clenched. They all knew a plunk when they saw one. Crowe dropped his bat, staring at the mound, but shook it off and jogged to first. Nico bounced on his toes, his fists clenched.

Jake appeared next to Nico as he asked Alvarez, "Some history I don't know about?"

Alvarez spit on the concrete, sunflower seed husks flying. "When we were in Baltimore last month there was a controversial play at second. Crowe slid and Markson put on a show, acting like Crowe gunned for him when the truth was Markson just didn't apply the tag fast enough. Insisted Crowe broke the new slide rules. No way, man. Markson's the one who has his cleats up for our guys. He's full of it. It went to a review, and they ruled it was clean. Baltimore yapped about it, crying about how it was dirty. Guess they wanted some payback."

The crowd was still unsettled and murmuring as the inning continued, the Caps unfortunately grounding into a double play and popping up to end it. Nico shrugged off his jacket and took the mound again for the top of the fifth—and promptly gave up a hit to Baltimore's catcher, a line drive down the middle.

Fuck, fuck, fuck.

After two balls and a strike, the batter popped up, thank Christ. Then a quick groundout from the next batter, and Baltimore's catcher advanced to second base with two outs.

As Markson of all people came up to the plate next, Nico clutched the ball in his glove. He'd made an ass of himself earlier with Lopez, but here was his chance to stand up for his team. Yes, this was his chance on a silver platter.

Jake called for a timeout and trotted over. He held his glove up to his face and stood close. Nico lifted his own glove and leaned in like gravity was pulling him.

"Do not hit him," Jake ordered. "I know you're dying to, but do not do it."

Shit, was Jake reading his mind? Although he supposed he wasn't exactly hiding the simmering anger at the moment. "But you know he beaned Crowe on purpose. You know it, I know it, the umps know it, crowd knows it. The seagulls shitting over the bullpen know it."

"Yes, but it doesn't matter. Rise above it. This is a one-run game. Do not hit him."

Nico huffed. "But they—" Pressing his lips together, he stopped himself.

Jake's eyebrows almost disappeared under the edge of his raised catcher's mask and helmet beneath it. "They what? They *started* it?"

"Well they did," Nico muttered.

"Yes, but since we're not ten-year-olds on the playground, it doesn't matter. You're better than that. Because if you hit any of their players today, the ump's going to eject your ass right away. Skip'll have to argue it, and he'll get tossed too. Then he'll definitely tear you a new one. Winning is the best revenge, so strike the fucker out."

As much as his inner pouty child wanted to argue, Nico nodded decisively.

Jake jogged back to the plate and crouched, his fingers flashing the signs rapidly: Two fingers, three, one, four, and then one again tapping his left inner thigh, indicating inside the plate. Since Nico and Jake used pumps when there was a runner at second, Nico knew the first sign was the number of pumps, making the one finger the actual sign. Fastball inside.

Drawing his left knee up above his waist, Nico raised his glove in his left hand and ball in his right, then pulled his arm back and exploded forward, hurling the ball toward the plate, his leg kicking up behind him.

Markson swung and missed.

Jake gave him another set of signs, including decoys. Three pumps, and the third sign was four wiggling fingers, which meant a changeup. Nico went into his windup again and released the ball. It just caught the outside of the plate with Markson looking.

Next was a fastball that missed low. Then Jake gave him the sign for a splitter.

Heart rabbiting, Nico spread his first two fingers wide on the ball. He unleashed it—and Markson swung hard, whipping his bat through thin air as the crowd roared, the inning over.

Markson shook his head as he stalked back to the visitors' dugout, muttering, and Nico couldn't hide a shit-eating grin. Jake waited for him by the plate, and Nico's heart skipped. Would Jake tell him off for gloating?

But Jake only grinned too and bumped their shoulders together as they returned to the dugout, the Astroturf feeling light as a cloud beneath Nico's cleats.

That happiness lasted until the next inning, when it all went to hell in a handbasket. By the time Skip walked out to relieve him, Nico had blown the slim lead and let Baltimore get a three-run advantage. The bleeding continued from there, the bullpen giving up four more runs in a rout. The locker room was quiet afterward, most of the guys hustling into the showers, grabbing a bite, and then heading home.

They had an afternoon game the next day, but since Nico wouldn't be pitching again for four games, he took his time, heading to the training room and the whirlpool after his shower. He wasn't hungry and he didn't feel like talking to anyone in the lounge, that was for sure.

Lopez was on one of the training room's handful of treatment tables, one of the assistant trainers digging his elbow into Lopez's shoulder. Lopez opened his eyes as Nico walked in, flip-flops slapping on the tile floor.

Lopez grimaced, and it wasn't clear if it was from the treatment or Nico's arrival. But then he said, "Sorry about that fly ball. I don't know what happened, man. I thought I had it."

As he dropped his towel and climbed into the rectangular six-man hot tub, Nico shook his head. "No. I'm sorry for the stink eye. Mistakes happen. I need to nut up about it." The water was deliciously hot, and he sighed as he lowered himself to the bench, sliding down so the water bubbled over his shoulders.

Lopez chuckled. "It's cool. We all have our moments. God knows I've had plenty."

"Your shoulder okay?"

"Oh yeah." He inhaled sharply. "Baranski here just likes to torture me."

Baranski snorted. "I live for it." He glanced up at the doorway. "Hey, Fitz. What do you need? Summers is in the office; I can call him over if you want?"

Naked but for the towel around his hips, Jake shook his head, scratching his chest, nails scraping a dark pink nipple. "I'm fine. Just going to ice and soak."

Nico closed his eyes, trying not to think about how the water droplets glimmered on Jake's bare skin, catching in the hair scattered over his pecs. Or how his wet hair turned a shade darker, which made his blue eyes pop even more, the stubble on his face thicker as midnight ticked closer.

Nope, Nico wasn't thinking about that stuff at all. Instead, he mentally rewound the game and all the things he'd done wrong.

"You know, that's supposed to be relaxing."

Nico wasn't sure how much time had passed when he opened his eyes again. He'd really zoned out, reliving every pitch, and now Lopez was gone, Baranski was in the adjacent office talking to Summers in low murmurs, and Jake stood by the hot tub. Nico blinked up at him.

Jake's eyebrows rose. "You were grinding your teeth. I could actually hear it from across the room."

Embarrassment sank through Nico like a rock. "Sorry."

Jake shook his head, making an exasperated sound. "Don't be *sorry.*" He climbed the first step of the entry to the hot tub, then hesitated. After a moment, he tossed his towel onto a nearby bench and climbed the other three steps.

Breathing was impossible as Nico stared at Jake's thick, cut cock and heavy balls, at the thatch of dark hair between his legs. Over the murmur of the hot tub's bubbles, blood rushed in Nico's ears.

Holy fuck.

There it was, his fantasy in the flesh. His heart thumped so hard it was painful, his head going light, whole body tingling. He couldn't look away, but he had to because he was staring, and Jake was climbing down into the water now.

Jake sat back against the far side of the tub, his feet brushing Nico's under the water as Nico jerked his gaze away, frozen.

"Sorry." Jake laughed awkwardly. "Long legs."

Nico somehow managed to scrape out a couple syllables. "S'okay." He also somehow managed to resist launching himself across the tub and onto Jake's lap.

As a kid, he'd wondered if Jake was cut or not, and now he knew. Now he wondered what it would feel like to tongue that slit, what it would taste like to swallow him to the root. To suck his balls.

What sounds would Jake make? What would it feel like to have those powerful arms around him, that body pressing him down...

Stop! You can't get hard in the clubhouse hot tub!

Jake cleared his throat. "Look, I know it's easy to say, but don't waste energy on your emotions out there. If the other team hits off you, if they score runs, you need to focus on turning it around. Not letting it get away from you. Command your pitches."

"I know, but—" Nico exhaled forcefully, pressing his lips together.

Jake didn't get impatient or raise his voice. "But what?"

"Forget it." Nico's skin itched, his body jangling with nerves and frustration and sticky desire with Jake naked right there but forever out of reach.

"You can tell me," Jake said quietly.

As Jake looked at him so calmly, his eyes kind and patient, Nico was able to catch a breath and focus on baseball even though he wanted to rub himself all over Jake's hairy, muscular body like a cat and its scratching post.

"When they score runs on me, it's like... Like the game's ruined. Fuck, it sounds stupid when I say it out loud."

"No it doesn't." Jake smiled softly. "We all want to be perfect. We never will be. Odds are, you're never going to pitch a perfect game where not a single batter reaches base. I mean, it's not *impossible*, but in the history of baseball, in more than a hundred years, there have been what, twenty-three perfect games, I think?"

"Twenty-one in the modern era starting in 1901. Felix Hernandez in 2012 was the last."

Jake laughed. "Not that you're counting. And how many no-hitters have been thrown in that time?"

"Two hundred and fifty-two."

"Out of how many games?"

"A few hundred thousand, I guess."

"Right. So those are pretty spectacularly shitty odds. You can still pitch a damn good game if you get scored on. You can still get the win. The team can still get the win. If you dropped an egg, would you throw the rest of the carton on the floor too?"

Nico blinked. "Well...no."

"That would be pretty counterproductive, right?" Jake shifted closer and squeezed Nico's shoulder. "You've got to let go of this all-or-nothing mindset."

The wet warmth and weight of Jake's hand felt so good, and Nico had to stop himself from leaning in for more. Jake was so close. What would it feel like just to hug? For Jake to take him in his arms? Hold him close, skin to skin...

Stop! Focus!

Nico said, "I hear you. I just... I need to be my best. I need to get Rookie of the Year."

Frowning, his hand still on Nico's shoulder, Jake said, "That would be great, but don't pressure yourself."

"But Marco and Dad both won it. I have to prove I'm as good as them."

"Your family won't care whether or not you win. It won't mean you're not a damn good ballplayer, or that you're not going to have a stellar career. And they'll love you just the same."

If they knew the truth they might not love me at all. Nico ached to tumble into Jake's arms, feel that warmth and strength surrounding him, enveloping him so he could stop thinking, stop worrying just for a minute. Instead he moved away, dislodging Jake's hand and reaching for one of the bottles of water kept on a shelf by the hot tub.

After he chugged half of it, he said, "I hear you. That all makes sense. I'll try."

"Winning isn't everything. In a given season, the majority of teams won't make the playoffs." Jake shrugged. "It's not the end of the world. It really isn't."

Nico opened his mouth and then closed it again. Sure, winning wasn't everything and all those clichés, but it was why they were there. Maybe it wasn't everything, but it was sure *something*. When he'd known Jake years ago, there had been a spark, a drive that was missing now.

Granted, Jake had been around the block and his body was wearing down, but he'd been on a losing team in San Francisco most of his career. The Caps really could be contenders. Shouldn't that matter to Jake? Put a bit of spring back in his step?

Even if they didn't make the playoffs, Nico sure as hell wanted to *try*. Not to mention there was Rookie of the Year to think about. He had to keep his eyes on the prize.

"Anyway, we have to take this game pitch by pitch." Jake winced. "Sorry, I keep saying that."

"No, it's good. Clearly I need to hear it about a million more times."

Jake's lips lifted in a smile. "Good thing I like repeating myself. Your next start is against Cleveland, right? I played them a couple weeks ago. We'll go over their lineup and make an action plan. Okay?"

Nico allowed himself a smile back. They had a plan. And a big part of it would be winning, at least as far as Nico was concerned.

CHAPTER SEVEN

"**L**EFTIES ARE REALLY struggling to even get a look at Palmer's slider." Ed Loyola, the Caps' pitching coach, examined an open folder on the desk in his little square of an office, reading glasses perched on the end of his nose. He ran a hand over his salt-and-pepper hair, which he kept almost in a buzz. "Let's keep that up."

"Absolutely." Jake scrawled a line in his small leather notebook. He wore his practice shorts and tee and would hit the gym for a bit before team stretch.

"And finally, we have Agresta." Ed cocked a smile, the creases on his wide face deepening. "You're doing a bang-up job with him, Fitz."

Ed was a trailblazer—one of the first African Americans to manage a professional baseball team—and had tried to retire but said he couldn't stay away. He'd won the annual pitching award as a player, and knew more about the game than Jake ever hoped to. The praise felt damn good.

Returning the smile, Jake said, "He's had some good outings. Kept his emotions in check. Well, mostly. More, at least." There had been a near-meltdown, and Nico was still rattled when things didn't go his way.

Ed smirked. "It's only been a month. You're one of the very best catchers in the game, but you're not Jesus. No one expects a miracle, son."

"Still, he worked through that jam in the third on Sunday and pitched another solid three innings."

Eyeing his ream of notes, Ed nodded. "He did indeed. Like I said, you're doing a fantastic job. Sometimes I think we should have kept him longer down in triple-A to get the maturity, but with that arm and ball control..."

"I hear you. And I'm working on it. *We're* working on it. And obviously you guys are as well."

"We are, but he really responds to you. Coming from me and the other coaching staff, I think sometimes it's just a lot of words from old farts. You're out there on the field with him in the moment. That connection can't be beat." He flipped a page in his folder. "Agresta was asking again about trying his splitter on a regular basis. Said you're in favor of it? I assume so since you had him use it against Baltimore to get out Markson a few weeks ago."

Jake sat back in the guest chair, propping his left ankle on his knee, ignoring the usual aches and pains, his lower back flaring. "I'm definitely open to it, especially in tense situations like that one. He has so much confidence in the pitch, and confidence makes or breaks him. But I understand your concerns."

Ed sat back as well, removing his glasses. "When you look at how many guys are having to get Tommy John surgery, I just want to do everything we can to avoid it. We thought it was the magic solution and ignored the root causes."

Jake nodded. A quarter of the pitchers in the league had had the ligaments in their elbow replaced, and the debate raged over whether the surgery had lulled baseball into a false sense of complacency.

"I definitely don't want to see Nico blow out his arm," Jake said. "But if he threw the splitter sparingly, it could be a great tool. McCrory in Seattle throws it about twenty-five times a game. But some of the guys in Japan rip it constantly and haven't had problems. So who knows. And there's the school of thought that it's all about the quality of the delivery, not the pitch itself. And I do think Nico's delivery on it is excellent." He smiled. "He was determined as a kid to nail it. And he didn't neglect his other pitches."

"Hmm. That's true, and there's a new report that says there's no evidence watching the pitch counts and babying a pitcher prevents injury. But I tend to think it can't hurt. At any rate, stick with the game plan for Agresta's start tonight. Let me think about the splitter."

"Sure thing."

"Again, great work." Ed closed the folder. "The starters and the bullpen all speak highly of you. I think it'll really benefit Baldoni as well having you to model. And the guys who catch Agresta down the line will undoubtedly be grateful."

Jake smiled and said goodbye, then headed toward the gym, nodding at teammates and staff as he went. While he warmed up with an easy jog on the treadmill, the idea of Nico and other catchers strangely nagged at him.

It was ridiculous—Jake would be retired in a couple of years, and Nico hopefully had a long career ahead of him. Of course he'd work with other catchers.

Yet…it bugged him. He increased the incline and speed of the treadmill, breathing deeply as he tried to banish the sensation. It felt a little like jealousy, which was insane. He'd worked with dozens of pitchers over his career and had been friendly with many of them. Sure, maybe he had a soft spot for Nico because he'd known him as a kid. It was cool seeing that shy, serious little kid grown up into a man.

Jake jabbed at the treadmill controls, thinking about Nico's rare smiles and the way a lock of his curly hair usually tumbled over his forehead when he wasn't wearing his cap. How his brown eyes were still so serious most of the time beneath those thick lashes, and how when Jake got close on the mound to talk to him, he could just make out light freckles across Nico's cheekbones.

Not that any of that mattered or had a thing to do with baseball. Maybe Nico was his pet project here in Ottawa, but he was just one part of the job.

"Whoa, what did that treadmill ever do to you?"

Jake jerked his head to the left to find Aaron Crowe on the treadmill beside him. He hadn't even noticed Crowe come in and realized he was pounding the treadmill, breathing hard and stabbing the console to go faster, faster, faster. Pressing the down button now until it was a light running speed, Jake forced a smile.

"Lost in my own world, I guess."

Crowe jogged. "No problem, man."

After a minute of silence as they ran, Jake glanced around the gym. Alvarez was on a bike listening to headphones, and a couple guys pumped iron and spotted for each other in the corner.

He asked Crowe, "Hey, what's your take on Agresta?" His pulse spiked, and he was stupidly nervous waiting for the reply. He wanted the rest of the team to like Nico.

"Wound pretty tight, but he's not a bad kid."

"He talk much when you guys go out to the bars and stuff?"

Chuckling, Crowe shook his head. "Nope. Usually just sits there and gets drunk until he leaves with a chick. Rinse and repeat."

The sharp twist of jealousy returned. Jake barely resisted the urge to roll his eyes at himself. Clearly he needed to get out more, because not only was Nico a teammate and too young for him, he was clearly straight. Not that it mattered. Jake said, "That's good he's got a stress release."

"I think Agresta could bang every single woman in Ottawa and still be ready to snap. He's going to burn himself out if he doesn't unclench." Crowe hopped his feet onto the side of the treadmill and turned it off. "I'm going to do a leg set before team stretch."

Later, after the stretch and batting practice and the usual rhythm of a home game, Jake got into uniform. It was quarter after six, and he bypassed a couple of guys playing a game on their tablets and talking smack to each other, a few others shooting the shit and listening to the new Jay-Z album.

The music faded away as the bathroom door swung shut behind Jake. He pissed at the urinal and thought he was alone until he heard a small cough. He realized the last stall was occupied, not thinking anything of it until the telltale splash.

Sure, maybe someone was just dropping a load, but after his father had been diagnosed, the aggressive chemo had made him nauseous all the time. Jake had stood by uselessly too many times to count while his father vomited.

Nico hadn't been in the locker room, and Jake's own stomach clenched. Was Nico sick? Had he eaten something off? He hadn't said a word, but some guys tried to tough out illness, usually to disastrous effect. Shit, if he wasn't feeling well, they had to tell Skip and get the bullpen up *now*.

Jake asked, "Nico? Is that you in there?"

Dead silence. Then a cleared throat. "Uh-huh. Be out in a second."

Jake waited by the sinks, and when the stall door opened, Nico gave him a flicker of a close-mouthed smile and said, "Hey. Almost ready?"

"Are you sick?" Nico's face was slightly flushed, but he looked fine otherwise. Jake stepped closer. "Did you throw up?"

"What?" Nico scoffed and brushed by him. He waved his hand for the motion-sensor tap to pump soap into his palm. "I'm fine."

"I'd be more convinced if you'd look me in the eye. Seriously, are you sick?"

Nico met Jake's gaze in the mirror as he scrubbed his hands.

"It's not a big deal."

"So you did puke. Look, if you've got a bug or this is food poisoning, you're not going to have the stamina you need. You may feel okay right now, but come the third inning, you'll be on empty."

Drying his hands with one of the fluffy towels stacked on a shelf, Nico shook his head. "I'm always fine. Don't worry about it."

"Wait, what?" Jake stepped in, lowering his voice. "What does 'always' mean? How often do you get sick like this?"

Nico shrugged. "Just before starts. It's better to get it out now so I don't hurl out there."

Jake's heart beat a little too fast. "Do you stick your finger down your throat?"

"*No.*" He rolled his eyes. "Stop looking at me like I'm bulimic or whatever. I get nervous, okay?"

"You throw up before every start?"

Nico shrugged again. "Some actors blow chunks before they go on stage. That's our stage out there." He tossed the hand towel into the laundry basket. "I'm good to go now."

Jake tried to process it. "You don't feel depleted? When I puke I just want to crawl into bed."

"Nah. I drink Gatorade. I'm good." He shifted from foot to foot. "We should get back out there."

"You never throw up other days?" Worry gnawed. "You don't force it?"

"I swear I don't."

"You're young now and have the energy to spare, but if you keep doing this, you'll start running out of gas on the mound. I don't like this."

"I don't much like it either, but like I said, I get nervous. I try not to, but my stomach always goes crazy, and at a certain point it's just better to clear it out." He tapped his thigh, his gaze dropping. "I threw up once on the mound, okay? In high school. There's a video on YouTube if you want a good laugh. I guess I should be glad it's not in HD."

"I wouldn't laugh." Jake's heart hurt for him. He could only imagine how mortifying it must have been.

Nico's smile was razor-sharp. "Everyone else did. Even the guys on my team. The grounds crew was the school janitor, and the game was delayed half an hour while he cleaned it up and a teacher wheeled out some fresh dirt." His face flushed beet red. "I was humiliated, my dad was horrified—it was the worst."

"God, I'm sorry." Jake squirmed thinking about it.

"Before my next start, Dad told me to throw up before I went out if I couldn't handle my nerves. It works. It's no big deal."

Jake gaped. "No big deal? Your *dad* told you to do it?"

Nico raised his eyebrows. "Dude, would you stop looking at me like I'm a messed-up teen in a crappy Lifetime movie?"

"Sorry. But winning isn't more important than your health. I'm sure your dad would agree."

Nico sighed. "My health is perfectly fine. Look, there's no way I'm letting it happen again." He shuddered. "No way."

"It was one time. You were a kid."

"I can't risk it. End of story. I have my game plan and it works."

"You put too much pressure on yourself. We do our jobs, and what happens happens."

Nico's brows drew together. "'What happens happens'? Is that seriously your mantra these days?"

"It's done pretty well for me," Jake replied defensively, his mother's voice echoing in his head. *You can still dream, sweetheart.* He quickly diverted the subject back to Nico. "Speaking of mantras, have you tried yoga or meditation to relax?"

"Yes, and I suck at being zen. I've tried a hundred times, and it just stresses me out more because I can't shut off my brain and breathe the right way or whatever."

"Okay. I get that. It's honestly not my favorite thing either. So how do you unwind at home? If you have a day off and you just want to relax."

Nico seemed to think about it. "Listen to music, I guess. Clean stuff—do something mindless and repetitive."

"What kind of music?"

"Rap or metal. Rock if it's loud."

"So you can lose yourself in it."

"I guess." Nico shrugged again. "It's stupid."

"No it isn't. Not at all. Look, we should get out there, but let me think about how to incorporate some rock and roll relaxation into our game plan. Okay?"

Nico's little smile didn't show his dimples, but it lit up his face all the same.

THE PLAN HAD been going so well.

Before Nico's next start five days later, Jake had arranged a relaxation session in the bowels of the supply area. Mike the bullpen catcher had said it was way beneath their pay grade, but agreed to give them a couple bags of pearls to scuff.

Tucked away in the corner of the concrete bunker where the team's uniforms, equipment, dry food, and boxes and boxes of other mystery things were kept, Jake set up his little portable iPod dock and speaker system and blasted Metallica while he and Nico dipped into the mud and scuffed balls.

There really was something soothing about the repetitive movements, and the driving music pumped Jake up for the game. Nico said he felt okay, but still went to vomit. It was an ingrained habit now, and Jake knew they wouldn't break it in a day.

Jake had watched the video of little Nico throwing up during the game in high school. He'd been sixteen, still skinny and awkward, zits visible on his chin even at a distance. Just after he'd issued a walk, he'd bent in half, heaving his guts out in the dirt, falling to his knees.

The laughter in the bleachers from his classmates had been raucous, even though an adult voice could be heard telling them to knock it off. On the shaky video, Mr. Agresta had stalked out to the mound before the coach could even get there, hauling Nico to his feet.

Jake's heart broke for that kid, and he was determined to help Nico now. He hoped that if they stuck to the plan and tried to relax Nico before starts, his stomach would be settled enough. Some game-day nerves were normal and not a bad thing at all, but he was going to give himself ulcers and drain his energy too much.

Despite puking, Nico had been on fire, in command and racking up strikeouts aside from two runs on a homer. Jake was certain the ball scuffing had still had a positive effect. Nico looked absolutely confident on the mound, his uniform hugging lean muscles, socks pulled up to his knees in the throwback style Jake found incredibly sexy despite himself. Nico was in control of the ballgame.

That was until the top of the eighth, when he gave up a walk and then a line drive that allowed the pinch runner to get from first to third with one out. The home crowd murmured, and Jake knew they were wondering if Skip would make the walk out to the mound to give Nico the hook.

Nico had thrown a great game, hanging in for more innings than usual for a starter, his pitch count still fairly low. He had to be exhausted, and there was no shame in letting a reliever take over. But Skip stayed put, so Jake focused on the next batter.

He flashed the signs to Nico. It was another near sell-out—on a Wednesday, no less—and the audience's restless energy set his hair on end, tension building. The Capitals were ahead 4-2. If they could hold the lead or better yet keep their bats going in the bottom of the eighth, they just needed three outs for the win in the top of the ninth.

The Atlanta batter, Gerard, was at 2-2, and Nico just needed to throw one more strike. Jake's left knee throbbed, and he balanced on his toes in his crouch, his shoulders hunched forward. With runners on, Jake switched to his hop stance, his feet flatter and positioned at three and nine, ready to spring up and pivot to six and twelve to throw out the runner currently at first if he tried to steal second. The guy probably wouldn't since he wasn't known for speed, but Jake had to be ready.

He flashed the signs and waited for the pitch, the crowd buzzing like cicadas in the surprisingly humid night. It was late June now, and this was apparently a taste of what was to come. Sweat dripped down Jake's forehead, and he wanted to push up his cage mask and swipe it out of his eyes.

Nico wound up and let the pitch rip, just missing the corner of the plate. Jake held the ball, twisting his wrist minutely toward the strike zone. But the ump behind him, his hand resting lightly on Jake's back, didn't say anything as he stood up straight, which meant it was a ball.

Fuck. Full count. If Nico walked the bases loaded, his night was over, and he'd be on the hook if these runners scored in the inning. Nico's shoulders were up, his fingers tapping his thigh restlessly. Jake wished he could communicate with him telepathically and tell him to breathe. Hell, he wished he could pitch for him, but all he could do was flash the signs and hope.

It was crazy to think Jake had only known Nico again for what, a month or so? Maybe it was the time they'd spent together years ago, because hell if Jake wasn't rooting harder for Nico than he had for any of his pitchers in far too long.

The crowd roared as the fastball streaked over the plate and hit Jake's glove, the batter caught looking and the ump pivoting with a guttural called third strike.

One more. Just one more out and they would escape the jam. Pop-up, fly ball, strikeout, groundout. Jake mentally reviewed the stats of the next batter and flashed Nico the sign for a two-seam fastball to try and generate weak contact in the bottom of the strike zone.

Nico nodded, wound up, and unleashed the ball toward the plate. Just like Jake had hoped, the batter jumped on the first pitch, hitting a grounder to third that ended the inning. Jumping to his feet, Jake shouted along with the crowd as Nico pumped his fist and walked toward the dugout. Jake pushed up his mask and joined him, slapping Nico's butt with his gloved hand.

"Great patience to get the out. Keep it up."

A grin brightening his face and dimpling his cheeks, Nico nodded. Jake firmly told himself to ignore the flutter in his belly.

But a minute later through the din of the crowd and an old CCR song, Nico's voice rose at the other end of the dugout. "No way. I want to stay in. I can do it!"

Jake looked over to find Nico on his feet, gesturing emphatically to Skip and Loyola. Murakami, the closer, was up in the bullpen, and Nico's face was turning alarmingly red. Jake wanted to go talk him down, but it wasn't his place to get involved when Skip was already over there. The other guys seemingly ignored the fracas, but Jake knew they were listening to every word.

"I can do it! I want the complete game!"

The coaches spoke reasonably, too low for Jake to hear. Nico shook his head emphatically, insistent that he could finish the game, but the decision had been made, and he grabbed a batting helmet and whipped it onto the floor, where it clattered and spun. "Fuck this!"

Jake's blood pressure spiked with equal parts irritation and disappointment. This juvenile bullshit should have been beneath any major leaguer, and Jake had thought Nico was better than that.

Chomping his gum so hard he was about to dislocate his jaw, Skip glared and hissed a warning to Nico, who slumped down on the bench, his lips pressed into a thin line and arms crossed, steam practically shooting out of his ears. The guys down there gave him a wide berth, and attention turned to the field as the team went up to bat. Jake was tempted to go over and tell Nico to cut the shit, but hopefully they'd score an insurance run or two and he'd get his head out of his ass.

Naturally that didn't happen. After a pop-up, a ground out, a walk, and a fly ball, it was time for Murakami to close it out in the top of the ninth. Jake pushed Nico from his mind. The crowd cheered Murakami's arrival from the bullpen, clapping along to musical interludes and doing the wave, excitement brimming. When he was ready, Jake flashed the signs. Three outs, and this one was in the bag.

Too bad the bag had a big fucking rip in the bottom.

Murakami was usually steady as a rock, his breaking balls fooling hitters from both sides of the plate. But after a walk and a hit, Atlanta's second baseman ripped a three-run homer. Head low, Murakami trudged to the dugout in the middle of the inning after retiring the other hitters, the dissatisfied crowd unnervingly quiet.

Jake patted Murakami's back, his jersey damp. "It's okay. A bad day at the office. Happens to all of us."

Murakami shook his head. "Tell that to Agresta."

"He'll survive. That's just the way it goes sometimes." Jake gave him another pat, then realized Nico was staring daggers at Murakami, who slumped on the bench. Jake briefly glared down the dugout at Nico and added, "We still have a shot to tie it up or pull ahead."

Unfortunately, it was three up, three down in the bottom of the ninth, and that was the ballgame. The crowd shuffled out of the stadium as the team retreated to the clubhouse. Nico's hands were balled into fists, and he kicked the side of the bench before disappearing down the steps.

Clenching his jaw, Jake stalked down the tunnel to the dugout with the guys, no one saying much of anything, the silence thick but for the dull echo of their cleats. Nico was just ahead, and he muttered, "Should have kept me in. Could have had it. I fucking had it."

As Nico shook his head and scuffed his foot, his cleats scraping the concrete, a bolt of anger fueled Jake's steps. Grabbing Nico's arm, Jake tugged him away from the entry to the locker room and down to the gym, deserted since they were going on the road in the morning.

Bypassing the main area of weights and cardio machines, he hauled Nico into the stretching room, slamming the door behind them and flipping on the overhead lights. Like everywhere else in the clubhouse, the room was accented in the team colors, and Jake blinked at the assault of red and white.

"What the fuck?" Nico yanked back his arm. His cap was pulled low over his face, his blazing eyes just visible under the brim.

"Stop acting like an asshole. Mura feels bad enough about the blown save without you sulking about it."

"He only had to get three fucking outs." Nico's hands cut through the air. "How hard is that?"

"Sometimes it's damn hard, as you well know."

"I needed this win!"

"*You* needed it? No, the *team* needed it. Team always comes first, and we all fuck up sometimes. So no glaring and guilt-tripping. Come on, you're better than this."

"It's wrong to care? Sorry if I give a shit about winning."

"And I don't?"

"Do you? Do you actually give a shit, Jake? You're all calm

and collected, but I remember you from back in the day. You were in it to win it. You lived and breathed baseball."

Jake scoffed. "Of course I did. I was a kid. A rookie just like you are now. Then I grew up."

"I didn't know growing up meant not caring. It's in your eyes, you know. You go through the motions and say all the right things, but deep down it doesn't matter to you if we make the playoffs or not. You're like, whatever. Maybe next year. Maybe not. Who gives a fuck. 'What happens happens,' right?"

As Nico's words hit far too close to home, Jake flushed with hot anger and shame. "And what would you know about growing up? Caring doesn't mean acting like a petulant brat. Just cut the shit, you hear me?"

"Or what?" Nico spat, raising his hands out to his sides.

His sweaty uniform clinging to him, pads still strapped on tightly, Jake slammed his catcher's mask and helmet to the floor, and they bounced on the studio's thick rubber tiles. "I'm pretty fucking tempted to take you over my knee!"

Nostrils flaring, chest heaving, Nico jutted out his chin. "I dare you."

Even as he closed the distance between them with one long stride, a voice in Jake's mind shouted for him to keep his cool. But then he had Nico's upper arms in his grip, and it was only another step to a bench.

Jake hauled him over his lap.

Nico's cap went flying, his short curls springing out. Jake's right palm came down hard, and Nico jerked, his uniform pants surely not cushioning the strike at all.

Although he wasn't as tall as Jake, Nico was still a big man, and he sprawled over Jake's thighs just above the knee pads, palms on the floor, legs twitching as Jake brought down his hand again—once, twice, three times.

Jake held him down, his left hand splayed over Nico's lower

back as he hit him on his firm, round ass. Nico gasped sharply with each blow.

Get a hold of yourself! This is wrong!

Blood rushed in Jake's ears, his chest heaving, and he realized his cock was swelling, pushing against the hard protective cup. His hand still hovering in the air, he muttered, "Fuck, *fuck!*" An apology was scraping its way out of his throat when Nico groaned and jerked his hips, humping against Jake's thighs.

A lightning bolt of desire ripped through Jake, his mind spinning. *What the fuck is happening? This isn't right.* "Shit. This is…" *This is fucked up beyond belief is what this is.*

He staggered up, Nico sliding off and dropping to his knees, staring up at him, pupils huge and dark, red lips parted, chest rising and falling rapidly. Jake's heart pounded as he fought the urge to shove Nico back on the floor and fuck him senseless.

Nico should have jumped to his feet and screamed at Jake for being such a prick, but he only knelt there like he was begging for it. No, this was impossible—

Jake's breath hitched painfully, his knees almost giving out as Nico reached tentatively for Jake's waistband. Still looking up, he licked his lips, thick eyelashes low. "Please?" he whispered, positively *pleading,* and Jesus Christ, Jake hadn't had a clue Nico was apparently batting for his team. His mind spun like a fastball thundering over the plate.

Words were beyond him as desire roared, and all he could do was nod helplessly, lust searing his veins, drowning out the garbled and distant voice of reason in his brain. Nico tore open the belt and snaps of Jake's uniform pants, unzipping them with a powerful tug and yanking them down to his knees. He made quick work of the cup as well.

Jake's cock curved up, and Nico rubbed his cheek against it, his stubble rasping the sensitive skin. Jake panted through his open mouth as Nico buried his face in his crotch desperately, kissing and licking with needy little whimpers that got Jake even harder.

He tongued Jake's slit, moaning, then took the shaft between his lips, almost choking himself as he sucked it deep, coughing and gagging. He pulled back and then tried again, sloppy and wet. Jake couldn't bite back his moan, and he wavered, the bench digging into the backs of his sore knees.

Ignoring the pain, he spread his feet as much as he could with his pants around the tops of his leg pads, his gaze locked on the sight of his dick filling Nico's mouth, stretching those red lips, spit dribbling down Nico's chin.

Wet, filthy smacking and slurping filled the cool air, loud in Jake's ears along with his own breathing. His hand still tingled from the spanking, and now he threaded it through Nico's curls, making him moan low in his throat and suck harder, the wet heat so tight around Jake's dick.

It was messy and raw, untrained, and Nico's teeth scraped, but Jake didn't care. He didn't care that they were in the goddamned gym at the stadium and anyone could walk in. It should have horrified him, but the thrill reverberating in his bones was undeniable.

He might as well have been in quicksand, stuck in place with Nico at his feet, sucking him so prettily—blowing him like his life depended on it.

Jake tightened his grip in Nico's hair, muttering, "That's it. So good. Fuck, Nic."

Breathing hard through his nose, Nico dug his fingers into Jake's hips, bobbing his head, his face red, freckles standing out high on his cheekbones. He looked up at Jake through those thick lashes, and their gazes locked, the suction of his mouth so perfect, the need in his eyes like a fist clenching Jake's heart.

The orgasm tore through him before he could give a warning, but Nico swallowed greedily, sucking and licking, Jake's cum dripping from the corner of his mouth. Jake still clutched Nico's hair, and he realized he'd pulled far too hard.

As the haze of pleasure cleared, his vision refocusing, Jake smoothed his palm over Nico's head, his dick slipping free from those thick, beautiful lips, white drops staining them, Nico still looking up at him as if at something wondrous.

Jake's knees did give out then, and he smacked down on the bench, his spent dick hanging out and Nico at his feet. His hand still tangled in Nico's hair, sweat and sex thick in the small room, the air conditioning humming in the walls.

"Fitz?"

The call was distant, but they scrambled apart. Yanking up his cup and pants, Jake cleared his throat and yelled, "We'll be out in a minute!"

Closer now: "Cool." It was Diego, and he added, "The media's getting restless, so don't take too long. Need their sound bites and all that shit."

Fumbling with his belt, Jake forced a cheery tone. "Yep! We're on our way."

There was silence again but for the A/C and their harsh breath as they straightened their uniforms. Jake turned to inspect Nico. His face was still red, but he scrubbed his lips clean with the back of his hand and watched Jake warily.

"Don't blame Mura. Talk about Atlanta's power hitting and what a tough lineup they have. We'll discuss..." He waved his hand in the air. "All *this* later."

Nico nodded, following when Jake led the way out of the stretching studio and through the empty gym, concentrating on his breathing. *What the fuck just happened? What did I just do?*

Exactly what the holy hell they'd say to each other later, Jake had no idea.

CHAPTER EIGHT

"**A**TLANTA'S GOT A great lineup. Real power hitters, and their bats were swinging tonight."

A reporter called out, "You have one of the best records so far this season in the league. Many people are pegging you as a strong contender for Rookie of the Year. How does it feel when the closer blows the save and you don't get the W?"

Nico robotically answered, "We win and lose as a team. Mura's a fantastic closer, and it just wasn't his night. But the great thing about baseball is that we get to do it all again tomorrow and give it a hundred and ten percent."

"Nico, you're not angry?"

"No."

Another voice said, "You seemed pretty angry in the dugout. Do you—"

"No," he insisted.

There were a few other questions, and Nico stuck to clichés and one-word answers. He genuinely didn't care anymore that he'd lost. How could he concentrate on baseball after *that*?

I sucked a guy's dick. I actually fucking did it.

And not just any guy. He was acutely aware of Jake nearby answering questions and giving the required answers. Jake didn't seem flustered in the slightest. He smiled, affable and open, and gave the media the comments they liked. It was like he spanked pitchers every day—no big thing.

Desire and queasy confusion simmering through him, threatening to blow, Nico backed away from the press scrum and escaped into the bathroom area of the locker room, where no media was permitted. His dick was still half-hard in his jock, and thank God for the cup so his uniform wasn't tented.

By the sinks, he turned his back on the mirrors and leaned against the counter.

I sucked Jake's dick and he let me.

And it had been better than Nico had ever imagined. The earthy taste, the way Jake's shaft had throbbed and filled in his mouth, stretching his lips. Those nights he'd fantasized or broken down and allowed himself to watch gay porn, he'd never imagined it could be so...what?

He knew it would be good, that it would turn him on. He'd had sex with women and knew what it was like to be touched, to get sweaty and intimate, to get a blow job.

But he hadn't suspected the sensation that would overpower him once he took a cock into his mouth would be *belonging.*

It thrummed through him now like a heartbeat, the certainty that this part of him had been a missing piece, a phantom limb. Having Jake's cock in his mouth, pubes brushing his nose, musky sweat filling his senses, swallowing cum—Nico relived every detail.

As he did, his dick swelled. Especially when he thought about the sting on his ass when Jake had hit him.

Leaning against the counter, his ass smarted, like he'd slipped on ice and landed on his butt. It probably wouldn't bruise or anything. But pushing back on the edge of the Formica, Nico wished it would.

How fucking weird is that? I'm such a loser.

He should have been outraged, furious. But when he'd been splayed over Jake's lap, Jake holding him, overpowering him, Nico had experienced the strangest release. The constant worry, the doubts that nagged at him morning to night, were eclipsed.

In those moments, he hadn't been in control, and letting go had been like riding a rollercoaster, air rushing in his face, fear and exhilaration too close to tell apart, pain spurring on jolts of pleasure.

He'd simply reacted after, reaching for Jake before his brain could order him not to.

And now what was Jake thinking? Surely he regretted it. Probably thought Nico was even more of a freak than he already did. Because Nico was pretty sure he could have come just from being spanked, and he wondered what the smack of Jake's hand would feel like against his bare skin.

Throat dry, his breath came faster. How red would his skin get? How hot would it feel? How much would it hurt? Would Jake like it too? Had he gotten off on spanking Nico tonight? Was he actually gay?

Is he like me?

Nico pushed away the fluttery, warm rush of hope. Jake had let Nico blow him, but that didn't necessarily mean anything. Sure, his dick had sprung up half-hard when Nico freed it. Could have been from the adrenaline rush.

"Agresta, you here?" One of the assistant managers poked his head in. "Skip wants to see you in his office."

Afraid he'd only squeak if he tried to talk, Nico nodded and hurried through the locker room and down the hall, surreptitiously adjusting his cup and commanding his dick to settle down. The rest of the team were probably in the lounge, and he didn't pass anyone as he went. Maybe he'd missed Jake or—

Or maybe Jake had been called to Skip's office too. Nico skidded to a stop in the doorway, his cleats digging into the carpet.

Skip sat at his desk, chomping gum like usual. "Close the door, son." The phone rang, and he glanced at the screen before answering it with a "Yeah?"

Oh fuck. Does he know? Did someone see us? Nico felt like a kid being called to the principal's office, and he cut a glance at Jake standing there like he wasn't bothered, his steady gaze on Skip. Nico pulled the door shut and stood a few feet away from Jake, his heart thundering as Skip listened to whoever was on the phone, tapping his desk with a pencil.

Nico fidgeted, looking everywhere but at Jake: couch, fridge, closet, bulletin board covered in reports and lineups, Skip's scrawl in some of the margins. Framed pictures of Skip from his playing days decorated the walls, and Nico examined the one over the couch featuring Skip in trademark flight, firing the ball to first with both his feet off the ground.

Crack!

Jumping, he jerked his gaze back to Skip, who leaned back in his chair, phone call apparently over. He blew another bubble.

"Nico, I know you were disappointed not to get the win tonight. I was disappointed. We all were. Mura too. Now I know you and Fitz disappeared for a bit there, and maybe you already had this convo. But I want to make sure we always put on our best face to the public, and that we always support our teammates. Blown saves aren't a day at the beach for any of us."

Nico nodded, his throat like a desert. He croaked, "I'm sorry. It won't happen again."

"Good, good." Skip nodded and pushed back his chair. "I can see improvement in you since Fitz came aboard. You've shown more patience and control on the mound. Sometimes, that is. Keep it up and make it more of the time. Make sure it extends to the dugout too. I don't want to see another hissy fit. You're a hell of a talent, but I'll bust you down to triple-A so fast your head will spin. Okay? Good. I'm going to get some chow. If you need more postgame analysis, there's beer in the fridge." With another smack of his gum, he was gone, the door swinging shut behind him.

"Jesus," Jake muttered, pacing and rubbing his palms over his face before dropping his hands to his sides. "Are you okay?"

Nico had no idea how to answer, so he nodded.

"I can't believe that happened. I can't believe I did that."

The tips of Nico's ears went hot, and he shifted from foot to foot, pretty sure he was going to puke Gatorade all over Skip's carpet. Questions ricocheted around his brain.

Is Jake into guys? What if he just didn't say no to getting blown? What if he tells everyone I'm a faggot?

"I didn't hurt you, did I?" Jake looked at him with clear concern shining from his blue eyes.

That's what he was worried about? After Nico just got on his knees and sucked him off? Well, at least it seemed like Nico wouldn't get punched for crossing the line.

"I know talking's not your best event, but can you please say something?" Jake's brows were knit together and he stepped closer. "Seriously, did I hurt you? God, I was completely out of line."

"No," Nico croaked. He cleared his throat. "I'm fine."

"Okay. Good. Do you want to say anything to me?"

Too many things to know where to begin, so Nico shook his head.

Jake exhaled noisily, keeping his voice low. "Come on. I *spanked* you, and then we—" He rubbed his face. "Can you please tell me what you're thinking? Because I have zero idea."

Nico captured one of the questions whipping around his mind like a hurricane. "Have you done that before?"

"Not like that. Never at work. Never in anger."

So Jake was talking about hitting him, but it still wasn't clear about the rest. "Are you—I mean, when I... You didn't..."

Jake's forehead creased. "Are you asking if I'm gay? Yes, I am."

Holy. Fuckballs. Jake Fitzgerald was actually gay. *I'm not the only one.* And of all people, it was Jake who was like him. Nico could only stand there staring at him mutely.

His expression soft and voice low as if he was holding out sugar cubes to a jittery horse, Jake asked, "Are you?"

Even with the rush of relief that he wasn't alone, a knee-jerk *no* still hovered on Nico's tongue. Looking into those eyes he'd fantasized about for years, he swallowed thickly. "I don't know." Heart tripping too fast and head too light, he added, "Maybe."

Nico's knees trembled and he really was close to vomiting, those barely whispered syllables loud as a gunshot to his ears, so close to the *YES* he should have shouted but was still caught inside him, its barbed hook wedged deep. "But I've never…"

Jake watched him seriously, stepping closer, tantalizingly within reach. "That was your first time?"

"I mean, I'm not some virgin." His cheeks flushed hot with a fresh wave of humiliation. "I've banged plenty of chicks."

"But it was your first time with a man?"

Nico nodded, twitching his fingers restlessly.

"Wow. I thought you seemed a bit… But I didn't think…"

Nico dropped his head and stared at the scuffed tips of his cleats. "Sorry." It was probably the worst BJ of Jake's life.

"No, that's not—" Jake's feet came into view, and his big palm covered Nico's shoulder, sending a shiver through him. "That wasn't a complaint." He gently tipped up Nico's chin, his eyes kind. "You were great. Okay? I just would never have—it was fucked up, and that's totally on me."

"But I liked it," Nico blurted. Blood rushing in his ears, he fisted his hands, blunt nails jamming into his palms. Jake was so close now, and God, he longed to touch.

Jake's fingers tightened on Nico's shoulder. "It doesn't matter. I should never have hit you. It was unbelievably unprofessional. I still can't believe I did it. We were at work, and I'm not your boss! I had no right to treat you like that. Jesus, not that being your boss would have made it any better."

Nico felt like it was his turn to say something, but he could only watch Jake mutely.

Jake whirled away, pacing in front of Skip's desk. "It was absolutely unacceptable. I've never lost control like that. You just got under my skin. I can't explain it. But God, that's no excuse. If you want to work with Baldoni from now on, I'll understand."

The urge to go hide in a dark room with a bottle of scotch tugged at Nico, hot needles of mortification stabbing all over. He'd finally given in and had sex with a man—with *Jake Fitzgerald*—and it had been something disgraceful. Something *wrong*, just like him. The earlier sensation of belonging, of rightness, curdled into ugly shame.

His throat felt full of broken glass as he choked out, "No, it was me. You hit me, but I'm the one who liked it. I'm the one who begged to suck your dick. I'm a freak, okay? Just forget about it." He backed up and yanked the door open, stumbling down the hall toward the locker room.

"No, no. Nico!" Giving chase, Jake hissed, "Wait!"

"Hey, Fitz, there you are. You gotta come see this." One of their teammates—Araya or maybe Washington, Nico didn't stop to look—called out, and Nico sped into the locker room, tugging off his dirty uniform and jumping into his street clothes without showering.

When he ducked back into the hall, Jake was surrounded by a few of the guys, who were showing him something on an iPad, but Jake broke away and caught Nico by the elevator down to the player parking lot. Jake's hand was a brand on Nico's arm even through his leather jacket.

"Please," Jake muttered. "We have to talk. But not here. Can I come to your place?"

He wanted to say no, because what more was there to talk about? Jake would try to make him feel better with hollow words, and Nico would still be a pathetic freakazoid. But they had to work together, so he had to hear him out. He rattled off his address on George Street. "It's a condo in the Market. I'll tell the concierge you're coming."

The elevator opened, and Nico jabbed at the buttons, keeping his eyes on his feet as the doors finally closed.

NODDING TO THE valet, Nico walked around his SUV and into the lobby, telling the solicitous guy behind the desk about Jake's visit before taking the elevator up to the sixteenth floor.

Inside his condo, he hung up his jacket when he usually would have tossed it over a chair, fiddling with the hanger and then a mark he noticed by the collar. Licking his thumb, he scrubbed at it uselessly before giving up.

His white, silver, and black condo was nice—two bedrooms and bathrooms, an open concept and dark hardwood throughout, and a huge island in the kitchen he only used to heat leftover takeout. The team had organized it all and hired someone to decorate it too.

Now that Jake was coming over, Nico eyed the abstract paintings critically, little splashes and slashes of color that could have been done by a kindergartner.

As if Jake gives a shit about my art.

Broad windows and a balcony lined the outer wall of the living room, a big screen TV dominating the inner, black leather sectional filling the space in-between. Nico peered out at the city lights and the dark ribbon of the river before closing the vertical blinds tightly.

He could have walked to and from the ballpark, but driving made it easier to avoid fans and maintain his privacy. Ottawa was a small city, so fans knew a lot of the players lived in the condos in and around ByWard Market. However, Nico wasn't keen on leading people right to his door.

He paced to the fridge, opening it to find beer, mustard, pickles, ketchup, and a Styrofoam container of Thai that had leaked reddish oil, drip, drip, dripping down to the top of the empty crisper. Not that he could eat anything if he tried, even though he knew he should.

The knock jolted him, dread churning his stomach. When he opened the door, Jake stood at the threshold, his hair sticking up in sweat-dried spikes. He'd apparently skipped a shower too, considering how quickly he'd made it over. His hands were shoved in the pockets of his jeans, his light jacket unzipped.

Nico waved at it. "Do you want…" He opened the closet and took out a hanger as Jake came in and handed over his jacket. He wore a purple Henley underneath, and he bent to untie his brown boots, the leather worn and soft-looking. Nico was suddenly strangely embarrassed that he was still wearing his sneakers, and he reached down to tug them loose.

"Sorry," Jake said. "Canadian habit I never got out of. We're big on taking our shoes off. Lots of snow. Not that you don't get snow in Chicago."

"No, it's good. Keeps the floors cleaner." His socks were sweaty and gross, so he peeled them off and stuffed them into his shoes. "Beer?"

"Sure." In his dark socks, Jake followed to the kitchen on the left side of the open space. "Nice place."

"Thanks. The team arranged it for me." He opened the fridge and popped the top off two bottles.

Jake said, "I told them I'd handle it myself, but I haven't seemed to find the time."

Nico passed a bottle over. Their fingers brushed, and he was pretty sure this was hell. Excruciating small talk with the guy he'd sucked off. The guy who'd *spanked* him because he was being such a brat. The guy who was Jake Fitzgerald of all people in the whole world. In his countless fantasies, hooking up with Jake had never ended like this.

By the fridge with the black, granite-topped island between them, Nico chugged half his beer and took a deep breath, forcing the words out in a rush. "I'm sorry I was such an asshole. Can we just move on and forget this?"

Still holding his untouched beer, Jake shook his head. "You don't have to be sorry. For throwing shade at Mura in the dugout, sure. But not for anything else. I initiated it all by acting completely inappropriately."

"It wasn't exactly 'appropriate' for me to get on my knees and beg to suck you either." His face burned, and he stared at the green glass bottle in his hand, feeling the weight of Jake's gaze like lasers. "It was wrong and weird and fucked up, like you said. So can't we just pretend it never happened?"

"Nic." Jake's voice was soft and a lot closer now, and butterflies swirled in Nico's belly. Jake had rounded the island, stopping a couple feet away. "It was wrong because we work together. Because we were *at* work. Because I was angry. We were both angry. But getting turned on by it in general isn't wrong."

Nico's breath came too fast, his body shaking as he forced himself to meet Jake's gaze. "You don't think I'm a weirdo for liking it? I never thought—I've never tried any of that stuff. I had no idea." He stepped closer without meaning to, only a foot between them now.

"*No*, you're not a weirdo. Plenty of people like it. I like it." Jake looked away and gulped his beer. "I was hard, wasn't I?"

He nodded, the memory of Jake's throbbing cock, the head flushed red, sending a shower of sparks through Nico's veins. He watched Jake's face, and when Jake looked at him again, they stared at each other, Nico's heart pumping harder with each beat, the air heavy.

Clearing his throat, Jake turned and took a few steps toward the living room. "Like I said, I've done things like that before, but never at work. Never in anger."

Jealousy roared through Nico, hating the nameless and faceless men Jake had been with. His voice was hoarse as he asked, "You do BDSM stuff?"

Jake took a gulp of beer, his eyes on the blinds covering the wide windows as if he could see beyond. He jammed his free hand into his pocket. "Yeah. I'm not into the full-on lifestyle with TPEs, but I enjoy it in the bedroom."

Swirling the letters around, Nico came up blank. "TPE?"

"Sorry—total power exchange. Sometimes a dom and sub will maintain those roles twenty-four hours a day, seven days a week. I'm not into that." He laughed weakly. "Sounds exhausting, honestly. But to each their own."

How was this actually a conversation they were having? In real life? "Oh."

Spinning and putting his beer on the counter, the glass clinking loudly on the granite, Jake scrubbed a hand through his hair. "Look, this shouldn't have happened, but I didn't mean to shame you. I'd never want to do that."

"It's not your fault."

"It is, though. You said you've never been with a guy before?"

Gripping his bottle, Nico shook his head. He knew how pathetic it must sound.

"But you've wanted to?"

That one little syllable was still hooked deep in his chest, unyielding: *Yes.* "I don't know."

"Have you wondered about it before?"

Memories of Jake flooded his mind: *squatting in the backyard with his catcher's mitt, laughing with Marco, kissing Nonna's papery cheek, slinging his arm around Nico's skinny shoulders, seeming like a giant, the sun catching in his sandy hair.*

"A couple times, I guess." God, he was such a liar. He'd sucked Jake's dick, but he still couldn't come clean.

Jake sighed. "I'm sorry. I know how tough it can be, especially if you're confused. Have you talked to Marco or Val, or—"

"Are you fucking crazy?" Laughing incredulously with a burst of nervous energy, Nico backed up, the handle of the fridge ramming his spine. "No way. I'm not... No way." He tried to catch his breath. "Does Marco know about you?"

"No. I wasn't comfortable telling anyone back then." Jake's twist of a smile was rueful. "Not that I'm super comfortable telling anyone now. My family knows, but I'm not exactly the poster boy for being out and proud."

"Oh."

Jake scratched behind his ear, then took a sip of his beer, his gaze skittering around. "Back then, I worried about how it would affect my career. How things could change with the guys in the locker room, with the fans. Every time I made a mistake on the field, I was afraid it would be all about my sexuality if I came out. But at this point I just want to finish up my career without controversy. It's selfish, I know."

"No, I get it." Tracing a seam in the hardwood with his big toe, Nico couldn't bear to look up.

"Nico..." Jake waited until Nico met his gaze, then gently said, "You know we can't ever do anything like that again. We're teammates, and I'm older, and it would be completely inappropriate on so many levels. We have to stay focused on our jobs."

"Uh-huh." He nodded vigorously, cringing at the way Jake was being so kind, like Nico was something terribly fragile he didn't want to break. Nico shrugged carelessly. "Just got caught up. No big deal."

"Okay." Jake ran a hand through his hair. "But if you ever want to talk, it's not like we can't be friends." He smiled faintly, and Nico was struck by regret that he hadn't had the chance to taste those lips just once. "My mom thinks I could use more of those, and she's usually right about everything. And..." He stepped closer again, his hand lifting before he curled his fingers and dropped his arm to his side. "I know what it's like, being in the closet."

"Right. I'm not. This was…" Nico tried to smile too, pretending his heart wasn't about to pound through his chest. "Anyway. Been a long day."

"Right, okay." Jake drained his bottle and headed for the door, where he grabbed his coat and stuffed his feet into his boots without doing them up, clearly just as eager to end the torture. He opened the door. "See you tomorrow. We can work some fastball drills."

"Great. See ya." Nico closed the door behind him and flipped the lock.

Tomorrow.

God, he'd have to see Jake not only tomorrow, but the next day, and the day after that, and practically every single fucking day until the season ended at the beginning of October.

Leaning back against the door, he tried to breathe evenly. He had to just forget it. Had to forget what it had felt like to be bent over Jake's knee, to have the sting of his hand on Nico's ass, and how it had turned him to butter, the hard block of tension inside him melting in a way he couldn't explain. He hadn't needed to be perfect in that moment—he just had to *be*.

Never in a million years had Nico thought he'd get off on that. He thought of the words Jake had used—dom and sub. He knew there were people who liked being tied up. Did Jake do things like that? His dick twitched, an electric coil of *want* in his belly at the idea of being restrained while Jake touched him. While Jake did anything he wanted. Did *everything* while Nico could simply let go.

The tension was back now, the thick brick jammed in his chest, immovable and crushing the desire. He had to forget it— the freedom and thrill of being controlled, of the taste of Jake's cock stretching his mouth, the rightness of it.

These weren't things he could have—not with Jake, not with anyone. But for the first time, he allowed himself to think of someday. Maybe he could have it then, once baseball was over.

Curled in bed after a cold shower, he imagined stubble rubbing against his in a hard kiss, sweat and muscles and maybe laughter, someone who understood him. Loved him, even.

And there in the darkness, his duvet pulled up to his ears, if he thought of Jake with him in that distant, impossible *someday*, no one had to know.

CHAPTER NINE

O PENING HIS EYES, Jake groaned loudly. The reason was threefold.

First, the team's flight was way too early. He would kill to roll over and sleep another three, four hours. Knees creaking, he rounded his back, a dull throb stretching from his tailbone to his ribs.

Second, he'd actually *spanked* Nico Agresta. Without consent. At the clubhouse. While they were working. He'd officially lost his mind.

Third, Nico had blew him. That had actually happened. It hadn't been some fever dream jerkoff session. No, Nico had taken Jake's cock in that pretty red mouth and had sucked like his life depended on it.

And there was a fourth reason Jake was groaning and wishing he could go back to sleep and forget everything: He wanted to do it all again.

Rubbing his face, he stared at the stark white ceiling. The image of Nico on his knees, trust and desire shining from his eyes, his lips parted as he whispered *"Please"* had been seared into Jake's cerebral cortex. Seeing Nico submissive like that had been a revelation.

Jake had always enjoyed sex. He'd liked a little BDSM with Ron and a few other guys over the years. Sex didn't always have to involve domination for him to get off, but if a partner liked being tied up or disciplined, the power and primal possessiveness in taking charge turned Jake's crank. He'd fantasized more than he should have about Brandon submitting to him, letting Jake control him. Letting Jake love him.

There was something heady about another person putting themselves in his hands. He supposed it was part of why he'd wanted to be a catcher despite his height. There had only been a handful of catchers that tall over the years in the majors, but once Jake had moved from third in the minors to fill a temporary gap behind the plate, he'd stayed put.

The trust the pitchers and managers placed in him to shape the game was a powerful thing. He kept the pitchers calm, talked them down when they started to panic, supported them and praised them, and helped them be their best selves.

It felt *good* to be that person. In the bedroom it was usually just about getting off, about pleasure. Ron was a successful man with his shit together, and Jake had enjoyed helping him unwind and let go. It had been fun and relaxing for both of them. No strings.

But thinking of Nico now, of his big brown eyes and sweet whimpers, of his shame and self-denial—his *pain*—all the strings in the world wrapped around Jake from head to toe, cutting off his circulation. The urge to take Nico in his arms and keep him safe echoed through Jake like aftershocks from an earthquake. Nico was so terribly afraid, and Jake wanted to make it better.

"I should have known." His voice was hoarse in the empty room.

He should have guessed from Nico's stares, the tension obvious in him, the pull between them that Jake had denied. But he hadn't known until Nico had begged to suck him, had exposed himself so completely, trusting Jake in those moments even if he hadn't been able to fully admit his sexuality later.

Jake understood why it was so hard to say it out loud, especially since Nico had never been with a guy before. Maybe it was just experimentation, but Jake's gut feeling was Nico had been repressing his desires for a long time.

And oh, the things it did to Jake—the knowledge that he was first. He exhaled a shuddering breath, his body humming and dick twitching. Maybe it shouldn't have intrigued him even more. Maybe it shouldn't have turned him on. Yet the idea that his cock had been the first in Nico's mouth, that he'd been the first to be gifted with that desperate passion, overwhelmed him.

First and last.

Kicking off the sheets, Jake shuffled to the bathroom, his stiff knees protesting. He had to stop this train of thought before it jumped the tracks and derailed his life. But as he pissed, his dick begging for attention, he couldn't corral a simmering jealousy. The idea of anyone else—male or female—touching Nico made him itchy, his skin too tight.

He glanced in the mirror at his scruffy face, his eyes bleary and hair on end. "You're being ridiculous," he said aloud. "You told him it can never happen again, and you were right. And now you're talking to yourself, which is never a good sign."

Smearing mint paste on his electric toothbrush, Jake hit the button, hoping the mechanical drone would drown out the rest of his thoughts. No such luck. Nico had said it himself—he wasn't a *virgin*. But the way he'd worshiped Jake's cock, it was as if Jake had watched a dam break, the flood unleashed.

If Nico had liked the taste of dick, what else would he like? Getting fucked? Having Jake's cock deep in his ass? Would he like other power exchanges? Would he like it if Jake took him over his knee again, but in the bedroom this time?

Jake spit out his toothpaste and rinsed his mouth. He leaned on the sink, breathing too fast. God, he wanted to feel that bare ass under his palm, see it redden, hear Nico's whimpers as his cock got hard against Jake's leg. Because it would. It would get so damn hard.

What about if Jake tied him up? Blindfolded him? Would Nico like it? Shit, he'd look so pretty spread out, trembling, giving himself over, trusting Jake to take care of him...

"Stop thinking about this." Jake glared at the mirror. "Now."

As he took a barely lukewarm shower, scrubbing his skin vigorously, the thoughts of sex took a backseat. Yet the protective impulse remained. Nico was so scared, and Jake had left him alone because Jake was afraid he wouldn't be able to control himself. He should have stayed and made sure he was okay.

The idea of talking to his family about it had shot Nico through with clear panic. Surely Marco and Val would be cool if Nico was gay or bi, but Mr. Agresta was definitely more old-fashioned, and certainly Nico's grandmother was.

Jake couldn't remember ever hearing them be hateful the summer he'd practically lived in their North Shore mansion, but it was a long time ago. Nico's father was a bulldog, but Jake had never thought he was a bigot. *Ugh.* He desperately hoped the Agrestas weren't homophobes behind closed doors.

Nico had barely smiled then, and he rarely did now either. But last night after he'd struck out Gerard, a smile had lit up his face, dimples creasing his cheeks. For a heartbeat, Nico had glowed with pure joy. Jake craved it now. He needed to see it again as much as he needed air.

After twisting off the shower, he rubbed a towel over his head. He had to stick to what he'd told Nico—that nothing could happen between them again. They could be friends. Nothing more.

And if that thought made Jake feel strangely hollow, it didn't mean a thing.

NICO HISSED, "WOULD you stop?"

Later that week, they were in the private terminal at the Detroit airport around midnight, waiting for their charter flight to Chicago. While most of the other guys played games, chatted, or tapped their phones, Nico sat in the far corner, ostensibly watching CNN on a wall-mounted TV.

After three games of rummy with Diego while the team waited for a mechanical problem on the plane to be fixed, Jake hadn't been able to resist getting closer to Nico. He'd taken a chair three seats away and pretended to read on his tablet.

He put on his best faux-innocent expression. "What?"

Nico shot him a narrow-eyed glance. "It's been days. Stop looking at me like I'm made of glass. I'm fine." He muttered, "My ass is fine too."

A completely inappropriate joke about how Nico's ass was indeed *fine* sprang into Jake's head. Fortunately he crushed it before it left his tongue. "I know. I'm not… I'm just sitting here."

Nico rolled his eyes. "You're pretending to read, but really you're hovering over me like you think I'm going to shatter any minute."

Okay, so he was worried. But Nico had a point. "I hear what you're saying. I wasn't trying to…hover."

"Then stop it, and stop feeling guilty. If you don't let it go, everything's going to keep being fucking weird, and other people will notice, and ugh."

"You're right." Sighing, Jake rubbed his face. "You're totally right."

"Stop worrying about it. We're good. You look like shit."

Jake huffed out a laugh. "Thanks."

"I mean like you haven't been sleeping well." A little smile tugged at Nico's mouth.

So you think I look good otherwise? Again, Jake obliterated the question before he could ask it out loud. Nico, on the other hand, looked the same as ever—too handsome to be allowed. He was his usual quiet, antisocial self.

Maybe he wasn't affected the way Jake was. Maybe he was glad to put the incident in the past and move on. Maybe he really wasn't gay or bi, and it had been a one and done type of thing.

But when Jake thought about Nico on his knees with that imploring expression on his beautiful face, the longing in that one word...

"Please."

The way he'd swallowed Jake's cock, choked on it desperately, like he'd been starving for it—like he'd die without it—when Jake thought about all that, he knew there was far more below Nico's taciturn surface.

Jake refocused. "You're right, I've been sleeping like crap. Sometimes I wish I could just unplug my brain."

"Yeah." Nico watched him like he wanted to say more, but didn't.

"Someone told me once to imagine the trunk of a car, and you pack all your worries into it and shut the lid. Then you walk away, and you keep walking, and you fall asleep with all the shit locked away."

Nico frowned. "That works?"

"Nope. I tried it, and I had to go back to the car so many times I was walking all night."

Nico smiled, just a little arch of his closed mouth. On CNN, a story about selection for the all-star game played, and he slouched lower in his chair, any trace of mirth vanished.

"I played in it twice," Jake said. "It was cool. You'll get there one day. No doubt." Rookies were rarely named to the all-star teams, but he knew Nico had probably put pressure on himself to make the cut.

Frowning again, Nico said, "Cool? That's it?"

He shrugged. "Yeah. It was fine. It was good. It was an honor for sure." He re-crossed his legs, brushing at a nonexistent stain on his jeans.

He knew what Nico was thinking, and had to admit that, yeah, he was jaded. As a kid, the idea of being on a big-league all-star team would have made him pee his pants in giddy elation. But by the time it had happened, Brandon and their friendship was long gone and Jake was going through the motions. He'd been covered in bubble wrap, not feeling much of anything.

"What?"

Blinking, Jake said, "Huh?"

"You said something about bubbles." Nico's brows were drawn together.

"Oh, nothing." He waved his hand dismissively. "So, are you excited to see your family tomorrow?"

Looking back up at the TV, Nico's shoulders seemed to creep up to his ears, his body awkward with tension as he shifted restlessly. "Sure."

"That sounds enthusiastic."

He shrugged. "I've got the start tomorrow. I can get pumped after I win that."

"Is your dad coming to the game?"

"He wouldn't miss it." Nico slumped lower in his chair.

Before Jake could say anything else, the flight was ready to depart, and they were on their way to the Windy City.

FROM HIS SPOT on a couch in the visiting clubhouse in Chicago, Jake could make out Nico's profile from the corner of his eye.

Perched like a statue on the chair in front of his locker, Nico barely seemed to blink. The space was comfortable and similar in layout to the Caps' locker room at home, but not quite as luxurious.

"Sevens?"

Jake refocused on Diego sitting on another couch across a low table. "Huh? Oh, right. Go fish."

Looking to his left, Diego peered at Nico. He glanced back at Jake, an eyebrow popping ever so slightly. Jake realized he'd been checking on Nico at least once a minute. Probably more like every ten seconds. He cleared his throat and asked, "Kings?"

"Go fish." Beside Diego, Jimenez watched a movie on his tablet, huge headphones covering his ears. Davis sat on the other end of Jake's couch, engrossed in whatever was happening on his phone.

Jake pulled a card and glanced back at Nico despite himself. Since they were on the road, he and Nico couldn't scuff balls in the storage room like usual. He knew that as game time approached—still more than an hour away—Nico's gut was likely churning.

The thought of Nico going to silently throw up before the game nagged at Jake. Even if it was only once every five days, that was too much. But with the lingering awkwardness between them, he wanted to give Nico his space. Maybe that was stupid. They were supposed to be friends, right? So they should hang out. They should—

"Hey, Agresta!" Diego called.

Rigid, Nico turned. He waited for Diego to say more.

"Want to come play cards?" Diego asked.

Forehead creased, Nico looked to Jake. Jake sat mutely. Nico shook his head. "Thanks, though."

Jake managed to find his voice. "Come on, we should do something to loosen you up before the game." As soon as the words were out of his mouth, his cheeks went hot. But none of the guys even blinked, and why would they? Why would anyone think "loosen up" meant anything sexual? And Jake hadn't intended it to be sexual, so why—

Why are you overthinking every single thing? Calm the hell down!

"Why don't you go for a walk?" Diego suggested. "Usually helps me unwind a bit." He checked the clock and gathered the cards. "I've got to call Liz anyway."

"Yeah, let's walk." Jake was on his feet, and after a few heartbeats, Nico stiffly rose and followed.

In the tunnels under the stadium, they walked quietly, still wearing their workout shorts and tees. Jake cast about for something to say. *This isn't a date. Chill out.* Finally he asked, "What's your favorite game?"

Nico stepped closer as a guy in a golf cart passed by. The furrow in his brow returned. "Baseball."

Jake had to laugh. "I mean other than the obvious. Like, do you play video games, or…"

"Not really. A doc told me it wasn't good for my hands. Could strain my fingers."

"Ah. That makes sense. Board games?"

Tracing his left fingertips along the tunnel wall, Nico said, "Yeah, but not lame ones."

"What are the lame ones? Snakes and Ladders? Parcheesi?"

"Yeah, and, like, Monopoly and Life. Connect Four. I guess that's not really a board game."

An image of the hospital smacked Jake in the face—sitting cross-legged on the floor outside his dad's room in the wee hours with Brandon, Connect Four between them as they quietly played game after game.

"Are you a big Monopoly fan?" Nico asked. He laughed awkwardly. "Don't cry about it, dude. You can like Monopoly."

Shaking his head, Jake dislodged the memory. "No, not a big fan either. I haven't played those kinds of games in years. But a friend in San Francisco introduced me to some awesome cooperative games. Dead of Winter, Legends of Andor. I love Pandemic."

Nico's face lit up as they turned down another tunnel, winding their way through the pathways. "You know Pandemic? It's awesome, right? Val and I used to play sometimes."

"Have you done Legacy or any of the expansion packs?"

"Uh-uh. Just the original." A little smile played on his lips. "It's been a few years since I played. We should—maybe we can play sometime. Not before a start, but I dunno. Sometime."

"That would be cool. And why not before a start? Takes too much brain power to save the world from deadly viruses?"

"Yup. I need to zone out."

"And you don't like cards?"

Nico shrugged, scratching at the back of his neck where his hair had recently been shorn. A stubborn curl crept over his forehead. "Cards are fine. I just can't concentrate before a start. Scuffing balls is mindless, you know?"

"Right. So let's play a mindless game."

"Like what?"

"I dunno. Tag."

"*Tag*?" Nico scoffed.

"Yep." Jake poked Nico's chest. "You're it." Then he was off and running through the tunnel, veering around the Chicago equipment manager and a skid of sunflower seeds. Realizing he'd look pretty stupid if Nico wasn't following, he glanced over his shoulder, a warm jolt of excitement and pleasure kicking up his heart as he saw Nico giving chase.

Through the mostly empty tunnels they raced, sneakers quiet on the concrete. Jake looked again, and Nico was closer and grinning now, dimples deep in his cheeks, making Jake's stomach flip-flop.

He careened around a corner to discover a dead-end ahead. It wouldn't have mattered anyway, since Nico pounced, gripping Jake's shoulders as they stumbled and almost smashed right into the wall.

Jake braced himself with palms out, but the momentum of

Nico right behind him sent his forehead into the wall. It was only a glancing blow, and he laughed as he turned and leaned back on the concrete. He rubbed his head theatrically. "Hope I don't end up on the DL."

But Nico wasn't smiling. Standing so close their shoes met, he reached up for Jake's forehead, brushing his fingers over the skin so lightly they were a whisper. "How bad did you hit? Shit. If you end up on the disabled list because of me…"

"It's nothing." Jake laughed awkwardly, vividly aware of Nico's fingers brushing back his hair now, Nico biting his lip as he peered at Jake's forehead.

"Maybe you should sit down while I run and get the trainer. Just to make sure."

"I've got a hard head. Don't worry. It was barely a scrape." Jake stared at Nico's thick eyelashes, and his throat went dry as their eyes locked. They were standing too close, and Nico should have backed up now, but his fingers rested at Jake's hairline, and he licked his lips—

"I hear there are a couple hooligans loose in the tunnels!"

At the sound of his brother's voice, Nico jerked back like he'd been burned, tripping over his own feet and ending up against the other wall. He ripped his gaze from Jake's as Marco rounded the corner, a grin lighting up his handsome face.

His thick, wavy hair was brushed back from his forehead. Dimples like Nico's creased his cheeks, and heavy brows framed brown eyes. He wore his gray uniform pants and a workout T-shirt.

As he yanked Nico into a hug, Jake realized Marco was actually a couple inches shorter now. Well, not that he had shrunk—Nico had sprouted up in his late teens.

Jake watched them slap each other's backs, then Marco hugged him and said, "So good to see you! And now you're playing with my baby brother." He stepped back, shaking his head. "Still hard to believe he's old enough to be in the big leagues and not popping zits back in Highland Park."

Nico rolled his eyes. "I haven't lived at home for four years."

"Shit, has it been that long?" Marco looked at Jake. "Hard to believe it's been mumble-mumble years since we played here together, huh?"

"It is." It was a million years ago, when Jake was hungry to win, Dad was alive, and Brandon didn't hate him. "How's Chi-town treating you?" Marco was one of the rare players who had been with the same team his whole big league career so far.

"I can't complain. This club's been very good to me. This city too. My city. I want Nico to come down here. The prodigal son returns." He slapped Nico's shoulder. "How freaking awesome would that be, for you, me, and Dad to all have worn the uniform?"

Nico nodded, the quiet intensity back in the stillness of his expression. "Awesome."

Jake wasn't sure he quite meant it. He'd tensed right up again, and his shoulders only inched higher when Marco said, "Think you can strike out your big brother, kid? Huh?" He elbowed Nico playfully.

Nico shrugged, but Jake said, "Hell yes he can, old timer."

"Oh, it's like that?" Marco laughed. "I believe your birthday's before mine, but okay. It's on." He checked his watch. "I should get back. Nic, Dad's on his way."

"Great." Nico's smile was so tense it was about to snap.

Marco added, "Since tomorrow's an afternoon game, family dinner out at the house afterwards. Fitz, you're coming, or Nonna will show up and drag you over by the ear. She may be in her eighties now, but her threats should never be underestimated."

He should have said no since he needed to keep his distance from Nico, but Jake chuckled. "Dinner tomorrow would be great. Thanks."

"Just like the old days, huh?" Grinning, Marco gave Nico another elbow. "This one still following you around like a lost duckling."

"I am not!" Nico's face went red all the way down his neck.

Before Jake could defend Nico from his brother's ribbing, Marco rolled his eyes and turned back down the tunnel. "Always so easy to wind up. I'm going to take you out of the park tonight, Nic."

As Nico stayed silent, his face still red, Jake called, "We'll see!" *God, please don't let him homer off Nico. Or even get on base.*

Marco spun back. "Oh, and no calla lilies tomorrow, Fitz."

"That was one time! Nine years ago!" Jake had to laugh as Marco winked and jogged off with a wave. Jake had made the grave mistake of bringing calla lilies for Nonna, who had crossed herself about a dozen times after putting the flowers down the trash compactor. Jake didn't take offense after Valentina had apologetically explained that in Italy, the flowers were usually reserved for funerals, at least where Nonna had grown up.

Eyes on the worn floor, Nico was still silent. Jake stepped closer and, after a moment of debate, squeezed his shoulder. Thumb resting on the bare skin by Nico's neck, he felt his pulse jumping. "You're going to kick ass tonight. Plus take names, and one of those names will be Marco's. Okay?"

Meeting Jake's gaze, Nico nodded.

They walked back to the clubhouse instead of running, shoulders brushing as they stepped aside to make room for a group of groundskeepers. When they returned to the locker room and Nico made a beeline for the bathroom, Jake grabbed a bottle of water and followed.

CHAPTER TEN

"I'M JUST SAYING, you could have thrown your only brother at least one nice pitch that didn't sink like it was returning home to the devil." Marco swirled red wine in his glass.

Nico was floating after the win yesterday—especially after getting Marco out on every at-bat with two strikeouts, a pop-up, and a ground ball. The reporters after the game had made a big deal of him shutting down Marco's offense, and he'd tried to be professional. But he'd been powerless to resist a shit-eating grin that had been captured on the front page of the Saturday paper.

Across the dining table, Valentina laughed. "Good for you, Nic."

"Oh, I see how it is." Marco shook his head sadly. "Lucky for me, I've got a healthy ego or this family betrayal might send me into a tailspin."

"If 'healthy' means gigantic, then sure." Val tossed her brown curls over one shoulder and winked at Nico.

He sipped his own wine, more content than he could remember being in ages. He'd gotten the win and kept his ERA under three, and Dad had seemed proud as he slapped Nico's back, no heat behind his bluster as he chided him about beating Chicago. There had been only five criticisms—mostly pitch selection, which had made Nico cringe since Jake called the game. Fortunately Jake hadn't heard.

As much as being home could stress Nico out, sitting around the glossy walnut dining table with Nonna at one end and Dad at the other, siblings in-between, was reassuringly familiar.

Nearing sixty, Nico's father still had a head of dark curls, which he slicked back. He also dyed his hair every two weeks, because Alfonso Agresta, Rookie of the Year, MVP, and Hall of Famer, wasn't about to age gracefully. He'd been tenacious on the field, and he gave no surrender now.

Although if Nico squinted, he could spot the gray in Dad's bushy eyebrows. Dad wasn't as tall as Nico or Marco, but he was still built like a brick house, solid and powerful and as intimidating as ever. He wore slacks with sharp creases and a blue button-up. Nico had put on a Polo shirt over khakis since he hadn't felt like ironing, but was perennially underdressed as far as his father was concerned.

The same paintings of the horses Nico's mother had loved filled gold frames on the walls in the spacious dining room, some of the silent reminders of her everywhere. The rich smell of Nonna's ziti made Nico's mouth water. It had always been his favorite, and he liked to think she'd made it especially for him. Despite his role in his mother's death, Nonna had always fed him well.

He stole a glance at Jake beside him, feeling thirteen again, hoping their knees would bump under the table. Jake wore a plaid shirt over dark jeans, his sleeves rolled halfway up his muscled forearms, the collar unbuttoned below his throat. Nico wanted to lick the hollow there.

Taking her seat after doling out the ziti, Nonna speared tomato slices with a serving fork and reached to her right to put them on Jake's plate. The floral arrangement Jake had brought—roses of different colors—sat in the middle of the table. He thanked her, and she eyed him speculatively over her half-glasses.

"Still no wife? Why?" She wore a dark, long-sleeved dress with red flowers, her salt-and-pepper hair twisted into a bun, wrinkles etched deeply on her tan face.

Clutching his fork, Nico's mouth went dry. But Jake just smiled easily and cut into a tomato. "I'm still enjoying being single." He took a bite. "Mmm. Are these tomatoes from your garden? Delicious."

"*Si.* But don't change the subject." She clucked her tongue. "Seventeen, I was married. You'll all be too old!"

Valentina laughed. "Thanks, Nonna. I am getting married in November, just in case you've forgotten. I know Ian couldn't be here tonight, but I hope you haven't disowned him already."

Ignoring Valentina, Nonna glared at Marco. "What about you?"

Marco's eyebrows shot up. "What about me? I was married! You couldn't stand Leslie."

Nonna huffed, but it was the truth. As she argued the point, Nico exhaled. Beside him, Jake ate quietly, as if he wasn't bothered at all. At least the attention seemed to be off them as Valentina declared she was definitely *not* too old to start having kids at thirty-two.

As Nonna, Dad, Valentina, and Marco talked over each other, Nico tuned out as usual. If his aunts and uncles and cousins had been there, he wouldn't have even been able to hear himself think. But after a few minutes, he did hear something.

"So these fags walk in, and I'm like—"

Val's knife clattered to her plate. "Dad, can you not?" She stared daggers at him. "It's not funny. There's nothing wrong with being gay."

Oh Jesus. Oh fuck. Nico's lungs were being crushed, and he couldn't bear to look at Jake beside him. He should have known home would turn toxic before they even served dessert.

Dad sneered. "Oh, I'm sorry we're not PC enough for you."

"It's not about being 'PC,' Dad." Valentina exhaled forcefully.

"Come on. What does it matter who someone has sex with? Who someone loves?" As Nonna crossed herself and muttered in Italian, Val pressed her lips in a thin line. "You two are ridiculous."

"Us two?" Laughing, because it was all just a big joke to him, Dad's thick eyebrows shot up. "Marco, you're good with queers now?"

Marco held up his hands. "Hey, leave me out of it." He scooped a mouthful of cheesy ziti into his mouth.

"How about you, Nic?" his father asked. "Are you all political-ly correct like young morons these days?"

Staring at his barely touched plate, there was a good chance Nico was actually going to vomit all over it. From the corner of his eye, he could see that Jake was motionless beside him, gripping his knife and fork.

"We have a guest," Valentina said sharply. "Let's change the subject."

As if nothing at all had happened, Marco asked, "Hey, did you hear Seattle traded for Nalasco? Never thought New York would give him up."

"Nalasco's not all he's cracked up to be if you ask me." Dad stabbed a piece of pasta with his fork. "His ERA's sky high this season. I think his best days are behind him."

As baseball took over the conversation, it wasn't until dessert Nico could really breathe freely again. He drained his wine glass too many times and didn't dare to glance at Jake, who contributed a few quiet comments when Dad asked for his opinion.

When dinner was over, Dad retreated to the living room, turning on ESPN with the volume loud enough to wake the dead. The rest of them pushed in their chairs, and Nonna disappeared into the kitchen with an armful of dishes, Jake insisting on following with more.

Valentina whispered to Marco, "I can't believe you."

Nico froze where he was stacking tacky old placemats his mom had loved depicting Rome landmarks, the Colosseum gripped in his hands.

Marco rolled his eyes. "Relax, Val. Dad's just being Dad. You can't let it get under your skin."

"So you don't agree with his views on the LGBT community?"

Marco huffed. "Of course not. But there's no point in arguing with him. Or Nonna, for that matter. She's eighty-three. She's not going to change her mind now."

"Of course there's a point!" Valentina hissed, slamming a serving spoon into a dish, where it spun and rattled. She looked at Nico then, her expression softening, pity clear in her green eyes so much like their mother's.

She knows.

Still holding the placemat, Nico realized he should have known—maybe years ago. Because shrewd Val had probably guessed before he'd even figured it out himself.

"Look, if you want to pick fights with Dad, be my guest," Marco muttered. "But I've learned there's something to be said for the path of least resistance. He's not going to change."

Val opened her mouth, then snapped it shut as Jake returned. He smiled without teeth. "Nonna wants the salad bowl."

They cleared the rest of the table in silence until Marco said, "Nic, go through that school stuff from the basement and see if you want anything. It's mostly notebooks and crappy essays. Val left the boxes in your room."

Glad of the excuse, Nico escaped upstairs, his father's braying laugh echoing as he told an empty living room what a bad pitcher Thompson was and how he'd be sent back down to the minors by the end of the month, mark his words. Nico shoved the door shut behind him, but it bounced back.

"Ouch." Jake filled the doorway, rubbing his nose.

"Shit, sorry. Come in." Head buzzing from the merlot, Nico stuffed his hands in his pockets.

Jake closed the door, muffling the roar of the too-loud TV and Dad's rumblings to a distant murmur. He watched Nico carefully. "So that was…surprising. And awful. It took everything I had not to lunge across the table and punch him. I don't remember him talking like that back in the day."

His shoulders hunched, Nico shrugged. "Guess you got lucky. He's said shit like that as long as I can remember. Not all the time or anything. But enough. And Nonna acts like Satan just cartwheeled through the room whenever the subject comes up."

"I'm so sorry. That must be terrible for you. I had no idea." He reached for Nico, but Nico sidestepped, knocking into the boxes.

"It's a mess in here. Sorry." He had no idea what he was saying, but he was going to start fucking crying if they didn't talk about something else.

Fortunately, Jake rolled with it, glancing around. "It's like you never left, huh?"

Nico's ears got hot as he saw his room through Jake's eyes. Despite the grandeur of the house, he'd always had a normal-sized room and simple twin bed that was way too small for him now. It jutted out from the right, a cluttered and dusty desk filling the exterior wall between two wide windows, a bulletin board over it.

Hands twitching for something to do, Nico went and pulled the wooden slats of the blinds shut. A dresser, messy walk-in closet, and ensuite bathroom filled the other side of the room, and faded posters of rappers and baseball players still hung from the walls.

"Yeah, I don't know why they don't change it. I haven't lived here in years, and it's not like I'll ever move in again."

"Your dad probably likes the memories."

Nico snorted. "He doesn't give a shit."

Forehead creased, Jake was silent for a few moments before saying, "Of course he does. No matter what ignorant garbage he spouts."

"All he cares about is that I don't embarrass him."

"He's your father. He loves you, despite what a jackass he can be."

Nico stalked over to the four boxes stacked by his dresser and unfolded the top flaps, ripping one clean off. "He has Marco and Val. I'm the accident."

He pawed through the box, pulling out reams of paper and tossing them aside, not really seeing them at all. Jake wasn't saying anything, and Nico felt the need to fill the silence, words tumbling off his tongue for a change, not stuck in his throat. "Marco and Val were boom, boom, and then ten years until me. Something happened when Val was born, and they didn't think they could have any more. But a decade later, I was like, surprise, bitches!"

"I'm sure it was a wonderful surprise."

"Not so much. Mom had to be on bed rest the whole time, and then she got cancer when I was still a baby. Cervical. She made it five years, which was pretty good, I guess. But if she'd never had me…"

Dropping to his knees, he tipped out the box, rooting through old notebooks, choking down the sudden swell of grief. Fuck, he tried so hard not to think about her, but memories crowded in.

Her voice hoarse, skin paler as she leaned over to tuck him into bed, dark curls that had just grown back falling out again, never returning.

He barely remembered, but she was everywhere here even after so many years without talking about her.

Jake's deep voice was close now. "My dad died of cancer. It was… Well, it was awful. Soul-crushing."

Nico could sense Jake just behind him, and he ached to lean back into that warmth. Instead, he crawled to the next box and tore it open. He had to get back in control. *Now.* Amazingly, he managed to keep his voice steady. "I'm sorry about your father."

"I know how hard it is. I'm sure your mother's illness had nothing to do with the pregnancy."

Nico tried to wave it off. "Yeah, you're probably right. It doesn't matter now. And like Marco said, Dad's just being Dad. I never do anything right."

"I'm sorry. I didn't realize it was like that. Especially now you're grown."

Nico sprang to his feet with an attempted smile, brushing past him. "No big."

His limbs twitched, and he needed to move. But he didn't want to go back downstairs, so he paced around the room as if he was looking for something, opening and closing drawers, then stalking into the walk-in, sliding hangers back and forth on a rod.

Cornered now, he went back into his room, closing the closet door and leaning back against it, his heart beating too fast. Jake still stood by the boxes, watching him with a pinched expression of concern.

"I wasn't ever even going to—" Nico ducked his head, his cheeks going hot, lust suddenly tugging at him, low and insidious. With Jake only a few feet away, he had to keep his shit together.

"What?" Jake asked softly. "Have sex with men?" After a few silent moments he added, "Do you enjoy having sex with women? Are you bi?"

Nico hitched his shoulders. "It's fine with women. I mean, suction, friction—it's never really *bad*."

"But if you had your choice?"

Meeting Jake's gaze again, those blue eyes watching him with a tenderness that sent a thrill spiraling through him, Nico finally told the truth. "I'd choose men." He shuddered, legs quivering. There it was. He'd said it out loud.

"Everything's going to be okay. I promise."

"I kept trying with girls, hoping... Hoping something will

change, I guess." He tried to laugh. "No luck so far, and now—" *Oh my God, stop talking. Jake regrets that anything ever happened!* "I just mean—I can't pretend anymore after we... I'm not saying..." He had no idea what he *was* trying to say, so he snapped his jaw shut.

Jake still watched him like Nico was about to break. "Nic, I know it must be scary, especially with your dad's prejudices."

"It's fine. I'm fine." Nico was talking too fast, and he swallowed hard. He shouldn't have had so much wine. His skin was too tight, the pressure expanding like soda in a shaken can, and something had to come out. He blurted, "If I can get Rookie of the Year like he and Marco did, I'll prove him wrong."

"Wrong about what?" Jake asked quietly.

Wasn't it obvious? "About me."

"What about you?"

"That I'm... You know. Bad."

Shaking his head, Jake stepped close, speaking fervently. "Nico, you're not bad. Do you really think that? Your dad and grandmother are wrong."

He shrugged violently. Fuck, how had he let himself get this raw? In front of Jake of all people? But there was something in Jake's gentle, patient gaze that had always stripped Nico's defenses. "Maybe I'm not bad, but I'm still not good enough." Closing his eyes, he knocked his head back against the door, *thump, thump, thump.*

"Hey, hey. It's okay." Jake's breath feathered over Nico's cheek, his palm cupping the back of Nico's head.

Nico had to open his eyes, had to look up at Jake so close to him, so tall, that little scar on his temple, stubble darkening his face. Jake was here in this room where Nico had yearned for it so desperately. Yearned for *him.* "I want to be right," he whispered.

Jake's other hand came up to stroke Nico's cheek. "You are. You're beautiful."

Then Jake kissed his forehead, a dry press of lips, and Nico was going to disintegrate right there, combust into a pile of ashes to be swept away. There was only an inch between them, their noses almost touching, and the last barrier tumbled, Nico reaching for Jake's waist as he pressed their lips together.

They stood locked there, Jake's hands on Nico's head and face as they kissed softly. Nico's lungs burned, his heart skipping hollowly, and he breathed through his nose, the musky, male scent of Jake filling him, their lips touching, parting gently.

When Jake eased back, sucking in a breath, he pulled Nico into his arms. Nico buried his face in the juncture of Jake's neck and shoulder, scruff against one cheek and smooth flannel the other, wrapping his arms around Jake's wide back, enveloped by him.

They'd hugged when Jake had arrived in Ottawa and years before at the end of that summer, a fleeting, backslapping clasp when baseball season was over. Nico hadn't even breathed he'd been strung so tightly, and now he clung to Jake's powerful body, his control slipping away with every heartbeat.

The wine really had loosened his tongue—or maybe it was the kiss—and Nico whispered, "I used to dream about you here."

He heard Jake's forceful swallow, and Jake eased back, dropping his arms. "Nico…"

Breath coming faster, Nico's hands seemed to move of their own accord, caressing Jake's flanks through his flannel shirt, his fingers splayed over tensed muscle. Jake stood motionless, his lips parted and gaze flicking down to Nico's mouth and back to his eyes.

Nico knew he should stop, but the confessions escaped. "Wondered what it would feel like to kiss you." He nosed in close, rubbing their cheeks together before brushing his lips over Jake's jaw, dragging back behind his ear. "How rough your stubble would be."

Still rigid, Jake trembled now as Nico held his hips. On a shaky exhalation, Jake whispered, "Did you touch yourself?"

"Fuck, yes. All the time. Imagined how big your cock was, and if you were cut or not. What it would taste like. Wanted to swallow your cum. Used to taste mine and pretend it was yours."

Jake's chest rose and fell faster. "Jesus. We can't."

But the truth was a river now, white water carving through rock. "When I found out you were traded and I'd see you again, I got so hard I had to jerk off. Shoved my finger in my ass and imagined it was your cock, and—"

With a guttural noise that was almost a growl, Jake grabbed his head and crushed their mouths together, pinning him against the door, his long leg shoving between Nico's thighs.

Gripping Jake's hips, Nico ground their swelling cocks together, opening his mouth for Jake's tongue, stroking and licking, the rasp of their stubble so fucking *perfect*.

The broadness of Jake's shoulders and the few extra inches of height had Nico deliciously trapped, wood unyielding at his back and Jake's lean muscles jammed against him as they rutted and gasped, more truth escaping through Nico's kiss-wet lips.

"I've never been fucked, and I want it to be you. Want you to come inside me."

Thrusting his hips, Jake's fingers tightened even more in Nico's hair, pulling on the edge of pleasure and pain. He pressed their foreheads together, muttering, "Christ, I want you. This isn't… It's never like this."

"You want to fuck me?" He dragged his hands over Jake's ass, pulling and squeezing, their dicks straining in their pants. "I need it. Need you."

"We can't." Jake moaned low in his throat, rocking his hips against Nico's, Nico so close to coming already.

Here in his teenage bedroom, with his Pedro Martinez and Eminem posters watching, between the four walls where he'd fantasized about cock and muscles—about Jake's—Nico was afraid he'd wake up alone in his old twin bed, the sheets sticky, shame blanketing him as he tried to go back to sleep, praying he'd wake up normal.

Praying he'd wake up the "right" way so he could play baseball, so he could be what his father wanted. Demanded.

Gulping for air, he spread his legs farther, his fingers digging into Jake's ass as they rubbed off together. It was really happening—he'd tasted Jake's mouth, and now Nico felt the hot puffs of his breath against his swollen lips. The little pants and groans Jake made filled his ears, surrounding him.

He'd waited so long to say it out loud that Nico was suddenly struck by a soul-shaking tremor of fear, panic rising that if he didn't get all the words out now, they'd somehow be swallowed too deep to ever surface. "I'm queer."

Nodding, Jake murmured, "That's it, baby."

Tears burned Nico's eyes. "I'm gay. I want cock. Always have. Always will."

Jake was kissing him again, their teeth bumping, spit stringing between them, the wet friction of their tongues echoing the motion of their hips. Nico needed their clothes off so he could finally feel Jake skin to skin, but it was too late. Panting, they rubbed off frantically, and Nico couldn't seem to stop talking.

"Want to suck your dick until it's choking me. You can spank me again. I'll do anything you tell me to, I'll—"

Shuddering heavily, Jake came, eyes closed and back arching, the long column of his throat exposed. Nico licked his Adam's apple. "Oh fuck, Nico." Jake was still thrusting, and he hoisted up Nico's leg, holding his thigh against his hip. "Come on. That's it."

Jake's lips were red and wet, his face flushed and pupils huge, and he was the most beautiful thing Nico could imagine. And after all the years of fantasy, he was touching Nico, looking at him so intently, kissing him and stealing his breath.

Nico's balls tightened and he went rigid, the orgasm sending his head back to thump against the door again, his eyes squeezed shut.

Then Jake's hand was there, cradling the back of his head. Nico dropped his leg down with a thud, and they slumped against each other, the only sounds their harsh breathing and the distant, watery rumble of the TV downstairs.

Eyes still closed, Nico repeated, "I'm gay."

Jake's lips pressed against Nico's face—forehead, chin, cheeks. Finally on his lips once more, so sweetly, and Nico kept his eyes squeezed shut, because he didn't want this dream to end.

CHAPTER ELEVEN

NICO HAD COME out, and they'd both come in their pants.

His underwear was a mess. Jake shifted uncomfortably, grateful his jeans were dark. Since they had another afternoon game the next day, they'd been able to duck out fairly early, and Marco offered to drive them back to their hotel on his way home.

Nico was in the backseat, staring wordlessly out the window. Jake forced himself to chat with Marco, who fortunately never seemed to run out of things to say.

The urge to turn around and reach for Nico's knee and ask him what he was thinking surged through Jake in waves as Marco expertly steered his huge SUV through suburban Chicago streets, claiming he knew all the best shortcuts.

"And I thought, serves her right!" Marco laughed expectantly.

"Seriously!" Jake agreed, having zero clue who Marco was talking about.

As Marco launched into another story, Jake stole a glance into the backseat. Nico sat behind the driver's seat and still stared into the darkness, passing headlights spotlighting his face for a moment. Was he relieved? Scared? Regretful? All of the above? None of the above?

"Don't you think?" Marco asked.

"Hmm?" Jake quickly turned his head. "Sorry, I'm thinking about tomorrow's game."

"Oh yeah? Anything in particular?" Marco asked so innocently.

"Hold on, let me write down the pitch selection I'm planning for the top of the order."

"No one has to know, Fitz. I mean, Chicago was once your team." Punching Jake's shoulder lightly, Marco turned into the curved driveway of the hotel. "Well, see you tomorrow on the field. May the best team win." He peered in the rearview mirror. "Good thing we won't have to face your ace on the mound again. Always knew my little brother would be a hell of a pitcher someday. Looks like that day is now. You crushed it yesterday, Nic."

Nico looked at his brother, finally smiling briefly. "Thanks."

"Sure. Next time I'm taking you out of the park if it's the last thing I do. Now get out, you bums."

In the elevator up to the eighteenth floor, they didn't say a word, Jake smiling and nodding to a young couple who clearly recognized them.

What's going to happen now? What do I want to happen? What does he want to happen?

They stepped off on their hushed floor, all sedate cream and brown. "I'm..." Nico pointed to his right. "This way."

Jake checked his key card, totally blanking on the number. "I'm that way."

As they stood there by the elevator bank, it felt ridiculously symbolic. Too many words crowded on Jake's tongue, and as he tried to pick a few, Nico said, "See you tomorrow," turning on his heel and disappearing through a door halfway down the hall.

Okay. So apparently Nico didn't want anything else to happen. That was... That was for the best, clearly. Jake hurried to his room, stripping off his clothes and turning on the shower. He scrubbed dried cum out of his pubes and told himself it was fine. It was good. Everything was good.

Naked and rubbing a towel over his damp hair, he stalked around his room, the brown carpet thick under his feet. He needed to ice his knees and get out his foam roller to work out the tightness in his quads and hamstrings, but his mind played the encounter in Nico's room on a loop.

Jake had been with his fair share of men, and he couldn't remember ever feeling that kind of buzz, that kind of connection. He didn't just want to fuck Nico. He wanted to talk to him. He wanted to say everything. Hear everything. He wanted all the things, and he didn't really know what they were, exactly.

But he *wanted*.

Nico had been so vulnerable, an honesty in his kisses that had Jake's lips still tingling. That he'd apparently wanted Jake for years was an undeniable turn-on. Although Nico didn't seem to want Jake now, given the way he'd taken off.

Unless he was embarrassed. Ashamed, even. The thought of Nico believing he was *bad* had Jake clenching his fists, a swell of sticky anger and frustration heating his neck and cheeks. What if Nico was hating himself now? What if he'd been waiting for Jake to make the first move? To tell him it was okay?

Nico had come out. Had Jake inadvertently rejected him?

Still pacing, he looked at the door as if Nico would suddenly materialize there. If Jake didn't go to him now, would Nico burrow back into his shell? Jake couldn't let that happen. It didn't matter what he wanted—he had to put Nico first and make sure he was okay. Make sure he didn't feel alone.

Shaking his head, he scoffed. "Oh yeah, you're a real *hero*. Because there's nothing in it for you to go fuck him now. It would be a complete sacrifice."

He hummed with the urge to get Nico naked and show him how good it could be between two men. Ached to bury himself in that tight ass and experience Nico's complete surrender. Taste his lips again, feel those thick eyelashes fluttering, hear the low moans in the back of his throat. See the dimples in his cheeks, the ever-present tension lifted.

Chugging a bottle of water, Jake cleared his parched throat. The first person he'd ever told he was gay had been Tony Tucker from Moose Jaw at some tournament in Winnipeg a million years ago. Jake had been seventeen, and he and Tony had ended up drinking too much beer and going for a midnight skinny dip. They'd jerked each other off and kissed with too much thrusting tongue, and it had been amazing.

But first was the terror. Although Jake had been mostly sure Tony was at least curious about boys, his heart had nearly beat right out of his chest and plopped into the water like a dying fish in the bottom of a boat. He could still remember the sweet swell of relief that Tony hadn't laughed or been disgusted or punched him—and that he'd kissed back.

Naked in the middle of his room, Jake stopped pacing. No matter what happened, he had to make sure Nico didn't feel abandoned.

A scant minute later he knocked quietly on Nico's door, hair damp and feet bare, commando under cargo shorts, a tank top on backwards, the tag scratching his chest. Nico appeared in a fluffy white bathrobe, his curls wet. He looked at Jake inscrutably, then stood back.

When the door was shut, Jake said, "I wanted to make sure you're okay."

Nico nodded.

"That's a lie, actually. I mean, I do want to make sure you're okay, but I want more than that." *Everything.*

Adam's apple bobbing, Nico asked, "What?"

"To fuck you. And I'm not sure if I should, or if that's what you want right now. What you need. And if you do want it, I'm not sure how to do it." He tugged at the neck of his tank top. "Should it be rough? Do you want me to spank you tonight? Do you want to see my face the first time? Because I want to see yours. But I could pound you too, get you on your hands and knees to take my cock. Am I going to hurt you? Do you want me to? Or do you want to go slow?"

Nico opened and closed his mouth. Finally, he whispered, "Yes."

"Which part?"

"All of it."

Breath catching, Jake managed to nod. "Get on the bed. Naked. However you want."

As Nico dropped the robe and crossed the room, Jake yanked off his clothes, too keyed up to wait, to stay dressed and teasing. Especially when Nico was presenting himself on his back, his legs spread, chest rising and falling rapidly, cock thickening and curving toward his belly.

It was an earth-toned hotel room like hundreds Jake had been in before, and the side table lamp cast a golden glow over Nico's bare skin. He looked so *perfect*, like someone had put a soft-light filter on the whole room.

"Good boy," Jake murmured before ducking into the bathroom to root through Nico's toilet bag. He came out with condoms and a bottle of pure aloe vera sunburn gel, tossing them on the other side of the king-sized mattress. Nico watched his movements avidly, his red lips parted.

"You've never had a man touch you like this before?" Jake sat on his heels between Nico's legs, nudging them wider and ignoring the needles of pain in his knees. He traced his fingertips up and down Nico's trembling inner thighs.

A shake of Nico's head.

"I want you to answer me. I want you to talk. You said a lot earlier. Didn't that feel good?"

Nico started to nod, then said, "Yes."

He pushed up Nico's knees, displaying his ass. "Do you think it'll feel good if I kiss your hole? If I lick it?"

Breath ragged, Nico whined, "*Yes.*"

"Any of your girls ever do that for you?"

"No." A drop of water fell from Nico's hair, sliding down his nose. His arms were spread, hands in fists.

After scooting back, Jake huffed hot air over the puckered skin of Nico's hole. He feathered little kisses around it, avoiding direct contact. Rubbing his cheek against the tender skin of Nico's inner thigh, he asked, "Do you like how rough my stubble is?"

A whimper. "Yes."

"What else do you like?" Jake continued his torment, teasing Nico's thighs and the sensitive skin behind his balls, barely brushing them with his face and lips.

For a moment, Nico sounded like he was choking. Then he gritted out, "Your hands. How big they are."

Jake flattened his palms on the back of Nico's thighs, pushing his legs even higher. "You like knowing these hands are in charge?"

"*Yes.*"

"Will you really do anything?" Jake wouldn't test the limits of Nico's boundaries tonight, but he still held his breath waiting for the answer.

"Yes. I trust you."

Rubbing Nico's hairy thighs gently, Jake caught his breath, his heart in his throat. Then he leaned down and made good on his promise, kissing Nico's hole with wet presses before licking over it again and again, dipping inside.

Nico cried out, moaning softly. "Please fuck me. Please, Jake."

His cock hard, the temptation to rear up and bury himself almost overpowered. He resisted, afraid he'd cause real damage. Instead he pushed his tongue deeper, licking into Nico's ass. He worked his way up, sucking Nico's balls, wiry hair tickling his nose. "Tell me what you're thinking."

Between gasps, Nico said, "Waited so long. Never thought I'd have this. Not with anyone."

"Why not?"

"Coward." His breath caught on what sounded like a sob.

Heart beating too fast, Jake raised up and braced himself over Nico, their hard cocks slapping together. He stared into Nico's glistening eyes. "Why not, baby?"

Nico squeezed his eyes shut. "Didn't deserve it. Not if I got to play baseball."

"Why?" Jake wanted to punch someone; wanted to turn back time and fix it. "Look at me. Why?"

Tears escaped, hanging on Nico's lashes. "No queers in baseball. Not allowed."

The fury burned white hot, but Jake tamped it down. "Fuck that. Fuck anyone who thinks that. Fuck your dad for thinking that. He's wrong. They're wrong." He kissed Nico, stroking his tongue as if he could erase the words Nico had said—that he didn't deserve it, that he wasn't allowed.

Jake exhaled harshly, pressing their foreheads together, rocking his hips, Nico's knees around Jake's ribs. "You deserve both. You get to have them. You get to have everything."

"Fuck me." Nico lifted his ass, his hands coming up to clutch Jake's hips. "Waited so long. Never thought in a million years it would be you."

Jake slicked his fingers and prodded at Nico's hole, forcing himself to go slowly even though he wanted to throw up Nico's legs and bury himself inside. "You wanted it to be me?"

Nico nodded, arching his back as Jake's finger breached him. "Wanted it so bad. You have no clue."

"I've got some idea if it was half as badly as I want you now." He kissed Nico deep and filthy as he squeezed in another finger.

"Do it," Nico begged. "Waited so long."

"I've got you." Jake fumbled for the condom, sitting back and rolling it on, squeezing the base of his dick as he fought for control. He squirted more aloe, slathering it onto his cock.

He knew Nico would be tight, and *Jesus,* the hot constriction as Jake nudged the head of his cock against that tight hole was heaven already. He cupped Nico's face, getting aloe all over his cheek. "Breathe. I'm here."

"I know." Nico gritted his teeth. "You're kind of hard to fucking miss right now."

The laughter was a beautiful release, and Jake kissed Nico lightly, not moving and letting him get used to the sensation, teasing a smile out of him. Jake rocked slightly, pushing. "Let me in. It'll be so much easier in a minute, I promise."

Nico nodded, looking up at him with those big brown eyes, his tears drying, trusting Jake to guide him. Their skin grew slick with sweat and stray aloe, and as Nico took a deep breath, Jake thrust, shoving the head of his dick past the ring of muscle.

Gasping, Nico's eyes went wide. "Jake!"

"What do you feel?" He inched in.

Nico licked his lips, the red flush on his skin spreading to his chest. "Feels like your cock's going all the way into my guts."

"Splitting you open, hmm?" Jake held Nico's hips and pushed a bit more, Nico tipping his head back and crying out. "That's it. You're doing so good. Being such a good boy for me. You know I won't let you break."

Nodding, Nico opened his eyes again, hands scrabbling in the sheets. "All the way."

Grunting, Jake filled him balls deep. Nico's cock had softened a bit, and Jake stroked it now, more aloe slicking the way. "You're taking it so well." He licked salty sweat from Nico's temple, fucking him with little movements until he started pushing back with long groans. "Tell me what you want," Jake muttered.

Nico grabbed at Jake's shoulders, heels drumming his back. "You."

Jake wanted to ask more questions but could only kiss him then, swallowing his cries, jerking Nico's throbbing cock and fucking his virgin ass. Sweat glistened on Nico's forehead.

Stroking Nico's shaft, Jake grunted. The hot grip of his ass was heaven, the slap of their slick skin music in the air. "You feel so good, Nic. You're beautiful." Jake kissed him messily.

Splayed and bent, wound tight as a wire, Nico came, spurting between them, moaning into Jake's mouth, biting Jake's lip.

The blossom of pain sent adrenaline shooting through Jake, the tingling in his balls becoming electricity jolting his legs. He clung to Nico, buried in him, rigid with pleasure and the burning relief of his orgasm as he emptied into the condom. Collapsing, he gasped against Nico's neck, ears ringing until the haze subsided.

His balls and dick ached enough for him to ease out of Nico as gently as possible, although he would have anyway. A tiny sigh escaped Nico as Jake tied off the condom and tossed it toward the garbage can by the desk, not bothering to see if he made the shot. He couldn't bring himself to give a shit, not with Nico flushed and fucked in front of him, still spread, semen drying in his chest hair.

Usually Jake wanted to sleep or eat or do anything but cuddle after sex. He and Ron had never lingered in the bedroom. But as he feasted on the sight of Nico wanton and satisfied, Jake could only pull him close, huddling down and pulling the sticky sheets over them, Nico's sweat tangy on his tongue as he kissed every inch of skin he could reach.

"Tell me how you feel," he whispered.

"Like there's no going back."

And as the words left Nico's kiss-swollen lips, Jake recognized that truth deep in his bones.

CHAPTER TWELVE

NICO'S HEART LEAPT at the rap on the door. It was still early, although with an afternoon game, the usual daily routine was shortened. He was in shorts and a tee, ready to head to the stadium for his customary pregame massage and physio. But maybe Jake was back. Maybe he missed him. Nico knew he was mooning, but couldn't wipe the smile off his face as he opened the door.

Valentina's eyebrows shot up. "Wow, I didn't think you'd be this happy to see me at nine o'clock in the morning." Her long curls were pulled back in a ponytail, and she wore a Chicago jersey, shorts, and sandals. She was half a foot shorter than him, and he stared down at her, trying to process.

Ducking her chin, she glanced at her shirt. "Sorry, but you know Dad would murder me if I showed up to the game in anything red and white." Looking left and right, she whispered, "But I'm secretly rooting for the Caps. Wearing red undies."

He laughed. "Thanks? What are you doing here? Not that it's not nice to see you." It would have been nicer if Jake had been sneaking back for a quickie, but since they'd blown each other before Jake had crept down to his room in the wee hours, maybe four rounds in twelve hours would be pushing it. A thrill sparked at the memory of Jake's mouth around him, and how he'd swallowed every drop of Nico's cum...

The memory cascaded into flashes of Jake on top of him, so wonderfully heavy and hairy, rough but gentle too, the pain and incredible fullness—

Nico realized Valentina had been talking, and now she was looking at him, eyebrows sky high again. He said, "Huh?"

"Are you okay?" She frowned. "Are you… If you're not alone, I can just leave these and see you after the game."

"Leave what? And no one's here."

She smiled tentatively, hoisting a white paper bag. "Okay, so do you want to let me in? I brought donuts."

"Oh. Thanks." He stepped back, heart skipping as he realized what a mess the bed was.

"Is there a—awesome, I figured there'd be a coffee machine." She went to the desk and pawed through the pods. "Can I have the dark French roast?"

"Sure." Shit, shit, shit—was the condom in the garbage over there? Not that a condom meant anything gay. At dinner, he'd been sure Val knew, but did she? And did it matter if she did? His mind whirled, pulse racing.

"Do you have to get going? You don't really work out much the day after you pitch, right?"

"Not a ton. I'll do a flush run and some shoulder stuff. Trainer gives me e-stim and ultrasound on my arm."

"Flush run? Does that have anything to do with the toilet?" Valentina held out her hand. "No, forget I asked."

He chuckled. "It's just a jog. I usually do half an hour. Flushes out the lactic acid and clears my head." Although he could probably run the perimeter of Lake Michigan today and still be thinking so many things at the same time it was impossible to get a handle on any of it.

"Ah. In that case, eat your donut. Powdered jelly, right? I brought a few."

He blinked. It had been his post-start tradition since high

school. "Yeah. How did you know?"

"I'm your sister." She put a cup under the coffee machine spout.

Nico joined her at the desk and unrolled the bag, moaning softly as he bit into still-warm dough, strawberry jelly sweet on his tongue, white powder dusting his lips. "I didn't think you noticed, or whatever."

Her brows drawn into a V, she asked, "Why would you say that?"

"You're older. You were busy with your own shit. It's fine, Val. I wasn't trying to give you a hard time." He lifted the half-eaten donut. "Thanks."

"You're welcome." She eyed the coffee machine, the dark liquid pouring out now in a steady stream. "I notice a lot of things."

Stomach clenching, Nico forced himself to have another bite, the sweetness like chalk in his mouth now. Were they actually going to talk about this?

Still watching the coffee, Valentina casually said, "I went up to your room last night while Dad and Marco were watching the game and Nonna was scrubbing pots because she refuses to use that massive dishwasher even though that's what it's for."

Nico squashed the remains of the donut in his fist, throat going dry.

Looking him straight in the eye, she calmly said, "It sounded like you and Fitz were having sex."

"I… We…" His face had to be beet red, the heat followed by a full-body chill.

Valentina stirred sugar into her coffee. "Has that been going on long?"

He shook his head.

"I really like Fitz. He's a great guy. So are you gay?"

Ears ringing, Nico managed to nod. Then he thought of Jake

getting him to talk, and croaked, "Yes."

His sister smiled—*smiled!*—and put down her cup before squeezing his upper arms. "Thank you for telling me. Not that I gave you much choice. You know I love and support you, right?"

Nodding, he unclenched his fist and laughed slightly hysterically at the sticky mess. First aloe and cum, now a jelly donut. "I've got to..." He hurried to the bathroom and scrubbed his hands clean.

Valentina leaned in the doorway. "I always thought maybe, but I wasn't sure. Have you... Have there always been guys? On the downlow?"

"No. Only Jake."

"Really? But not..." She stood up straight, going rigid. "Tell me nothing happened back in the day. You were still a baby."

"Of course not. I had a massive crush on him, but nothing ever happened. He had no idea."

She exhaled. "Oh, thank God. I was going to have to strongly revise my 'great guy' evaluation. Then go down the hall and punch him in the nuts."

"Yeah, please don't do that." He wiped his hands on a towel and leaned back against the counter.

"So Fitz is gay too." At Nico's nod, she asked, "Have you guys been hooking up for long?"

"No." He was still getting used to the idea, and the surrealness of discussing it with his sister made him squirm. But he was an adult. He could handle this.

"Did you like being with girls before? Sorry, I know this is weird. I just want to understand. And I'm your nosy big sister, so deal with it."

Nico smiled. "With girls it was... It wasn't what I wanted, but I was trying. I thought maybe if I tried hard enough... If one of the Jennys was perfect enough, then I could make it work. Then I could not be queer."

Her face pinched in sadness, Valentina asked, "Jennys?"

"I just mean the girls I've hooked up with. The last one was named Jenny. The ones before... I don't even remember their names. It's shitty, I know. I'm an asshole."

"I'm not saying that. You were—maybe confused is the wrong word. But you were hurting, right? And I know why. I know exactly why."

"Yeah." Picking up the hand towel, he twisted it. "They'll never accept it."

"You don't know that. They don't understand. I think if they realized gay people aren't this *other,* this nameless, faceless *them,* then they'd start to see. They love you, Nic. They're ignorant. I'm not saying it's an excuse, but we can teach them."

"No way. Dad'll hate me even more than he does already."

She jerked. "What are you talking about? Dad doesn't *hate* you. That's crazy."

"Of course he does." He shrugged. "I'd hate me too."

"But he doesn't know you're gay. I really don't think he does. So whatever narrative you've dreamed up, it's in your head."

"Not because I'm gay." Nico unfurled the towel before twisting it the other way as if he was wringing it out. "Because I killed her."

"Who?" The confusion on Val's face transformed into horror, her eyes wide as she flattened her palm on her chest. "*Mom*? Is that what you're saying? You think... You think that was your fault?"

Throat unbearably tight, he shrugged. "Yeah. Of course."

"What? '*Of course*'? No, Nic. Not of course! Not even a tiny bit! Why are you saying this?"

"Because it's true." He shook his head in confusion. "You know it is."

"No! I don't know any such thing!" She was suddenly in his face, gripping his shoulders. "Mom died of cancer."

"Because she got sick when she was pregnant with me. She had to be in bed the whole time. She never got better."

"She was on bed rest because she had preeclampsia. It had nothing to do with the cancer. It was a coincidence. Nothing more. Look at me. Do you hear me? *It was not your fault.*"

"But it was." How could she not see it?

Valentina breathed hard. "Did someone tell you that? Who said that? Who made you believe this bullshit? Dad can be a real asshole, but he wouldn't. God, he didn't, did he?"

"No."

"Then who?" She shook him with surprising strength.

"No one. I just always knew."

Her eyes flooded with tears. "You've thought this all along? All this time? It's not true. It wasn't your fault. She had bad luck. It was no one's fault. Do you know how happy she was to have you? Early on, the doctors thought she should terminate, but she wouldn't. She loved you so much. She laid in that bed day in and day out for months, and she never complained. She couldn't wait to meet you. We were all excited. And when she got sick after, it really fucking sucked, but it was not your fault, and we never blamed you."

Eyes burning, he tried to speak. "But she had cancer down there. Maybe if she hadn't had me, they would have found it earlier."

Valentina shook him again. "It had nothing to do with you or the pregnancy. Nothing. Do you hear me? Why would you think that?"

"I don't remember. I really don't. It was just always something I knew. Like the sky being blue. It just…was."

Tears slipped down her cheeks. "It wasn't your fault at all. Do you believe me?"

Looking down into her glistening green eyes, something crumbled inside Nico, a hard knot becoming dust. "I believe you." His breath stuttered. "But why didn't we talk about her? If it wasn't because of me?"

"Because we're emotionally fucking repressed. Dad and Nonna wouldn't even say her name, and the rest of us were afraid to. We're fucked up. But we never blamed you, Nic. We're not *that* fucked up." Going up on her tiptoes, she wrapped her arms around him, and Nico hugged her back.

She smelled like baby powder and coffee and *Val*, and he inhaled deeply.

"I can't believe you've been carrying all this around." She sniffled. "Christ, that breaks my heart."

He blinked back tears. "I'm fine."

"Oh, Nic." Valentina held on tighter, and they stood like that by the sink for a long moment.

It wasn't my fault.

Maybe it should have been harder to accept, but his worldview was shifting like a kaleidoscope after having sex with Jake, so he rolled with it. God, he was so tired of fighting.

Easing back, Nico gave her a smile, hardly having to work at it. "I'm fine. You don't have to worry."

"I'm going to anyway." She ran her pinky finger under her eyelids, blinking at the ceiling rapidly. "Waterproof mascara put to the test."

"You look beautiful."

Holding his chin, she kissed his cheek. "So do you. Jake Fitzgerald's a lucky man."

It was still super weird that they were talking about it out loud. *We had sex. I got fucked. I'm not an ass virgin anymore. That's probably not even a thing.* But it was how he felt. "I'm lucky too. I never thought..." He realized he was grinning.

"You really like him, huh?" She tugged his hand. "Come on, let's eat the rest of the donuts."

Nico followed, and they sat on the end of the bed, scarfing down the treats and licking powdered sugar from their fingers like they were kids again.

"Have you thought about telling Dad and Nonna? Marco?" She rolled her eyes. "He's so clueless, I swear. But he loves you. We all do."

"I always assumed I'd never do anything, so there was no reason to tell."

"You mean you didn't plan on being with any guys? Not ever?"

"That was the plan." It seemed ludicrous now, impossible. "Then Jake came to Ottawa, and then—" He shifted uncomfortably. "Then something happened, and I thought maybe one day."

"You don't have to wait. We can sit down with them tonight and—"

"*Tonight?*" His breath caught. "Not tonight. I can't."

"Okay. That's fair. But hey, you're staying around during the all-star break, right? It's only a few days. Stay. I'm not saying you have to tell them, but we can hang. No pressure. And whenever you're ready, I'll be there. Okay?"

"Okay." He leaned into her shoulder briefly, and she leaned back.

"I wish Ian wasn't away at that conference. You've barely met him."

"You'll be married to him forever, so we'll make up for lost time eventually."

She laughed softly. "Well, forever's the idea. Oh, hey! Fitz is already coming to my wedding, so that works out. I swear, I didn't even realize. Clearly I'm brilliant. You're welcome." She brushed white powder off her dark shorts. "So, are you guys serious? Are you in looove?"

Shoving another bite of donut in his mouth, Nico rolled the questions around in his mind. He hoped the answer to the first question was yes. He knew it was to the second.

Sitting there with his sister, jelly dripping down his chin, he thought of Jake—the tenor of his laugh, the clear blue of his steady gaze, his reassuring presence. Jake's strong hands calling the signs and catching everything Nico hurled at him, those same hands firm and demanding on Nico's body, sometimes tender, but always reliable. Always helping.

Simply nodding, certainty flowed deeper with each beat of his heart. Nico was a hundred and ten percent in love.

CHAPTER THIRTEEN

*C*RACK!

C Heart soaring as he drove the ball through the gap for a single, Jake ran to first base, head down in the bright sunshine. There really was nothing quite like it—the sensation of the bat smacking the ball but good, vibrations ringing up his arms. Then either the roar of the crowd or the groan.

In this case, the Chicago fans grumbled restlessly, but a vocal contingent of Ottawa supporters who'd made the trip cheered, big groups of red shirts visible in the stands.

With two on base and no outs, Chicago's manager took his slow walk to the mound to pull the starting pitcher and send in a replacement. The Caps were only up by a run, but now was the time to blow it open.

Excitement sparked in Jake's veins. The Caps were having a damn good season, and while winning their division was likely just out of reach, they could grab the wild card spot into the playoffs. Jake wanted it—*really* wanted it—for the first time in years.

Granted, it hadn't been more than a pipe dream in San Fran, the team never in the running in the back stretch of the season. But the Caps were in contention. Jake looked to the dugout, where Nico sat watching him with his laser focus. Pulse surging, Jake wondered if anyone noticed, and forced himself to look away. The Caps were hungry, and so was Jake—for more than just the win.

He nodded to Vasquez, the Chicago first baseman, who patted Jake's butt with his glove. They'd have a few minutes to kill while the new pitcher made his way from the bullpen beyond the outfield.

He and Vasquez had never played together, so Jake didn't know him well, but he'd always seemed like a good guy. "How's it going?" Jake asked.

"Can't complain. Nice clean hit you got."

"Thanks." He took off his batting helmet for a second to swipe his damp forehead with his red sleeve. The air was thick and sticky, the sun beating down. "Hey, any recommendations for dinner?"

"Definitely. New place on Randolph. In West Loop? The charcuterie is to die for. It's called Meat and Cheese, so it's easy to remember if you want to hit it up this weekend."

Jake chuckled. "Cool, thanks."

"How's it going up there? You guys get good turnouts, I hear."

"Definitely. We're really lucky." Jake kept his eye on the third base coach for any signs while the reliever approached the mound, glancing at the first base coach nearby every so often as well. "The city's damn eager for it. Whole country, really, with only two teams."

"I bet. You're from there, right?"

"Yep. It's good to be back." He realized as he said it that he actually meant it this time.

"Going well with Marco's little brother, huh?"

Jake's heart skipped a beat. *He's talking about baseball. Relax.* "Yeah. He's got a hell of an arm."

The first base coach, Arakawa, stepped over. "He does, and Fitz has a hell of a way with him. Kid's always had great ball control, but now his head's in the game."

Jake tried to shrug it off. "He's got the talent. I just catch the balls."

Arakawa laughed. "Yeah, yeah, you're the conductor and he's the orchestra, right? Well, have you ever seen an orchestra play without a leader? You're instrumental."

Vasquez chortled. "Instrumental, get it?"

They all laughed, and Arakawa added, "Seriously, I was afraid Agresta was going the way of Gellar."

Jake and Vasquez groaned. Vasquez said, "He's unreal. My buddy Lee's over there in Cleveland, and the clubhouse is sick to death of his shit. Did you see him plunk Medina last week?" He laughed. "And when Medina rushed the mound, the Cleveland guys were all, like..." He jogged on the spot in slow motion. "Took their sweet time getting over there, and I don't blame 'em. Medina got in some vicious hits before it was broken up."

"Trust me, Nico's nothing like that asshole Gellar." Jake realized he'd used Nico's first name, which wasn't necessarily unusual since first names and surnames were often used interchangeably. Still, he cleared his throat and added, "Agresta's working hard to be a team player." The catcher and relief pitcher were warming up with a few pitches now, and Jake checked third base again for signs.

As they got ready to resume play, Arakawa faded back into foul territory and Jake took a lead off the bag. Diego was on second, still having a few words with the baseman, so even if Jake had wanted to steal, he couldn't. At his size, he wasn't the quickest on the base paths anyway. Tugging down his helmet, he focused as Lopez stepped into the batter's box.

Crack!

Lopez took the very first pitch down the first base line, and Jake raced for second as soon as the bat hit the ball. He looked to the third base coach for a signal that the ball had been foul, but he was waving Jake on, Diego already speeding toward home. Adrenaline erased the aches in Jake's back and knees as he rounded second and powered to third.

The coach windmilled his arm instead of holding up his palms to tell Jake to hold at third. The ball must have gone into the corner, and Jake didn't slow as he stepped on third and veered wide before bringing himself back in line with the base path, adrenaline thundering, muscles burning as he ran full out.

The Chicago catcher still waited for the throw, so he couldn't block the plate yet. Jake shifted his weight back, sliding into the dirt toward home as the ball rocketed from the outfield, the crowd screaming, willing it there before Jake.

Choking on dirt, his foot crossed the plate as the catcher applied the tag, hitting Jake's shin with his glove, the ball gripped inside. In a tangle, they whipped their heads up for the umpire's call.

The ump threw his arms out to the side, and as the fans groaned and the catcher protested, Jake leapt to his feet to highten Diego and Crowe, who was waiting in the on-deck circle.

He and Diego jogged back to the visitors' dugout, where enthusiastic butt slaps and high-fives waited. Nico stood near the end of the dugout, his socks pulled up to his knees like always, uniform hugging his lean body, the sun rich on his skin, a dark curl poking out from beneath his cap visor.

And God *damn* if Jake didn't want to haul him into his arms and lay one on him. God damn if Nico wasn't the most gorgeous thing Jake had ever seen, especially with those dimples digging into his cheeks as he raised his hand.

Their palms slapped, and as Jake angled away to high-five one of the coaching staff coming up behind him, Nico smacked Jake's ass. Jake's breath caught in his throat. It wasn't anything out of the ordinary at all in a dugout. No one would think twice, and Jake forced himself to tuck his batting helmet away in his cubby and not react.

With the dugout buzzing from the runs, guys laughing and

chatting, Jake turned back to Nico and reached past him to fill a little white paper cup with orange Gatorade.

Nico bit his lip, a positively mischievous look on his face. A swell of affection hit Jake like a strike slamming into his glove, a warm glow at seeing his boy so relaxed and happy.

As he moved back, Jake murmured, "You're going to pay for that tonight."

"Is that a promise?" Nico looked out at the field as Crowe's at-bat began.

Jake sipped his Gatorade. "You bet your sweet ass." Maybe he'd take him to Meat and Cheese for dinner first. They might be recognized, but teammates out for a meal during a road trip wasn't strange. They could eat, have a few drinks. Build up the anticipation. He could really *play* with Nico in a way they hadn't yet.

His heart did a hop, skip, and jump, and he couldn't decide whether he wanted to haul Nico into his arms to keep him calm and happy and safe, or if he wanted to fuck his brains out. *Both.*
Careful.

He wasn't supposed to feel like this. Not for Nico or anyone. This was getting messier by the day. Hell, by the hour. The minute.

Jake sat on the bench beside Nico, their knees barely brushing. Desire and affection zipped through him, the lingering adrenaline from scoring pumping his heart. He didn't dare look directly at Nico or he might drag him over his lap right then and there. His dick swelled uncomfortably in his cup, and Jake shifted, reaching down to scratch his thigh and surreptitiously adjust himself.

From the corner of his eye, he saw Nico's shit-eating grin.

Jake banished his worries. He'd deal with all of that…later. Because forget taking Nico to dinner. They were going straight to dessert.

WHEN THE SOFT knock came at his hotel room door, Jake was tempted to wait. Let Nico sweat it out a bit. But he didn't want him standing out in the hall where teammates and anyone could come by and wonder what he was doing. Especially since, peeking through the peephole, Jake could see Nico looked as sweaty as a priest in a brothel.

He opened the door, and Nico came inside, saying, "Um, hey." He wore jeans and an Old Navy T-shirt, and kicked off his flip-flops.

Jake shut the door and flipped over the extra lock with a sharp rap, making Nico jump a little. God, he was *delicious.* Smothering his smile, Jake stepped close and pressed their lips together for a moment. Then he leaned down close to Nico's ear. "Nervous?"

Breathing unevenly, Nico nodded.

"You should be." Their bodies brushed, but Jake kept just enough distance. "Have you been thinking about what we're going to do together tonight?"

A vigorous nod.

Jake trailed a hand down Nico's arm, feeling him shiver as Jake touched his bare skin. "Have you been thinking about how I'm going to own your ass?"

A shuddering exhale, pupils blowing wide and dark. "Yes."

"Good boy. And how do you feel about that?" He stroked his hand lower over Nico's butt.

"I want it. I want—" He broke off, cheeks going red.

"What?" Jake rubbed Nico's ass rhythmically. "You can tell me. You can always tell me." He wanted to know everything. Excavate Nico's brain, discover his secrets. Hell, as much as he was dying to fuck him, Jake wanted to *talk* to him almost as much. Almost. "What do you want?"

Another lick of lips. "To let go."

"To just feel and not think?"

Nico's breath quickened. "Yes. You know what I mean?"

"I do." He stroked Nico's hip. "You'll be with me. I won't let you fall."

"I know." Trust shone from Nico's eyes, a smile of relief and joy flickering across his beautiful face.

Jake wanted to crush him in his arms. He wasn't supposed to feel so much. He wasn't supposed to fall for this kid. But as he kissed him again, longer this time, deeper, their tongues and bodies meeting, Jake knew the dominoes had been tipped, and gravity was in control.

Nico was already hard, and Jake reached down to stroke him through the denim. "Did you put on underwear?"

Lips parted, he shook his head.

Fuck, it made Jake's dick swell to see how eager Nico was. "You ready to play?"

"Yes," he breathed, thrusting his hips into Jake's steady touch, the denim straining. Jake stopped moving, and Nico frowned.

Jake said, "We need a safe word."

"Oh." Nico blinked. "Okay. Something random, right? Like, armadillo or whatever?"

Laughing, Jake kissed his nose. "Armadillo it is."

"I'm not saying it has to be that!" Nico sputtered, laughing too.

"No, it's good. I like it." He squeezed Nico's dick, their laughter fading. "Does that feel good?"

"Uh-huh." Nico leaned into him, his breath hot on Jake's neck. Tentatively, he nuzzled and sucked, their stubble rasping.

Jake bit back a moan. Part of him wanted to let Nico suck a hickey onto his skin, but it wasn't professional to show up on the field with a love bite. Besides, it was time to take charge. He leaned back and lifted Nico's chin with his finger, angling his head to see the desk.

The room was like countless others over the years—a king bed with cream duvet, pale carpet, and art displayed on the faintly striped wallpaper, abstract swirls of green and gold trees in this case. The desk was like any other too, off to the side against the bathroom wall, sturdy dark wood with a lamp, room service menu, blank pad of hotel paper, and a branded pen.

But the chair was missing, tucked in a far corner. A fluffy white towel rested on the desk's polished surface, folded in half. By the lamp stood a new bottle of lube and a foil-wrapped condom. As Nico swallowed forcefully, his eyes flicking wide, Jake took the back of his neck, whispering, "Get naked. Now."

Almost tripping out of his jeans, Nico ripped off his clothes. His cock stood, curving out from the thatch of dark hair, his balls hanging low. He waited, gaze flicking back between Jake and the desk, chest rising and falling rapidly.

Jake ran a fingertip down Nico's hairy chest, taking in the firm, lean muscles with a sly smile. "You know what to do."

Still dressed in jeans and a tank top, Jake's bare toes curled into the plush carpet as he watched Nico approach the desk, two steps that were almost a run, and then slower.

With a glance back at Jake, Nico bent over the shiny wood, displaying his round, muscular ass in all its glory. Jake couldn't quite swallow his groan and ground the heel of his hand into his crotch through his jeans. Nico pressed one cheek into the towel, his feet spread and hands splayed on the corners of the desk, gripping.

Mastering the compulsion to stride over, pull Nico's cheeks apart, and slam inside, Jake slowly removed his own clothes, Nico craning his neck to watch. Jake gave him a show, arching his back as he peeled off the white cotton tank, then undoing his jeans with slow, deliberate movements. He hadn't bothered with underwear either, and Nico's breath caught as Jake kicked off his jeans.

Stroking his hardening shaft slowly, he prowled toward the desk. He'd always loved these moments, when his partner was positioned and waiting, trusting him, giving themselves over to him. And with Nico, Jake's blood ran even hotter and thicker.

Nico's young, wide eyes as he watched Jake over his shoulder, licking his parted lips, fired the primal urge to dominate and protect. It was a drum pounding in Jake, stronger with each beat of his heart.

Nico fidgeted as Jake stood behind him, a few inches between them. Reaching out, Jake feathered a fingertip down Nico's spine to the crack of his ass, then back up again. Their thighs grazing, Jake's cock nudging Nico, he slipped his other hand underneath to caress Nico's nipple. Nico moaned, his back arching.

When Jake pinched hard, Nico's gasp sent a pulse of hot need straight to Jake's balls. He did the same with the other nipple, Nico trembling in anticipation as he lightly teased, making him wait for it. When the pinch came, Nico jerked, his mouth falling open and eyes closed.

Jake repeated the pattern on both sides again, rubbing slow circles on Nico's ass with his cock. "Open yourself for me. Let me see you."

Hands shaking, Nico reached back and spread his cheeks, displaying his hairy crack and dusky hole. Jake crouched, ignoring the protest from his knees. This view was sure as hell worth it.

His hands gentle on the back of Nico's thighs, rubbing and making circles with his thumbs, Jake leaned in so he knew Nico could feel his breath fluttering against his hole. Just once, Jake licked it, then pressed a kiss to it before standing.

Without warning, he struck with his flat palm. The smack was as sharp in the air as Nico's cry. Jake hit his ass again in the same place, the tan skin already pinking up.

"Remember—armadillo," Jake said, his throat already going dry.

"Don't stop," Nico begged. "I love it."

"Yeah?" Jake spanked his other cheek once, twice. "You love this? Want me to slap your ass until it's red as a cherry?"

Nico moaned, "*Please.*"

Another strike, loud in the stillness of the anonymous room. "You won't be able to sit on the bench tomorrow." *Smack!* "And I'm not going to just spank your ass. I'm going to fuck you. Going to fuck you so hard you won't sit down for a week."

"*Uh,* uh, God. *Yes.*" The prettiest little noises flowed from Nico, and he humped the desk.

"You want that? Want to take my cock?"

Nico nodded desperately, wriggling his ass. Jake smacked him again on each side, the red skin warm now. His palm tingled, and he could imagine how the strikes must burn for Nico, how his ass must have been on fire.

But Nico trusted him not to go too far, which filled Jake's chest with a sweet pressure. He had to bend over him for a kiss, tangling his fingers in Nico's hair to yank up his head. With the awkward angle, it was all teeth and tongues, wet and messy.

Jake dug his teeth into Nico's lower lip, pulling it until he whimpered, then straightened up and gave Nico's upper thighs their smacks as well. "Wish you could see how red your skin is. How pretty you look bent over for me. I'm going to fuck your tight hole. Going to pull out and come all over your bruised ass when I'm ready. You want that?"

"Yes!" Hands scrabbling on the desk, Nico pushed back. "Do it!"

"I will. You have to be patient."

Nico glared over his shoulder.

Jake grinned. "Just for that, I'm going to take even longer." As Nico whined, Jake flicked open the bottle of lube and spread some on his fingers. He pressed two just behind Nico's balls, holding for a few seconds.

Time to explore. Pressing harder and then softer, testing different pressure and movement, Jake massaged Nico's perineum between his hole and his balls, looking for the sweet spot. Nico panted softly, the little sounds going straight to Jake's dick.

Rubbing his fingers in small circles around Nico's hole, Jake murmured, "Are you still hard?"

"Is that a trick fucking question?" Nico gasped as Jake massaged with more pressure. "Please. Need you inside me. Do it."

With his forefinger teasing Nico's hole, Jake used his thumb to press on the sensitive flesh below, still looking for just the right spot to externally massage the prostate. When Nico cried out, Jake pressed harder, asking, "How does that feel?"

"Fuck!" Nico shuddered. "Like I have to piss, but it's so good. Oh, Jesus. Jake, please. Please fuck me now."

"I will, baby. Going to fuck you so hard as soon as you're ready."

"I'm ready!" He shoved back with his ass. "I can take it."

"Hmm." Jake continued rubbing without penetrating him yet, loosening Nico's hole and massaging his taint until he kicked back restlessly, his heel striking Jake's calf.

"Shit." Nico froze. "I'm sorry."

"You're forgiven." Jake leaned over, whispering in his ear. "Just this once. I'm in charge, remember? No kicking."

He nodded. "I'm sorry. But..." Nico bit his lower lip.

"What?" Jake circled his fingers around Nico's rim.

"I'm ready. Please, *please*. Need it."

He relented. "Put your toes together. Heels out." Nico scrambled to comply. "That's it." Jake rubbed up and down the ridges of his spine. "This way it's harder for you to clench. Hold on to the desk."

Nodding frantically, Nico's fingers went white as he gripped the wood.

"Not going slow this time. Not going easy on you." Jake grabbed the condom and tore the package, rolling the latex on his painfully hard dick. He squeezed the base, taking a long breath before flicking open the lube again and coating himself. With one slick finger, he pushed into Nico's ass now, shoving right past the ring of tight muscle as Nico cried out.

"That's only my finger. Think about how my cock's going to split you open. You still want it?" Nico was so tight it had to be painful even with the massage, and Jake eased out his finger, waiting to see if he balked.

Nico glared over his shoulder, eyes wild, and gritted out, "Don't you fucking stop."

Grinning, Jake spread Nico's ass and thrust inside, making sure not to push with full force despite what he'd said about not going easy. They both cried out this time, Nico gasping, his body rigid.

"How does that feel?" Jake asked, shaking with the struggle to control himself. "Can you take it?"

"Just shut up and fuck me!"

Laughing, Jake didn't give him any mercy now, pulling back and slamming in again, digging his fingers into Nico's hips. He was so fucking tight and amazing. Jake braced his legs wider, pistoning his hips, their skin slapping together loudly.

Nico's pants and cries increased as Jake angled deeper and tried to hit just the right spot. He knew the moment he found it when Nico actually screamed and threw his head back.

Jake slapped his hand over Nico's wet mouth, going for his prostate again and again, pinning him down, fucking him relentlessly.

Nico spasmed, wracked by full-body quakes as Jake lifted Nico's hips to jerk his cock with his free hand. It only took two strokes before Nico's toes curled and his whole body tensed as he shot his load, spraying the towel. He moaned against Jake's hand, going limp, his eyes shut.

Letting go of Nico's mouth, Jake leaned his palms on the desk, circling his hips, rubbing Nico's tender prostate, making him twitch and whimper.

"Jake... *Fuck*."

"You've always called me that," Jake whispered, his lips at Nico's ear. "Everyone else but my mother calls me 'Fitz.' But never you." Brandon didn't either, but that was a distant memory now. All that mattered now was Nico.

Nico opened his eyes. "Should I?"

"No." He rammed suddenly with his hips. "I like it."

"You were always Jake to me. I don't know why."

Jake's heart swelled, and he couldn't explain it either. Suddenly he needed to come, needed to mark Nico. Rearing up, he pulled out and ripped off the condom. "Watch," he ordered.

As he jerked off, Nico did as he was told, lifting his head and staring over his shoulder, gaze torn between Jake's eyes and his cock. The tingling in Jake's balls transformed into an unstoppable flood, and he groaned, spraying his cum on Nico's red cheeks in thick white stripes. "Oh, baby. Fuck, look at you," Jake muttered.

When he'd squeezed out every drop, he spread his seed over Nico's hot flesh as Nico shivered. Then he dropped to his knees on the forgivingly thick carpet and dragged his tongue over that red ass, tasting his own cum, gathering it in his mouth.

On his feet again, he hauled up a boneless Nico, turning him and supporting his weight. Jake gave him a salty kiss, and Nico groaned, licking into his mouth hungrily even as he sagged in Jake's arms.

Easing back, Jake kissed Nico's cheeks and forehead, stroking his back gently. "Did you like that, baby?"

"*Nnngh*." He nodded with a giddy laugh, heavy in Jake's embrace, but clearly so much lighter.

CHAPTER FOURTEEN

HOW LONG CAN you have pins and needles before it causes permanent damage?

Nico's foot was tingling where it was tucked underneath his knee as he lay on his back on the soft mattress. He'd move, but Jake was sprawled naked with his head in Nico's lap, heavy arm thrown across his thighs.

There was plenty of room on the other side, but Jake seemed drawn to Nico like a magnet in his sleep. As he mumbled against Nico's belly, breathing heavily, there was no place Nico would rather be. Pins and needles weren't so bad.

Besides, a little cramping working its way up his calf was nothing compared to the glorious throb in his ass. He'd been well and truly fucked, and he felt it with every breath. He really *would* have trouble sitting on the bench. The thought brought a smile to his lips.

It'd be like feeling Jake still inside him in front of all those people. They wouldn't have a clue, but Nico would feel so deliciously...*queer*. After all the years of denying it, after all the Jennys, it was real now. *He* was real.

And fuck, was he in love.

Last night had been incredible. The heat and pounding, the surrender. Nico had wanted to shout his love to Jake, but he'd nearly chewed through his own lip muzzling himself. He couldn't get too far ahead. He couldn't expect anything more from Jake than sex.

Right?

Unable to resist, he ran his hand through Jake's mussed hair rhythmically. It was still early, and they had a couple hours before they had to be at the stadium. Nico could watch Jake on the field, knowing that no one else got to see him like this—loose and vulnerable. Well, he supposed other men Jake had fucked had possibly woken like this too.

Shifting slightly, Nico winced, trying to shove away the thought. It didn't matter who Jake had been with in the past. It was just the two of them now.

What about tomorrow? And the next day? What if Jake gets bored? What if he meets someone he likes better?

Flexing his cramped foot beneath him, Nico squeezed his eyes shut, trying to think about anything else. Tomorrow wasn't there yet. Neither was the next day. He stretched out his right arm, flexing the muscles.

His next start wasn't for five days since no teams would play Monday, Tuesday, or Wednesday due to Tuesday's all-star game. Loyola had talked to him about his splitter, giving him the go-ahead to try it up to a dozen times on Friday. Excitement mingled with fear, almost indistinguishable.

What if it doesn't work? What if Boston gets a read on it? Shit, what if they get a bunch of runs? What if they win? What if—

"I can hear you thinking," Jake mumbled, rubbing Nico's thigh with his powerful hand.

Nico had to smile. "Sorry." He shifted, wincing as he straightened his leg.

Suddenly wide awake, Jake's head shot up. "Are you hurt?"

"No, no." Nico wriggled his leg, shaking feeling back into it. "Just pins and needles."

Grimacing, Jake pushed himself up to sitting. "Sorry. Elbow

me next time."

Next time. Nico nodded, his belly fluttering.

Jake ran his palm over Nico's chest, playing with the hair there. "How's your ass?"

"Fine," he answered too quickly.

"Let me see." Not waiting for an answer, Jake rolled Nico onto his side. Nico's leg still prickled, but he ignored it as Jake's fingers gently spread his cheeks and caressed his hole.

Nico's breath stuttered, and he wasn't sure if it was from the soreness or the imaginary weight of Jake's gaze. "It's fine, see?"

"It's swollen. Was it too much? Did I hurt you?"

"No, I told you."

A deep furrow between his eyes, Jake loomed over him. "I want you to tell me if I do. Armadillo, okay?"

He nodded. "Armadillo. But really, I'm fine. I like it. I like that it stings. Makes me think of you. Feels…" He couldn't find the right words. "You know."

Gently, Jake caressed Nico's hole and leaned down for a kiss. He whispered against his lips. "You like having a cock inside you?"

"Yes."

"Is it how you imagined?"

Nico's half-hard morning wood swelled. "Better. Especially because it's you."

They kissed, breath stale, and Nico didn't give a shit, because then Jake was rolling on top of him, Nico on his back again. He'd kiss Jake all day if he could.

He moaned discontentedly when Jake broke away, but pleasure flooded as Jake worked his way down, licking and sucking.

Jake spread Nico's legs and lapped at his balls, teasing until his dick leaked. Then he swallowed the head, cheeks hollowing, reaching down with his finger to push just barely inside Nico's hole. It was as though he was claiming his territory, and a sudden orgasm ripped through Nico.

Only choking a little, Jake swallowed, inching his finger in farther, the sting sending another pulse of pure pleasure through Nico and out his cock. He groaned, mouth open. Then Jake pulled off, removing his finger. Nico wanted it back, but Jake moved up over him, straddling his chest with long legs, his thick thighs pinning Nico's arms.

"You want my cock?"

Nodding desperately, Nico gazed up at him eagerly.

"I'm going to fuck your mouth. That's right, keep it open for me."

He tried to relax his face as Jake fed him his cock, stretching his lips. Saliva gathered in Nico's mouth, his nostrils flaring as Jake filled him completely, reaching up for leverage on the headboard as he rocked his hips.

"That's it. You're doing so good, baby. Let go."

Absolutely pinned down, Nico gagged, Jake's thick shaft hitting the back of his throat. His eyes watered and he bent his knees, kicking his heels into the mattress as he struggled to breathe.

"Look at me. You're okay. I'm here. I've got you."

Staring into Jake's blue eyes, his cheeks flushed pink, lips parted as he fucked Nico's mouth, Nico relaxed his throat as much as he could and let his legs fall to the mattress, still. Jake's balls slapped his chin, and the musky, sweaty taste of his cock overwhelmed Nico's senses. Pliant, he let Jake take control, tension draining away.

When Jake shook and shot down his throat, grunting like an animal, a wave of warmth washed over Nico, like another orgasm that had nothing to do with his dick.

Flopping down next to him on the mattress, Jake breathed heavily. "Jesus. I've never..."

Nico's heart thumped, and he waited for him to say more, but Jake kissed him messily instead, stroking deep into Nico's mouth with his tongue. When they caught their breath, Jake stretched out, eyes closed, smiling.

Nico smiled too, but soon his brain started whirling again. "Do you ever like being fucked?"

Jake opened his eyes, trailing his knuckles down Nico's sternum. "Not really. I'm not vehemently opposed to it or anything. Just never felt as good as doing the fucking."

"You don't like other stuff either? Like last night?"

"Being spanked, you mean?"

"Uh-huh."

"No. I like taking control. Why? Do you want to fuck me? Spank me?"

Nico thought about it. "It wouldn't be bad, but no. I want you in charge. You call the signs, but with sex stuff. You know what I mean? That probably doesn't make any sense."

Smiling, Jake kissed his nose. "Baby, that makes perfect sense."

Nico cuddled close on his side, his cheek on Jake's shoulder. Unlike with the Jennys, he loved it when Jake called him that. He felt calm and cared for and…

Loved.

His stomach tightened. "Baby" was just a word. He shouldn't read too much into it. Maybe it was just how Jake talked with guys he fucked. Maybe he'd had a dozen "babies." As many babies as Nico had had Jennys.

"Stop thinking," Jake said quietly.

"I can't. I try, but…"

"What are you thinking about?" Jake trailed his fingers down Nico's arm.

"Friday's start," he lied.

"Worry about it when it comes."

Nico shifted restlessly in the arc of Jake's arm. Of course now he *was* thinking about Friday. "I really want the win."

Jake rolled onto his side and propped his head on his hand, his gaze even. "Naturally. We all want to win every time we step on the field."

"Yeah, but I *need* to win. It's like…breathing. You might want to win or whatever, but I don't think it's the same."

"Right, because I'm not giving myself an ulcer."

Annoyance rumbled through Nico. "It didn't bug you? All those years in San Francisco, being on such a shitty team?" Jake pressed his lips together, and Nico added, "I know it was the owners being cheap and not getting enough talent. You couldn't carry the whole team. But didn't it? Get to you? Playing all those seasons, knowing the odds of making it into October were practically zero?"

Jake's gaze skittered around, and he shrugged tensely. "At first. For a few years, and then…"

"What?"

Rolling onto his back, Jake stared at the ceiling, clenching and releasing his hands. "My best friend got traded and it just wasn't the same."

Nico seemed to have stumbled onto a sore spot, and he wondered if he should just drop it. But no, Jake pushed him to talk about his shit, so it was only fair. "Who?"

"Brandon Kennedy."

"I don't really know him. He got traded to Toronto, right? A few years back? I didn't realize you were friends."

"About five years, and we're not. Not anymore."

"Oh." Nico was dying to ask why, but before he could, the alarm on Jake's phone chimed on the nightstand.

"Shit. Time to get moving."

"Right." Nico wanted to know more—wanted to know everything—but he'd have to wait.

Neither of them moved, their skin pressing together, Jake sliding his knee between Nico's legs. He said, "Wish we could stay here all day."

Nico smiled. "Me too."

"Are Val and your dad coming down again? Does Nonna ever come?"

"Just Dad today. And no, Nonna hates crowds." His heart skipped, and he cleared his throat. "About Val, I was going to tell you last night, but I never got a chance."

Jake grinned and nipped at Nico's lips. "Sorry I distracted you. What's up?"

There was no good way to say it, so he spit it out. "Val knows. About me. About us."

Jake leaned back, concern etched on his face. "Okay. And how did that go?"

"Good? She heard us in my room. I didn't tell her. But she doesn't mind. She thinks it's great, actually. And she won't tell, don't worry."

"I trust her. I always liked your sister." He traced his finger over Nico's cheeks. "You feel good about it? About talking to her?"

"Yeah. Surprisingly. We talked about a lot of stuff." He inhaled, relishing the lack of resistance in his chest, his guilt over his mother faded. Not vanished, but maybe eventually.

"Glad to hear it." Jake's phone rang, and he groaned, rolling out of bed. Standing there naked, strong and steady, he answered, and Nico let himself look.

Jake listened to whoever had called, a low rumble of a distant voice. "Okay. Yes. I understand. Right." He glanced at Nico. "I think Agresta would certainly be able to pitch Thursday if you want to bump him up. Even without the all-star break, he's young. He bounces back faster than the rest of the rotation."

Adrenaline zooming through him, Nico bolted up like an arrow. One of the other guys in their five-man starting rotation had to be hurt. Shit, fuck, shit. Was it bad? Who was it?

Jake hung up and faced him. "Carter strained his hamstring. He's going on the DL, so they're bumping up Palmer in the rotation to today. Bullpen's shallow right now, so they need to look at the roster and figure out who to send down to bring up another arm. I've got to get in there and go over Chicago's lineup for this afternoon with Skip, Palmer, and the coaches. I was expecting to DH today since Baldoni catches Carter."

"Shit, hope he's okay." Nico and Carter didn't talk much, but Carter was a good guy. Even if he wasn't, Nico never wanted to see another pitcher end up on the disabled list. "Yeah, of course I can pitch Thursday. It's only Sunday now. Easy." As if to spite him, his shoulder twinged, and he rolled it, tension stiffening his spine.

Jake crawled back onto the mattress. "Don't start worrying."

Nico's mind spun through Boston's likely batting order. It would have probably been the same Friday, but now that it was a day sooner, his plan felt compromised, and his pulse galloped.

"We'll handle it. Okay?" Jake rubbed Nico's knee.

He nodded, but his breath came faster, and he scrubbed his nails over the back of his neck. He'd been feeling so much better, so relaxed. But suddenly he wanted to leap out of his skin. What the fuck was wrong with him? So he was pitching a day earlier than planned. It didn't matter! Why was he freaking out? Frustration clawed at his throat, and he wanted to scream.

"Hey, hey. Breathe." Jake smoothed his palm over Nico's leg, pressing down, his fingers curling over Nico's tender inner thigh. "Don't psyche yourself out. Take it one pitch at a time. I'll be there with you." He squeezed gently. "Okay? Pitch by pitch."

Nico licked his lips, his breathing slowing. "Okay."

Jake kept his hand on Nico's leg as if he could ground him. "I have faith in you. You can do it. Just don't get ahead of yourself. Don't start thinking about a million other things."

Inhaling and exhaling slowly, the panic receding, Nico tried to smile. "When it's just you and me like this, I can almost believe it's possible."

"It *is* possible. If I could, I'd fuck those worries out of you on the mound. But I think Skip might object. The league too. Police. Public decency laws and all that."

Nico's shoulders shook with laughter, tension easing bit by bit.

"Hey, I can give you a sign." He pressed firmly against Nico's inner thigh. "When I do this to my own leg, imagine it's you I'm touching. That I'm right here with you, and you can breathe, and everything's okay."

Nico looked down at where Jake's hand cupped his thigh. "Our own sign? Just for me?"

He pressed firmly. "Only for you. It'll be quick, but you'll feel it like you do now. You'll remember how good it is when you let go. When you let me take control."

Nico swallowed thickly. "I'll feel it," he whispered, his gaze locking with Jake's.

Jake kissed him then, his palm still heavy on Nico's leg as their lips met. There was only the next breath and wet sweetness, baseball a million miles away.

NICO LUNGED FOR his phone on the coffee table as the screen lit up, tuning out the too-loud horse race his dad was glued to. There were two couches in the large, sunken living room, decorated in dark leather everything. Dad sat back on the other couch, paying avid attention to the prerace buildup, his slacks and button-up shirt neatly pressed as always.

He scanned the text from Jake:

Landed in TO. Dreading this charity dinner, but duty calls.

After unlocking his phone, Nico's thumbs flew. He wanted to say: *MISS YOU ALREADY! YOU'RE GOING TO THINK I'M CRAZY, BUT I LOVE YOU!*

Instead he typed out a message without all-caps, telling Jake to try and have fun and get to bed early. As the message was delivered, he chewed his thumbnail. Was that too naggy? Too...boyfriendy? Were they boyfriends? Were they dating? Did Jake want any of that? He'd stayed single so many years, and maybe he had no desire to change it. Maybe—

The three bubbles popped up, undulating.

Don't worry, no partying for me tonight. Are you back home? Enjoy the cannoli, you bastard. Jealous.

Nico exhaled and typed: *Yeah, staying until Wednesday. Morning flight back to Ottawa.* He weighed his next words. *Guess I'll see you then?* Was that too casual? *Wish you were here.* No. Too...clingy, or something. Finally he just hit send without another line. He waited.

Cool. Talk to you soon.

As his dad muttered something about gait, Nico read Jake's last text repeatedly, as if he expected the words to change at some point. Would Jake call later? Should Nico? Did "talk" mean actually speak, or did it mean text? Should Nico go to Toronto and surprise him? No, that was definitely too clingy.

He checked the screen again, forcing himself to put the phone in his jeans pocket. Nonna's garlic tomato sauce that had been simmering on the stove for days permeated the house, rich with onion and fresh herbs Nico couldn't identify but smelled like home.

Valentina and Marco wouldn't arrive for dinner for a few hours, and even though a bunch of cousins were coming too, maybe he could get Val alone for a minute to get her advice about Jake.

He and Jake had fucked twice that morning before Jake had to catch his flight, and Nico's ass still felt it. His lips looked normal in the mirror, but felt deliciously swollen.

"What're you grinning about over there? There's no way Idle-wood's going to win this race. Forget the Triple Crown." Socked feet on a wide leather ottoman, Dad gulped from his beer bottle.

After breaking down and checking his lock screen—still empty but for an aerial shot of the Caps' stadium—Nico sipped from his own beer.

Nonna was weeding out in the massive garden, and maybe he should go help her, even though she'd swatted away his earlier offer. She was probably too old to be kneeling so long, but no one dared tell her that. And more power to her. That garden was her baby, and she still hummed when she tended it.

"Maybe if they didn't have this fairy riding her, Idlewood would stand a chance. He won't use enough crop. I know it. Too light-wristed like they all are."

Nico's bottle clattered and almost tipped as he slammed it onto a marble coaster.

"What crawled up your ass now?"

You wouldn't believe me if I told you. Not that Jake had crawled so much as hammered. God, he wanted Jake's cock again. He wanted it all day, every day.

"The silent treatment, huh? Okay."

"No," Nico grumbled. "First I'm too happy, now this."

Dad popped a few sunflower seeds in his mouth. It'd been tobacco back in the day, but Nico's mother had forbidden it when they married. Sometimes Nico wondered why Dad hadn't gone back to it once she was gone.

He spit the husks into a little bowl. "I didn't say that."

"Fine, whatever."

Attention back on the TV, Dad groused, "I'm telling you, this guy's too much of a pussy to get the job done."

Nico bolted up straight, on the edge of the couch now. "Would you stop with the name-calling?"

Shoulders shaking, Dad had a good laugh. "What?"

His whole life, Nico had never objected. Never said a word. But suddenly it was too much, and something hard inside him gave way, snapping right in half this time. "Stop with the homophobic and misogynistic bullshit! Stop calling people names. Stop being such an asshole!"

Any traces of laughter vanished. "What did you say to me?"

Nico's heart drummed. "You heard me."

"So you're *offended*? Is that it? You sneeze nowadays and someone's fucking offended. Tough shit."

He kept his voice even, little more than a whisper. "What if I was a fairy? A queer, a faggot, a cocksucker?"

Dad stared, not blinking. Then he picked up the remote and muted the TV on the wall. "What did you say?"

"You heard me."

He scoffed. "Cut the shit. I get your point. I'll try not to offend your delicate fucking sensibilities in the future."

Broken glass coated his tongue, but Nico went on. "You don't get it. I'm all those things. I'm those awful, disgusting things. You don't want queers in baseball, but you're looking at one. A queer in the family too. Sorry to disappoint."

Running his tongue over his teeth, Dad turned back to the TV, breathing hard through his nose. He was silent for a few heartbeats, going completely still. "I never said that."

Rage rocketed Nico to his feet, resentment choking him. "You said it right here, Dad! Right in this room. '*Queers wanting to get married—next thing we know, they'll want to play baseball too!*'" He struggled to breathe. "That's what you said. And Val wasn't even paying attention—she was so used to you spouting hateful garbage, and she ignored it back then. Nonna crossed herself the way she does every time something gay comes up. And I was sitting right there—" He jabbed his finger at the corner where an armchair had once sat. "I was right there, and I knew I had to hide who I was, because I was a little queer, and you'd hate me more than you already did."

Palms sweaty, Nico quivered, refusing to sit back down. He'd opened the wound, and the poison gushed out.

Still on the couch, Dad stared up at him, demanding, "What does that mean? Hate you more?"

"For Mom. For being born, for making her sick. Val says no one blames me, but I knew it was my fault."

His craggy face turning red, Dad shoved to his feet. "What the hell are you talking about? It was cancer. It wasn't you. She—" He broke off, eyes on the polished hardwood.

"You can't even say her name. You never say it. She was all around us in this house, but we acted like she'd never been here at all. Like we weren't missing anything."

"Of course we missed her," Dad gritted out, jabbing his finger toward Nico. "Don't you dare stand there and tell me I don't miss her."

"That's not what I'm saying. It just… We never talked about it. About anything! She was just gone and we weren't allowed to say her name."

"That's bullshit!" Dad's chest heaved. "When did I ever say you weren't allowed?"

"But you and Nonna never even mentioned her!" He wanted to punch the coffee table. Wanted to rip the damn TV off the wall and throw it through the bay windows.

"Because we missed her!" Dad's nostrils flared. "Because it hurt too fucking much!"

"Why didn't you say that? I blamed myself, and maybe it made no sense, but I was a little kid. Someone should have told me how it was. How she died."

"I was supposed to read your goddamned mind?" He swallowed thickly, speaking more quietly than Nico had maybe ever heard. "I can't read your mind, Nic."

The anger ebbed, Nico trembling in its wake. "I know."

"Your mother… Angela died of cancer, and it didn't have a damn thing to do with you. You hear me?"

He nodded, hugging himself, fighting the urge to curl up into a ball and weep.

"Good," Dad said. "Good." The bluster returned in a flash, veins bulging in his neck. "Now about this other nonsense—"

"It's true." Nico cleared his throat, willing strength and surety into his voice. "Whether you want to believe it or not, I'm gay."

The gasp came from behind him, and he turned to find Nonna in the wide entry that led down the hall to the kitchen, clutching a bouquet of fresh peonies, still wearing her gardening apron over her plain dress. She crossed herself, and Nico wasn't sure whether to cry or scream.

Backing up toward the TV so he could talk to them both, blood rushed in his ears. It was happening. He was saying it all out loud. Being with Jake, being touched by him and fucked by him like he'd dreamed for so long had apparently opened the floodgates, and there was no stopping it now.

"I'm gay. I've always been gay, and I always will be. I want men. A man. A man to be with, to love, maybe even marry one day. And I know you think it's a sin and it's wrong, but it's who I am. It's not a phase. I'm not confused. I tried to deny it, to hide it." He pounded his chest, tears burning. "I tried to bury it so deep, because I knew you'd never accept me, but I can't do it."

"It's not true." Dad grimaced. "It's not true," he repeated, more forcefully this time. "It can't be. You're a baseball player for fuck's sake. You can't be..." He wiggled his hand, his wrist limp.

"I am. I'm gay." Nico looked between them, Dad's shoulders rising and falling, Nonna an absolute statue, the poor peonies wilting in her iron grip. "I can't hide it anymore." Lungs constricting suddenly, he gasped. "I can't. Jesus, I can't. It's only my rookie year. I can't pretend for another decade or more. That's a lifetime."

Little white spots crowded his sight, his vision tunneling. "I can't do it. I can't!" His head light, a wave of dizziness swayed him, his bare feet trying to grip the polished wood. "I tried so hard to be perfect—to be what you wanted."

Then Nonna was there with her gnarled hand on his arm, the peonies scattered. "Breathe," she ordered.

He did, and the swirling faded, leaving nausea behind. He should probably stop talking, but the words stumbled off his tongue, undeniable. "I want to be honest. I want to be free. I *need* to be. I want to be with Jake, and…" As he realized what he'd said, bile rose in his throat. *Fuck, fuck, fuck!*

"Jake?" Dad's face paled. "Fitz?"

"Yes." Nico was proud of how he didn't tremble, even though he'd never intended to out Jake.

"Fitz is a…"

"A fag? Yeah, Dad." He glanced at Nonna, still digging her fingers into his left arm. "He is. We… We're together."

Mumbling something in Italian that sounded like a curse or a prayer or maybe both, Nonna pressed her lips together, still grabbing him. "I don't understand, Nicolito. How?"

"I know it must be confusing. I'm sorry." He looked to his father, who simply stared with his mouth open.

Before Nico could say anything more, the drone of an engine approached, a car coming up the long drive. Nonna sprang into action, bending to collect the fallen flowers like she was half her age. She muttered, "The sauce," and disappeared toward the kitchen.

Nico prayed it would be Val, but a carload of cousins appeared on the front walk through the bay windows. Running his hand down the front of his shirt, then over his hair, Dad drained the rest of his beer and headed to the door.

With a second to spare, Nico dashed up the wide stairway, escaping to his childhood room as he heard his father's booming welcome.

CHAPTER FIFTEEN

T HE CLOSING ELEVATOR doors bounced back open, and Jake
slipped inside, realizing too late the other passenger was
Brandon. They stared at each other in their tailored suits until
Jake turned to face the doors, his left hip pressing into the rail
beside him, as far from Brandon as he could be while still in the
metal box.

Several inches shorter than Jake, Brandon was as handsome as
ever, his face still boyish despite a goatee. Looking from the corner
of his eye, Jake could almost imagine nothing had changed, and
Brandon was about to crack a wide smile and tell one of his punny
jokes.

But Brandon's jaw was set, his hands clasped behind him,
thumb tapping, gaze locked straight ahead as if Jake wasn't even
there. Damn if that didn't sharpen the ache in Jake's chest to a
razor's edge.

The elevator stopped on its way down for a middle-aged
woman with an ice bucket who got off on the next floor. Jake's
heart thumped, his fingers tingling and skin hot. He had to say
something. He had to at least try, didn't he? He had to.

"Congrats, by the way," he blurted.

Brandon went very still as the elevator stopped on another
floor. The doors opened, but there was no one there. "For what,"
he asked carefully.

"You had twins, right? A boy and a girl?"

"Yes. Two years ago."

"Right. Well, that's great."

Rubbing a hand over his trimmed goatee, Brandon said, "I don't know what you're trying to do, but stop."

The elevator was apparently on the milk run, and it stopped again, letting on a young couple who only had eyes for each other, and who were apparently also only taking the elevator one floor.

Brandon was right. He should forget it. It'd been too long, and he'd fucked things up far too royally. But as the doors swept shut behind the couple, surety bolted through Jake like lightning, fear electric in his veins. This was his last chance. If he stayed silent now and they walked out of the elevator, that was it. Game over forever.

He jammed the emergency button with his palm. A shrill alarm sounded as the elevator brakes engaged. Brandon stared, his mouth agape.

"What the hell? Is this some joke?"

"No." Jake was flying now, out of his body on an adrenaline burst, his heart exploding. "I loved you."

"What?" Brandon's forehead creased, and he looked around the elevator as if there would be some answer on the mirrored walls. "This is a joke." Shaking his head, his eyes met Jake's and his fists clenched. "I swear to God, man, I don't know what you're pulling, but get me the fuck off this elevator. I have nothing to say to you."

The words were marbles on Jake's tongue, slippery and hard, tumbling out in a clatter. "I'm gay, and I was in love with you."

Brandon stared, his eyebrows almost at his hairline.

The shrill alarm sounded again, making them both jump. A tinny voice from the elevator control panel asked, "What's your emergency?"

They both looked at the panel, and Jake cleared his throat.

"Sorry, I hit the button by accident. We're fine."

It must have happened regularly, because the elevator started moving again without further comment. They reached the ground floor before Jake could formulate another sentence, but he only moved to press the button to return to his floor. A few people streamed in, and Brandon hadn't gotten off. Brandon stared straight ahead as the elevator went back up.

"I'm sorry to bother you, but aren't you Jake Fitzgerald and Brandon Kennedy?" An older woman beamed at them. "I'm such a fan. So wonderful to have two Canadian teams now! Hopefully one of you will make it to the playoffs! Or both!"

Brandon smiled and nodded. "We hope so, ma'am. Thank you."

Jake smiled too and edged past the woman and her companions as the doors opened for his floor. He didn't look back, because what else could he say? He exhaled noisily, the adrenaline rush crashing into nausea. There was a sound behind him, and Jake turned to find Brandon standing there, the elevator doors shut.

The thick hotel carpet whispering under his feet, Jake walked to his room, hoping Brandon would follow. Hoping he hadn't just made everything worse. But really, how much worse could it get?

Their friendship was over a long time ago, and at least Jake could tell the truth. Maybe it was selfish to want to unburden himself, but he couldn't help but hope deep down that his old friend would want to know what had really happened and why.

Inside his suite, they stood by the breakfast table, the door closing with a gentle whoosh and click. Breathing deeply, Jake tried to think of the right words, or any words, really.

"You're gay." Brandon watched him carefully, as if he still expected a TV crew to jump out from behind the couch and shout it was all a prank.

"Yes."

"Since when?"

"Since always. I came out to my parents before I left for college."

Brandon's eyebrows soared again. "You knew back then? You were out? Other people knew?"

"No. Just my parents and my family in England. I didn't want it to get in the way of baseball. Didn't want it to affect my career."

"Okay. I get that." Brandon gestured sharply. "But you could have told me. We were friends. At least I thought we were. Maybe I had it wrong from the start."

"No, we were. You were my best friend. I wanted to tell you, believe me. But I couldn't." He shoved his hands in his pockets, gripping the hard plastic of his key card.

"Because you were in love with me."

He swallowed hard. "Yes."

Shaking his head, Brandon rocked on his feet. "If this is some joke, it's seriously not funny."

"I was in love with you, and I was too afraid to tell you. I was afraid it would make everything awkward. Ruin our friendship. Which of course I destroyed in the end anyway." The plastic key dug into his palm, and he took a shuddering breath. "I can't tell you how sorry I am. I was a coward, and you deserved better."

"What did you think I'd do if you told me?"

"I don't know. Worst-case scenarios used to spin through my head when I tried to sleep. I knew you didn't feel the same way about me."

"You could have at least said you were gay. I'm not some ignorant fool. You were my boy, Jake. I would never have turned my back on you."

Regret lodged in his throat, and Jake could only croak out, "I know."

"I mean, yeah, it would have been weird at first if I knew you were into me. But we'd have pushed through it. Instead you were a dick. Denise was always like, 'Did I do something to offend him? Why doesn't Jake like me?' She tried so hard to get in good with you because she knew how tight we were."

Shame sank through him down to his toes. "I'm sorry. She didn't deserve that. I was jealous and petty, and I have no excuse for it. None. Especially not for the awful things I said after your engagement party. I deserved that punch. It was all on me."

Brandon clenched his jaw. "So why'd you get me traded?"

"I swear, I asked them to trade *me*. On my mother's life. I said I wasn't happy, and I didn't mention you at all. But obviously they'd heard about the party and what happened. But I didn't ask them to trade you. Not that it matters after all this, I know."

Rubbing a hand over his shorn hair, Brandon walked a few steps and then back again restlessly. "It matters."

"You believe me?"

"You were never a liar, Jake." He laughed humorlessly. "Although I guess you were, huh? Had me fooled."

Jake had to turn away as unshed tears burned his eyes. He paced around, staring up. When he had control, he said, "I truly am sorry." He still looked at the ceiling, a swirled pattern of white circles. "I'd give anything to go back and change it."

A sing-songy chime echoed in the silence, and Brandon swore under his breath. "We've got to get to this fucking dinner."

When Jake faced him, Brandon's thumbs were flying on his screen. "Denise is waiting."

"Right. You should go. I'll go down soon." He was nodding like an idiot, and he clenched his hand over the key card again, bending the hard plastic.

At the door, Brandon said, "I don't know what to think. But I'm glad you told me."

Then he was gone, and Jake had to loosen his tie, slumping against the wall as he tried to catch his breath. He didn't expect the truth to change anything with Brandon, to bridge a gap so hopelessly vast.

But he'd buried that truth so deeply in roots of shame and guilt, and now the layers were pulled back, the nerve exposed. He realized another truth down in his gut, in his soul.

He wanted love. Sex wasn't enough—he wanted it all. The laughter and fights and comfort and the cap off the toothpaste and the same person to kiss goodnight and good morning. He wanted someone to protect and hold close, someone to hold him back. Someone to fuck and kiss and learn to cook for, someone to make his half-life full.

Not just *someone*.

With each deeper breath, calm spreading through his limbs, he knew exactly who he wanted. But Nico had barely texted. Jake told himself Nico was busy catching up with his family, but worry nagged. Was he having regrets? Or maybe now that he'd lowered his inhibitions, he was ready to explore. Maybe he didn't want to be tied down.

Jake groaned. Not that they were even officially a couple. Why would Nico want to be restricted? Sure, sex with Jake was the culmination of longtime fantasies. But usually when something culminated, it ended. Nico might want to move on now that he'd gotten what he'd wanted. And Jake would have to be fine with that.

He fought to catch his breath. Damn it, Jake knew who he wanted. Now he just had to keep him.

INSTEAD OF ROOM service, it was Brandon at the door the next morning in jeans and a Toronto team jacket, rocking back on his heels the way he did when he was nervous. "This a bad time?"

"No. Come in."

Brandon shoved his hands in his pockets once the door closed.

"So. Not gonna lie—that was trippy, finding out all that stuff."

"Right." Jake shifted uneasily, tugging anxiously on the hem of his T-shirt. "I can imagine."

"You know what's funny? Denise wasn't even surprised." He shook his head with a little smile. "She said she thought maybe that was it, but she was so pissed after I was traded that she didn't care anymore."

"I don't blame her."

Brandon's shoulders hitched up as he sucked in a breath and blew it out. "Look, man. It really sucks that you never told me the truth. And it's weird to think of you being, like, *in love* with me. Wanting to get with me. It's hard to wrap my head around it."

"I know. And I don't feel that anymore." Standing there with gorgeous Brandon almost in arm's reach, he realized it was true. There was still a nostalgic tug of affection, but that soul-scouring need, the bittersweet yearning, was gone. "I really don't."

Brandon nodded. "Okay. I'm glad, because you know as pissed as I was at you all these years, *fuck*, I hate thinking about you in pain because of me. I hate it. You were hurting back then and I never knew a damn thing." Shaking his head, he put his hands on his hips. "Shit, Jake. I really hate that." He pressed his lips together, tears glistening as he groaned and wiped his eyes roughly. "Now you've got me cryin'. Shit."

Jake tried to laugh through the swell of emotion. "Jesus, don't make me cry too." Then they were both laughing, Brandon's brown eyes shining, and God, Jake had missed his friend so damn much. "I missed you, B."

"Yeah, I missed your dumb ass too."

Jake laughed again, tension seeping away. "Has it been good? In Toronto? Denise and the kids? Is it...are you good?"

"Yeah. I'm great. It's a quality city, good ball club. Awesome fans all across the country. You get that too in Ottawa, I bet. And my family's the best. Have you seen them? The twins? We did that one magazine photo shoot when they were babies. They're walking now. Shit, *running*. Every-fucking-where and shoving their fingers every place they shouldn't put them." He pulled out his phone and tapped. "This is from the other day."

Jake stood beside him and leaned in, smiling at the picture of two curly-haired toddlers grinning at the camera with what looked like chocolate smeared all over their hands and faces. "Wow. They're adorable."

"Right? I know, I'm supposed to be modest, but shit, those are some cute kids."

"They really are."

Jake's bagel and coffee arrived, and he poured Brandon a cup from the carafe. Brandon plucked an apple from a fruit bowl and sat across from Jake at the small breakfast table.

"So if you're not into me anymore, who is it? I realize I left some big shoes to fill."

Laughing, Jake smeared cream cheese on his bagel. "As humble as ever, I see."

"Hey, it's just reality." Brandon kept a straight face as he indicated his body. "God made me this way, Jake. Don't hate the player." He cracked, a bark of a laugh getting through. "But seriously. You have a boyfriend?"

There was the million-dollar question. Jake wished he knew the answer. "Boyfriend" sounded juvenile on one hand, but "partner" was too serious at this stage. "I just started seeing someone. It's…complicated."

He'd never *missed* anyone like this. It had only been a couple days, and he was anxious to get back to Ottawa.

But his mom was coming down for lunch and shopping since Midland was only a two-hour drive, and Nico would be in Chicago for another day anyway. Despite all the logic his brain coughed up, Jake itched to see Nico, to kiss him and wake up in his arms again.

After swallowing a mouthful of apple, Brandon asked, "Complicated how?"

Jake took a deep breath. "Complicated because he's a teammate."

Brandon's jaw dropped. "For real? Yeah, I'd say that's a little complicated. I can't see Skip Jankowski approving of monkey business in his clubhouse."

"We don't do anything there." Jake flushed. "Okay, once. The first time. It wasn't planned!" He was glad Brandon couldn't read his mind, because the memory of Nico sprawled across his lap, loving what Jake gave him, then on his knees begging, swallowing Jake's cock was… Clearing his throat, he shifted in his chair. "We definitely won't again."

Laughing, Brandon took a bite of his apple. "Mmm-hmm." He swallowed. "Now you have to tell me who it is."

"I don't think so. It's not that I don't trust you, but it's not for me to tell anyone he's gay."

"I get it, man. That's cool." Brandon took another bite. "Is it Lopez? No wait—Crowe. That's what's hot these days, right? That bullshit lumberjack thing?"

Laughing, Jake shook his head. "It's not them. And stop guessing."

"All right, all right." He toyed with the apple stem, twisting it off. "You think people will care? Nowadays? Maybe I'm too optimistic, but I don't think they will. Wouldn't bother me. Might bug a few guys, but I bet they'd keep their ignorant traps shut. Times are a-changin.' But I know that's easy for me to say. Hey, next time the Caps are at Toronto, you should come for dinner. Bring your mystery man if he's cool with it."

The thought was both exciting and terrifying. "Are you sure Denise would be okay with that?"

"Absolutely. She's not big on grudges. And you know, maybe it's a cliché, but having kids really helps you see what's important and what's bullshit. And holding grudges is crap. All that shit's in the past, and we can't change it. But I can give my kids an awesome Uncle Jake. Those kids are what matters. Everything's black and white to them, you know? If I told them about you, and that we'd had a big fight, they'd look at me with those serious eyes, and they'd say something like, 'Daddy, is he good or bad?' And I know what the answer is. So come the fuck over for dinner, all right?"

The lump in Jake's throat took a moment to swallow around. "All right."

It was later that day when Jake's phone lit up with a message from an unknown number.

Knock, knock

His heart in his throat, Jake typed back: *Who's there?*

Little old lady

Thumbs clumsy as his hands shook, Jake sent back: *Little old lady who?*

Dude, I didn't know you could yodel!

The laughter was sweet relief, like rain in August. Jake texted back a smiling emoji before creating a new contact in his phone.

CHAPTER SIXTEEN

"**C**OME IN."

Rolling over, Nico found Valentina in the doorway of his old bedroom. He'd gotten dressed, but hadn't ventured downstairs. It had been almost twenty-four hours, and he was starving.

She shut the door behind her. "Dad said you're sick. What's going on?" Wincing, she kicked off her high heels, then reached under the skirt of her power suit and peeled off her pantyhose. "Whew. That's better. Sorry I couldn't make dinner last night. Work bullshit. But today I told them to go fuck themselves. We have an all-star game to watch." She approached the bed, lips pursed. "What's wrong?"

Before Nico could answer, Marco burst through the door. He stared at them both, then focused on Nico, his hands out, palms up. "You're gay? Seriously? Is this for real?"

Valentina swallowed a little gasp. "You told them? Oh my God." She perched on the side of Nico's bed and brushed back his hair. "How did it go? Okay, that was a stupid question. I'm going to guess not so well."

Nico asked, "What did Dad say?"

Marco put his hands on his hips. "He said, 'Your brother's a homosexual.' Nonna crossed herself and practically ran to the kitchen—haven't seen her move that fast in years—and Dad went back to SportsCenter."

A homosexual. Nico shifted uncomfortably. That's what he was, but the idea of his father thinking about it—about him and Jake—flooded acid into his empty stomach. It was out there now. No going back.

"Well, it's a good sign he's saying it out loud." Valentina gave Nico's arm a squeeze.

"You knew about this?" Marco huffed. "Nic, why didn't you tell me?"

Val narrowed her gaze. "Oh, gee, let's see. Maybe because when Dad spouts his homophobic bullshit, you never argue with him?"

"It's just *Dad.* I ignore him when he gets like that. It doesn't mean I agree."

"Well, your silence speaks volumes, Marc." Val rubbed her face. "Not that I always spoke up. Back in the day I didn't argue either. I'm sorry, Nic."

"It's okay. I don't blame you guys."

Marco came to sit on the bed too, the three of them barely fitting, so Nico sat up against the headboard. Marco slapped Nico's shin. "You're my brother. You know I love you no matter what, you moron."

"I know." Nico laughed softly. "It's been a long time since the three of us were together like this. Since before I went to the minors. No ex-wife, no fiancée." He gazed around at the posters and old bulletin board, yellowed concert tickets tacked up with photos of high school friends he hadn't thought of since he left. "This room is trippy."

Val smiled. "Little time capsules in this house. I told Dad he should redo our rooms so they're presentable, but he says the other guest rooms are enough." Her smile faded. "What happened?"

Nico picked at a loose thread in his old green duvet. "Dad started going off about this guy on TV. Fairy. Pussy. You know, the usual. I just couldn't anymore. I'd always planned to keep it locked down. Keep *me* locked down. But it's too hard. Lying to everyone all the time. I can't do it."

"Nor should you," Val assured him. "They'll come around."

"Absolutely," Marco agreed.

She said, "Dad's always liked Fitz. Maybe that'll help him see how ignorant and small-minded he's been."

Marco's forehead creased. "Fitz? What's he got to do with it?" The other shoe apparently dropped, and his eyes widened. "Wait, Fitz is gay too? Holy shit, is everyone gay? How big is that closet?"

Val snorted. "In professional male sports? Pretty frickin' ginormous."

"Huh." Marco looked into space, clearly processing. "Maybe there were some clues there now that you mention it. Never seen Fitz with a woman."

"A few clues, yes," Val said wryly. To Nico she added, "Dad and Nonna will come around. They don't have a choice. You and Fitz stay strong and be happy together, and to hell with everyone else."

Marco chimed in, "Exactly. Look, I didn't see this coming with you, so I can imagine they *really* didn't see it coming. But—" He broke off, blinking. "Wait, what? You and Fitz?" He waved his hand through the air. "You *and* Fitz? Like..."

The little ripple of laughter felt good. Nico said, "Yeah. Me and Jake. We're...well, I don't know. We haven't officially talked about it or whatever."

"But you're fucking?" Marco asked.

Val rolled her eyes. "Always with the delicate touch, our brother."

Nico's laughter grew stronger. "Yeah, Marc. Jake and I are...you know. Hooking up." *And I'm already in love with him and I have no idea what our status is.*

Granted, he'd barely looked at his phone all day and had given short replies to Jake's texts. He'd wanted to call Jake and spill it all, confess that he'd outed him while coming out himself, but the thought had made him curl up and go back to sleep.

Marco's cheeks puffed out. "Wow. Okay. You're hitting me with a lot tonight, but I can take it. You and Fitz." He seemed to ponder it. "So... Are you still the pitcher?"

"Oh my God!" Valentina exclaimed. "I can't believe you actually just said that. Out loud!"

"What?" Marco was the picture of innocence, mouth open and hands out. "It's a valid question!"

"Nope. Not even a little." To Nico she said, "Ignore him."

Mortified, his ears going hot, Nico muttered, "I've ignored him for years."

"Hey!" Marco grumbled, "Okay, okay, you and Fitz. That's good. Fitz is a stand-up guy. And he'd better stay that way, or else."

With a giggle, Val loosed her hair from its clasp. "That's right. Or else your big brother and sister will kick his ass. He's bigger than all of us, but we'll manage. The Agrestas are scrappers."

"Yeah we are." Marco puffed up his chest.

Nico chuckled. "I appreciate it, but I don't think you'll need to defend my honor. Jake's..." He ducked his head and pulled the duvet thread looser. "You know. He's cool." It was beyond surreal that they were having this conversation.

"Cool?" Val asked. "Mmm-hmm. If by 'cool' you mean smokin' hot, super sweet, and an all-around dreamboat, then sure."

"*Dreamboat?*" Marco put on a high-pitched voice. "Is Ian a dreamboat too?"

Valentina smacked him with a pillow, and naturally it quickly disintegrated into a three-way fight, pillows flying as they tumbled to the floor. They were tangled in a pile, Marco and Nico ganging up against Valentina and tickling her feet when the door banged open. They looked up at their father filling the doorway, and Nico *really* felt twelve again.

"Sounded like you were killing each other up here." Dad stared down at them, and the silence was almost thick enough to see. He cleared his throat. "I ordered the pizza. The usual. Meat lovers for me and Val, pepperoni for Marc and Nonna, and Hawaiian for Nic."

Wearing his usual slacks and a red button-up, their father's hair was neatly slicked back as always. But he shifted from foot to foot, shoving his hands in his pockets, a tremble visible in his hunched shoulders. The wrinkles in his face seemed impossibly deeper, the gray edges of his hair somehow having spread overnight.

He watched them with eyes both eager and afraid, his voice little more than a rasp. "You kids going to come watch the pregame?"

Nico realized he'd never seen his father so vulnerable as long as he could remember. Even in the hazy memories surrounding his mother's death, Dad had been stoic and determined, always sure of himself.

Letting go of Val's foot, Nico extricated himself and stood, reaching carefully for the fragile olive branch. "Pizza sounds great, Dad."

EVEN THOUGH HE should have been exhausted after three-plus hours of pretending everything was normal while they ate pizza and ignored the giant pink elephant lumbering through the living room, Nico wasn't ready for bed.

His muscles twitched and his throwing arm was stiff. In his bare feet, he pulled on a ratty old Chicago T-shirt over his pajama bottoms and padded downstairs. From a skylight high above in the vaulted ceiling, moonlight glinted off the gold-framed photos lining the wide staircase.

Near the bottom of the stairs, Nico stopped, raising his fingers to trace the faded rectangle where only a hook remained. He was sure all the photos had been there earlier, and he was sure which one was gone.

Breathing shallowly, he tiptoed into the hall toward the sunken living room. His father sat in his favorite spot on the couch closest to the bay windows, his back to Nico. The TV was off for a change, and the only light came from the distant moon.

Nico hovered there on the top step, his heart too loud in his ears. He could creep back up, but since he'd shouted the truth earlier, he felt like a boat cut free of its rope, the current carrying him forward.

Nonna had left her knitting bag on the floor by the other couch, and Nico accidentally kicked it over as he sat. Catching a ball of wool before it unraveled too far, he turned it over in his hands. "I don't know how she still knits so fast." Her knuckles were swollen most days, but she seemed to ignore the arthritis completely. Mind over matter. Just like she was ignoring Nico's truth.

Dad didn't say anything. He was still in his slacks and button-up, and he cradled the missing picture in his hands. After several heartbeats, he turned it to Nico. "You and your mother, when we brought you home from the hospital."

Nico could just make out the outlines of the familiar photograph, an eight by ten blowup of his mother in the old green armchair, her dark curls tumbled around her face, her teeth white in a beaming smile, dimples cutting her cheeks. She held Nico in her arms, a little squishy-faced bundle, barely a person yet. The old longing flowed through him, the regret sharp-edged.

His father said, "This picture has hung there all these years."

He seemed to be waiting for Nico to respond, so Nico said, "I know."

"Why would you think we blamed you for any of it?"

Nico had been puzzling over that question since his talk with Val at the hotel, tugging at the loose thread in his mind. "I honestly don't know. Now that I think about it, the only thing I can remember is being outside the kitchen window." He remembered it now, the snatch of memory so distant he wasn't sure it was real.

But maybe it was, because he could imagine the cool grass between his bare toes in the sliver of shade by the house, the bricks rough on his arm as he bent to grab his Transformer where his cousin Jimmy had hurled it to see how strong Optimus Prime really was. The robot was in one piece, and Nico remembered the surge of relief as his fingers closed over the hard plastic.

"It was after Mom died. I heard you and someone talking. Aunt Rosie, maybe. She said, 'She was in bed for so long. After Nico, she was never well again.' And you didn't say anything. I kneeled in the grass, dying to hear more because no one ever talked about Mom. But that was it. Nonna came in and you guys started talking about dinner or something. And I guess I thought, 'That explains it. I was the one who made her sick.' It made sense to me."

"Christ," Dad muttered. "That's not what Rosie meant."

"I know. But I didn't know it then. Later, I asked Jimmy why Mom had been in bed for so long, and he said something about how I was poison. I know he didn't mean it—it was just a dumb insult he tossed out. But I thought it was true. And later, I couldn't remember not feeling that way, like I was responsible for Mom dying. It was just something I knew."

"You should have told me." Dad's voice was gruff, and he ran his fingers over the glass in the frame, staring down at the picture. "When we lost her... It was too hard." He reached to the table beside him, but the bowl of sunflower seeds was empty. He curled his fingers into a fist. "I'm no good at this shit. And now with this queer stuff, I don't know. I don't get it. It doesn't make any sense. Why?"

"Why am I gay?" Nico squeezed the ball of wool, trying to breathe. "I was born this way, Dad."

Rolling his tongue over his teeth in his familiar way, he nodded. "Okay, so you were always like this. That's what they say, right? People are just...born different. Is that what they say?"

"Yes."

"Never really thought much about it. About how it happens. Didn't have anything to do with me or my family. Those freaks were other people. No one I knew."

Don't cry. Don't cry. Nico knew if he spoke he'd lose it, so he waited silently.

Dad said, "But you're my boy, and you're telling me you're one of those people."

He barely scraped the word out. "Yes."

"Fitz too, huh? Can't wrap my head around it. It's like you're suddenly from outer space. Like I don't know you at all."

Nico's throat closed, and he blinked desperately to banish the tears.

"But you're sitting right there, and of course I fucking know you. You're my kid. You're the best damn pitcher this league has seen in years. You're going to be better than your brother and I ever were. And I know I'm hard on you. It's because I want you to be the best."

Sucking in air, Nico whispered, "I try so hard to be perfect. To make you proud."

"No one's fucking perfect. And you're damn right you make me proud. I don't get this gay thing, and I can't pretend I'm gonna turn into some granola-crunching liberal loon." Breathing hard, Dad looked down at the frame he was still clutching. After a few moments, he said quietly, "You're my son, and I'll try to understand."

Nico sniffed, swallowing down the moisture in the back of his throat and nose. "Thank you."

"Your grandmother's going to want a drive to Mass every damn day now. She loves you, but what the church says goes. Maybe that hippie pope's changing things. I don't know. Just try not to…you know. Don't do gay things in front of her."

It hurt—of course it did—but Nico laughed softly. "I'll try to control myself."

"Alma's a good woman. Been good to us all these years. Worked her fingers to the bone even though we had money for housekeepers and shit. You know she was going to move back to Italy when your grandfather died? She and your mother didn't get along too well." He smiled fondly, his gaze distant. "Angela never liked being told what to do, and her mother sure liked telling. Angela's brothers and sisters were older, still in Italy with their families, so Alma said she was going to go back where she was wanted. Then Angela had to be in bed for months with you, and Alma moved in to help. They argued all the damn time, but they never held a grudge. Then Angela got sick, so her mother never left."

Nico rolled around the new information. "I don't think I've ever seen you and Nonna argue."

"Nope." He laughed, a deep rumble. "I never sassed my mother either. Or my father. My brothers did all the time. I was the smart one." He scoffed fondly. "Eh, you know your uncles. Not too bright. Never made it past Buffalo. Me, I couldn't wait to get out. Once I hit the minors, people thought it sounded glamorous, being from Niagara Falls." He barked out a laugh. "I said they clearly never went past the tourist traps, and even then it's better on the Canadian side." After few moments he abruptly asked, "So what's the right word?"

"Huh?"

"What am I supposed to call you? Is 'gay' allowed?"

Tucking his foot up under him, Nico unspooled a length of soft wool and rolled it back up. "Yeah. That's the right word. Some people like to call themselves queer, but you shouldn't."

He seemed to ponder this. "Okay. I'll stick to 'gay,' but tell me if it changes. Words are always changing." He laid the picture frame gently on the cushion beside him and stared out the window toward the shadowy branches of the oak towering over the winding driveway. "Wop. You don't hear that one much nowadays. Never even knew what it meant, but I used to get it every day at school. I remember once I was walking home, and there were some biddies sitting on a porch. Those little concrete pieces of shit with a couple of cheap folding chairs, you know?"

Nico had grown up in this huge house on the North Shore, so he didn't really, but he nodded.

"And these were old women and housewives, not kids. I must have been eight or nine. They shouted, 'Hey, wop! Go back to Italy!' as I walked by."

"Seriously?" It was tough to imagine his dad as a child, but Nico felt a swell of anger on behalf of that little boy.

"I was so goddamn confused. I thought, I've never been to Italy. I don't even know how to get there. How could I go back when I haven't gone in the first place?" He shook his head. "Sometimes people threw tomatoes at our house. When we got a color TV—first one on the block—the neighbors sneered that Pop was in the mafia. My dad was a butcher and they knew it. Bought his steaks because they were the best, but whispered behind his back."

"Wow." Nico had only been to Niagara Falls once as a kid to visit the dozens of relatives he barely knew. But at that point, Dad had given his siblings more than enough money for them to live in nice suburban houses.

"Junior year of high school, I dated a gal called Samantha.

Went over to her house for dinner once. Afterward, her father offered me an Italian liqueur. Just Frangelico or some shit. He was explaining what it was, and I said I'd had it before. Then it came out that I was Italian. Samantha had told them my last name was Andrews, so this was news to them. Her father stood there holding that bottle of Frangelico like he wanted to throw it across the room. Turns out his brother was killed in Italy during the war. He hated Italians."

"Why were they drinking Frangelico if they hated Italians so much?" No one had ever said a thing to Nico about his Italian heritage, and his mind boggled at the thought of houses being tomatoed because of it.

Dad laughed. "Good question. Who can resist hazelnut, right? Anyway, we sat there sipping from our little glasses, Samantha's dad not breathing a word, her mom smiling too much, complimenting me on not having an accent."

"But you were *born* here."

He shrugged. "I was still way too Italian for them. 'Go back where you came from!' people would shout. And of course we were too American for the Italians in the neighborhood. We only spoke English at home, and my dad read three different newspapers every day. He was determined to lose his accent."

"Wow. I've never heard this stuff before."

"Eh." Dad waved his hand dismissively. "No point in rehashing all that business. But I guess this stuff with you has me remembering." He stared out the window quietly for a few moments. "Dad took me and my brothers to our first baseball game when I was nine. Just single-A ball, but to me it was the big leagues. The slogan painted on the wood fence said: *America's Pastime*. Big crowd in the stands—or it seemed big to me."

His father went quiet. Nico waited in the shadows, the distant ticking of the clock in the hall counting his heartbeats.

Finally his dad went on. "They cheered and clapped so loud

when David Parker—I still remember his name—when David Parker hit a three-run homer. Everyone went crazy. We were all on our feet, and I stood on the bleacher so I could see Parker round the bases. That's when I thought, 'I want to play baseball. I want them to cheer for *me*. I want to be a real American.' The best fucking American they ever saw."

In the stillness of the night, the pale moonlight ghosting over his father's weathered face, Nico couldn't look away. He'd never seen his father more…real. More human. He wanted to say something profound, but nothing came.

Dad said, "You know, all those years in the majors, I never cared about color or religion or where a guy was from. If he could get his bat on the ball, the ball in his glove, and his feet around the bases, I was proud to have him on my team. Proud to call him brother. But fa—gay guys? Nah, I didn't want any of them around."

The lump in Nico's throat was too big to swallow, the pain from years of denial and hiding rising, expanding, searching for a way out.

"What a fucking hypocrite I am, huh?" Dad asked. He sniffed loudly, and to Nico's astonishment, tears shone in his father's eyes. "Guess we all want someone to look down on. Someone to be better than. But here you are. And there's no one better than you. You hear me? Huh?"

Nico opened and closed his mouth mutely.

"You listening?" At Nico's nod, he said, "Good. That's settled. You better get some sleep. I'll drive you to the airport in the morning."

Finally, Nico was able to speak. "It's okay. I can take an Uber. You probably have stuff to do."

"I'm driving my kid to the airport. Now get to bed. That Boston lineup's looking good, but if you can neutralize the top of the order, I think you guys'll sweep the series. But not if you don't sleep."

The familiar tension returned, jamming Nico's neck. He rolled his shoulders restlessly. He wasn't starting for a few days, but he had to get the win—and he hadn't been doing his training at all. He'd stayed in bed for more than a day. Unacceptable. He knew he wouldn't win every start, but he always did his work.

Maybe it's okay to get upset and deal with it. Wallow in it a bit. Like Dad said himself, no one's perfect.

But I can still win Rookie of the Year. I can do it. I can make Dad proud.

Trying to shake off the competing thoughts ricocheting through his mind, he tucked Nonna's wool back into her knitting bag, the same one with penguins on the side she'd used for years. *Why penguins? Where did she even get this bag?*

Nico breathed deeply, trying to focus as he stood. He needed to say something to his dad. Something smart and just right. "I... Um..." He went with the only thing that spoke louder than the other noise crowding his mind. "I love you." No matter what, it was true.

Clearing his throat, Dad said, "Of course you do. I love you too. Now get your ass upstairs." He wouldn't look up, but Nico saw the tears overflowing.

He waited until he was back in that tiny twin bed to let his own fall.

CHAPTER SEVENTEEN

"H EY." NICO STEPPED back and let Jake into his condo. Kicking off his shoes and propping his bag in the corner, Jake smiled nervously. "I should see if there's another unit in this building. I can't live in that hotel forever. How was your trip from Chicago? Flight out of TO was delayed, of course. Waited in the lounge for three times longer than the flight itself. Had a rip-roaring headache too." *Why am I babbling?* He forced himself to stop.

"That sucks. My trip was fine." Nico had barely smiled, and he stood there with his hands at his sides, his fingers tapping like they did in the bullpen before a start. Jake wanted to kiss him, breathe into him, but did Nico want that? He honestly couldn't tell.

Maybe he'd asked Jake over to tell him *they* were over because it was a colossally bad idea to secretly date a teammate. Or maybe he was afraid to make the first move. Or maybe he wanted to see other guys, or—

Screw it.

His hand slipping behind Nico's head, Jake kissed him, long and sweet. He brushed their noses together. "Hi."

Nico swayed into him, his hands coming up around Jake's waist. "Hi." Then he took a shuddering breath and his face fell. "I outed you," he blurted.

Jake's heart skipped. "What?" He slid his hand down to Nico's neck, keeping his grip loose.

"To the rest of my family. I didn't mean to, but when I told them about me, it just came out." He grimaced. "Ugh, I didn't mean that as a pun or whatever."

"You told them?" The momentary surge of panic disappeared as Jake breathed deeply. "It's okay. I'm not mad." He kissed Nico again, a soft press of lips.

Even though it was Nico's condo, Jake guided him to the big leather sofa by the bank of rain-splattered windows, heavy gray clouds filling the sky without a hint of blue. They sat with their hips and shoulders pressed together, legs touching.

Jake stroked Nico's leg. "How did it go down?"

After a few deep breaths, Nico told him about his conversations with his family. When he was finished, Jake kissed him softly. "I'm proud of you. I know how hard that was."

"Was it for you? With your parents?"

"Not in hindsight. They were completely supportive. But before I told them? Terrifying. It kept me up for hours most nights. Finally I was so sleep-deprived I just blurted it out on the way to Dairy Queen. My mom said, 'Okay, dear.' Dad asked, 'Is there a lucky fella?' and then we got Crispy Crunch Blizzards."

Nico smiled. "I'm glad." He examined his blunt fingernails. "Val's fine, obviously, and Marco is too. Dad and Nonna... Honestly, I think Nonna's going to pretend I never said it. When I left this morning, she couldn't even look at me. But she hugged me, at least. Dad's... He's going to try. He's trying."

"Good. All that shit he says—I hate that you had to hear it. From anyone, but especially from him. I wish I'd known. Wish I could have done something." He was still awfully tempted to go down there and give Al Agresta a piece of his mind. And his fists. "I can only imagine what that was like."

"Yeah," Nico said quietly, head down. "It sucked. People

always say how he speaks his mind and 'calls it like he sees it.' Reporters loved him because he gave them great quotes after games. It was something he was proud of, that he didn't pull his punches."

"He definitely had a larger-than-life persona."

Nico sighed. "With the antigay stuff, I think the worst part is how casual it was. It wasn't like he was one of those religious nuts picketing people's funerals, all up in arms. He didn't even really care that much, you know? He'd say these things the same way he yells at an ump for needing glasses. Like it's nothing. He'd call people fags and queers, and the next second he was onto something else. It didn't even matter. It sure mattered to me."

Jake squeezed Nico's inner thigh—their sign. "I wish there was something I could say to fix it."

"You're here." Nico pressed their lips together. "That fixes a whole lot."

They kissed for a minute, simple caresses and tastes with no heat, cuddling in peaceful silence. A question formed in Jake's mind, and he weighed it before asking, "Now that your family knows, have you considered coming out publicly?"

Nico's eyes widened. "You want to? Man, I don't know. I never even thought I'd let myself act on it. Being gay." He fidgeted, tapping his bare foot against the metal leg of the coffee table. "I haven't thought about coming out to the whole world. I... That's scary." He shook his head hard. "I don't think I'm ready."

"That's all right." Jake brushed a curl off Nico's forehead. "I'm not saying I want to—I just think we should discuss it. I've never come out because I'd rather keep the focus on baseball. There would be a ton of attention being the first active gay players in the majors."

Nico exhaled shakily. "I get that. I was always terrified of what my dad would say. I guess more than other people, you know? In my head it was never an option to tell anyone." He seemed to ponder it, his brow creasing. "I think most of the guys would be okay with it? The fans too? When I was drafted, the league made me a watch a video on diversity and stuff. And when that kid in the minors came out last year, they seemed cool."

"Yeah, the league said all the right things. I still wonder if it was all roses behind the scenes, but…maybe it was. Maybe the times really have changed enough. Part of me thinks we should do it. No more hiding. Deal with the fallout and attention and move on. But it's more complicated than that. Being gay is one thing. Fucking your teammate's another."

Both Nico's feet tapped now. "Yeah, Skip would not like that."

"Nope. Honestly, I wouldn't blame him. Clubhouse dynamics can be complicated enough without bringing relationships into it."

"Totally. Let's see what happens. Telling my dad was enough for now, you know? I need some time to process and stuff."

"I agree." He rubbed Nico's inner thigh again, squeezing. "Did I mention how proud I am of you?"

Nico gave him a little smile. "Thanks. It's so weird that he knows. And that he didn't throw me out. I always thought that's how it would go if I ever slipped up. But he was way better than I expected."

"Amazing, isn't it? What goes on in other people's heads?"

"How's your head, by the way? I mean your actual head. Not your issues."

Jake chuckled. "It's good. Headache from this morning's gone. My issues are actually better too after that dinner in Toronto. I saw my old friend Brandon."

"Right, you mentioned him the other day. What's up there?"

Jake whistled. "So much. Where to start? He was my best friend, and boy did I fuck that up royally. I was in love with him, and I couldn't tell him." As Nico stiffened, Jake took his hand, threading their fingers together. "There's nothing between us. Never was, and there never will be. Brandon's straight and happily married."

Still rigid, Nico asked, "But you... You love him?"

"I did. I don't anymore. I care about him, but only as a friend." It was the truth. God, it felt *good.*

Nodding, Nico exhaled. "Okay. I mean, not that... We're..." He opened and closed his mouth. "What are we?"

Jake's pulse thrummed. "I really like you." *Jesus, could I try to sound more like a twelve-year-old?* "I want to be with you. I want to see where this goes. I hope you want that too."

"I do," Nico said quickly. He laughed awkwardly. "I never thought I'd have a boyfriend."

Relief coursing through him, Jake snorted. "Me either. I was dead set against it." He found himself grinning. "We're quite a pair. It's amazing we even fit in your condo with all the baggage we're lugging around. Jesus, I haven't talked as much about my feelings as I have this week in... I'm going to say ever."

"Ditto. Apparently the all-star break doubles as therapy. I really have to make that team next year." Nico slouched and dropped his head to the back of the couch, propping his feet on the glass table.

Laughter flowed through Jake, warm and welcome. He slid down too, his fingers still entwined with Nico's. "You'll make it."

"Maybe you will too. Would be cool if we both did next year."

"It would be." He hadn't really paid attention to the all-star game in years, even though he'd been a contender more than once.

Nico asked, "So is that what we are? Boyfriends, I mean. Like, you don't want to see other people?"

Jake steeled himself. "I don't, but if you do, we can discuss it." Yes. Like mature adults, though the bottom of his stomach dropped. Then he blurted, "But I'll want to punch anyone who even looks at you too long." He tried to laugh it off with a sad little *ha-ha*.

But Nico didn't look offended or angry. He positively beamed. "I don't want anyone else." He bit his lip. "You own my ass, remember?"

"Do I ever." Possessiveness surged, a primal instinct Jake honestly never knew he had. Dominating during sex was one thing. It had always been more about play for him, about fun. But with Nico, he didn't just want to dominate—he wanted to protect and cherish. Support and shield Nico from anything that might hurt him.

Maybe part of it was because Nico was so much younger, but whatever it was, Jake was in over his head. And instead of fighting it, he wanted to go deeper. He kissed Nico slowly, their tongues winding together until they had to breathe.

Nico murmured, "I really want to stay here all afternoon with you. But I should do some prep for tomorrow."

"Me too. We can play catch, hit the gym. Do some fielding drills. Nothing too heavy. It'll be good to get back out there." He realized he was looking forward to tomorrow's game—to the crowd and the dirt and the sweat—in a way he hadn't in too long.

"So we're together now, but we're not telling the team, right?" Nico asked.

"Right. I don't think we should tell anyone else for the time being. We have to keep it professional in the clubhouse and on the field."

"I agree. Besides, can you imagine all the 'who's the pitcher and who's the catcher' comments we'd have to hear?"

"Oh my God. I never even thought of that." Jake groaned. "That settles it. Definitely not telling anyone."

Nico toyed with Jake's fingers. "I was thinking we could drive out to this great burger place—Vera's. It's in a gourmet butcher's shop in the burbs. The double burger and sweet potato fries are amazing."

"Sold. You had me at meat, honestly."

"Then, if you're into it, we could come back here and save the world? I picked up one of the Pandemic expansion packs. The one with the virulent strain."

"Oh baby, I'm into it." Jake nipped at Nico's ear. "And I really want to fuck you, but we should wait until tomorrow night after the game." He let go of Nico's hand and rubbed up and down his thigh. "Is your ass still sore from the last time?"

"All better now," Nico breathed, his lips parting. "I really want to do it again. I'll do whatever you want. I'll do...everything."

Jake's cock twitched, heat sparking. Trust shone from Nico's eyes, and the protectiveness returned like a wave flowing to shore. Jake wanted to wrap him in his arms and keep him safe. Keep Nico *his*. All the years he'd loved Brandon, it had never been like this. Not even close.

Jake's heart kicked like a mule. Was he really in love now?

"Jake?" Nico frowned. "Did I say something wrong?"

"No, of course not." He refocused. "You want to do everything, huh?" He licked across Nico's lower lip. "I'll plan a little something for tomorrow night. Don't need you limping out to the mound. We can try something new. If you're game."

"Anything."

"Hmm. I have a few ideas."

Nico breathlessly asked, "What?"

He grinned. "That's for me to know and you to find out."

CHAPTER EIGHTEEN

WITH A BIT of mud lingering under his fingernails, Nico hummed as he and Jake walked back to the clubhouse via the tunnel from the storage area. Still in their workout gear, they'd listened to music and scuffed a few bags of pearls after team stretch and batting practice. Nico's stomach was calm, and he didn't have the sweats.

His little iPod dock tucked under his arm, Jake asked, "You liked that album?"

"Yeah. I love that one song especially—the opera-ish one?"

He grinned. "'Bohemian Rhapsody.' Everyone loves that song."

"It's really good. I didn't recognize most of the other ones, but I liked them." He couldn't resist teasing. "Not bad for old music."

"Hey, this is before my time too, I'll have you know."

"Sure, sure. I believe you."

Lightly taking the back of Nico's neck, Jake leaned in. "Watch yourself, or I'll have to punish you later."

Nico couldn't hide his smile. "Promises, promises."

"Hey, Ricky!" Jake smoothly dropped his hand and put a foot between them before Nico even realized Palmer had appeared at the tunnel bend.

"How's it hanging? Agresta, you ready to strike those fuckers out?" Palmer raised his hand for a high-five.

Ricky Palmer was relatively tiny at only five-seven, and fresh out of the minors, a streak of bright purple still dyed into his short afro. He'd lost a bet, but decided it was his lucky charm now. Nico slapped his palm. "You know it." He sounded confident, but a knot looped tightly in his gut.

Jake raised his arm straight above his head. "Up high."

Laughing, Ricky bent his knees and exploded up to slap Jake's hand. "Gotta love the plyometrics! Hey, Loyola and I've been tweaking my curveball."

As Ricky chattered away like usual, falling in step with them as they reached the clubhouse and headed for the locker room, Nico tuned him out, concentrating on his breathing, playing the Queen song over again in his head. He was ready for this. He was going to pitch a great game.

What if I don't? Their lineup's been hitting homers almost every night.

He thought about the scouting reports, the strengths and weaknesses of the Boston hitters reeling through his mind like a PowerPoint presentation on crack. Laughter and music and the beeping of video games filled the air in the locker room, and Nico automatically looked at the clock. Twelve minutes after six.

"Fitz, come look at Barcena's fastball," Alvarez called from where he and some other guys huddled over a tablet. Barcena was on the mound for Boston, and his fastball was a smoker. Nico was jealous of the pure power, although he could lack control.

Ricky was still talking a mile a minute, and Jake looked between him and the guys on the couch, and then at Nico. Nico waved him off. "See you in a bit." He made a beeline for his locker in the back corner, rolling his shoulders and stretching his neck one side and then the other.

He was fine. He was ready. He could do this. He didn't have to be perfect. His father still loved him the way he was.

Breathing deeply, he changed into his uniform, visualizing

Boston batters swinging at the air or caught looking, the ump fisting his hand to indicate the strike. Nico tied his cleats and pulled his red socks up to his knees over his pants, images of success running through his mind.

He looked at the clock.

His feet seemed to move of their own accord, and he glanced at Jake, still huddled with the other guys, dissecting the Boston pitcher's heater. Then Nico was in the bathroom, going straight to the last stall. He latched the door and lifted the seat.

Hands on his knees, he contracted his abs. It was 6:15, and he had to do it. His stomach didn't actually feel that bad, only a little acidy, but it was better this way. Better out than in. This way, he could let go. Release his anxiety and have a clean slate.

He kept quiet as he opened his throat and mouth, emptying his lunch into the toilet with a series of little splashes. Wiping his mouth with toilet paper, he breathed more easily, the sense of release and relief flowing through him. It was better than puking on the mound.

But would I really? I didn't feel that bad. I felt pretty good until I started looking at the clock.

Flushing and escaping the stall, Nico froze in his tracks. Jake leaned against the sinks, his arms crossed and jaw tight. He nodded to the bottle of water on the counter beside him.

Nico forced himself to move. Feeling Jake's gaze intensely, he unscrewed the bottle and took a gulp before spitting into the sink.

"Thanks. Sorry, I got anxious."

"Don't be sorry."

Nico washed his hands, lathering the soap until it released little bubbles. "You're not mad?"

Sighing, Jake said, "It's not about being mad, Nic. I'm worried. This isn't healthy. I'm sure your dad would agree if he knew you were still doing it after all this time."

"What, are you going to tell on me?" He scrubbed his hands,

getting under his blunt nails, squirming under Jake's scrutiny.

"Of course not."

"I just can't deal with humiliating myself like that again." Nico rinsed his hands, soap bubbles cascading down the drain.

"I know it must have been awful. The way your dad marched out there and hauled you up, I—"

Nico turned his head so fast his neck strained. "You watched it?" Even though he'd just emptied his stomach, bile surged up his throat. He gulped more water and spit into the sink, dropping his head, staring at himself in the mirror through his lashes.

"I'm sorry." Jake turned and rubbed the back of Nico's neck, but Nico wrenched away.

"It's fine. I'm fine. Forget it." *God,* please *forget that fucking video.* His skin crawled, memories of his teammates' laughter echoing, dirt beneath his hands and knees, vomit soaking into the mound, ruining it. Ruining everything.

Nico pumped more soap into his palm and scrubbed again. "I'm a weirdo, okay?" He tried to laugh it off, glancing around to make sure they were still alone. "I mean, I like getting spanked and stuff. I'm a freak."

Jake sharply said, "Hey. That's not true." He leaned in close, his breath warm on Nico's face. "You're not a weirdo or a freak or anything bad. You hear me? Not any more than I am for getting off on dominating. Lots of people do stuff that's way more intense. There's nothing wrong with it. We have fun together. We...connect. I'm not apologizing for it, and neither should you. As for this other thing, we've got a game to play. Now let's get out there and do it."

Nico nodded, rinsing off his hands and breathing more easily. "Let's do it." He chanced a smile, relieved to drop the subject. "You're sleeping over tonight after?"

"Yes. Don't think about that yet." Peeking over his shoulder, Jake slid his hand down Nico's thigh, squeezing their sign.

Voices preceded the bathroom door banging open by a few seconds, and they sprang apart, Nico busying himself drying his hands as Jake talked to the guys who'd just come in.

The minutes ticked by mercilessly, and soon he and Jake walked to the bullpen to warm up. Fans trickled into the stands, red shirts everywhere. Nico glanced at a white-haired lady who waved vigorously and turned around to point to her back, his name and number 33 emblazoned on her jersey. He smiled and waved, breathing in the warm breeze, the dome open to the summer evening.

An hour later, he wondered if the nice lady in the stands was cursing him now. Three runs had scored and there were two on at first and second with only one out in the top of the third. And he was down in the count, two balls to zero strikes. If he wasn't careful, he'd walk the bases loaded. Part of him wanted a timeout to talk to Jake, but no, he had to deal with this. He could do it.

Jake flashed the signs between his thighs, separating his thumb and finger to indicate a splitter. Nico nodded. His splitter hardly ever missed. He had this.

He wound up and unleashed the ball, his fingers wide. It sank perfectly and painted the corner of the plate while the batter didn't move. Nico waited for the ump to call the strike, but after a few interminable seconds, the man straightened up.

Ball three.

What the actual fuck?

The crowded booed the call, and Nico pressed his mouth into a line thin, choking down the swell of fury. That was a mother-fucking strike, and the ump's zone was bullshit tonight. It wasn't *fair*, and now Nico was going to walk this asshole and it would all fall apart and it would be ruined and—

He focused on Jake's hand pressing against his inner thigh. Puffing out his cheeks, imagining Jake was there with him on the mound, grounding him, Nico nodded. He read the signs as Jake's fingers flew.

At the end of the sequence, Jake pressed his thigh again, just for a second. The coaches would wonder about it, but Nico knew Jake would come up with some explanation.

Spreading his fingers on the ball, Nico threw another splitter. The batter swung and missed, cursing to himself as he kicked dirt off his cleats and regrouped. Then Jake called for a changeup on the inside, and Nico nodded.

Crack!

The ball rocketed straight to him, and Nico threw up his glove on instinct, the ball thwacking the leather. He pivoted and stepped toward second base, firing the ball straight over the base to Diego, who caught it perfectly, his foot on the base, and whipped the ball to first, dodging the hard slide of the runner.

The batter was fast, and the ball just beat him in time, the crowd screaming as the ump held up his fist for the out. Nico whooped and hopped off the mound, the inning over just like that. They'd gotten three runs off him, but it was okay. The Caps could make it up. It wasn't ruined yet.

Jake met him on the way to the dugout, giving him a light smack on the hip. "Good focus."

Nico nodded, trying not to smile too much since the game was far from over. But he imagined he could feel the imprint of Jake's hand, and knew no matter what, they'd get through it together.

NICO WASN'T SURE what exactly he'd said to the reporters after the game, but he'd tried to stay calm as he'd told them what they wanted to hear about a tough loss and a powerful Boston lineup, and that tomorrow was a new day and the team would focus on that.

He took the elevator up to his condo now, itching with restless energy. Skip had pulled him in the sixth with the Caps clinging to a one-run lead, and in the end Boston had squeaked it out with a homer in the ninth. Nico told himself it was just one of those things, and he'd done his best. The team had done their best.

But fuck, he still hated losing. There would be five days to think about it and regroup, but he wished he could pitch again tomorrow for a do-over. His arm didn't like the idea one bit, and he rolled his shoulder.

Sitting in the dugout watching the game slip away had sucked large, but he'd kept his frustration in check. Granted, he'd bitten the inside of his cheek almost raw, but he hadn't said a word. And he knew the guys really had tried their best, and that sometimes your best still meant you lost.

Still, the urge to break something now and vent the frustration was almost overwhelming. But it would be okay. Jake was coming, and Nico would be able to release the tension, like a blister being popped.

Inside his condo, he opened a beer, pacing by the kitchen island. Waiting.

It wasn't long before the concierge called up. Another minute before the tap at the door. Nico had forced himself to wait in the kitchen and not be hovering right there to answer the knock. He didn't want to seem too eager. But fuck, he was dying to get his hands on Jake—to get Jake's hands on him.

Jake filled the doorway, carrying a small leather duffel. He closed the door behind him and unlaced his sneakers, and Nico hovered now. They'd decided they were a couple, but he suddenly felt awkward and unsure.

"Did you eat?" Jake asked.

Nico couldn't quite swallow his groan. "*Yes.* I grabbed a sandwich in the lounge while you were still doing press. I'm fine."

"You'd be better if you didn't make yourself puke before

games."

"It's, like, barely more than once a week." He stalked back to the counter and chugged his beer. "It's gotten me this far, so whatever."

Jake stood watching him silently for an uncomfortably long time. "I'd argue that how far you've gotten has nothing to do with *that*. In fact, I'd argue it's in spite of it."

Nico tore off a strip from the label on the beer bottle. "Is that what we're going to do? Argue?"

Jake softened and came closer. "No. I just think you underestimate yourself. I *know* you do. Look at how you handled that jam tonight. I was so proud of you."

Another strip of paper came off with a sharp rip, Nico's gaze on the bottle. "You're not now?"

"That's not what I meant." Jake was right there then, easing the bottle from Nico's hands, squeezing them. "I'm sorry. I'm being a dick." He pulled Nico into his arms, and they held each other tightly. "I definitely didn't come here to argue or lecture you."

"Good. That's not what I thought you had in mind when you said you had something planned." He leaned his head on Jake's shoulder, nuzzling his neck and inhaling the minty soap from the clubhouse.

Chuckling, Jake murmured, "Not quite."

"Are you going to tell me?" He nipped at Jake's throat, then kissed and sucked the little mark. Jake's arms were powerful around him, and Nico loved that Jake was bigger. He'd seemed like a giant when Nico was a kid, and somehow still did now even though he only had a few inches on him.

Pulling back to look him seriously in the eye, Jake asked, "Did you always use condoms when you had sex?"

"Yes."

"Every time?"

"Always. No way I was going to get some girl pregnant."

"I've always been safe too, and I was tested when I joined the team, for the insurance and all that."

"Right. Uh-huh. I got tested recently too. Had a checkup." He quivered in anticipation. "Do you want to fuck without one?"

Jake cupped Nico's cheek, brushing his lips with his thumb. "Yes. But only if you feel comfortable. We're not seeing anyone else, and we'd have to trust each other."

"Yes. Absolutely. I want to." He rocked on his heels. "Now. Now would be good."

The smile that lit up Jake's face creased the skin by his blue eyes. "Okay. That's settled."

"Yep. Was that what you were talking about? What you had planned? Because I'm ready. Now."

"I did have something else in mind too." Humming, Jake walked Nico back into the wall by the fridge. He lifted Nico's arms over his head and held his wrists with one hand. "You ever been tied up?"

Oh sweet Mary, mother of Jesus. Nico hadn't been to church in years, and he thought of Nonna, guilt prickling. It sure as hell wasn't the time for it, and he hit the mental delete button.

Jake's grip loosened as his forehead creased, but he didn't release Nico's hands. "Where did you go? If you're not into it, it's okay. We don't have to."

"No, no. I'm into it. Totally into it." Nico flexed his wrists in Jake's grasp, already digging being restrained.

"You like the idea?"

His answer was little more than a trembling exhalation. "Yes."

Gripping Nico's wrists tighter in one hand, Jake slipped his other under Nico's T-shirt, tickling his belly. "I could do...anything. You'd be helpless."

Twitching, Nico's breath hitched. "Yes."

Jake barely brushed his skin, making him shudder. "You'd

have to let go. Do you want that?"

"Please." His throat was too thick, lust and some unnamed emotion building with each heartbeat.

"Go into the bedroom and get naked. Wait for me on the bed on your stomach." Jake stepped back, releasing Nico.

Heart about to explode, Nico scurried into the bedroom, flipping on the soft pot lights in the ceiling. The gray walls were decorated with some abstract art that he didn't love, and the queen bed had a burgundy duvet. He peeled it off and pulled down the sheets. When he'd stripped his clothes, he followed Jake's instructions and stretched out on his stomach, dick hard already, nervous excitement fluttering his limbs.

Jake had insisted he wasn't a weirdo, and Nico didn't care if he was. He wanted this. *Needed* it. Was so grateful he could have it—and with *Jake*. For a stupid second, Nico had to blink rapidly to stop from crying.

Footsteps, almost silent on the thick carpet, approached. The mattress dipped, and Nico turned his head to see Jake with one knee on the side of the bed, smiling down. Jake threaded his fingers through Nico's hair and lifted his head for a slow kiss.

He whispered, "Remember: armadillo," and Nico nodded.

Jake moved back out of sight. There was the sound of a zipper lowering, and Nico waited, breathing shallowly. The mattress dipped again, behind him this time, and Jake's big hands spread Nico's legs farther, kneeling between them, still in his jeans and Henley. Nico craned his neck, watching over his shoulder as Jake lifted velvety-looking red ropes out of the duffel bag beside him.

Lungs stuttering, Nico didn't move an inch.

"Sit up. Put your arms behind your back and grab your elbows. Tell me if it's too much on your arm."

Nico did as he was told, his legs folded under him. "It's fine."

"If that changes, tell me. A little discomfort is okay, but you pitched tonight. We have to be careful."

The mattress shifted, and Jake's breath wafted over Nico's neck as he loomed over him and circled the rope twice around Nico's chest. He tied what felt like knots in the middle of Nico's back, then looped the rope down over Nico's wrists, securing them, arms immobilized and folded behind him. Nico could let go of his elbows now, his arms staying in position.

"This is called a box tie. It should allow for good blood flow. How does it feel?" With powerful hands, Jake eased Nico onto his stomach, and Nico kicked out his legs wide.

The rope was taut around Nico's chest, and he arched his back, the weight of his wrists tugging on the binds, but not painfully. "I like it." And shit, he did. His dick got harder by the minute, and he circled his hips against the soft cotton sheets.

Jake's lips brushed his neck. "That's it." He left the bed, and Nico closed his eyes. He desperately wanted to ask what Jake would do next, but bit the inside of his already raw mouth. He didn't resist as Jake lifted his hips and propped his ass up with pillows under his groin.

"Bend your knees. That's it, all the way." Jake took hold of Nico's left ankle, the rope slipping around it. "This is a frog tie. I'm going to bind your lower legs to your thighs. One rope will go just above the ankles and around your upper thighs; the other below and above your knees. Your feet will still be free." He worked as he talked softly. "You won't be able to raise your head very far at all. Standing is obviously out of the question. You're not going anywhere."

Shivery anticipation bolted through Nico. Sure enough, his chest pressed into the mattress, his ass in the air. When Jake was done, Nico's legs were completely bent and lashed together, his heels by his butt. He was utterly exposed, his hands and arms trapped behind him and legs caught, and panic briefly cork-screwed through him with a whimper.

"Shh." Jake stroked Nico's ass. "You're okay. You know the

safe word. You know I'd never hurt you."

He did, and Nico breathed through it and relaxed. Jake's weight left the mattress, and Nico wanted to look, but he kept his eyes closed. Clothing rustled, and the water ran in the bathroom sink. Then nothing. And more nothing.

Nothing.

Fidgeting, he wanted to demand what was taking so long. He jumped when Jake finally touched him again, his hands running lightly over Nico's bonds.

"Look at you. I wish you could see how beautiful you are. You're being so good. Such a good little slut." His fingers teased Nico's crack. "Maybe next time I'll stick a plug in you. Or fuck you with a nice big dildo."

Nico moaned. "Anything."

"That's right. But tonight my cock is aching for your ass." He sucked loudly, then a wet finger circled Nico's hole.

Rubbing his rough cheek against the cotton, Nico could only beg, "Please. I need it."

"I know." He kissed Nico's cheeks, stubble scraping. "How does it feel to be tied like this? Knowing I could do anything?"

"I... I don't know."

Jake spread Nico's ass open, licking his hole. "What words come into your mind?"

"Um..." He shuddered. "Open. Exposed." Nico sucked in a gasp as Jake stabbed at his hole with his tongue. "Trust."

"That's it." Jake caressed Nico's ass. "You're doing so good."

"Free."

And he was—free and flying even though he couldn't move, could only take what Jake gave him.

When Jake stopped teasing and fucked him, pushing his thick, slick cock inside, Nico willed himself to relax. The sensation of skin on skin had his eyes rolling back as he gasped and cried out, filled with Jake's dick. Completely at his mercy. Why it was liberating, Nico had no idea, but he already wanted more. Needed it.

On his chest with his ass in the air and cheek pressed to the mattress, Jake's cock stretching him, Nico grunted softly, little whimpers and moans escaping, his arms locked behind him. Jake grasped Nico's hips with his powerful hands as he fucked him.

Nico's thighs began to cramp, but he breathed through it. He didn't have to strain or push or fight. He didn't have to meet anyone's expectations—or even his own. He didn't have to be perfect. He just had to *be*.

He listened to Jake's grunts, focusing on the sensation of Jake impaling him. Owning him. What he'd craved for so long was finally his, and there was nothing between them. He was filled to the brim, and nothing else existed but Jake's cock, and Jake's hand pulling Nico's hair now as he fucked him.

"Give it to me," Nico begged hoarsely. "Until it drips out."

Chanting urgent little nonsensical words, Jake thrust power-fully, tugging Nico's head up. Nico's back arched like a bow as Jake shot him full of cum, shuddering and emptying himself, moaning.

Nico was bereft when Jake pulled out, but he could feel semen dripping down his crack. Knowing it was inside him turned him on fiercely, his cock straining beneath him.

Jake untied Nico's legs and rolled him onto his back, arms still bound behind. Nico's aching legs splayed, his cock standing up, the leaking head a dark, reddish pink. He gasped as Jake, on his hands and knees, swallowed him to the root, sucking almost painfully hard.

All Nico could do was take it, heat rushing through his veins and exploding through his cock, choking Jake and coming on his face when he pulled off, spurts of white painting his dark stubble and dripping down his neck. Jake took it all, milking him until it was too much.

"No more," Nico whimpered.

JAKE GENTLY UNTIED his arms and rubbed Nico's limbs carefully, paying special attention to Nico's throwing arm. Absolutely boneless, Nico laid there, watching Jake inspect him with such concern. He whispered, "I'm good."

A smile playing on his lips, Jake kissed him. "You are. You're so good."

They were both sticky with semen, and Jake disappeared into the bathroom for a washcloth. When they were clean enough, he tugged the covers over them, holding Nico close. Nico knew morning had to come, but he almost hoped it wouldn't.

CHAPTER NINETEEN

"**H**EY, MAN." JAKE answered the Skype call on his tablet, propping it on its stand on the little table in his suite as he finished a protein shake with a loud slurp through the straw. In his boxers, he scratched his bare chest and glanced toward the bathroom.

The door stood ajar, the shower running full blast, Nico humming a tuneless song. Jake had needed to pick up some clothes after that night's game, and they hadn't possessed the will power to wait until they made it to Nico's condo. After fucking against the wall and then the floor, they'd collapsed and finally made it to bed.

Ron laughed, sitting in front of his desktop computer, the familiar bookshelves behind him. "Breakfast of champions, huh?"

"Indeed. What are you doing up this early? It's barely six o'clock over there."

"On deadline for a profile on a hot football prospect. No rest for the weary, et cetera. Speaking of which, you'll be back here next week, right? You guys are looking great heading into September. For any team, but especially such a new one. The pennant race in your division is heating up something fierce. I really think you've got a shot at the wild card at least."

Jake couldn't help but grin. "I think we do too. I forgot what this felt like."

"I can tell. You look giddy as a schoolgirl."

After giving Ron the finger, Jake asked, "How are things? I can't believe it's been months."

"Can't complain. I've had a few tryouts with some guys to scratch my itch, but none of them enjoy reality shows. Have you been watching the new *Top Chef*?"

"Sadly, no. As you may or may not be able to see, I'm still living in a hotel room, so no watching my shows. It's been busy. It'll be great to get back home to my place."

"I bet. So I was thinking we could get together after one of your games next week?"

"Oh, right. I..." Shit. He didn't want to hurt Ron's feelings, but no. As much fun as they'd had in the past, Jake wasn't even a little tempted. To even consider it felt like a betrayal of Nico.

Laughing awkwardly, Ron held up his hands. "Hey, if you're not into it anymore, no problem."

"No, it's not that. I mean, it is, but it isn't."

"I'm following." Ron raised a thick eyebrow. "Except not at all."

"It's just that I'm kind of..." He realized he hadn't talked to anyone about Nico, and the words got all tangled on his tongue.

"Wait—are you seeing someone?"

"Yeah. I am. It's not public or anything, obviously."

"Well, well, well." Ron grinned, the wrinkles around his eyes fanning deeper. "Someone found a chink in the armor."

"Yeah, it's... It's good." Jake's cheeks flushed hot. "So anyway—"

"No, no, no. You're not off the hook yet. Who is it? Anyone I would know?" His eyes widened. "It is, isn't it? You look like the kid with his hand in the cookie jar. Who's the chocolate chip?"

Jake knew he shouldn't tell, but the urge to talk to a friend about Nico won out. He knew he could trust Ron, but still said, "You can't tell anyone. I mean it."

"Cross my heart." Ron's expression became serious. "Really, you know I wouldn't."

Jake rubbed his bare feet on the carpet, fisting his toes, and played with the straw in his empty glass. "It's Nico Agresta."

Ron's jaw dropped. "Holy shitballs. You and the rookie? Damn, Fitz. Good for you. Mmm, I bet he's fun to play with, huh?"

Shifting uncomfortably, Jake shrugged. "Anyway, like I said—"

"Whoa, whoa." Ron leaned in closer to the camera. "Is this more than sex? You falling for the kid?"

"Maybe." Jake huffed out a laugh. "Yes." It was good to say it out loud, and he couldn't hide his smile. "I never expected it."

"Well, you've been doing outstanding work with him on the field. His record's what, seventeen and five this season?"

"Only four losses, actually." Jake couldn't help but glow with pride. "ERA's 2.91. His ball control is amazing."

Ron rolled his tongue in his cheek. "Please note my restraint in not making a sexual comment here. But yeah, he's impressive. Seems intense. His old man never shut up, and his brother's a goofball. What's Nico like?" ·

"He's…" Jake could still hear the water running. "He's smart and hardworking. Stresses himself out. Perfectionist. But we're working on it."

"I bet you are. He's pretty hot too, yes? You're exclusive?"

"We are. We're seeing where it goes, you know?"

"Good for you. I'd love to meet him. We could do dinner with Steve when you guys are here? You know Steve won't tell a soul, and it would be great to get together. If that won't be too weird."

"That would be awesome. I'll talk to Nico about it. Make sure it won't freak him out too much. He can be a little skittish."

"Understandable."

"Hey, he's into games too." Jake shook his head with a laugh.

"I mean board games."

Ron chortled. "Sure you do."

"We're going to start Pandemic Legacy in the off-season. I bought Dead of Winter too. Maybe we can all play when we're in San Fran."

"Absolutely. You guys come over so Steve can try the new recipes from America's Test Kitchen that have been burning a hole in his tablet." Ron took a sip from a mug declaring *World's Okayest Brother* and waggled his eyebrows. "So what's it like being on the field with your secret lover?"

Jake laughed. "It's good. A little stressful, making sure we don't give ourselves away. Of course it's baseball, so slapping each other on the ass is expected."

"Lucky for you! Okay, I'd better finish this piece. See you soon, Fitz. My ass misses you, but I'm really glad it's working out in Ottawa."

"Thanks, man." Jake realized the water was off, and when he turned, Nico was standing in the bathroom doorway, a towel slung around his lean hips. "Look, I've gotta go."

Ron said, "Wait, is he there? Hi, Nico!"

Tentatively, Nico approached the table, his gaze darting between the tablet and Jake. He stopped by Jake's shoulder. "Um, hey."

Jake motioned at the screen. "Nic, this is my friend Ron from San Francisco. We were just talking about getting together for dinner and games with him and his husband when we're in town."

"Oh. Cool." He didn't crack a smile.

Ron grinned. "I look forward to meeting you. Big fan of your work." He winked. "And Jake's. You're in good hands."

Jake groaned internally but put on a smile. "Okay, we'll see you soon." He closed the window and reached his hand around Nico's damp waist, but Nico sidestepped.

"What did he mean by that?" Nico asked quietly. Too quietly.

"Hmm? Oh, ignore Ron. Since we're up early, I was thinking—"

"Why does his ass miss you?" Nico folded his arms, droplets of water flying. "That's what he said. I heard him."

Jake sighed and tried to laugh. This shouldn't have been a big deal. Why was he letting it be one? Keeping his tone casual, he said, "We used to have sex."

"You—" Nico looked at the tablet's home screen, then back at Jake. "He was your boyfriend?"

"No. We used to have sex. We're just friends and have never been more."

"Friends who fuck." Nico clenched his jaw. "How is that not 'more'?"

"We had an arrangement. Ron's happily married, but he and Steve have an open relationship. Steve isn't as into sex, and he isn't into Ron's kinks. So we hooked up when I was in town, and it was never more than having fun."

"His kinks," Nico echoed, his voice too low. "Did you—the things *we* do? With him?"

"Some of them. Nic, it's not the same. At all."

"Did you—" He sucked in a breath, barely whispering. "Did you tie him up? Spank him?"

"I have, yes." Jake told himself to be calm and patient, but irritation scratched with sharp nails. "Did you think I just googled how to tie those knots? Yes, I've had practice. I'm a grown man."

Nico jerked. "And I'm not? Because I'd never been with a guy before?"

"*No.* Don't put words in my mouth."

"Gee, sorry I'm new at this. I'm sure *Ron* will be happy to step in. If you want to fuck him again, just say so."

Jake gripped his empty glass, tempted to hurl it across the room like he was throwing out a runner at second. "Jesus Christ, stop being ridiculous. Ron is a friend. Nothing more. And if I wanted to fuck him, I would."

"Who's stopping you?" Nico's face went red as he jerked off his towel and stalked over to the tangle of his clothes on the floor. "If you want to see other people after all, go for it. Whatever." He yanked on his jeans without bothering with briefs.

"You're being ridiculous. There's no reason to be jealous."

"I'm not jealous!" Nico shouted. "I just thought we had an agreement that we weren't going to see other people."

Jake shoved back his chair. "We do. We're not!"

"What do you call that?" Nico jabbed through the air in the tablet's direction.

"We were talking! About dinner plans with you and his husband!"

Nico's shout was only slightly muffled as he pulled a long-sleeved Caps shirt over his head, punching his arms through the sleeves. "Is his ass on the menu?"

"For fuck's sake." Jake dug his nails into his fists.

Jamming his bare feet into sneakers, Nico snapped, "It's fine. It's cool. We're on the same page now. I get it. Later."

"Nic—"

Nico slammed out, and Jake growled in frustration. "That went well," he said to the empty room.

"THE ONE THING we've heard over and over from the pitching staff since you joined the team is how instrumental you've been. The starting rotation is having a great year, and they credit your game-calling and pitch-framing, and your overall presence behind the plate. What do you say to that?"

Jake shifted uncomfortably, kicking at the turf with his cleat, smiling at the reporter who was starting her series of interviews with him for a profile piece for a national Canadian magazine.

"Well, we're all competitors, and we all want to win. I'm doing my job, but they're the ones throwing the balls. I'm guiding them, but they have to execute."

"Agresta's having a stellar debut season. Might even grab Rookie of the Year if he keeps it up as we look toward the pennant race. Before you joined the team, he was pitching well, but seemed easily flustered and at times combative. He's really calmed down, and many credit that to your influence."

Jake's pulse hopped, and he worked to keep his tone steady. *He's not so calm right now.* "He's getting his fastball consistently down in the zone, and when he throws ninety-five with late movement, he's able to get weak contact. The thing with baseball is, when you've got top hitters at the plate who can get the bat on great pitches, sometimes you get bloopers and that kind of stuff. That can be really frustrating, and it's challenging to control your emotions. Agresta's young and he's working on not letting those situations get the best of him."

Nico had been holed up in the gym, and when Jake had gone for a light jog on the treadmill, Nico had refused to even glance his way. Jake was awfully tempted to haul him into a closet and spank him until he saw reason, but had restrained himself thus far. Barely.

The reporter said, "This is a crucial series against Boston before you briefly head to the west coast. Boston and Baltimore have been duking it out for the division lead all season, but the Caps are right there with them. What do you think will be the key to hanging in with the top teams as the pennant race heats up?"

"We just have to play our game and not worry about what everyone else is doing. From the first pitch to the last in every inning, we have to be focused and positive."

"This is quite a young team, both the players and the franchise. Do you feel added pressure as one of the veterans?"

"You know, we're grinding through this together down the

stretch, and it's about the team, not individuals. We all have our roles to play."

"You've actually never been to the postseason in your career. How does it feel to be playing for a contending team again?"

He grinned. "Michelle, it feels pretty darn great."

She moved on to questions about growing up playing baseball in a hockey town—hockey country, really—and Jake rattled off his standard answers. Game time was nearing, and the crowd was filing in, the dome open to a blue sky, the parliament buildings rising in the distance.

Excitement rippled through him despite the fight with Nico. The pennant race was on, and they really could win. They could really do it for the city and the fans and the country. And themselves, of course.

There was no time now, but he'd speak to Nico after the game. Jake had to admit that if he'd heard Nico laughing and chatting with a former lover in such a friendly way, he'd have been jealous too. They'd talk it out once Nico had calmed down. Fuck it out too.

Smiling to himself, Jake imagined how red Nico's ass would become when he got him to submit. Could definitely turn the morning's lemons into lemonade.

He jogged back to the locker room to strap on his pads and collect that day's starter, Ricky Palmer. Palmer jabbered all the way to the bullpen as he always did, and Jake smiled and nodded and let him talk out his nerves.

In the bullpen, Jake tossed the ball to him casually, warming him up slowly, taking the pace down a notch. Sure enough, Ricky's breathing calmed, and he got into the rhythm.

Jake stood from his crouch for the anthems, ignoring the sharp twinge in his lower back and his creaking knees. His aches and pains didn't matter. The stupid fight with Nico didn't matter.

It was game time.

FULL COUNT.

The crowd stomped and shifted, willing Palmer to hurl that last strike. There were runners on, so Jake adjusted his crouch to shield the coded signs he flashed. Ricky shook his head. Okay, he didn't want to throw a sinker. Jake went to his backup for the lefty batter, a slider. Ricky nodded.

Hamilton waved his bat over his shoulder, shifting his weight. Some batters twitched at the plate, and others were almost like statues waiting for the ball. Hamilton had been on a majorly hot streak all month, and it was intimidating, especially with no outs and a runner not only on second, but Ephram Wrigley ninety feet away at third, itching to score.

Jake tucked his hand behind his right leg to protect it as best he could, his middle finger stinging from a foul tip in the second inning. He'd shaken it off and assured the trainer he was fine. He held out his glove with his left hand as Ricky wound up. The ball rocketed from the mound and—

Crack!

It was a chopper to third, bouncing to Crowe, who fired it right back to Jake. Jake held out his glove, bracing with his legs apart, close to the plate but not blocking it yet, adrenaline spiking as the ball hit his glove and—

His knee blew out, the blunt force of Wrigley's cleat and the twist of gravity combining as the bone crunched and ligament tore like flayed, useless rubber on a tire rim shooting sparks on the asphalt. His pads were no match for the impact, the white-hot agony seismic as he flipped and rolled, crashing to the dirt on his stomach, mask flying off.

A scream tore from his throat, a kaleidoscope of color filling his vision before inky tendrils of black smothered everything.

Distantly, he heard voices shouting, felt hands touching him gingerly, and then one familiar voice in his ear. "You're okay. I'm here."

Nic. He must have flown out of the dugout. Jake wanted to cry, and as someone eased him onto his back, he realized he was, wetness breaking free from his tightly closed eyes, streaming down his cheeks uncontrollably. He thrashed and kicked with his right leg, his left ruined. His glove was somehow still on his hand, and he pounded the dirt with his other.

"Breathe," Nico ordered, stilling Jake's arm and taking his hand. "Come on."

Bile choking him, Jake managed to open his eyes, his vision blurred for a frightening few seconds before the world came into focus. The world being Nico hovering over him, his brown eyes wide, the trainer on Jake's other side, his mouth moving. But Jake couldn't make out the words, and he looked to Nico.

"Can you hear us?" Nico asked. He dug his fingers into the back of Jake's hand. "Jake?"

"Uh-huh." It didn't sound like his own voice, but Jake supposed it was. The trainer was asking him questions about what he felt. Beyond, teammates hovered with pinched faces—Diego, Alvarez, Palmer, Crowe, and some other guys crowded in behind. The Boston trainer had come out too, his mouth pressed into a grim line.

In the terrible silence, an oppressive stillness flattened the stadium, thirty-five thousand people holding their breath.

His chest pad strangled him, and Jake opened his mouth, gasping. Nico said something he couldn't understand, and Jake needed to get back in control, but he was frozen. A bolt of panic exploded, and he shook his arms and legs, reassuring himself that he could. The pain blasting from his knee was a punch to the throat.

Fuck, everyone was watching. In the stadium and on TV. He needed to get up. He needed to take charge. But all he could do was lay there, powerless and trembling, what was left of his knee shrieking, gnawing on his lip so he didn't scream as well.

Then the EMTs were there with the team doctor, more faces hovering over him, more voices blending into an indistinguishable haze. The only thing sharp and focused was the agony in his knee and Nico's eyes, Nico's fingers gripping him, holding him together.

Jake realized everyone could see Nico holding his hand, but considering how much pain he was in, no one would likely think anything of it. Even if they did, Jake wasn't letting go.

Something caught Nico's attention, and he twisted his neck, snarling behind him. "Step the fuck back, you cowardly piece of shit."

It had to be Wrigley. As someone removed Jake's glove, he asked, "Is he out? Did I hold on to the ball long enough?"

"Don't worry about that, son." Skip's voice, and the familiar manic chomping of gum as he leaned closer.

"But that's the go-ahead run." Jake's throat was dry, and his voice still sounded wrong. Panic clawed, and he clung to Nico's hand. He hadn't cared for so long, and now it felt more important than anything, even the soul-shredding agony in his knee. They'd worked so hard and come so far—for what?

"We've got it covered," Skip assured him. He glanced at Nico. "Agresta, ride with Jake in the ambulance and we'll see you there after the game."

It was only when they hoisted Jake onto the stretcher that Nico had to let go of his hand. Jake closed his eyes while he was strapped on. He couldn't bear to look as he was wheeled off the field before the stunned crowd, who applauded their support.

In the tunnel, voices told him to hang in there. Jake felt like he was on the ceiling, watching as they approached the loading dock where an ambulance waited. He saw Nico beside him in his uniform, the white still untouched by dirt since Nico had been riding the bench and wouldn't pitch again for another couple days.

I won't be able to catch him.

Panic and grief flapped through Jake, and he wanted to scream. He'd ruined everything. He was abandoning Nico and the team. He squeezed his eyes shut, blocking out the scene and praying to wake up, praying the throbbing agony in his knee was nothing more than a nightmare.

When he opened his eyes again, he'd returned to his broken body, the pain overwhelming but for a strong warmth around his hand. He stared at the ambulance roof, then at the back of the EMT, who'd turned to root through a drawer as the doors were closed. Nico was on Jake's other side, squeezing his fingers, their palms connected.

"It's okay," Nico croaked. "You're okay." He leaned over and pressed their lips together for the space of a heartbeat. Sitting straight, he tried to smile. "I'm here. I've got you."

Sirens wailing, the ambulance sped away from the stadium. Jake almost floated to the ceiling again, but the grip of Nico's hand and the lingering sweetness of his kiss grounded him.

IT'S OVER.

The grief churned like white water, unrelenting, as Jake endured an x-ray and pokes and prods, painkillers dulling the torment enough that he could breathe. Nurses and doctors spoke calmly, none of them saying what Jake already knew.

It was over.

At the very least, his ACL had blown, that much he knew for sure. At his age, this wasn't an injury that would land him on the fifteen-day disabled list. This was the end.

He was in the ER behind a curtain, the left leg of his uniform pants sliced off, his pads removed. He kept his eyes on the ceiling tiles, unwilling to look at the ruin of his knee. Turning his head left and right, he searched for Nico, who had been there with him until the tests but then disappeared. Jake knew he should be strong, but he longed to hold Nico's hand again.

"Mr. Fitzgerald? Jake?"

He blinked, trying to focus on the middle-aged woman leaning over him, her dark hair swaying in a short bob. "I'm Jake," he replied stupidly.

She smiled fleetingly, without teeth. "I'm Dr. Choudhury. We need to do surgery on your knee to properly assess the damage and repair it."

A commotion rumbled up from nearby, voices raised, a woman saying, "Sir, I told you that you need to stay in the waiting room."

"No!" Nico nearly shouted. "I need to see Jake. Get out of my way!"

Dr. Choudhury grimaced. "Your teammate is very persistent." She yanked back the curtain. "Sir, lower your voice and please leave. You'll have to wait until after surgery."

"No, I want to see him," Jake rasped. Please. And some water?"

Nico pushed into the space, exhaling sharply. "They wouldn't tell me anything."

"Of course we won't," Dr. Choudhury admonished. "You aren't family, and we still need to discuss treatment with Mr. Fitzgerald."

Jake sucked the ice chip a nurse held to his dry lips and said, "He can hear. I want him to stay."

The doctor nodded. "All right. Well, the damage appears extensive, Jake. I think you know that the ligament has been severely torn. We don't need an MRI to confirm since the x-ray shows a small piece of bone has been pulled off the lateral tibial plateau at the top of your shin bone, indicating the ACL has been torn. Chips of your kneecap were also broken off by the impact and need to be removed. Given your age and profession, I suspect the meniscus—cartilage—is likely weak. We'll repair what we can tonight and assess."

"How long will it take to for him to recover?" Nico asked.

She glanced at Jake. "We can't say right now. We have to get in there and see what we're working with. It might require more than one surgery. I think recovery will be at least six months, if not longer." She hesitated, and Jake knew exactly what she was thinking. "Whether or not you can play baseball again will have to be assessed down the road. Let's take it one step at a time, okay?"

Jake nodded because he couldn't speak. His throat tightened as he looked at Nico's stricken expression, but he had to be strong. Guilt sliced through him jaggedly to think he was abandoning Nico on the field.

This is karma. This is what you get for checking out all those years.

Nico looked between Jake and the doctor, then nodded.

"We're going to take you upstairs now, Jake." Dr. Choudhury gave his arm a pat and strode out.

You wanted to retire early. This is what you get for not appreciating everything you had.

"I—I'll be here when you wake up," Nico said, his voice steady after a shaky start. "Everything'll be okay." He glanced at the nurse, then gave Jake's forearm a squeeze, his palm damp and warm.

Jake was supposed to take care of Nico, not the other way around. "I'm sorry."

Nico's brow furrowed. "Why? I'm the one who's sorry. This morning, I—" He looked at the nurse again, but then Jake was being wheeled away, and Nico wasn't allowed to follow.

Nico called out, "I'll be here!" and Jake could only lay there and go where they took him. Powerless to fix it. *Should have gotten out of the way! Must have been in Wrigley's path. I was sloppy.* He ached to turn back time and make the play again. To do something—*anything*—differently.

He couldn't even sit up by himself. There was nothing he could do. Upstairs, another nurse cut through the rest of Jake's uniform with precise, economical movements.

Snip, snip, snip.

She tossed the red and white fabric aside like garbage. Motionless, Jake wanted to weep, but knew it was what he deserved.

He'd played his last game and he'd lost.

CHAPTER TWENTY

J AKE PATTED HIS stomach. "Thanks. I needed that. This food is…well, it's not Vera's burgers. At least yesterday I was too groggy to eat much."

Sitting in the too-hard guest chair beside Jake's bed, Nico toyed with a fry in a splotch of ketchup on the burger wrapper spread on his lap. "Yeah, you were pretty out of it."

Jake had slept for hours and hours after surgery, but Nico had still resented going to the ballpark for another game. He'd skipped team stretch and BP, barely making it for the anthems. But Skip had only squeezed Nico's shoulder and asked for a status update on Jake.

Despite all the rest, Jake's face was too pale, dark circles under his eyes, his scruff growing. The pain from his knee tightened his jaw every time he moved. Nico hated that there was nothing he could do to fix it.

"Poor nurses had to deal with my mom calling every five minutes for updates, I'm sure," Jake said. "I told her not to cut her vacation in Halifax short, but of course she's ignoring me."

"That's how a mom should be. Nonna totally ignores us if she thinks she knows best." The fondness and love for her now swirled with apprehension. He tried to laugh it off. "Now I guess she might ignore me altogether."

"Give it time. She'll come around."

"Yeah, maybe." Nico pushed the thoughts away, only able to deal with so much crap at once. "Sorry I couldn't be here much yesterday."

"You had to work. Another day, another game, no matter who got their knee busted the night before. That's baseball. Besides, I was out of it, like you said." He shifted, going rigid and gritting his teeth. "I hate hospitals—not that anyone loves them. ACL surgery doesn't usually even require an overnight."

"But you didn't just tear your ACL. It was all pretty messed up."

Jake sighed. "Yeah, it was a lot more complicated than a straight tear. At least I'm getting out tomorrow." He plucked at the blue hospital gown, grimacing.

And where will you go? Nico kept his gaze on anything but Jake's leg wrapped in bandages and a hard brace that extended all the way to the top of his thigh and down to midshin.

It was a day off for the team, and guys had been streaming in and out to visit. It'd gotten too crowded, and Nico had felt too weird being there without being able to really *be* there. He wanted to sit by Jake's side the way a boyfriend or partner or whatever they wanted to call it would.

And what were they after that dumb fight? At least they were alone again for the moment. Nico spread more ketchup, tapping his foot restlessly. "I was a moron," he blurted. "About your friend on Skype."

Jake actually smiled. "Forget about it. I have." He waved a hand at his knee. "Perspective."

"You were right—I was totally jealous. Just for the record." The memory of the tantrum he'd thrown had him squirming on the hard chair. "I hated the thought of you with anyone else."

The smile became a grin on Jake's face. "I know. There's absolutely nothing to be jealous of. And I despise the thought of anyone else touching you. For the record."

The little rush of pleasure didn't last long. Nico smiled back, but worry gnawed. Jake was taking it all so well. Too well. Why wasn't he freaking out? His career was over, barring some kind of miracle. It was done, and there was nothing that could change it.

The thought of never being able to play again sent shivers down Nico's spine, and he popped his last fry in his mouth, trying to banish the clammy panic. He shoved their garbage into the paper bag and sat back, trying to smile. "Whew."

"That filled a corner, as my mom would say?"

"Definitely."

Jake hesitated before asking, "And when you're full like this, you don't feel the need to throw up?"

Nico sighed. "*No.* I told you, I'm not bulimic or whatever. It's just nerves."

"And a ritual?"

"What? No." Fighting the urge to get up and pace, Nico glanced to make sure no one was hovering around the open doorway. "That would be stupid."

"Mmm. So what would happen if you couldn't puke before a game? Say the bathroom was out of service, there was no time, and you had to get on the field."

Anxiety flapped through him, but Nico tried to remain nonchalant. "I don't know. Probably toss my cookies all over the mound. Grounds crew would love that. I'd end up on YouTube in HD this time, not just some blurry handheld video from high school. Dad would love it. There'd be a bunch of internet memes. It would suck. And it would be beyond embarrassing, going back out there once they'd cleaned up. I'd lose the game for sure."

"Why?"

"What do you mean? I just told you."

"You could puke on the field and still win the game. You puke in the bathroom before games and win. Why would you lose for sure?"

Crossing his arms, Nico swallowed back a huff. "I just *would.*"

"Because you didn't do the ritual the right way?"

"I don't know! Maybe." He lowered his voice, tapping his foot vigorously on the linoleum, the rubber sole of his sneaker bouncing. "It's just the way it is. I feel sick, and I puke, and then it's okay."

"But you don't always win. Even when you follow the ritual."

"Would you stop calling it that?" Nico snapped.

"I'm sorry. I'm not trying to be an asshole."

"Still doing a pretty good job," Nico grumbled. He sighed. "Sorry. I know you're not. I'm just…" Completely defensive? On edge? Not cool with being called on his bullshit? "I really do feel sick before starts. Even when we scuffed balls and I tried to relax. As soon as it's fifty, forty-five minutes before the first pitch, my stomach rebels."

"Your stomach or your mind? Maybe it's because you're following the same pattern. You could go to the bullpen earlier. Mix things up. See what happens? Don't let the ritual control you."

"But—" He clenched his jaw at the use of that word again. "You don't get it, okay?"

"Okay. Hey, I'm sorry."

Jake reached out and smoothed his hand over Nico's leg, fingers curving over his inner thigh. Their sign. One Nico would never see on the field again. The thought brought a pang of grief like a bell, and he swallowed thickly. There was no sense in being upset about it. Jake wasn't, so why should he be?

The warm weight of Jake's hand through Nico's jeans should have soothed, but frustration churned his guts. Maybe he'd puke now after all. He blurted, "I know you don't get it and you think I'm crazy. But I genuinely feel sick before starts. I'm not forcing it. And I don't get you!"

His hand still pressing on Nico's thigh, Jake frowned. "Okay. In what way?"

"This!" Nico waved his hand through the air. Pushing back the chair, he jumped to his feet, pacing the length of the bed.

Jake crossed his arms. "I don't think I'm following."

The urge to lean over and *shake him* had Nico's hands clenching into fists. "You're so damn calm. It's like you're not upset at all. Like you don't even care! Your career is over! You're never playing baseball again. Doesn't that bother you? Doesn't that make you feel *something*?"

His voice controlled, Jake answered, "Of course it does."

"Does it?" Nico held out his hands. "Could've fooled me. So how do you feel? Angry? Scared? Devastated? Because I do. I hate that you're never going to play again. That you'll never be behind the plate giving me signs. I don't want to go out there without you. And I know I'd have to eventually, but it wasn't supposed to be like this. It was supposed to be on your terms. But one dick slide from that asshole and your choice was taken away. I hate it. It's not fair!"

"I impeded the runner. It happens."

Nico sputtered. "What are you talking about? That sack of shit knew you were going to beat him with the tag, so he took you out."

It had happened too fast. Jake tried to remember, but the only thing he could recall was the exploding agony of the impact. "What did the umps rule?"

"He was out. Jake, he's getting suspended. I thought you knew."

"No. No one's really told me anything. I was conked out from the surgery."

"It wasn't your fault, if that's where this is coming from."

"Where what's coming from?"

Growling in frustration, Nico waved his hand through the air at Jake. "*This!* Your whole zen whatever-the-fuck this is."

"Uh... I'll just..." A nurse hovered in the doorway. She

backed out, closing the door behind her.

Nico scrubbed a hand over his face. "I feel like I'm a freaking basket case because I can't keep this shit inside. I tried, and I can't. Maybe I kept too much in there for too many years, and now I just…can't."

Jake reached out to soothe him. "I know I might seem calm…"

"Yes! You do. Still!" Nico paced. "You never lose your shit."

"That's not true." He raised his eyebrows. "You might recall a spanking I gave you in the clubhouse gym."

"Okay, once. I just…" Nico sucked in a deep breath, trying to steady his racing heart. "Don't you care? Even a little?"

Turning his head to the window, Jake swallowed hard. "Yes. But it's not… What's the point? It won't change anything."

He tried to find the right words. "Lots of times people get sad about stuff they can't change. Mad too."

"True. But I don't get to be upset. I don't deserve it."

Nico still itched to shake him, but managed to speak calmly. "Why not?"

Jake mumbled, "Because I checked out. I wanted to retire early. So I guess I got what I wanted. Careful what you wish for and all that."

The anger and frustration receded like a wave abandoning the beach, and Nico perched on the edge of the chair, reaching for Jake's hand, easing Jake's arms open from where he'd crossed them, little half-moon fingernail marks left on his biceps. "This isn't what you wanted."

Jake let Nico hold his hand, and he blinked away tears, his head still turned to the window. "Not now. But for a long time I went through the motions. When I got traded to the Caps, it sucked. I didn't care about the game anymore, and now I had to come up here and smile and fake it with new people. I was so *done*. Then it changed. Thanks to you. The team. The fans. I really thought we could do it—make it to the postseason. And you guys still can. But I won't."

Nico rubbed his thumb over Jake's hand, wanting to say so much, but afraid to interrupt.

"I'm getting what I deserve for taking it all for granted."

"What?" Okay, forget staying quiet. "You don't deserve this. No way."

"I didn't appreciate what I had," Jake said softly. "We both know guys who bust their balls and never make it out of the minors. Kids who dream of making it to the Show. Not just making it, but staying for years. Having good long careers playing a game we're supposed to love. I stopped loving it. Stopped loving everything."

"But you said things changed when you came here, right?"

Turning his head on the pillow, Jake swiped at the tears escaping his eyes. "When I started loving you, I loved the game again."

Nico was pretty sure the floor had just evaporated and he was falling through space, his heart pounding in his ears. "You love me?" he whispered.

"Of course. I honestly never thought I'd love anyone again. I didn't want to. But you're undeniable."

Laughing, Nico said, "I guess I'll take that as a compliment? Since you love me and all." *Jake loves me.* The giddy rush of hearing the words had his head buzzing. "I fell in love with you when I was thirteen. Never really stopped."

Jake squeezed Nico's hand. "Now I kind of feel like a pervert, but what can you do?" He laughed, and then a fresh burst of tears welled in his eyes. "I want to play. I want to get back on the field. But I never will."

"I know. Shh. I'm sorry." With his free hand, Nico brushed back Jake's greasy, rumpled hair.

"When I was traded, I sat there in the manager's office thinking about how that had been my last game with San Fran and I didn't even know it. Hadn't been given the chance to appreciate it. And now that seems like nothing, because yesterday was my last game *ever*. I should have savored it more. The crack of the bat on contact. Rounding the bases and hearing the crowd cheer—*feeling* them roar in my bones. Crouching behind the plate in the dirt, giving the signs, the whole field laid out in front of me. I'll never see that view again, not from that low, from right *there.*" A sob escaped. "It's over, and I don't want it to be."

Nico didn't have any words, so he leaned over and kissed Jake's salty lips, then held him close, letting him get it out, murmuring little soothing noises. He was leaning so far off the chair it was about to tip over, but he dug in his feet. He wasn't moving.

After a minute, Jake eased back, swiping at his eyes and laughing awkwardly. "I guess I have some feelings about all this."

"You're allowed, you know. You don't always have to be the strong one. If it gets too much, you can say armadillo too. You know what I mean?"

Jake's smile grew, and he brushed back the curl that never wanted to do what Nico told it. "Yes, I know." He shifted and sucked in his breath, grimacing.

"Okay?" Nico reached for Jake's leg as if he could do something to fix it.

Inhaling forcefully, Jake nodded. "Think the pain killers are wearing off. This might be an armadillo moment."

"I'll get the nurse." Nico moved to stand, still holding Jake's hand, and Jake tightened his grip.

"Not yet. Stay. She'll be back soon. I can take it for another minute or two."

Pulling the chair right up to the bed, Nico nodded. He wasn't going anywhere.

"SWEETHEART, OF COURSE you're coming home with me." Helen Fitzgerald stood with hands on hips, wearing running shoes and capri pants with a blue golf shirt tucked in. Her thick blond hair had gray roots, and her eyes crinkled the same way Jake's did. Nico had scooted around to the far side of the bed so she could have the chair, but she didn't seem in any rush to use it.

"Mom, I'm still technically part of the team, and I'll see the trainers every day for physio. The brass has to pretend there's a chance."

"Of course there's a chance." She sighed. "I'm not saying it's likely, but stranger things have happened." Her light British accent was musical to Nico's ears.

"Okay," Jake said, clearly placating her. "Regardless, I'm not going home with you."

"And what? Seeing the trainers every day is all well and good, but how will you get there? Who knows when you'll be able to drive again?"

"They'll make house calls at first."

"To where?" She motioned with her hands. "Hmm? That hotel? It's been months and you haven't even found a place."

Jake rubbed his scruffy face. "It doesn't matter now."

"But you need someone to take care of you. Cook for you, help you to the bathroom. I can't leave you alone. I'm sure we can get a two-room suite."

"He can stay with me," Nico said before he could think twice. Helen looked at him as if she'd forgotten he was there. She smiled kindly. "Oh, how sweet. What a good teammate. But I'm not sure you know what you're getting into. My bullheaded son's going to need a lot of attention."

Nico caught Jake's gaze. Jake was just watching him and didn't seem pissed, but Nico still probably should have kept his big mouth shut. Jake raised an eyebrow, as if he was asking something. Nico was pretty sure he knew what it was, and he nodded.

Jake said, "Mom? Don't get excited, okay?"

Screwing up her face as if she'd chewed a lemon, Helen replied, "My son's been seriously injured. What on Earth would I have to be excited about?"

Jake reached out, and Nico took his hand, threading their fingers together, his mouth going dry. Helen knew Jake was gay, but this still might be a—

"Oh my God." Her face lit up, and she actually pressed her palms to her cheeks. "Are you serious? I'm in no mood for cruel jokes, young man."

Smiling, Jake squeezed Nico's fingers. "I'm dead serious. Nico and I are together."

"Well, isn't that wonderful news?" She shrugged up her shoulders, beaming. "It's about time." Her gaze examined Nico again, much more closely this time. "You're quite young, aren't you?"

"Um..." Nico looked to Jake, who huffed.

"Mother, if you get picky now—"

"No! I'm delighted. You've been acting like a grumpy old man for too long. Some youthful vitality and optimism is just what you need. Thank you, Nico."

He hesitated. "You're welcome?" Was that really all she was going to say? Was she really okay with it? He marveled as she beamed at him and kissed Jake's forehead. It seemed she was not only okay with it, but truly thrilled. Nico couldn't wipe the smile from his own face.

Helen plopped into the guest chair. "Now I can stop worrying. Excellent. I really didn't want to move here for who knows how long. I'm chair of the activities committee for the seniors' group, you know. Nico, I'm sure you'll take good care of him. Don't let him give you any grief. Give me your phone number and you can text or call anytime for moral support." She pulled out her smartphone, thumbs at the ready.

Trying not to smile, Nico rattled off his number, and Jake groaned. "No, no. The two of you don't get to start complaining about me behind my back."

Helen tapped her screen and absently said, "We'll do it right in front of your face, sweetheart." She jabbed the phone and put it back in her purse. "There. We're all set. Nico, tell me a little bit about yourself. You've been having a wonderful season. Of course I have to give catchers the number-one slot, but pitching is the second hardest job in baseball, I think."

"Pitching? Don't you mean bowling?" Jake asked with a twinkle in his blue eyes.

Still holding Jake's hand, Nico looked between them. "I'm not following."

Helen rolled her eyes artfully. "It was decades ago, but Jake still loves to tell this story."

"Stories. Plural." He addressed Nico. "Okay, a neighbor gave Mom a pair of tickets to a game, and we drove down to Toronto in the morning. I was around twelve. I'd been to a couple of games over the years, but there was still nothing like it. Mom bought me a hot dog and peanuts and cotton candy, and we had amazing seats by first base."

"Sounds good so far," Nico said.

"It was very good!" Helen crossed her arms with a theatrical, long-suffering sigh. "Do you know how much they charge for concessions? It's highway robbery. Even worse now, of course."

Jake went on. "So, Toronto was playing Detroit. Our pitcher didn't get off to a good start, and she starts complaining— loudly—about how they should take out the bowler and put in another."

Nico asked, "Is that like in cricket?"

"Exactly." Jake grinned. "So she's going on and on about the bowler, and everyone around us is like, 'Who is this crazy British lady, and why is she talking about bowling?' Meanwhile, I'm giving people apologetic looks and hissing to her that it's the pitcher in baseball."

Helen chuckled. "Poor little Jake, so embarrassed by his mother."

"But it gets better." As he spoke, Jake rubbed the back of Nico's hand with his thumb, sending warmth up Nico's arm. "They did replace the Toronto pitcher, and we started turning it around. Our catcher was on a smokin' hot streak. You know the type, when just seeing him in the on-deck circle gives you hives."

"Yup," Nico answered.

"So Detroit decides to intentionally walk him, and they start the whole routine. Mom freaks out. 'They're not letting him hit! Why aren't they letting him hit?' She's shouting this so loudly that I have no doubt everyone on the infield could hear. The first baseman's looking over, security's coming down the aisle, and I'm getting ready to be ejected."

Laughing, Helen shrugged. "What can I say? I get wrapped up in sports."

"She was so *indignant!*" Jake gave his mom a wink.

"I still don't like that rule, for the record," she said.

Nico's laughter died in his throat as he looked up and realized Skip and Martin Tyson, the Caps' GM, were in the doorway. And that they could see Nico and Jake were holding hands. Nico tugged his hand free, shoving both in the pockets of his jeans.

"It's all right, we already know," Skip announced as he bustled in, chomping on gum as usual. Nico realized it was the first time he'd seen the man out of uniform, although he still wore a Caps jacket in red and white. Skip added, "In fact, everyone does."

Nico's breath caught, his ears ringing. What did Skip say?

Tyson closed the door behind him. "Mrs. Fitzgerald? How nice to meet you."

As Tyson made introductions, Nico met Jake's wide eyes, his pulse pounding. Everyone knew? What the actual fuck?

Tyson smiled smoothly and asked, "Jake, how are you feeling?"

"Like shit. What happened? How does everyone know?"

"I only just found out five minutes ago," Helen said.

Tyson adjusted his tie, smoothing a palm down his expensive charcoal suit. "Seems that someone in the loading dock of the stadium was filming on their camera when Jake was put into the ambulance. They shot through the back window, capturing a moment when Nico briefly kissed Fitz."

"Now it's a goddamn tree," Skip muttered, chewing madly.

"Vine," Tyson corrected. "And it's gone viral. We're taking all measures to find out who took the video and apparently sold it to a gossip site."

"Oh my God." Nico's head spun. "I'm so sorry." He looked to Jake, who still watched Tyson.

Skip's craggy face creased even more. "Sorry for what? Some cowardly asshole invaded your privacy. Their ass is grass when we figure out who it is." He blew a forceful bubble. "I had a feeling something was going on with you two, but decided as long as it wasn't impacting the team, I'd stay out of it until it did."

Nico stared at Skip. "You knew?" The other shoe dropped. "That's why you told me to go with Jake in the ambulance."

Skip shrugged. "Figured you'd be the best person."

"Thank you." Nico shifted from foot to foot. They really weren't in trouble for lying?

Tyson cleared his throat. "As I said, we're taking all measures to discover the culprit. This is obviously a stressful time already, and I wish this hadn't happened. But the Ottawa Capitals support you both a hundred percent."

"You do?" Jake asked warily.

"Absolutely," Tyson answered. "I can't say we're thrilled with the idea of teammates dating." He glanced at Skip. "Or that it wasn't disclosed, but that's an issue for another time."

"It won't be a problem," Jake said. "I'll never be able to play again." He held up a hand. "And I know you're all going to argue and say anything is possible, and blah, blah, blah. But we know what the reality is."

Nico did want to argue. He wanted to yell at the top of his lungs that it wasn't true, but it wouldn't change anything.

"Yes, well." Tyson sighed. "We're going to issue a statement saying our players' personal lives are none of our business and our priority is Fitz's health and well-being. The PR manager will work with you both on your statements. For now, try to avoid the press and don't engage in any way online."

They nodded, and after a few more inquiries into Jake's leg, Skip and Tyson were gone. Nico dropped onto the side of Jake's bed, his knees weak. "I'm so sorry. I had no idea."

Jake took his hand again. "I know you didn't. And everything's okay. Don't worry about me. God, I was always afraid of this." He exhaled. "But it'll be all right. We'll get through it together. Of course that's easy for me to say—you're the one who still has to go out on the field. And shit, your dad."

"I'm sure he'll support you unless he's a complete fool," Helen said with a frown.

Nico pulled his phone from his pocket. The battery had died the night of Jake's injury, and he'd only gotten around to recharging it that morning, not eager to talk to anyone anyway.

The screen lit up with dozens of messages, and he looked for his dad's name in the list of texts. Trembling, he tapped. There were two, the first from two nights ago.

That slide would have been dirty even before all these namby-pamby new rules.

Nico smiled. It was his dad's way of saying he was sorry about Jake's injury. Then he scrolled down to the next message.

That was a pretty stupid move getting recorded like that. But you and Fitz tell anyone who doesn't like it to go to hell.

"And?" Jake asked.

"He sends his best. In his own way."

Helen rounded the bed and pulled Nico into a gentle hug. "It's all right, dear. It'll be better now that it's out in the open, you mark my words."

Trying to quell the rising dread as he leaned into her sweet softness, he could almost believe it.

IT'S JUST ANOTHER DAY. *Just another game.*

But when Nico walked into the clubhouse a few days later, all eyes were on him. Skip had let him stay away while he got Jake settled in his place instead of riding the bench between starts, but now it was Nico's turn in the rotation.

Staffers nodded to him with too-bright smiles as he walked the hallway, and inside the locker room, conversations stopped. He'd come in later than his usual, and most of the guys were there.

Silence descended but for the murmur of SportsCenter on one of the TVs. Sweat prickled Nico's neck, and his mouth was a desert. He'd stopped instead of going right to his locker, and now he stood there like an idiot.

"Hey, brother." Crowe jumped up from a couch, his bushy red beard swaying. "Good to have you back." He came right up to Nico and gave him a hug and slap. "How's Fitz?"

It took a second to croak out, "Fine. I mean, he's not, but. You know."

Palmer bounded up right behind Crowe, the streak in his afro now dyed purple. He hugged Nico too. "Welcome back."

From behind, Diego said, "Hey, man! Good to see you." Another hug and slap. "Don't let Fitz give you too much trouble. I'll be over tomorrow to make sure he's behaving."

Nico tried to laugh, but was afraid he might cry as one by one, the team greeted him. The odd smile or handshake seemed forced, but the vast majority of his teammates welcomed him back with open arms, literally.

"Fitz said you've been doing a bang-up job scuffing balls before your starts." Baldoni clapped Nico on the arm and held up Jake's iPod dock. "He told me to get it out of his locker. We'll head to storage after BP, yeah? I've got you covered."

Nico nodded. "Thanks. I... Thanks." He glanced around. "To everyone. I know this must be freaky."

Crowe shrugged. "Only thing freaky here is the stench of Banner's feet. Jesus Christ, son—how does that smell occur in nature outside a trash heap?"

Banner scoffed. "And you smell like fuckin' roses."

Some guys joined in the ribbing, and others wandered back to their games and tablets and SportsCenter.

And that was it.

Nico made his way to his locker just like any other day, sweet relief cushioning his steps, gratitude filling him. He and Jake had released a statement via the PR team that they were just two of the many gay and bi players in baseball, and they hoped all players would be accepted and supported, etc., etc.

The PR people had written it, and as long as Nico didn't have to say anything himself, that worked for him. The media had been strictly instructed to only ask about baseball after the game. Maybe one day he would give some big interview and talk about his feelings, but...not yet. For now, it was just another day at the ballpark, and he had a job to do.

The memory that it wasn't any other day because Jake wasn't there was a stab of grief in Nico's abdomen. Not that he didn't appreciate Baldoni's support, and had done just fine with him before, but Baldoni wasn't Jake.

Nico sat on his leather chair and ran his fingers over his waiting uniform, hanging proudly. If all went to plan, he'd be playing for at least a decade, if not almost two if he protected his arm.

He'd likely partner with dozens of catchers, and he hated so fucking much that none of them would be Jake. But that was baseball, and this was the first day of the rest of his career. It would never be the same, but he had to deal with it.

If he played his cards right, at least he'd have Jake at home, and that was far more than he'd ever thought possible.

"Hey, want to come play the new racing game they put in the lounge?" Diego asked as he approached.

Normally he'd say no. Nico glanced at Jake's locker, where his uniform still hung, his glove and bats and pads all tucked inside. There would eventually be another name there. This was the new normal. He pushed to his feet. "Sure, man. That would be cool."

By six, Nico was back at his locker, changing into his uniform. He and Baldoni had scuffed balls and listened to Blink-182, and it hadn't been the same at all—but it hadn't been bad either. Now he was counting down the minutes, thinking of Jake at home.

Home. Was it their home now? Were they living together? Jake had moved in, but was it permanent? There was a month left of the regular season, and then what? Nico hadn't even thought about where he'd live in the winter.

Socks pulled up and belt buckled, he checked the clock again. Quarter after six.

Stomach churning, he walked calmly to the bathroom, nodding at guys on the way and sidestepping a game of dominoes that had sprawled onto the carpet. Alvarez was finishing up at the urinal, and Nico ducked into the last stall—*his* stall.

Leaning against the door, he breathed deeply. He hated that Jake wasn't waiting by the sinks. For once, Nico would welcome the disapproving sigh and frown lines.

What will happen if I don't puke?

The thought ping-ponged around his mind as he stared at the empty toilet, the seat up, metal handle gleaming, faint smell of disinfectant in the air. He inhaled again, counting as he exhaled.

Then again. And again.

I don't have to be perfect.

Shoulders back, he rolled his head ear to ear, breathing steadily. After a minute, he realized the churning had subsided, only a faint flap of butterflies in its wake. It was normal to be nervous. To be excited.

He stared into the toilet again. Part of him, a low, scared growl, commanded that he bend over and let go, purge the bad energy.

Is it really bad? What will happen if I don't puke?

If Crowe laced his right cleat before his left, would that really make a difference in the game? Sucking in another long breath, Nico knew the answer was no. And would it really make a difference if Nico went out on the mound with food in his belly? Maybe he'd even pitch better, wouldn't have to chug Gatorade.

I don't need this.

Closing his eyes, he visualized the field, the mound, home plate. He was allowed to be nervous. It was okay. He wasn't going to throw up out there. He was going to pitch his best, and the chips would fall where they did.

I don't need this.

Excitement fueling his steps out of the bathroom, almost running, he grabbed his phone from the shelf in his locker, thumbs flying as he texted Jake.

Going out there. Won't be as hungry afterwards. I don't need the ritual. Wish me luck.

The three little dots appeared almost immediately. Then:

Break a leg, baby. Oh wait, I've covered that. You've got this.

"Ready to warm up?"

Nico looked up to find Baldoni standing there, pads in place along with a smile. Nico nodded. As he put the phone back on the shelf, it vibrated again.

So proud of you.

Sliding on his glove and flexing his fingers in the worn leather, he returned Baldoni's smile. "Ready."

As he walked from the bullpen to the mound half an hour later, Nico concentrated on breathing steadily, eyes on the turf. He soon became aware of the crowd buzzing and applauding, which was strange since the first pitch hadn't been thrown yet. When he looked up, he did a double-take, almost tripping over his own feet as he jerked to a stop.

Rainbow flags filled the stadium, thousands of them being waved enthusiastically, ripples of color all around.

"Dude, this is amazing!" Grinning, Baldoni slapped him on the back, and they started walking again. "Gotta love Canada."

And God, it really was amazing. Thirty thousand strangers clapped and hooted and waved rainbow flags for him. At the mound, he could only stare in wonder, emotion thick in his throat.

Lifting his cap, he raised it to all four sides of the stadium, one after the other in a slow circle as the crowd showed him so much love.

When Nico had the ball and everyone was in place, the ump called, "Play!" And even though it wasn't Jake giving him the signs, Nico felt him in every cheer and each pitch.

CHAPTER TWENTY-ONE

"WHERE TO, SIR?"

Sitting against the side door of Diego's SUV with his leg stretched across the backseat and crutches on the floor, Jake said, "Ha, ha."

"If I'm playing chauffeur, it's usually with my kids, and I'll have you know that joke kills every time. Oh, they were here on the weekend, so I hope there's not a stray sippy cup jammed up your ass or anything. How they manage to leave shit everywhere all the time is beyond me."

"I'm good. Thanks for the ride."

"Anytime. Nico's already down there?"

"Yeah, pitchers' meeting. How are the kids doing? And Liz?"

"They're okay. Liz sends her best. Next time we'll have to get together." Diego turned out of Nico's condo driveway and started the short drive to the stadium.

"Definitely. Are you going to move them up here?"

"We're not sure yet. I'll go back down to Texas when the season ends in a couple weeks. Hopefully we'll make the playoffs first. Either way, we're going to take a couple months to really think about it."

"Good idea." Jake's phone pinged, and he read the text laughing. He read out, "Why couldn't the pony sing himself a lullaby?"

Diego answered, "I don't know. Why?"

"Because he was a little hoarse."

They laughed, and Diego said, "That sounds like a Brandon Kennedy joke if ever I heard one." He gave Jake a look in the rearview mirror. "He texted me after your injury to get a status update. You guys made up?"

"We did." A flush of happiness warmed his chest. "I told him the truth. We've been texting, and he invited me and Nico over for dinner with his family next time we're in Toronto."

"That's awesome, man. I'm so glad to hear it." Diego pulled up to a red light. "And you and Nico are living together now, huh? How's that going?" He laughed. "Wait, no need to answer. I can tell it's going well by the huge, goofy smile on your face."

Jake laughed too. "Yeah, things are good. Turns out I'm in love with him, and he's in love with me, so."

Diego half turned and extended his fist for Jake to bump.

"I'm kind of dreading you guys going back on the road tomorrow," Jake said. "It'll be weird, you know?"

"Yeah. You going to be okay on your own?"

"I'll manage. Every day it's feeling a little better. Team hired a nurse to come by and clean my bandages, wash me and all that. One of the assistant trainers will stay in town to come over and do my physio. The Caps are going all out."

"Of course they are. We all want you back on your feet ASAP."

Flexing his quad, Jake adjusted his leg, wincing. The too-big track pants that fit over his brace were cinched tightly at his waist, the cord digging in. "But you know this is it for me. I'm not saying that to get sympathy or whatever. It's reality."

Diego sighed, turning into the stadium's underground parking. "I know. I mean, it's not impossible. But at your height especially, it's amazing your body held up to the wear and tear of catching this many years. Factor in this injury and your age…"

"Exactly. If I were ten years younger—hell, five even. But it's going to be a long haul just to be able to walk normally and bend my knee. It's feeling better than it was, but there's a long way to go. Doc thinks I can make a full recovery for a normal person, but that playing again will be too much. Might fuck up my knee for life just trying it."

"Man. That royally sucks."

"Yep. Trying to stay positive, but..." He shook his head. "Life's funny. A few months ago, the idea of never playing baseball again sounded pretty good. Now that the choice has been taken away, it's damn tough to swallow."

"That's human nature, right? We don't want something, but tell us we *can't* have it—whoa, that changes everything. Whether we're five or fifty."

Jake chuckled. "Hopefully I'm handling it a little better than a five-year-old."

"I'll give you a slight edge."

"Thanks. Anyway, it is what it is. I can't change it. Don't get me wrong, I have my moments of feeling awfully sorry for myself. It's going to be a huge adjustment. Have to take it one day at a time. Wow, could I use a few more clichés? I'm also going to give it a hundred and ten percent."

"Leave it all on the field. And you know, the best defense is a good offense."

"That's what they say."

Pulling into his spot with a laugh, Diego asked, "Ready to be the center of attention?"

"Always. Actually, wait."

Diego killed the engine and turned in his seat. "Sure. What's up?"

"How's Nico doing? Not on the mound—in the clubhouse. He said it's been good, that you and Crowe and guys like Palmer have made sure everything's cool. But I want to get your take on it."

"Yeah, it's been good. Maybe a couple guys don't like it so much, but Skip's made it clear he won't tolerate any bullshit, and we won't either. Hopefully the guys who are uncomfortable are learning that it's not a big deal. Nico's still the same dude he was before. So are you. Everyone respects you. I think this is a great thing all around the league."

"Cool." Jake exhaled. "Thanks. I just worry about Nico out there without me."

"I hear you. But I'm pleasantly surprised by how the brass are really putting their money where their mouth is about inclusion."

"Me too, actually. They've said all the right things in the press and have reached out to be supportive. Probably makes it a little easier that I can't play now. If Nico and I were on the field together..."

"True." Diego grinned. "The pitcher/catcher jokes alone, although I guess you're still getting those. I'd stay off Twitter for a while."

"Ugh. Sometimes the internet's great. Other times..."

"Seriously. There are trolls out there hating, but it's always something. This week it's gay players in baseball, and next week it'll be something else. Fuck 'em. The real fans have been incredible. You and Nico know who matters."

"We do. Thank you. For everything. You've always been a good friend even when I wasn't."

Diego waved him off. "Whatever, man. I know you've got my back. Hey, are you two going to do an interview? You must be getting hounded."

"Luckily the PR team's handling all that. We'll do something in the off-season; for now we have enough to worry about. We do want to say more eventually. Especially for the queer kids out there."

"Totally. Oh, and I'm curious. How did Nico's old man take it? He strikes me as rather...conservative."

Jake smiled wryly. "Indeed. Nico came out to him just before all this went down. Al isn't exactly the warm and fuzzy type, but he's been way better than Nico expected. Weirdly enough, I think us getting outed actually helped. He's protective of his kids, like any father. If he sees anyone hating on his son, he won't stand for it."

"I bet. I wouldn't fuck with Al Agresta." He grinned. "You'd better watch your step, Fitz. That's a hell of a father-in-law to have."

"Okay, okay, we're not married yet."

"'Yet,' hmm?"

"Slow down, *Mom*. Let us live together for a year or two first." But Jake couldn't deny the idea of marriage was much more appealing than ever before.

He'd never been able to imagine it—sharing a bed every night, having someone else in his life always there. Putting a ring on Nico's finger, making him officially Jake's. He knew they shouldn't get ahead of themselves, and they wouldn't, but it echoed faintly in the back of his mind: *one day.*

"All right, all right, let's get you inside."

Walking—well, hobbling—into the clubhouse again was surreal. It had only been a couple weeks, but it felt like a lifetime. Everyone was there—Skip and the coaches, Tyson and front office staff, all Jake's teammates.

As they lined up to hug him, he still felt like part of the team. The idea struck with an eager jolt of optimism that maybe he could be a coach eventually. Maybe his career in baseball didn't have to be over, only changed.

The Caps still had to sort out his contract, which wouldn't happen until he was completely healed and assessed for his ability to play. But down the road...

One day.

Nico gave him a smile, hanging back and letting the other

guys have their moments.

"Fitz, it's damn good to see you up on your feet." Skip's gruff voice rang out, and everyone stopped talking to listen. "I know I speak for all of us when I say we've missed the hell out of you. We want you back in the clubhouse and the dugout when you're ready." He held up a uniform with Jake's name and number. "Had some new pants made to fit over your brace. You're a vital part of this team, and you still have a lot to contribute as we try for that wild card spot. Whaddya say?"

For a moment, Jake's throat was too thick to speak. "I say that would be just what the doctor ordered."

After a little more talk, it was time for everyone to get back to their pre-game routines. Leaning heavily on his crutches, the throb in his knee dull and manageable, Jake made his way to his locker and lowered himself into his chair, Nico hovering behind him.

He squeezed Jake's shoulder and murmured, "Are you sure you're up for this?"

"I can sit on my ass and watch a baseball game. Absolutely. Although I need a foot stool in the dugout and you might have to help me get those new pants on." He winked. "Just keep your hands to yourself."

"For now," Nico muttered under his breath, and they shared a secret smile.

STRETCHING HIS LEG gingerly as he lay back in his boxers, Jake winced. "Shit, it's still itchy." At least the bandages and initial hard brace were off, and the cutting-edge new brace he'd been fitted with was softer and only extended to mid-thigh. On his long legs, it was well below his groin and much more comfortable.

"Is there anything I can do?" Nico offered another pillow, but Jake waved it off, yawning widely.

He was thrilled to have Nico back from the Caps' road trip, but wished his eyes weren't so heavy. "I'm fine. Pick something to watch. I'll probably fall asleep halfway through it, so I don't care what."

"Okay, Grandpa." Still in his jeans and tee, Nico picked up the remote. With only a week left in the regular season, it was going to be close for the wild card spot, while the division win was definitely out of reach. Jake had expected Nico to be much more on edge, but he was handling the stress remarkably well.

Jake tried to sound indignant and not smile. "Hey, they gave me a sedative for those tests."

"Uh-huh. Sure."

Laughing, Jake wished he'd taken an extra pillow so he could throw it at Nico now. "And don't choose that crappy sci-fi show with thirty-year-old actors playing teenagers."

"I thought you didn't care?" Nico smirked. "Now I totally have to pick that. And I'm putting the remote over on the dresser."

"If I could get up without a cane, you'd pay for that."

"Oh yeah? What would you do?" Nico challenged with a smile.

"What would I do if you were a bad, bad boy?"

Adam's apple bobbing, Nico swallowed. "Yeah."

Jake's heart skipped. "Hmm, where to start?"

Nico's teasing smile transformed, and he licked his lips, a glint in his eyes as he took a deeper breath. "Tell me."

The channel guide was up on the TV, SportsCenter playing in the top corner. "Turn it off." To hell with the sedatives. Jake was wide awake now, and so was his neglected dick. They'd kissed and touched since the injury, but without heat. Jake had been in too much pain, but it was manageable now.

The TV went dark, and Nico went to flip off the pot lights, but Jake shook his head. Nico stood at the foot of the bed with his arms at his sides, fingers twitching. Waiting.

Heat sparked in Jake's veins, and he worked to keep his tone even. "Take your clothes off."

Yanking off his purple tee and dropping it to the floor, Nico unzipped his jeans and shed them along with his briefs, leaving everything in a pile on the carpet. Well, Jake couldn't see beyond the end of the bed, but assumed they were in a pile.

As Nico straightened, Jake said, "No, no. Fold everything nicely." Nico did, opening a drawer in the dresser and placing them inside even though the clothes would have to go in the hamper later.

Naked, he returned to the foot of the bed.

"Come over here." Jake nodded to his left. "That's good." He raked his eyes down and back up Nico's body slowly.

Fuck, he was gorgeous. The tufts of hair on his chest, red nipples matching his moist lips. More hair dusting his arms and legs, and a trail leading down from his belly to the thatch around his cock, which was getting hard with each passing moment. "What do you think I should do to you?"

Taking a shaky breath, Nico said, "Spank me."

"Would that teach you a lesson?" Jake's cock swelled in his boxers.

Nico nodded vigorously.

"Maybe I can give you a couple swats now. Would you like that?"

"Yes," he breathed.

"Come here." Jake reached out his left hand, rubbing it over Nico's hip as he complied, then up over his chest and neck. He could just reach Nico's chin, and he pulled him down for a soft, wet kiss. Brushing his thumb over Nico's bottom lip, he whispered, "Do you want to let go?"

Another nod, Nico's eyes bright, his pupils wide.

"Turn around. Brace yourself on your knees."

Jake smoothed his hand over Nico's ass, savoring the faint tremble he felt. Gripping Nico's hip with his left hand, he smacked his other palm down. Nico gasped so prettily, barely moving.

Jake hit him again, and again, each gasp louder than the others. He could see Nico's mouth open, his eyes closed. The sparse hair on his ass emphasized the reddening skin. Jake caressed the heated flesh, soothing before giving him one last crack that garnered a yelp and breathy moan.

Releasing Nico's hip, Jake tugged his arm. "On me."

Nico turned, frowning. "But your knee. I don't…"

"You'll do as you're told. I'm in charge. Now come here." He urged Nico to straddle him at the waist, well clear of the brace, his ass heavy on Jake's dick. Jake inhaled through a throb in his knee as they settled. He'd pop an extra pill. This was worth it.

With Nico sitting on him, Nico's flushed and straining cock was tantalizingly close. But Jake didn't touch it. No, he had a better idea. "You used to jerk off and think of me?"

A nod and hard swallow. Nico kept his hands on his thighs, his fingers digging in, nails white.

"Show me."

Nico's eyes widened for a moment, and his chest rose and fell faster. Lifting his right hand, he slowly licked it from palm to fingertips, then spit a few times. He spit onto his cock as well, some of it missing and landing on Jake's stomach. Then Nico took his shaft in hand, stroking with a little twist of his wrist.

He groaned, his eyes fluttering, free hand still clutching his own thigh. The slaps as he worked himself mingled with their heavy breathing, the only sounds in the room. His ass pushed back against Jake's hard cock, and Jake barely resisted the urge to buck. Maybe soon Nico could ride him, but this would be enough strain on his leg for tonight.

"I can't wait to fuck you again," Jake muttered. "Spank your ass so red. Tie you up in all sorts of ways. You want that?"

Nico groaned. "*Yes,* yes."

"I'm going to take you so hard. Make you scream."

"Yes. Please. Oh, fuck." He jerked himself faster, the motion vibrating through Jake, the sweet endorphins of desire enough to blot out any discomfort.

Jake kept talking. "I'm going to spread you open. Fuck you with my tongue first. Push your knees up to your shoulders and shove my cock in. Going to tie your ankles to your wrists. Make you beg."

"Please!" Biting his lip, Nico moaned, flushed and sweaty.

"Give me your other hand."

Nico whipped it up, almost smacking Jake in the chin. Jake sucked his index finger, wrapping his tongue around it and getting it as slick as he could while Nico gasped, his rhythm stuttering, their eyes locked together.

Jake released him. "Fuck yourself." Panting, Nico reached back, crying out as he pushed his finger inside. Jake said, "Think about how much bigger my cock will be. Think about what it feels like raw. Nothing between us. I've only ever done that with you. Only you."

"Oh God." Finger still in his ass, Nico jerked his dick again, the head dark red now, curving up so deliciously.

"Want me to come inside you? You're such a good boy. Should I give you my cum?"

Nico tipped his head back, mouth open as he shuddered with his orgasm, painting Jake's skin in thick pulses. Leaning forward, he pressed his palms to Jake's chest. "Fuck," he whispered, breathing hard.

Part of Jake wanted to just watch Nico come down from the high, but he ordered, "Get off. On your knees beside me." He patted the mattress.

Looking torn between scrambling to comply and being gentle,

Nico lifted his leg and scooted back until he knelt by Jake's hip. Jake's dick was already glistening with pre-cum. "Suck me."

Nico did, and it was glorious. Watching his lips stretch, his mouth fill as he took Jake deep, watching him swallow as much as he could when Jake came until it dribbled out. Jake tangled his fingers in Nico's sweaty hair and eased him down for a long, deep kiss, loving the taste of himself on Nico's tongue.

Nico flopped onto his side, licking Jake's sticky chest before resting his cheek there. "Thank you."

"Thank *you*. I needed that. We both did."

"How bad does it hurt?"

"It's fine."

Nico raised his head, eyes narrowed.

Jake laughed, wincing as he shifted and tested his leg. "Okay, it hurts. Physio kicked my ass today, and after that... I think you'll have to help me get out of bed." He brushed back Nico's curls. "It was worth it."

"Good thing bed's exactly where I want you." Nico winked and pressed a kiss to Jake's nipple before resting his cheek again.

When the pressure on Jake's bladder became too much, he sighed. "I don't want to move, but it's time to get Grandpa out of bed so he can piss and have an early night."

Nico nodded seriously. "I'll get a glass for your dentures. Did you have enough fiber today?" He crawled off the mattress. "Oh, how is the bench in the shower stall? The guy came while I was gone?"

"The bench and everything is great. It's heaven being able to shower myself. You didn't have to go to the trouble."

Nico screwed up his face. "It wasn't trouble. You live here now. If it's something you need, we'll get it." He hesitated, watching Jake carefully. "Now that I think about it, I guess we never discussed it officially. I just think it makes sense. For you to move in for good." He shrugged nervously, looking at his feet. "If it's too fast…"

"No."

Nico frowned. "Can you be more specific?"

A laugh shook Jake. "Sorry. I mean, no, it's not too fast. It's perfect. Once the season's over, we could go down to California. I have a great house near the water. I don't think we want to experience an Ottawa winter, so we could live there until spring training." That he wouldn't be on the field sent a powerful pang of regret through him, but he shook it off.

A smile bloomed over Nico's face, his dimples out in full force. "Winter in San Francisco would be awesome."

"So it's settled."

"I guess it is." Nico laughed. "Should we talk about it more or something?"

"Nah. I think we're good, right? Just don't leave dishes in the sink. I hate that."

"Cool. I guess we'll figure out pretty fast what drives us nuts about each other. Just tell me, and I'll tell you. Like you always said, we'll take it pitch by pitch."

"Deal." Jake extended his hand.

Smiling, Nico shook it firmly, then looped his arm under Jake's shoulders. "Ready?"

Even with the damn cane in one hand, Jake had to lean on Nico all the way to the bathroom. As he pissed, Nico stood by him, a steady hand on his shoulder. The thought of months of limping and rehab to come were depressing as hell.

"Sure you're up for living with an old man?" Jake asked.

Nico's grip was unwavering. "Shut up."

Jake's life had been smashed right out of the park again, but with Nico, it was a grand slam.

EPILOGUE

"HI, NONNA."

Nico held his breath as she turned, her eyes widening. He'd seen her again a few times since he came out, and as he'd guessed, she'd avoided the subject entirely and pretended nothing had changed.

But this time, Jake was beside him.

Jake smiled widely. "It's wonderful to see you."

She stared at them both, her gaze flicking back and forth, smoothing her hands over her floral silk dress. It was the rehearsal dinner for Valentina's massive wedding, and most people would think this was the wedding itself, with a string quartet playing in the corner and servers circulating with trays of appetizers and champagne.

Tomorrow they'd be in the country club's grand ballroom, but tonight they were in a glass-walled restaurant, the sun setting over the browning golf course. The forecast called for blue skies and perfect autumn weather for Val's big day.

As the seconds ticked by, Nico's heart thumped. Would she turn away? Not say anything at all? Would—

"Nicolito." She took his face in her gnarled hands, bringing him down for a kiss. Then she did the same to Jake. "You were always good boys."

Someone clinked their glass, calling for attention, and that was that. Nonna grabbed a puff pastry off a passing tray, muttering that she could have made them better, as Valentina's future father-in-law thanked everyone for attending and blah, blah, blah.

Not listening anymore, Nico tried to calm his speeding heart as relief flowed. Nonna probably wouldn't be marching in any Pride parades, but he'd take it.

Jake reached for Nico's wrist just below the cuff of his suit jacket, rubbing his thumb over the tender skin on the inside, tracing the little black and white circle that matched the tattoo on his own wrist.

Most people who noticed the tattoos thought they were little yin/yang symbols. But on closer inspection, the ridges of the armadillo's protective shell could be spotted, its long face tucked in, tail circling around. Nico gave Jake a little smile, his heart slowing, constricting now in happiness, not fear.

Maybe it had been foolish to get matching tattoos so soon. It had only been six weeks since the Caps' season had ended half a game back of the wild card berth. An incredibly bitter pill to swallow, but that was sports for you.

Moving down to San Francisco, he and Jake had settled into Jake's wood-beamed, big-windowed house. The tattoos had come one night while making their way slowly down the street after tapas in the Mission District, Jake leaning on his cane and insisting he was perfectly fine to go for a damn walk. The parlor was open late, and they'd had two bottles of wine.

The next morning, they'd only grinned when they saw the tattoos and fucked before breakfast, Jake's knee getting a workout. No regrets.

"Hey, Rookie of the Year!" Marco swooped in as the speech ended, giving Nico and Jake slaps on the back.

Val rolled her eyes as she appeared in his wake, looking beautiful in an emerald dress that swirled around her knees, her dark curls pulled back. "He and Ian's brothers started over at the bar a little early."

"Just getting to know our new family," Marco said. "Being a responsible big brother." Ignoring Val's snort, he asked Nico, "So, how does it feel? We haven't had a chance to talk since you won."

Nico shrugged, but had to smile. "Feels good. Can't help but wonder if I won because I'm gay and the league is knocking itself out being inclusive. Not that I should complain about that. They've been amazing."

Jake shook his head. "No way. Your stats hold up. You came close to the pitching award too. Anyone that says you didn't deserve to win doesn't know a damn thing about baseball."

"I know, I know." Nico patted his arm. "It doesn't matter what idiots say on Twitter. It's fine."

Jake cleared his throat. "Sorry. I just get…" He waved his hand.

"Adorably protective?" Val supplied with a grin, her nose scrunching.

Nico's belly fluttered pleasantly. "All right, leave him alone. Anyway, it feels good to win. But it's also, like… It's nice and all, but you get up the next day and your life is the same. It's a huge honor, but I guess it's not as big a deal as I always thought it would be. It's not important compared to you guys and the team."

Pressing her lips together, Val blinked rapidly, her eyes filling with tears. "Our baby brother is growing up, Marc!" She pulled Nico into a hug and kissed his cheek.

Marco grinned. "I'm not gonna cry about it, but he is."

Nico muttered into her hair, "Jeez, you're supposed to be getting emotional about your wedding, not me."

Releasing him, Val licked her thumb and rubbed his cheek where she'd kissed. "I'm the bride. I get to be emotional about everything."

Their father appeared, smiling tightly. "Damn right you do, princess." He gave Nico a brief hug—complete with a back slap, of course—then extended his hand to Jake. "How's the knee, Fitz?"

"Good." Jake shook his hand. "Well, better. Slowly but surely and all that." He lifted his cane. "Don't need it all the time now, but since it might be a long night…"

"He's way better, though," Nico added. "He's working so hard at rehab."

Dad said, "He always was a hard worker."

"He's been talking to Skip about coaching too," Nico said proudly.

"We'll see." Jake waved a dismissive hand. "It's all preliminary, but he thinks I have a knack."

Nico elbowed him lightly. "Of course you do. Look how much you've helped me."

"Yes, well." Dad cleared his throat. "All right, have fun. I'd better go check on the rest of the family." He plucked a champagne flute off a server's tray, draining it as he walked away.

"That…went pretty good?" Jake squeezed Nico's wrist again.

Nico exhaled a long breath. "Definitely could have gone worse."

"Are you guys staying at a hotel?" Marco asked.

"Totally. Would be way too weird at the house. Maybe down the road, but not now." Nico laughed, some of the tension easing. "Besides, my bed's a little too small for the two of us." They all chuckled, and he added, "He's trying. Although he did call the other day to remind me not to do anything gay at the wedding."

"Oh, for the love of—" Val pressed her lips into a flat line, hands on her hips. "I expect you two on the dance floor tomorrow. Fitz, you're excused from the fast numbers, but you can stand and sway during slow songs, right? And hold hands. And kiss. Because last time I checked, straight people do those things too. Anyone who doesn't like it can pucker up and lay one on my bridezilla ass. That includes our family."

Jake grinned. "I'll drink to that."

"Where's that bubbly?" she asked, and Marco motioned to a server.

With flutes in hand, they raised them together in a silent toast, clinking their glasses. Fizzy champagne sweet on his tongue, Nico took Jake's hand and pressed their lips together. And if anyone didn't like it, they could kiss his ass too.

THE END

About the Author

Keira aims for the perfect mix of character, plot, and heat in her M/M romances. She writes everything from swashbuckling pirates to heartwarming holiday escapism. Her fave tropes are enemies to lovers, age gaps, forced proximity, and passionate virgins. Although she loves delicious angst along the way, Keira guarantees happy endings!

Find out more at: www.keiraandrews.com

Made in the USA
Middletown, DE
25 June 2022

67768383R00177